I0731278

THE END

OF

SHADOWS

After the Last Day, Book Three

By Don Hayward

Reader reviews of the trilogy

"Awesome epic book. It doesn't just deal with a collapse, but follows society for several generations, from the viewpoint of multiple characters.

This is a unique story in that it includes people with disabilities, people of various First Nations, people who are immigrants, people who are visible minorities, and people of widely varying backgrounds, ethnic heritages, political views, and religions beliefs, and treats them as actual people with stories rather than background decoration. This gives so many more opportunities to develop the story, and the author fully takes advantage of it. After reading this, I realized how much it gets repetitive reading books where the same generic heroic man fights to survive, with kids and womenfolk only there to cheer him on. I think this is the first post-apocalyptic book I've read where more than half the narrative is from the viewpoint of women.

Anton Chekov wrote, "If you say in the first chapter that there is a rifle hanging on the wall, in the second or third chapter it absolutely must go off.". In this book, the wall would be destroyed by a train driving through it. The author keeps things interesting by setting up the story so you expect one thing, but then knocks the legs out from under it. For example, a community develops its own currency to replace the nearly-worthless dollar, using some old store coupons they found. The characters carefully sign each one, keep track of how many are issued, monitor the relative value of the coupons to available food resources, and secretly mark the coupons to prevent duplication. You expect that they will soon have problems with counterfeit coupons, or hyperinflation. But, just like real life, events take place that invalidate your predictions.

This is really, really, really good value for the money. A lot of good story for your dollar."

***

"Gripping story, and all too plausible. There are no plot points where one says "no, that isn't possible"; more like "OMG, that could really happen"...
...On the whole, highly recommended. Prepare to have your thinking about society provoked."

***

"The books are interesting to read. The narrative is for ordinary people, and the plot is credible."

"The End of Shadows, After the Last Day Book Three," by Don Hayward.
ISBN 978-1-7752459-5-7 (Soft cover)
Published 2023 by Don Hayward, 8 Huron Lane, Goderich, Ontario, Canada N7A 3Y2

©2023, Don Hayward.
All rights reserved. No part of this publication
may be reproduced, stored in a retrieval system, or transmitted in any form or by any means, electronic, mechanical, recording or otherwise, without the prior written permission of Don Hayward.

This book is a work of fiction. Any resemblance to actual events or persons, living or dead, is entirely coincidental.

Cover photo courtesy of jillWellington Pixabay.com

I dedicate this book of the After the Last Day trilogy to my children and grandchildren as they enter an uncertain future.

Acknowledgement: To Alex, who read the manuscript, highlighted corrections and made suggestions for improvement.

To my wife Diane, who patiently attempted to discover all of my technical errors, confusing text and provided many helpful suggestions.

Any errors are the author's own.

Also by Don Hayward

Collapse
Book One of After the Last Day
ISBN 978-1-7752459-2-6

Under Shadows
Book Two of After the last Day
ISBN 978-1-7752459-4-0

The Seventh Path
A follow on story to the After the Last Day trilogy
ISBN 978-1-62137-949-2

Journey's End
Sequel to The Seventh Path
ISBN: 978-1-7752459-3-3

Return
Science fiction sequel to Spielberg's Taken series
ISBN 978-1-7752459-7-1

Murder on the Goderich Local
ISBN 978-1-62137-993-5

Sherwood Green
ISBN 978-1-7752459-0-2

Echo of the Whip-poor-Will
ISBN 978-1-7752459-1-9

Contact Don with comments or to order paper books.

https://www.danddhayward.ca/
haywardon@gmail.com

Introduction

This is the third story in the trilogy set in southern Ontario after a global economic collapse, previously published in a single volume as **After the Last Day**, still available as an ebook. The trilogy version is physically easier to handle, improved and updated. It would be best to read the trilogy in sequence, starting with book one, **Collapse** and continuing in book two, **Under Shadows**.

In **Collapse,** a global economic and climactic crisis that had been deepening for years suddenly transformed into widespread collapse on a late September day. Residents of the small Ontario town of Weyburne, although shocked and despondent, began an effort to survive under the guidance of Warren Dunne, a man previously derided as a "doomer" and a little crazy.

The Canadian federation fragmented and the world collapsed into chaos, but the residents overcame plotting by local business people intent on profiting from other's misfortune and achieved some stability involving hard work and life never far from hunger. That about 80 percent of the original local population disappeared in the first year, either by fleeing to cities in the desire to find work or through murder, suicide, hunger and disease made the task easier. As they made progress, a sinister threat developed from the local enclave of the former financial elite.

The local progressive organization weakened as more members joined the elite camp, attracted by paid wages and the aura of strength and control. The influence of the elite increased in Weyburne through the efforts of a local contractor, Roger Smith, who used bribery, bullying, and murder to gather support.

As the fascist People's Liberation Movement took control of Ontario, the local fascists, under the leadership of Alphonse Angel, seized control of Weyburne.

The handful of local leaders confronted the reality of fleeing or dying. Five families of leaders and other individuals fled north into a seemingly safer territory focused on Owen Sound and most of the former Grey and Bruce counties north of the Saugeen River. The refugees settled on a complex of three farms in the lower Beaver River valley. The shadows of their past, including the threat from the racist dictatorship, would colour their lives for the next several years.

Book Two, **Under Shadows,** follows the struggle to survive through salvaging and learning to endure. This takes place against the backdrop of unifying a safe, strengthening Huron Territory and culminates in what they believe to be the ultimate battle for existence against the fascist People's Liberation Movement that has seized southern Ontario. The survival of Huron Territory and the personal safety of everyone, especially the refugees from Weyburne, are uncertain.

Nature's fortune benefits the people of Huron and in the story, **The End of Shadows,** they enter the future taking advantage of an uneasy peace to overcome the lingering but rapidly fading emotional and physical shadows of the lives that they had been living before the last day of industrial society. Much of this is the personal journey of the travelling scribe, Brandi Shadly. She explores a world where the need for political, economic and emotional security remains a constant struggle

.

Chapter One

As you know, we closed the old building a long time ago. It is just a skeleton now, with only the concrete and steel standing. There is some talk of salvaging the steel for the Hamilton mills. The room where you held the founding meeting has gone, along with Granddad's office where you first met him.

Your depiction of the event and the signatures look even better now, framed under glass in our timber and stone meetinghouse. They hang above the Chair at the front of the Council Assembly Hall. I know my grandfather was not a formal delegate, but I smile every time I see him in your drawing. Thank you for including him. He was proud of that. Your portrait of Chester is still on the one side, but you may not know the Council recently ordered your self-portrait placed beside his. It is one of you on that big quarter horse from years ago.

We get many visitors, and I tell them the story of the first convention and the founding of Huron. We show your notes and other drawings, and I always read your last line aloud. Thank you for your kindness and for making this so real for my family and me. I know, to you, this is now a place of sadness.

From: A private letter to Brandi Shadly from Paul Jenkins III, then custodian of the Huron General Council meeting hall and offices. He is the grandson of the late Paul Jenkins, the original director of the museum.

They gathered in grief, full of uncertainty and fear, but they did a good thing.

From: "The Founding of Huron" (The Journals of Brandi Shadly, Vol. 6, p. 112)

Note: the Truth Talker Players re-enact portions of the Huron Founding Convention as recorded by Brandi Shadly. Their performance is part of the opening ceremony of the annual council meeting held each March.–E.T.

"Conditions are changing, and we need to get organized." Chester stood at the front of the auditorium of the old museum near Owen Sound. His voice filled the room. He gazed out over an audience of about one hundred delegates from the various villages and other watershed organizations. It especially pleased him to see the delegation from the lower Saugeen watershed, including his old friend Corrine from Chippewa Hill. The melting of the snow pack had finally allowed for this conference. Chester had been organizing the event since Christmas. Late winter proved the best time for meetings, allowing for travel yet not cutting into the farm work.

"It's time we formed a central council to coordinate bigger issues." He received a general murmur of agreement. "This meeting has no legitimacy from any previous authority. We may have to convince outsiders of our legality. Anyone elected may be in a tricky legal situation."

"There ain't no legal government left anyway!" Everyone laughed at the shouted response.

"Still," Chester went on, "I want a motion formally designating this gathering as the accurate representation of the wishes of the inhabitants. We will have a small group work on the boundaries of the territory to adopt later. It will probably change anyway." A unanimous vote adopted the motion. "Thank you," Chester beckoned to the mayor of Owen Sound. "Robert Paisley will chair the meeting until we organize."

Chester sat at a desk on one side of Robert and took notes. He could see Brandi Shadly seated against a wall furiously scribbling and drawing into her notebook.

She will make a better record than mine, better than a video.

Paisley's call for an agenda raised a hubbub, "what's our name?", "who's the leader?", "How big are we?", "what about my land?"

"Hold on! Hold on!" Paisley shouted above the din. "Let's be orderly and get this done right. What we want to end up with is a constitution of sorts. Let's go one step at a time. The PLM will attack in the spring; we have to get this done and get ready."

They easily picked the name. It took no time at all to decide on Huron Territory and to call the top body The Huron General Council. Two subsequent days of argument nearly derailed the whole affair as everyone tried to decide how to structure and elect the council.

Huron Ecology Institute sent Warren Dunne as a delegate. The previous ad hoc council had informally created the Institute. The school wanted a formal charter from a legalized territory. Warren had considered these issues for many years and had benefitted from input from others on the defunct computer internet. As the delegates had their say, and became repetitive, Warren sought the floor.

"Ladies and gentlemen," Dunne spoke softly, forcing everyone to be quiet. "I am not a constitutional expert, but I've been thinking for a long time about what might work after our industrial society crashed."

"So you caused the problem." Someone shouted.

"That's stupid!" Another voice rose, reacting to the pained look on Warren's face.

"I was kidding." The joker apologised.

Warren stumbled, remembering a meeting in Weyburne. He did not like speaking at large gatherings.

"The basic unit should be the watershed." Warren said. "Each watershed should have a council that would send representatives to the general council. A watershed council could veto any proposal from Huron Council, affecting the water quality and environment of their drainage system. The General Council could veto anything a watershed wanted to do if it would negatively affect the lake. It's good we call ourselves Huron because Lake Huron is the common resource we must protect."

"This is radical." Someone spoke up. "It sounds like anarchy. How will it feed my family?" A murmur of discontent swept through the hall.

"That's a good point." Warren looked at the speaker. "Surviving has been our immediate problem and will be for some time. We have done things to survive we might regret, but for now have been necessary. We must fix these issues later and avoid hurting the environment more and thus condemning our children to suffer."

The murmur of agreement swung in Warren's direction.

"If we can't sustain ourselves in a good way, we will die anyway." The crowd became quiet.

"There's a lot to work out, and we must make sure we carve nothing into stone. We'll make mistakes and must be flexible. The second biggest bit of fighting here, besides last fall's battle, involved taking control of the Beaver River watershed after the sewage incident at Flesherton."

"Sorry," the Flesherton delegate apologized. Laughter filled the room.

"Thank you," Warren smiled, "but we must let go of old grudges if this is going to work. We'll have enough to argue about, and I'm sure there will be fights and even hatreds over serious issues." He paused, thinking he sounded too stiff and formal. Lighten up, Dunne. Then he remembered some facilitator training. Tell a joke.

"I have to say though," he smiled at the Flesherton delegate, "downstream we now call toilets Flushertons."

"We sure do." A woman from the lower valley laughed. People joined in. His attempt at humour satisfied Warren, but sparked a heated discussion.

They had to solve the problem of the disparity in the size of both area and population between watersheds. The Beaver and Saugeen were by far the largest represented, and no one wanted them to gang up on the smaller entities. Extending the veto power to the watersheds of the tributaries eventually won support, and all watershed councils would submit any spending of resources to a gathering of the residents. Those meetings could reject any spending proposal.

This pre-spring session would set the Huron General Council budget, but beyond overall security, including external relations, the central authority had no power to take any action. The most important power this body would have was the veto over any lake threatening development in a watershed. Some saw the potential for civil war; the vast majority of delegates adopted it as prudent and realistic.

"Nothing will ever get done." One delegate complained. "Decisions could take months."

Many, especially those who had been in political office, seemed to agree they needed a more streamlined system. Chester made the counter-arguments.

"Passing a law should happen slowly and deliberately." Chester summed up his position. "It's better to be slow and get it right, with everyone understanding and feeling as if they had their say than just pass something to appear efficient. Politics is considering and balancing everyone's needs.

It isn't about having our idea or advantage winning. That kind of thinking caused the collapse." He took a sip of water and looked around the room. Many seemed unconvinced.

"Deciding is like firing a rifle. Once let loose, the bullet can do a lot of damage before it stops. It's better to make sure of the target and what kind of bullet to use before pulling the trigger." Chester carried the issue despite the sceptics.

They established the size and composition of the General Counsel. The representatives from Beaver Valley included one each from Thornbury, Flesherton and Feversham district, as well as one representing Kimberly and the upper valley, and there was one to speak for Heathcote, including Longview.

The lower Saugeen had adequate representation pending the freeing of the upper watershed, stretching almost to Weyburne. All the smaller watersheds had at least one voice. Anyone over the age of sixteen years, the age they joined the security forces, had voting rights. Newcomers became voting residents of Huron when they had been in the territory for one year. They required the vouching by two citizens before assuming full citizenship.

They elected Chester Amik as the first chairperson of Huron Territory. No one stood in serious opposition, and an impassioned speech by the Meaford mayor sealed his fate. Everyone agreed that Amik's personal efforts since the beginning of the crisis had reduced suffering and pointed the way towards a hopeful future. Chester assumed control of the meeting; however, it remained as a general convention. The General Council would not assume its place until the final vote of the group of one hundred formally handed over power and dissolved itself.

These divisive discussions had been easy compared to what solved the fundamental issues of trade, money and property. The vast majority of residents squatted on land vacated by disappeared owners. Others had defaulted on mortgages and no longer owned the land. Only a handful of residents had ownership free, but unpaid taxes to the old municipalities clouded their titles.

"I hope I have some goodwill left over from my last proposal," Warren regained the floor. "What I am proposing now will be hard to accept."

There would have been no attempt to present Warren's radical ideas if Chester and the other ad hoc council members had not been supportive.

Those running the territory for the past several years understood the flimsy legal structure beneath everything. They were eager to move ahead on land ownership. If the Province of Ontario ever regained control or the PLM won, everyone would face eviction.

"I propose," Warren hesitated.

"We propose," Chester corrected Dunne.

"We propose," Warren glanced gratefully at Chester, "title to all the land belongs to the territory which grants the right to occupy it in usufruct to its present and future occupants."

Chaos erupted, with comments ranging from: "what the hell does that mean" to "hey I own my land". Chester allowed the energy to dissipate and then called for order.

"This is going to take a long time," he glanced around the room, "but it's key to everyone's security and survival."

"I own my place outright, and so do others." A man from south of Owen Sound leapt to his feet, not bothering to be recognized. His angry look bordered on hatred. "I won't hand it over."

"We have a mortgage," Jake Costello added. "Maybe we'll get it back."

"We're all squatting," another speaker jumped up, "even you folks who are still on mortgaged land. There's a lot of abandoned land, and we need people. We need to find a way for all of us to know we are secure. What happens to us if someone returns claiming ownership?"

"Or worse," Brandi Shadly spoke, recalling Maud Dillingham's story of the PLM's seizure of Dufferin County. "The PLM has rounded up bank records and is stealing defaulted property and giving it to their friends. They would do it here."

"If we're just renting, there's no reason to fix it up. I've already done a lot of work at my place."

The young speaker, a hard worker and supporter during the years of hardship, represented what Chester saw as the hope for the territory.

"Usufruct isn't renting." Warren reluctantly assumed the role of instructor. "Traditionally, in most usufruct systems, people had control of and the use of the land in perpetuity, as long as they took care of it and made it productive. I think everyone I know in Huron already fits this description."

"Native communities have used the system for thousands of years, and it goes back before the Romans. The community would grant usufruct, and not some greedy noble who would treat us like serfs. Even you who have paid up land only own it by the convenience of the Crown. The government could expropriate it. With usufruct, we would be free men and women working for ourselves and the community."

Anarchy-syndicalism, thought Warren, but he would not say it aloud and start heated debates about meaningless political definitions.

Delegates pondered the unfamiliar. Several gathered into a group of hostile landowners.

"We would need a process to make sure that we didn't get kicked off just because someone didn't like us." The woman who raised this issue was one of the less liked people in the region. She and her family successfully farmed the land they squatted on out past Maxwell and contributed their share of resources and effort to the common cause. Her husband fell wounded in the recent fighting, and they had reluctantly accepted help from neighbours.

"Yes, we do." Several voices supported the woman.

"We would need a complete set of rules," Warren agreed. "The question of how we hand down a usufruct to the next generation is a problem. If a person with a holding marries another who has a holding, then what happens?" This issue gravely befuddled Warren. The quick suggestion surprised him.

"They pick one property and live there. The other one goes to someone else. We don't want any empire builders or marrying to get land." The suggestion came from Jake Costello. "If we don't nip it in the bud, we'll have feudalism pretty shortly."

"What about we who own our land?" The freeholders had picked an advocate.

"What about this idea?" Chester used his position as chair to intervene. He had been working on this problem ever since he noticed the landowners forming their little quorum. "People who have a free title or a mortgage will get to keep their property and are exempt from the productivity and other performance clauses of usufruct."

"No way, not fair." The sentiment swept out from the larger audience. "Everyone should be the same."

"If we were starting from a clean slate, I would agree," Chester knew he had to persevere, "but it's a big mess. We have to make some allowances."

"C'est une grosse poutine, sans the gravy." Roger LaFarge muttered from the back of the room.

Brandi caught the comment and would later present Roger with a drawing of him holding a plate that contained a likeness of Chester lying in a bed of French fries covered in gravy and lumps of cheese.

Chester carried on. "We don't need to worry. If they're not productive, they'll starve. People in this category will still have to pay the levy and do security and other labour obligations. You owners must understand, if we adopt usufruct, there will be no real estate market, ever. If an owner abandons the land, the territory will assume jurisdiction."

"What good is it if we can't sell?" The owner's group cried. "You're a bunch of commies!"

"Who's going to buy your land?" Chester ignored the insult. The man seemed to prepare to walk out, but stopped short and turned back.

"What does that mean?" He appeared to be scared.

"All you guys are greedy and just care about yourselves." One squatter jumped to her feet, glaring at the group of owners. "You don't want to make any sacrifice or help others, just yourselves." She spat her words out. Her animated face flamed red; and she leaned forward on the balls of her feet.

"You don't know what you are talking about." One man leapt up and shouted back. He took some steps towards the woman, and his fists balled into tight knots. "We have given and sacrificed..." His words faltered as he choked up, "we have sacrificed..." Sobbing made his speech slurred. "We have sacrificed." He was near tears. "My son died at the barrier last fall. Johnny, my little Johnny..." The man tried to tell the story, but his words choked off. He slumped into a chair. Several delegates put hands on his shoulders. His sobbing sounded throughout the hall.

The woman rocked back on her heels in stunned silence, beaten and deflated. Tears streamed down her scarlet cheeks. The room fell silent except for the man's sounds of grief. Chester called a recess. The few months since October had not been enough time to grieve. An hour after the confrontation, Chester called the meeting back to order.

"We were discussing selling land, and who could buy it?" Chester consulted his notes. "Who has the money or a bank to get a mortgage?" Chester glanced around the room. The little group of owners sat as if reality had hit home. The grieving father had stayed.

"The advantage for you is, if the Province ever regained control and did things legally, you would be the owners. Remember, those PLM folks make up their own rules, so don't depend on the law if they win. Those with mortgages can opt-out of this, but things are never going back. We need to build a future for ourselves."

There was a smattering of applause. The cluster of owners looked resigned and offered no more arguments. Still, Chester saw the freeholder's looks of sullen surrender.

I hope they don't become a problem later.

At that moment, Chester knew the proposal would pass as the best of political settlements, with no one completely happy but everyone willing to accept the decision as practical.

He was correct in assuming victory, but it took two days of arguing and re-writing rules and procedures before the usufruct idea became the foundation of the territory. A judicial body would review any attempt to remove landholders for failure to perform. Last appeal would go to a meeting of the watershed residents.

The land distribution idea almost died by the refusal of the two native bands represented to accept Huron's title over their tribal lands. Chester had to deal with some racist remarks. The suggestion to respect traditional community boundaries and the band assuming control of the usufruct system on their territory seemed to be acceptable. An amendment gave native bands representation on the General Council independent of their watershed obligations. In return, they agreed to submit all usufruct disputes to the General Council to arbitrate, and agreed non-natives could hold usufruct on native land.

Corrine Wilson and the other native representative had raised the issue. Both felt they had no authority to give away control of their territory, no matter what their own beliefs might be. They plainly stated they believed the whole thing was meaningless since Ottawa no longer functioned, making their treaties defunct.

Uncertainty thrust the natives into the camp of the freeholders. The "what if" question preyed on people's minds, and no one wanted to make a mistake. The number of surviving natives south of the Bruce Peninsula was small, and the lone representative from the northern reaches had no contact with most of their population. Ojibwe in remote settlements would eventually get their say.

After the fuss about land, no one wanted to consider a central currency. Personal promissory notes and direct trade worked well enough. A fiat currency could wait for another time, especially since no one had any idea how to produce physical money.

Warren's dire warning about the dangers of fiat currency encouraged the postponement of a decision. The only formal mechanism related to money was the creation of a Justice of the Peace to help keep disputes from becoming violent and to referee settlements if they accused someone of defaulting on a promise.

A person's reputation was the real currency behind their promises. It worked well at the local level. The few people who had not lived up to their promises went hungry or changed their ways. It had become a cruel, unforgiving world, but a sense of mutual responsibility developed.

After an exhausting two weeks, the gathering formally dissolved itself. The Huron Territory and the Huron General Council came into existence. A call for a unanimous vote failed, with the landowning group submitting written objections. The Chairman hoped the dissenters would elect one of their own to the council, so the group would not feel voiceless. Most of the delegates looked forward to a few weeks of hard spring farm work after the past weeks of rancorous debate.

They had pride in their effort, and even the dissenters gladly signed Brandi's drawing of the gathering. The councillors hung this work in the Council room to be the symbol of its authority.

"I travelled back to Kimberly with Warren. The results pleased him, but he told me making it work overwhelmed him. He said we had just written the first line of an epic story. Warren depressed me when he said he hoped we lived to write the second line."

"We all expected horrible fighting in the spring. No one thought we would win."

From: "The Founding of Huron" (The Journals of Brandi Shadly, Vol. 6, p. 114)

Chapter Two

We did not realize it, but the standoff with the PLM and making it through that eighth winter was the turning point in our history. Even though the security situation remained nervous for years, we had quietly passed into the era of the actual building.

Upon reflection, privately, I call it the beginning of the Brandi years. Her wanderings and spreading of everyone's stories resembled the growth of the nervous system and renewal of the body. In my mind, her work and the scribes she trained are the straw that bind our clay together.

From: "Conversations with Chester Amik," in the "Voices of the Founders," series by Erin Thomas

I am writing this, huddled by the wood stove, trying to survive what Erin is calling "the volcanic winter". We don't know if we will survive and writing and reflection take my mind off the worst.

We killed Shade last week. His death reminded me of the horses that I loved and the three who served me so well. I think of Dodger, and his violent end that gave birth to Nimise Makwa, of Niibin and her gentle passing on the sunny spring meadow, and now Shade's sacrifice so that we humans may live.

My mind drifts back to the beginnings of our ordeal and our journey of promise, back to Weyburne, now The Corners, and how, even after our flight from the village, it later gained new importance in our survival. Al Wright and the dangerous espionage of Jennifer and Barry Young and

Rob Bossley were vital to our safety, avoiding conflict with the PLM. The sacrifices of Evy tortured to death, and the hundreds who met similar ends are un-repayable. The millions who disappeared in that first decade after the last day of the Before Time were part of an unavoidable horror so we lucky ones could survive.

History flows like a stream, with unexpected tributaries, cutoffs and meanderings. Like the natural watershed that is the basis of our survival, we must understand and honour it. Near the end, I have more honouring than understanding.

From: - "Winter Thoughts - Towards the High Ground."
- Brandi Shadly archives

"They call this the Little Beaver River." Chester twisted in his chair and surveyed the scene. "It's more of a creek."

Amik, Roger LaFarge and Helen Niemczyk sat in handmade wooden chairs arranged around a table under a tree at one end of a small concrete dam. Dead trees stuck out of the water in the large pond behind the dam, their weathered trunks decaying memories of lower water levels. The pond reflected the blue sky. A light breeze rippled the water. Sunlight sparkled and flashed from the surface, finally disappearing where small hills and thicker bush touched the shore. A rivulet trickled over the dam, splashing on the rocks below. The trio watched a work gang along the slope rising away from the pond. Warren Dunne directed half a dozen locals planting tree seedlings between spring planting and the haying. Crews elsewhere around the watershed mimicked this effort.

"Warren's work will increase the flow." Chester frowned. Dunne struggled as he worked. "This was a respectable stream before they cleared the land."

"It'll take years for this to make a difference." Helen's army experience made her want instant results.

"Warren uses the saying about planting trees for your grandchildren. We hope planting above Eugenia will increase the water available to the hydroelectric station. The saw mill and machine-shops there are critical."

Chester picked up the top sheet from a small pile of paper and read it with a puzzled frown.

"We are at war, yet the enemy is not fighting."

"Yes, we have seen no patrols." Helen looked puzzled. "To get any action at all, we have to get close and fire a few rounds at them. Usually, there's no return fire. They just duck. It's like poking a snake with a stick, coil, but no strike."

She took the paper from Chester in her red and stiff right hand. The injury from last fall's attack on the tank healed slowly. Helen took meagre satisfaction in the battle, ending in a standoff.

"Where did we get this info?"

"They're from our spy in Weyburne."

"Can we trust the guy?" Roger read the page.

"Matt swears he's reliable, but only he, Jeff, and Ted know him. It's better that way, but the PLM cannot capture Jeff and Ted. We should not send them where the PLM could capture and torture them."

"They are both with Matt." Helen had sent them south to cause mayhem around Orangeville and felt guilty. Helen knew of Barry Young, but kept it to herself. The PLM would never capture her.

"Hopefully, they'll be okay. When Ted and Jeff get back, don't send them out again until it's safe."

"Gladly," Helen responded eagerly. Chester smiled. He knew about her and Ted Macedo and could only guess how hard it must be, ordering a lover into harm's way.

"So they've withdrawn and have left a small rearguard? It seems strange, after their big push last fall."

"It appears so." Chester brightened at the thought of a reduced threat. "As you can see, there are only a few hundred fighters north of Orangeville, most protecting Angel at Weyburne, with only a hundred in Dundalk."

"We could take Dundalk." Helen loved offence.

"Council doesn't want to stir them up. The pause gives us time to recover. Every day, we get more deserters and refugees. Time is on our side." Chester hesitated. "We can't let our guard down. Keep raiding but capture people alive."

"Yes," Roger enthused, "many lower ranks desert when we attack. The leaders may go down fighting, but most surrender easily. The PLM zealots have disappeared."

"Okay," Chester held out the next sheet, "here is some stuff you haven't heard. Matt's runner brings longer messages. They're getting information from the south. Don't ask me how. Matt doesn't even know. We think it's reliable and helps us understand the propaganda on the radio." Chester passed several sheets of paper around the table. No one knew about the book-code messages and how extensively Rob Bossley in Hamilton had upgraded Barry Young's library.

"Good God! They might as well have given us their maps." Helen said.

"Yes, they've pulled back east of the Grand River and south of old highway eight. Goderich is still in their territory. They're garrisoning Collingwood and Simcoe, guarding the grid there after your attack last fall, Roger, but they are struggling to keep their population under control."

"I would say the pressure is off for now." Roger smiled.

"That's the good news." Chester looked at both of the commanders and felt concern.

"The worst thing is, they aligned with your old buddies running Ottawa." Chester looked grim and reached for more papers. The proposed agreement had personal implications for his military commanders.

"We have the outline of their agreement. It seems this will be the basis of the alliance." Chester handed the papers to Helen. "They will shoot deserters from the old Canadian army."

"It's better than being hung!" Roger put on a brave face. The paper condemned him, Helen, and a dozen friends at Meaford base.

"They aren't bright," Helen scoffed. "They should offer carrots for us to desert. We would be useful to them."

"Maybe they assume we understood what deserting means." Roger smiled at Helen. "It's Bennett and Waters in charge." The old soldiers laughed. The Brigadier Generals had a reputation for incompetence.

"More serious than you two getting shot," Chester tried to be lighthearted, "the PLM might get better fighters and equipment."

"If they get decent weapons, we will have to contact old acquaintances and get them to defect. In the meantime, we can't worry." Roger said.

"I don't think any of you ex-military, or even any refugees or deserters from the PLM, should go on missions into their territory. It would be more dangerous than for the rest of us. Don't expose them to extra punishment. Unless all-out war starts up again, we need to keep them safe."

Chester came to the final few papers.

"The General Council wants me to broker a truce with the PLM." Amik peered at the two officers, trying to catch their immediate reactions.

"Mon Dieu," an emotional Roger reverted to his native tongue. "Embrassons le Diable."

"Or we could cage the devil." Helen pondered. "I don't think we can trust them. Do they want a truce?"

"Nothing direct so far," Chester shared the last of the papers, "but this is a decoded message from the south. There's talk of a truce with us. There are more groups like Matt's and at least one enclave like ours in the south-west corner from Windsor east to Point Pelee. They can't fight us because of trouble at home."

"It looks like the natural gas issue is their biggest problem, making many people upset," Helen digested the message, "and another epidemic of cholera, it seems."

Chester imagined the brutality the message implied. "They're cutting trees for heat and shipping wood from Dufferin. It's a disaster. They're human locusts."

"We still need to worry about them militarily." Helen passed the papers to Roger.

"I am guessing we'll hear soon. We might see a white flag somewhere along the frontier. Give the order to bring envoys in safely and to call us."

"We need to merge the new territory to look after and allies on the Saugeen who are on the front lines. They need help. It is all new down there."

Chapter Three

The Great Spirit is in all things; he is in the air we breathe. The Great Spirit is our Father, but the Earth is our Mother. She nourishes us. That which we put into the ground, she returns to us.
From: a conversation between Brandi Shadly and Corrine Wilson, who was quoting Big Thunder (Bedagi) (Wabanaki Algonquin); The Journals of Brandi Shadly (Vol. 5 p. 87)

Dodger picked his way over the crumbling asphalt. The highway had deteriorated since Brandi last visited Chippewa Hill. She guided Dodger around of the rougher places. His steel shoes crunched on loose crumbs of pavement. Occasionally, a piece of stone flew away, under the horse's weight. Brandi had fitted protective socks over Dodger's lower legs.

The sound of drumming grew loud. The beat rose and diminished in cadence. Brandi came upon horses, wagons and bicycles between the road and the riverbank. An old pickup truck sat amongst the horses. She wondered who could afford fuel or where they would find it, but they had converted the truck into a wagon. They had replaced the engine and hood with a captain's chair reserved for the driver. A Belgian mare stood quietly in the shade, hooked up to the front end of the vehicle. A whippletree made of steel tube connected it to the traces. Car bench seats filled the truck box. The automobile had come full circle.

Brandi chuckled as she dismounted. With Dodger lapping water from a bucket, she headed towards the music.

In the amphitheatre, a crowd focused on three women seated on a raised platform. One woman struck a large skin and wooden drum with a steady muffled beat, the volume rising and falling and the rhythm following. A decorative band of dyed quills and feathers embellished the rim of the instrument. A second woman sat cross-legged, eyes closed. Corrine sat on the other side, watching. She smiled when she saw Brandi.

Brandi sat on a large stone at the back. There was no singing. Later, Corrine explained, no one had received a song, and the drum allowed the audience to live in their thoughts. The woman put the drum away. Brandi sat with the three old friends feeling close to these much older women. Stan Gregson joined them.

"I come here to get recharged," Stan smiled at Brandi, lines near his eyes deepening; curled lips peeking through his full beard. "The townspeople come for the same reason. There's something to quiet the spirit."

Corrine did not tease her friend, but stared beyond him. Two young native men stood beside the stage. One looked animated; the other, older and more subdued.

"Those two boys arrived last week," Corrine nodded, "from fighting alongside the Mohawk at the Grand River. It became a rout, and few survived. These two are hurting and angry. I hope they aren't trouble."

"I knew that young one, Frank, before he left." Stan glanced at the boys. "I had him in the lock-up a few times. He was a hothead then and looks the same. I don't know the other one."

"He's a Mohawk," Corrine replied, "named Ben. Lost his family from what I can get out of him. I can't read him; he's a coiled spring."

"I'll have a chat with Ben if I can get him away from Frank."

"What are you up to here, young lady?" Stan saw Brandi as his niece.

"Two things," Brandi sucked on Timothy grass, "Chester Amik asked me to check out the Saugeen and spread our story along the river. The Institute wants me to get things started here. Corrine, I am hoping you'll follow-up on last summer's ideas. The horrible fighting last fall, and the disastrous winter, has delayed our school plans."

Brandi removed her straw hat and tousled her long hair. Sweat made it damp and stringy. She glanced at the river, hoping to swim and wash.

"I've already started." Using Stan's glowing remnant, Corrine lit her newly rolled cigarette and ignited a ball of tinder. She blew the embers into flame and placed dried twigs on top. Satisfied she had the fire to light more smokes, she returned to Brandi. "We teach gardening and drumming. We have half a dozen students."

"We teach reading, writing and math in town using old school rooms for the summer, but we'll have to find something we can heat. There are about thirty pupils, including adults." Stan added.

"The goal of the HEI is to teach teachers and skills. You've made a good start." It impressed Brandi. "Could some of you come down to Kimberly before winter to get a better idea of what we are trying to do?"

"I'll get there for sure, and bring some others."

They sat around the fire, chatting and smoking. Corrine led the Chippewa Hill Ojibwe Council using the guidelines of the Huron Territory and had a list of native and non-native squatter residents. She had encouraged the two men from the south to join, but it was too soon. Stan noticed Frank had drifted away. The cop excused himself to befriend Ben.

"Come," Corrine led Brandi. "We'll go up the river."

"Good, I need a bath and wash my hair. Kathy at Longview has made nice herbal soap."

"We can swim later," Corrine waited as Brandi checked Dodger then headed along the bluff. Mid-July sun sparkled off the river and through the trees. Despite her age, Corrine hurried along. They burst from the thick trees into a blueberry patch high above the river. Struggling through a hardwood thicket, they came upon a small cabin made of barn board, painted brown with a cedar-shingled roof. Vegetable and herb gardens surrounded the building. A ring of fruit and nut trees circled the little clearing like a garland. Two walnut trees grew in front of the south-facing cabin. A colourful rose hedge surrounded the garden. Brandi could taste rose hip tea and jam.

"We recently discovered Colleen and Walt Bryson. They've been living here on their own for seven years."

"Hello, is anyone home?"

"Hello, Corrine," a woman in late middle age emerged from the maple bush in the river's direction. "Who's your friend? I'm Colleen." The woman shifted fishing rods to her left hand and extended her, not waiting for an answer. A man carrying a string of fish followed.

"This is Walter," Colleen said.

"I am Brandi Shadly, from Kimberly." They shook hands.

"This place is like Union Station since Corrine found us." Colleen continued. "She's too nosey and blew our cover."

"It was an accident," Corrine pretended amazement. "I was looking for berries, not nuts. I found you anyway."

"See Walt, I told you she thought we were nuts."

"Did you water your children?" Walter stooped to examine the bare dirt at the base of the walnut trees.

Walt hung the fish in a pail down the hand-dug well. "These will keep until supper," Walt offered water to the women. "Would you like a tour?" For the pretence of not having wanted to be discovered, the man eagerly showed off their domain, explaining every detail in a steady patter. The couple raised ducks, geese, chickens, goats, and pigs. The waterfowl scoured the gardens for grubs, bugs, and weeds.

"Sometimes the geese eat what they shouldn't, but they do a good job on the weeds. We keep them out of the gardens until the crop plants mature. These are Chinese. We use Emden too, in the tree areas and over in the blueberry patch. We usually take them there when we pick because of fox and coyotes. They weed our spelt and barley fields."

The tour reached a clearing where two hectares of grain headed up in the July sunshine. Brandi would suggest bird-weeding to Longview.

"You might have noticed herbs and succulents under the trees. We have shade crops wherever we can." Walt evaluated the seed-heads. "The crop might be good this season. We're trying for balance. The birds seem to have the best sustainability. They eat pests and marginal vegetation, and we can winter over enough for breeding. The goats are the best grass eaters, but wintering requires a lot of work. Fishing is important, time-consuming but relaxing. We slaughter pigs in the fall and trade upriver for little ones in the spring."

Brandi thought about how much of this paralleled practice in Longview and at Kimberly and raised her respect for Warren.

Beyond the maple, black ash and birch trees, they reached an almost imperceptible route down the bank to the river's edge. Terraces of grapevines filled the bank. The succulent fruit had not yet fully formed, and higher up tender fruit trees flourished.

"We tried these peaches and plum trees here." Colleen pointed to the small plants. "We hope that climate change and the extra heat from the sand riverbank will keep them alive. The actual risk here comes from a massive spring flood. The watershed is huge, but swamps and bush upstream help even out the spring run. Sand dries quickly. We have a hand-dug slough up in the trees, lined with clay from the river bottom to catch rain for droughts. Otherwise, we have to carry river-water up the slope."

"This is sophisticated." It amazed Brandi that two innovative had done all the labour. "Where did you learn this? How did you do the work?"

"This is our version of Permaculture." Walt stood with his hands on his hips, looking over their vineyard. "We're certified Permaculture instructors and had a large group of students in Owen Sound. I taught high school, and Colleen worked for the city. We taught and intended to retire here. It would have been about five years from now. Students camped at the blueberry patch, coming here in the spring and summer to help and learn. We all shared the harvest."

"When the economy went bust," Colleen picked up the story, "our students vanished." She looked sad. "We lost our jobs, so came here and have made a go of it."

"It looks like a lot of work"

"Yes," Walt said. "It stretches us to the limit, but for the past few years, we felt it safer to be invisible, living alone."

"How did you remain hidden near Southampton for so long?"

"We didn't completely isolate." Colleen checked the clover growing under the grapevines. "We walked to Port Elgin to trade. Southampton was too close. The people in the Port thought we lived near Paisley. That suited us, and we hoped the fighting would end before people found us. Those trading visits kept us sane."

"The fighting is over, for now." Brandi was sure. Chester had briefed her to prepare her for the trip. "We know the PLM has pulled back past Goderich. The whole Saugeen watershed almost to Weyburne is open territory. Officially, you are part of the Huron Territory. The Saugeen Watershed Council runs this end."

"Yes, Corrine filled us in. It's safe, plus you blew our cover. There's nothing to do but make the most of it." Brandi decided that making the most of it was their strength.

"How would you like to teach again?"

"Gladly." Walt hugged Colleen by the waist. "After so many years like this, a few crowds would be nice."

Brandi explained the concept of the Huron Ecology Institute, highlighting the ideas mimicking Permaculture, raising Walt's interest. Brandi declined an invitation to dinner. Dodger required her attention.

***

"Be careful." Stan Gregson hugged Brandi.

"I'm more worried about Corrine and the Hill." Brandi frowned. "Those young guys are trouble."

"Frank's a question mark," Stan patted the horse's neck, "but Ben is older and more mature. He's grieving. Ben lost all of his family horribly when the PLM over-ran their community on the Grand River." Stan looked down the side street to where he could see a little sliver of lake and horizon. He blinked away tears. "Anyway, he's an electrician and an expert on renewable electricity. We're asking him to sort out and fix our solar and wind turbines. Frank's attached to Ben. I'm hoping Ben can help him. Maybe, for the first time, Frank will make sound decisions. Corrine's monitoring them. Ben's taking over an empty place near her. What way are you going?"

"The back roads along the lake towards Kincardine and east to Paisley, up the river to Mount Forest, and then back to Flesherton." Dodger twitched. Brandi ensured the ties on her overfilled pack of supplies.

"That's a long ride, and we aren't sure of the upper valley. When will you be home?"

"I'm aiming for early September. If I meet anyone interesting, it might be longer. I don't know. It gets lonely out there sometimes." Brandi looked hesitant, but her face was determined.

"I'll be down to Kimberly in October. See you then."

Brandi swung Dodger towards the lake-road. The early morning sun cast her shadow larger than life. It kept pace before fading behind as she climbed from the water to flat farmland. Several large wind turbines stood guard over the dead transmission lines to Toronto. The scene seemed strange, but she could not decide why. Brandi stopped at a guard post near the road to the nuclear generating station.

"I'm from Southampton," Brandi dismounted. The guards kept their rifles near. She left her Savage in the scabbard.

"How are things up there?" A woman stepped from behind the barrier. "We get up to the Port occasionally, but no further." They seemed friendly, and Brandi relaxed.

"They're getting organized. Port Elgin seems busier. How are things down at the plant?" In the old days, no one talked openly about the place. Perhaps now it did not matter.

"We have it under control." The woman did not seem reluctant. "It's still hot. There's fuel in the reactors, but we are slowly getting it out. Not my job, thank God! We're running a couple of wind turbines and back-feed for station service. The power keeps the pumps running, and we can use the other motorized equipment. It's safer and easier, but we can only work when the wind blows." The comment resolved Brandi's original puzzlement. Two wind turbines were turning, something she had not seen since the economy crashed eight years before.

"The reactor online scrammed last fall during the fighting and the ice took out most of the line, finishing us unless the world goes back. We need to get the fuel out and make it safe, so it won't poison us."

Brandi camped at the gate and spent an enjoyable evening swapping stories. The workers and bosses had endured the PLM and rejoiced when the goons left.

When her new friend produced a propaganda pamphlet from the PLM, Brandi took out her drawing kit. The leaflet had a picture of a smiling, benign-looking leader extolling everyone to join the PLM's Canadian Christian Crusade. She drew the dictator's face, snarling menacingly from a mushroom cloud flanked by wind turbines behind a portrait of her new friend. If folded over, it would just show the woman's portrait. In the morning, a new admirer bid Brandi farewell.

Brandi headed east, staying close to the Saugeen River. Two days and new friends later, she rode down the hill into the town of Paisley. The river's wide meanders flowed through the eastern half of the town. A creek spilt over a substantial dam into the river, and she stopped to learn about the efforts to restore the watermill.

Representatives from Southampton had recently visited, and a local committee had a list of ideas and demands. The usufruct concept received much discussion. Brandi heard no new arguments. She recounted the deliberations of the founding convention and could clarify that the usufruct system Huron used gave stability to squatters and reassured freehold landowners. Original property owners seemed to be more common around Paisley and made property rights a larger issue. Squatters and defaulted mortgage holders outnumbered the owners, making the usufruct idea popular.

Brandi would ask Chester to visit and reinforce the Saugeen Administration. Her suggestion led to what Karen Lefevre laughingly called "The Royal Tour", the next summer.

After several days of helping to hand-square logs, Brandi and Dodger moved on, following the county road south, turning east through Walkerton and Hanover. This area seemed to have kept more population than she had seen elsewhere. Many families had lived in the area for generations. Some clung to their land in desperation, waiting for the good times to return. Others had already adapted and were utilizing the substantial workforce from the towns to make their farms productive. They had had no contact with the authority from Southampton. The area had only received a call to a meeting. Brandi did not mention any of the details about the territory's rules, leaving it to the people in Southampton. While she believed deeply in the founding principles of Huron and would argue them all day long if necessary, she wanted to listen to people.

Hanover provided a surprising diversion. Brandi arrived between the second haying and the beginning of the harvest. The locals had always been horse-racing fans, and her visit coincided with the third annual summer race meet and fair. Perhaps a thousand people, mostly families, thronged the raceway. Many horses stood on display, and there were ongoing races between everything from standard bred trotters to saddle ponies, with sprints between large draft animals pulling hay wagons. For safety, these races were just a quick charge down a straightaway. Pulling stone-boats with heavy loads was a popular event. Watching a team of large Percherons demolish a lighter team, Brandi imagined her brother and Don Hunter enthusiastically taking part. Her tales of this event would inspire Muffin and Don Hunter to bring a team down for the fun in the following year, starting a Hunter tradition making the Hanover meet legendary in Huron Territory. One of the few excuses people would have for travelling long distances.

Brandi resisted a challenge for Dodger to compete with other quarter horses, citing the risk of her mount pulling a muscle, or worse. She took up a challenge made by a local artist in the competitive spirit of the day.

He had admired her drawings of the events. They sat atop two hay wagons and sketched the dynamic scene of the crowd and horses and after an hour, they would decide who had the more finished work. To encourage them, several old-time fiddlers and a guitarist gathered on a wagon and kept up a steady flow of lively music.

In the end, judges declared the local man the winner while agreeing; Brandi had created better detail. The onlookers loved a little vignette in her drawing of a boy pulling his sister's pigtails, and mom scolding them both. After a few embellishments, Brandi traded her picture to the mother for smoked pork, sourdough starter and oats for Dodger, enough to see her through to Flesherton unless something delayed her.

Brandi and the local artist became lifelong friends. The man would travel to Kimberly for a session, Brandi's first recruit to the band of artists and storytellers, who would find a welcome throughout the territory.

The ending almost spoiled the day, after families had drifted home with darkness. Dancing and the consumption of local beer and applejack had taken hold. Brandi enjoyed the scene and danced with her new friend and several others. It started as a grand party; however, drunkenness grew, and soon a brawl broke out. The locals tried to bring things under control, but it all deteriorated into the happy drunks trying to control angry drunks. Brandi scurried off to find Dodger and led him to a safe place for the night. At dawn, she left in the general direction of Mount Forest.

Brandi knew the river would lead her ever upward to the heights of the escarpment, but the hills and valleys of the landscape seemed to deny it. Brandi and Dodger wandered along the back roads, twisting and turning, mimicking the meandering of the Saugeen. She visited farming enclaves, most hosting several families. Twice she visited multi-generational family farms, spending a few days and enjoying the interplay between great-grandparents and the youngest of the children. This experience highlighted the sadness of the "missing generation" as one grandparent put it. There were no men and women between the ages of fourteen and thirty. The PLM army had drafted them and taken everyone to Toronto during the previous fall's pullback. The family had no news and deep sadness.

They warned her of a landowner, "A bad-man a few farms over" who kept people as slaves. Brandi would get the information to Stan Gregson. Dodger and Brandi backtracked towards the river. The roads led her through a small village with a dilapidated water mill. Locals struggled to restore it to working condition. The old mill and dam were impressive, and Brandi encouraged the locals with accounts of similar successful efforts. She spent a few days helping, telling stories and listening. The weight of isolation dragged people low. She always left happier people when she moved on.

Most places had an absence of younger people and hated the PLM.

Brandi found some of the country devoid of human occupants. At first, there were active farms interspersed with abandoned properties. Soon, there were no occupied houses at all. Everyone had vanished, leaving farms in ghostly silence. In several places, she found signs of a struggle and hasty flight.

Brandi's worry grew when she came upon a once prosperous farm, now silent and abandoned. A red and white sign wobbled in the afternoon breeze, dangling from the gatepost on a single rusting nail. It read, "Government, keep your hands off MY property." Brandi turned up the lane to understand. The once impressive farmhouse had burnt several years before, destroying the roof and crumbling the brickwork. Vegetation filled the gutted cellar, but the rear portion remained intact. With Dodger secured to the rusting wrought-iron railing of the pointless front steps, Brand un-shouldered her rifle, "spooked", as Jani would have said.

In the tangled yard behind the house, a flock of feral chickens scratched and argued, a living hint there had once been a farm operation. Brandi thought the birds had never seen a human. Cautiously, she entered the barn. Thick fly-filled cobwebs shrouded the dust-caked windows, and the skeletons of several cattle had a sobering effect.

Machinery rusted, scattered about in typical working farm fashion. Brandi discovered chickens were not the only living remnants of domestic conditions. The old kitchen garden had several onions and potato vines re-grown from their seed. Brandi harvested the offering into an old grain sack and filled her hat with raspberries. She easily caught a chicken and found a large stainless-steel pot in the ruined kitchen.

Late afternoon shadows spread between the buildings. Death had visited here, and Brandi would not stay overnight. She and Dodger retreated, but she pried the sign off the gatepost.

They made an encampment on the high riverbank with fewer mosquitoes. The pot boiled with a wonderful aroma of chicken and Brandi enjoyed one of her most contented encampments. After her meal, she reclined against her saddle, munching the sweet raspberries beneath the August sky full of shooting stars. Only her lingering disquiet over the destroyed farm and the empty countryside lessened her contentment. The day had no human contact, and loneliness replaced the setting sun.

Chapter Four

What is the use of a book, thought Alice, without pictures or conversations?
Lewis Carroll, Alice in Wonderland, Ch. 1" – ET

"Damn, Rob is making these messages too long!" Barry Young sat at the kitchen table with a coal oil lantern spreading pale yellow light over an open book.

"For an engineer, he talks a lot." Jennifer Young smiled, writing words down as Barry found them.

"Yes, I'm the strong, silent type." Barry winked. "Difficult," he added the word. They worked well into the night deciphering their friend's latest message, following the same routine whenever the engineer delivered a book. The PLM had named Barry the superintendent of operations for the railroad. Knowing Rob Bossley had worked harder coding the message reduced their frustration.

"It seems they want to negotiate," Jennifer finished the last phrase. "Do you think it's genuine?"

"The message is from Rob." Barry was confident.

The first letter of the first word in the message was "R", and the first letter of the tenth word was "B", the verification code. If someone forced Rob to write the message, or another had written, they would not know the signal. Rob might reveal it if tortured, but they had to draw a line of trust somewhere.

It took a day to re-encode using the matrix with an added message from the Young's to their son. Reverend Wright made his daily walk to the fifth line house drop-off. Matt Long rode through the driving rain to Flesherton. The fiasco of the fall battle lessened the danger, but he swung well west of Dundalk to avoid accidental encounters.

***

"They're coming to talk." Chester sat in the Flesherton office with most of the General Counsel. Absent representatives hurried to the meeting. The Security Council of Roger, Helen, and Jeff sat to one side with Matt Long. Ted Macedo led a security detail outside.

"How do we respond?" Bob Paisley sounded positive.

"We talk to them. From this message," Chester waived the paper, "they want a cease-fire and to finish the railway to the Sound with our help."

"When will this be?"

"The representative must be in Weyburne already." Chester glanced at the paper. "They plan to come up to the Ten Barrier and ask to talk."

"Let's go meet them," Bob was eager.

"We have to wait," Helen piped up. "Our being ready might make them guess we have spies. We must wait for them and delay our answer."

There was no argument. The leaders felt nervous optimism. A truce would buy time and save many lives.

***

"... and his name that sat on him was Death, and Hell followed with him."

From the Christian holy book. The Book of Revelation Chapter 6, part Verse 8–E.T.

Brandi sat gazing out the open door of the driving shed. She broke camp in the night and rushed Dodger to safety as a ferocious storm bore down on them. The hard drizzle from the back of the system made a dreary morning. They would need to go back to the campsite and retrieve her cooking kit. She hoped that the stew had survived, and she would have a meal of leftovers. To fill her time, she worked on a sketch of the Hanover races. The happy theme cheered her spirits.

In the early afternoon, they rode beneath clouds, with a brisk northwest wind at their backs. From the brow of a small hill, Brandi examined a little abandoned village below strung out along the road by the river.

Brandi paused at the edge of the built-up area to examine a sign, a beautifully carved and painted piece of pine bearing the name Paradise chiselled deeply into the wooden oval and painted green, contrasting with the yellow background. Someone had defaced the work with a roughly carved word wandering across the board. It said, „Hell'. The scene beyond seemed like hell.

Every building had burned out. Weeds obscured the ground. Low clouds scudded silently above. Only the wind's rustling the jumbled vegetation broke the oppressive silence. Brandi cautiously walked down the road, leading Dodger, afraid to look. The remains of what had once been a brick bungalow suggested someone had destroyed it several years before. Perhaps the timing corresponded to the destroyed farm.

Brandi counted thirty ravaged houses and a larger building. A natural disaster or accident was unlikely, considering the many bullet marks on the standing walls.

Stepping gingerly through the tangle of burdock and bindweed, Brandi attempted to reach a less damaged building. Her foot rolled as her weight bore down onto a hard, round object. She gasped. Her boot rested on a small shinbone beside the small bones of the foot of a child. Tears flowed as Brandi ran back to the road.

It is too horrible! Her thoughts tumbled. She could barely see Dodger through the tears.

"I HATE YOU!" she screamed at the ruins and the dark clouds churning in the sky. Dodger started and skittered at her unfamiliar eruption of emotion. His protests reinforced her outburst, mingling with her sobs. It took Brandi a long time to calm down. She leaned against Dodger, her tears wetting his coat. The big horse did not move, feeling her trembling body and sensing her need.

Without a word, she swung onto his back and cantered out of town. Brandi could not look back. Dodger carried her swiftly through the dismal afternoon. He could not feel the heavyweight of the girl's heart; perhaps he could sense her sadness. They hurried on, resting only for his benefit. She wanted to get as far away as possible, and often looked back as if some evil force pursued her.

Brandi could not outrun her feelings. The growing distance did not reduce her horror. Hunger finally reminded her of the day's end. She had passed many abandoned farms, each appearing to be hostile and dangerous. The threat of rain forced her to camp in an empty storage shed. They would be dry for the night.

"At least," she told Dodger, "there are no dead people."

The dilapidated, corrugated-steel structure proved comfortable. Not risking a fire, Brandi ate the last of the chicken stew, cold, telling Dodger it was not, "half bad". The big horse snickered, as if he doubted her taste, and munched his ration of oats. The storm had left ample water in the ditch. Dodger was content.

Brandi led her friend inside the building as darkness fell and slid the big door closed. Never had she felt so vulnerable. The girl reclined against a wall; the Savage rifle cradled in her arms. Dodger found the dirt floor to his liking and lay down. Brandi started and worried at every sound until fatigue finally won out. She joined the big horse in merciful rest. Fitful dreams plagued her through the night, but fortune kept her from remembering details. Her waking came with the sound of sheet metal scraping softly in the morning breeze. The wind had shifted to the southwest. A glance out the dusty window told her the sky had cleared and the dawn would be bright. She shivered and stretched. Dodger remained at rest.

She slipped out with her drawing case to sit in the strengthening light. An hour of furious drawing, Brandi produced what she would later describe as the darkest image of her career, a screaming child whose eyes, full of unspeakable fear, were staring off at an unseen horror. Sharon recognized the child as a young Brandi whose heart lay with little bones sleeping in the weeds.

***

"Welcome, my name is Aaron Martin."

Aaron stepped onto the road, startling Brandi. He had been whitewashing the gateposts marking the farm on the highway west of Mount Forest. Aaron wore black, threadbare trousers patched several times, held up by equally dark suspenders contrasting nicely over a clean, long-sleeved, white shirt with fraying collar and cuffs. A straw hat shaded his friendly face.

"We don't see many travellers these days. Come in and meet the family." He stood to one side, indicating the well-kept laneway. Brandi dismounted and extended her hand.

"I'm Brandi Shadly, travelling down from the west heading to Mount Forest." The man's work-hardened hand gripped hers in a firm greeting.

"Which way did you come?" They walked towards a large farmhouse. He frowned at the rifle in the scabbard.

"From Hanover, the last place I came through was called Paradise. Someone destroyed it."

"That's a sad place," His face darkened, "a sad place."

"What happened? Why is all that country up there abandoned? The farms all look good."

"There'll be time later." Aaron opened the gate into a neat paddock near the barn. "There's always time for sadness. First, we must have some happy times."

He helped Brandi strip the saddle from Dodger and rub him down. He carefully examined every inch of Dodger.

"You take good care of him." It was both a statement and praise. "He'll need work on that left rear hoof. Avoid too rough of a trail."

A cohort of children in traditional Mennonite clothing watched them from the house gate, patiently waiting for their father and this strange woman. Brandi would make lifelong friends today.

The path from the barn to the house passed through a bountiful vegetable garden. Gourds, tomatoes, cucumbers, and various root crops stretched all around the house. Fruit trees filled a neat orchard past the garden. Beyond, a vast field of pumpkin and then grains stretched away out of sight. There seemed to be too many people working in various places. Brandi thought that no one family could be so big. Four multi-generational families shared the work and bounty of the farm. Two families lived in this house; two shared the dwelling on the adjacent forty-hectare allotment. Twenty adults and sixteen children thrived on slightly more than a hundred hectares of fertile land.

"You have come a long way." Aaron sat in a large cane chair on the west porch of the big house. Sunset washed the sky with deep purples overhead merging with a golden horizon. From Brandi's position on a gently rocking porch swing, the man was a silhouette.

"This is my longest journey so far." Brandi shifted to make room for two of the older girls to slide in beside her. "I plan to get to Mount Forest and then to Flesherton."

"I take it the trip from Hanover wasn't the best." Aaron acknowledged an older man who had drawn up a straight-backed chair. Aaron seemed to be the leader, but Brandi decided this other was the true patriarch of the clan. He had ceded the head of the table to Aaron and sat near the foot, opposite the traveller. Brandi could feel the honour and respect the family had for this man. It had been a deliberate honour and breaking of tradition, seating her opposite at the meal.

"It was good down through the mill town. I met friendly people on a farm run a lot like yours." Aaron seemed to perk up at that statement.

"Was that a group of us?" He asked quietly.

"Nope, they are good folks. I'm not sure about what they believe. They said grace at meals, though. I reached the burnt-out place called Paradise, and it all changed. I have been upset ever since. Paradise, the other abandoned places and the burnt-out farms hit me hard."

The sounds of the night filled a long pause.

"It was terrible then, about three years ago." The old man spoke. "There were lots of bad people around, and new ones came in and stirred them up." His chair made scraping sounds as he drew it closer to the swing. "Jehovah's Witness adherents moved into that little village beginning the year of the change and they thrived, worked hard and looked after themselves. Many of the farms here are of our faith, but we got along with those up there. Just because they had the wrong end of the belief stick didn't mean they were no good."

The old man paused. One girl ran off, returning with a tall glass of water. When Aaron frowned at her, both girls disappeared, reappearing with drinks for everyone.

"Lots of the locals resented the folks in Paradise. The preaching could get on your nerves, but they were mostly too busy trying to survive to preach. When the outsiders came, the evil men recruited locals into a security force. They were a bunch of thieving no goods, demanding a levy and bullied folks, including us. Everyone had to fight or pay up. We don't fight, but the Paradise folks argued with them." The patriarch paused, concerned that he had passed judgment.

"The rest of the story is only second hand." Aaron took over when the old man dozed off. "A couple of people escaped and passed by here. They are hiding somewhere south. One day, a bunch of those bandits showed up in Paradise, drunk, demanding a tax and molesting women. The Witness men defended their own in an all-out fight. The posse had more guns, and the fight didn't last long. They killed everyone they could find and burned the place down. The two we saw survived by pretending to be dead."

For the first time, Brandi saw some emotion from Aaron. She empathized. Her memories and horror gripped her heart once more. The two girls sobbed.

"After, things got even worse around. They kept trying to find out if anyone knew about it. A few months later, they killed a couple of farmers they thought knew the story, including one of our families."

"What about those abandoned farms? I found one burnt out and a sign warning the government off."

"The bad guys hurt themselves when they destroyed Paradise. They had fewer people to rob and became more demanding. They upped the levy from us all. We paid and suffered. It wasn't so easy for some."

A girl took her empty water glass, and a glass of sweet raspberry drink replaced it. The girls smiled at Brandi and seemed eager to be with her. Later, one would admit even though they loved their family and knew their place, they felt isolated. Brandi brought excitement.

"Many people around here coveted their land. We share, but they seemed to think to own a few acres made them better. The sign you saw sums up their thinking. They resented those intruders who weren't even the legitimate government, so they fought back, but each one seems to have tried to defend their places alone. Same thing happened to them as at Paradise. It just took a little longer, one at a time."

Brandi shuddered, remembering the murder of the Quinn's at Weyburne.

"The terrorism ended after the big storm. The devils left, a big surprise, God's gift. We feel safe."

Brandi recounted the fighting and the failure of the electrical system causing turmoil in the cities.

"The mystery of prayer, but we didn't ask for killing," Aaron said no more about it.

Brandi remained for several days, working and learning. She told Aaron she would tell the Costello's and other horse people about the farm.

Everyone always wanted to search out new strains. The Mennonites had a
few good, light working horses. Brandi's stories of her travels, Huron
Territory and her flight from Weyburne entertained a group eager for
news.

The girls especially insisted on working closely with her. Unknown to
Brandi, a strong, single, independent female caused much debate amongst
the leaders uneasy about the example she might set for their young,
especially the girls.

"We sure are enjoying your visit." Annalise, the oldest of the girls, stood
and stretched in her spot between rows of cabbage. She tucked a lock of
hair into her gingham cap and used the back of her hand to wipe sweat
from her brow.

"Isn't your dress hot?" Brandi stretched and took a swig of water,
offering some to the girl.

"Sometimes," the girl replied, "but it is necessary to be modest. You
dress like a man. Poppa says that is unbecoming, but it is your way, and
we should respect you."

"He says the boys' struggle and should not be encouraged to sin."

"I'll try to not flirt with them." Brandi winked, and they both laughed.

Brandi had noted they never left two older boys in their late teens alone
with her. Whenever one of them came near, Brandi would look up and see
an adult in sight. She decided they distrusted the boys more than the
stranger, although they did not yet know her well enough to trust. Annalise
accidentally revealed an unexpected impact of her visit. One morning,
while working beside Brandi in the garden, she yawned profusely. She
said they rarely stayed up late, and yet no one wanted to miss any of
Brandi's late evening stories on the porch.

On the fourth morning, Brandi saddled Dodger and led him down the
lane, escorted by the family, laughing and joking. The hugs from the
women were warm, and the men nodded farewell. Aaron's wife held
Brandi's parting gift, a drawing where children laboured in the garden and
the Patriarch stood at the top of the steps with the adult women. Men
worked with horses beyond the fence. Aaron stood with one foot on the
bottom step, looking up at his father. The woman approved this depiction
of family and industry.

"Return soon." Everyone said at once.

"You'll see me again for sure," Brandi smiled and encouraged Dodger onto the road towards Mount Forest.

Chapter Five

"All warfare is based on deception. Hence, when we are able to attack, we must seem unable; when using our forces, we must appear inactive; when we are near, we must make the enemy believe we are far away; when far away, we must make him believe we are near."
Sun Tzu's The Art of War (From Roger LaFarge's library) - ET

A warm south-west breeze blew smartly as the Huron delegation approached the hilltop and a group of ten individuals. They had erected an open pavilion on the old highway. A large flag stood out stiffly in the wind; its white field supported a red maple leaf cut by a jagged black bar. Jeff Shadly tried not to show his disgust as he escorted Chester and Rob Paisley up the slight grade. His group had no flag save a white cloth. They paused fifty meters short of their goal.

"We have to go alone," Chester said. "Keep an eye out. They asked for this, so I'm not worried. They don't know how much we know."

Chester failed to spot Roger's commando squad. Ted and the other snipers remained invisible, but a brigade stood, visible, a kilometre down the road. PLM fighters waited in the opposite direction.

"I don't like you being up there unarmed." Jeff considered Chester a genuine friend. He had wanted to command the security for the negotiations but did not like being this exposed.

The negotiators headed up the hill. Jeff and two soldiers stood ready. The delegation reached the canopy, and two seated men stood to shake hands. The exchange was curt. No one smiled.

"You called this meeting." Rob Paisley did not waste time on pleasantries. "What do you want?"

"Please have a seat." The man made an expansive gesture towards two comfortable padded chairs. Chester smiled at the corporate style and laughed as he realized the refreshment pavilion stood twenty-five meters behind the meeting spot. Two white-clad figures laboured over a stove.

"I am Alphonse Angel; this is my assistant. By the grace of the people, I govern Dufferin County." The negotiations were too important for underlings, and Angel used the word "people" as if it implied democracy.

"I have full power to decide here and now." He implied they had to come to some agreement. His voice conveyed urgency.

Paisley, the experienced politician, guessed Toronto had mandated the talks and Angel needed an agreement.

"We have an offer and a proposal." Angel handed two copies of a brief document to the Huron delegates. The white paper contrasted with the dark maroon of the tablecloth. "We propose a cease fire and a truce for five years, and then renegotiated. There are frontier guarantees, a demilitarized zone and exchanges of security information."

"What do you mean by security information?" Chester frowned.

"We reveal the positions of fixed control points and travel routes and any movements of troops to the frontier and a commitment not to patrol the demilitarized area. We have a list of criminals who fled from our justice."

"You can give us the list," Chester looked grim, "but we won't commit to handing anyone over." He thought of Jeff waiting a few meters away.

"It would be hard to trust anyone who would harbour criminals." Angel's tone was fair, but his face showed anger. "How can you support murders and thugs?"

Chester resisted the urge to call Angel a murderer and thug.

"We can resolve that later." Paisley saw Chester's struggle and used his skills in talking with people he disliked. "We want only a hundred fighters stationed at Weyburne with none in the border zone." Rob smiled casually. "Also, you agree to post only a hundred in Orangeville. The truce zone border the Noisy River and along County Road Nine and Eight, down the Grand River to Highway 9."

"There is no way I can agree with those numbers." Angel burst out, but the look in his eye told Rob that Angel had already accepted but would lie, anyway. He already had several hundred fighters guarding his compounds in the hills. Rob hoped Angel would think the numbers revealed how few fighters Huron could muster. He intentionally low balled the proposal, hoping they would assume Huron's weakness. He gambled the low number might encourage an attack, but knew the PLM did not want war.

"Well then, we can't go any further." Chester stood.

"Hold on," Angel was a skilled negotiator, "I didn't say no. We need a hundred soldiers at Weyburne and two hundred at Orangeville?"

"And no heavy weapons or flying over us," Paisley smiled inside.

Both sides wanted peace, and they resolved the details in the morning. Chester and Rob had an open mandate. They would only take serious matters back to the Council waiting in Flesherton. The agreement would give them time to grow stronger. Even if it collapsed within five years, it would help. They would not let down their guard.

The cooks brought lunch to the table, a choice of roast beef with all the trimmings or roast duck. Angel wanted to impress the Huron negotiators. The two ate with relish and no regret, but they knew ordinary people under the PLM jurisdiction did not eat as well as the average resident of Huron. Despite their name, the People's Liberation Movement had one standard for their elite and another for the masses. The well-fed Angel had a soft life. The PLM pair drank wine. Chester and Rob declined and drank water.

"You have an offer," Chester said, as the lunch remains disappeared.

"We will complete the railway to Owen Sound for you." Angel made it sound like a generous gift.

"We didn't ask for one." Rob chuckled, annoying Angel.

"But you need one," he sounded too eager. Chester was glad they had not drunk wine. "Think of all the good it will do for you. All the great things we can ship to you." Angel did not seem to have a plan to sell the railway idea. The Huron negotiators understood more than this man did. They knew, from the intelligence reports, the Detroit River was unsafe, and the PLM could not negotiate the opening of the railway from Sudbury to Thunder Bay. They needed the railroad to bring iron ore to Hamilton through Owen Sound, bypassing the stubborn northerners.

"What are you proposing?" Chester wanted details.

"We supply material and experts. You guarantee safe conditions. We will need labourers."

"We don't have many people to spare." Chester knew Angel was also short of labour. The PLM would never complete the project without Huron's workers. He also guessed Angel was sure he could keep a hold of his engineers, but workers might desert, especially his slave labour.

"We don't have the skilled workers," Rob understood Angel's fear, "you have to supply half of the labour force and the engineers."

Angel flashed a smug look at his assistant. He had won. In fact, he was right about one point. The Huron General Council saw benefits in having material available from the south. People missed things like coffee and tea and sugar and fruit. There could be some trade. Huron could sell firewood and food. The ex-business people on the council dreamed of profits. They had instructed Chester and Rob to agree to the railway unless the cost was too high. Angel wrote out the document; the four men signed.

Barry Young would lead surveyors up the old right of way. Huron soldiers would escort them north of Proton Station. Young's group would assess the material and labour required. They wanted to begin work before winter. Proton Station would be the official border crossing.

"We know Young won't run away," Angel smiled, "with his family still in Weyburne." Chester and Rob winced at the implied threat of hostages. Angel repelled them.

They finally accepted the wine. Peering at Angel over his glass, Chester hoped he would see the man hung.

Chapter Six

I fear the stranger
I fear the danger
I fear the shadows of the night
I hide behind gates and bars
And never, ever see the stars

Brandi stayed briefly in Mount Forest where a few hundred families involved in local farming or basic trades made up the population. Metalworking and salvage were the principal activities, supported by surpluses from the farms.

They occupied dwellings near the river. Water was easier to carry shorter distances, and the safety of the river water had improved. This stream-focused community accepted the organized watershed concept. Brandi shared part of her journey home with representatives travelling to the meeting at Southampton.

"Won't you ride up to Durham with us?" The head of the Mount Forest delegation shook Brandi's hand.

"I've enjoyed our visit, but Durham is not a mystery. There has been lots of contact with Priceville. I want to meet unconnected folks elsewhere."

Brandi planned to wander through the back country, looking forward to a few peaceful days on her own. She watched the small band disappear to the north. The past week with friendly people had repaired her spirit.

Early afternoon found Brandi and Dodger well up on what had been an important but now little-used road. She paused, sitting silently on Dodger, listening and sniffing the faint odour of wood smoke. Gauging by the slight movement of the trees, it was coming from a thick bush to the east. She dismounted and eased along until discovering a disused lane. Once past the thicket at the road, the way was more open for Dodger. Aspens lined the edges, and smaller beech saplings, chest-high on Dodger, reclaimed the seldom-used path.

The smell of smoke increased. Brandi reached a clearing in front of a large wooden shed, hitched Dodger to the doorway, and headed around the building. It was not clear if Brandi or the small woman she met were more startled. The woman yelped and scurried backwards a few paces. She wore a long, much-worn cotton dress with torn seams and rough patching. Her hair was long and unkempt, with smudges of dirt on a rather pretty face.

"Hello," Brandi eased forward gently. "I'm Brandi. I'm sorry to arrive unannounced." She smiled, but the girl seemed confused, staring at the rifle slung innocently over Brandi's shoulder.

"How... who... why...?"

The startled creature suddenly yelped and turned tail, running towards another building and disappeared inside. A half-dozen people tumbled out, excited and looking scared. A man in his mid-thirties stepped forward, hostile but hesitant.

"How did you find us?"

"I wasn't looking for you, although I want to meet new people. Your smoke and the path led me here. I'm Brandi Shadly." She stepped forward. They eased back.

"No one found us before," he said. "We hid ourselves."

"An Ojibwe woman and my brother taught me how to track." Brandi tried to sound friendly. "I'm travelling to meet people who need help."

She saw that this group was undernourished and barely able to keep their clothes together. The man wore an outfit in worse shape than the woman's dress.

"I am sorry," he said. "We aren't unfriendly. You're the first stranger we've met in seven years. I'm Rune."

He shook her hand. Seven people lived in this desperate condition. Once over the shock, they eagerly showed her around. Seven years of talking to only a few other people became boring, if not debilitating.

No one offered refreshments. Everyone provided commentary as they guided Brandi through the grounds. She recognized Permaculture techniques like those the Bryson's used. Raised vegetable and herb beds complimented nut and fruit trees surrounded by swales dug to hold water; a variety of semi-aquatic and moisture-loving plants grew in the dampness. Nut trees hosted a scurry of squirrels. One resident attempted to chase the animals away. The creatures felt no fear.

The well-maintained gardens did not have as much yield as Brandi saw elsewhere. Pests had eaten many vegetables and fruit. She had not seen ducks or geese to eat weeds and insects, providing their waste as nutrients, and no animal enclosures or barns. The explanation came at supper.

"We thank Vega for her bounty and promise to continue protecting her children." The girl's voice sounded weary, almost lethargic.

The group held hands at a large table made of rough, un-sanded wood. Benches of half logs on maple branch legs ran along each side of the table. Two large chairs made from branches occupied the end positions. The furniture showed little skill and no finishing with linseed oil.

Everyone used a wooden bowl. Larger bowls held vegetables and grains. Everyone wrapped flatbread from a central pile around vegetables or tore bits to eat with handfuls of nuts and greens. They ate the unappealing fare without utensils. Brandi ate politely, anticipating smoked meat and other delights in her food bag.

"I know it's bland." Rune appeared to be the leader. "In the city, we had tofu, veggie burgers and lots of nuts for protein. Our supplies ran out in the first year. We didn't realize our dependency on stores and factories. Our nut trees are the major source, but as you saw the squirrels like them too." His attitude suggested surrender to the animals. "We don't eat meat or use animals. That poor horse you exploit needs to be free."

He unsettled Brandi, but she kept silent. The only other male in the group was Aeon. He was much younger, perhaps in his mid-twenties and with wild red hair and an unkempt, flaming full beard. Brandi did not know if these were nicknames. No one in the group used a family name. The four women's names reflected their beliefs.

"We raided many places to set enslaved animals free." The woman named Echo sounded proud. She was in her early thirties, dressed plainly in failing garments, with no makeup. They all wore handmade jewellery of wire, colourful stones and wood.

"What's your story?" Rune changed the subject, perhaps unsure of revealing too much to a stranger.

Brandi told the story of Huron. As she described routine farming and attempts to survive, her listeners burst out in anger. She had last heard such expletives from the prisoners taken in the aborted helicopter attack at Flesherton. Her hosts did not want to hear about farm animals or eating meat, milk and eggs, or hunting. When she talked about electricity and horse-powered technology, the atmosphere became hostile.

"Technology is a sin against Gaia." The woman named April Sky exclaimed. "Those who use such things are condemning themselves to death." Brandi was not sure if she meant it was an unsustainable idea or someone should kill the sinners. She thought of the congregation at Irish Lake condemning Al Wright.

"What did you do before the crash and how did you get here?" Brandi hoped to change the subject from her poorly received story. All eyes turned towards Rune, asking permission to speak.

"We are a commando group fighting for Gaia and all of her animals." Rune's description sounded grand.

"We raided lots of labs where they tortured animals and set them free," Echo was proud. "We were notorious. The stupid cops and animal murderers could never catch us."

"So, how did you end up here?"

"We set this up many years ago as a hideout, in case the cops got close." Rune spoke well. He had been a teaching assistant at a university with a Ph.D. in philosophy. "We tried to rescue abandoned animals after the collapse. It was too dangerous."

"People ate their pets," Echo flared. "Remember Tich? He died trying to stop one." Rage circled the table.

"We made a run for it." Rune took up the story. "We came in twos as planned. It took two months at the end of the first winter, but we all made it. We've been here since, growing our food by Gaia's law, waiting to get back to the city when the time is ripe."

"When do you think things will be back to normal?" April Sky looked at Brandi with large bright eyes. Brandi wondered if she should soften the blow. Honesty prevailed.

"Never," she said quietly, "that time is over. Things will never again be like they were." The girl gasped. Rune nodded.

"You are in rough shape," Brandi stated the obvious. "You could connect with the locals and get help."

"We are doing okay." Rune was forceful. "We don't need help, especially from animal killers."

Brandi had had enough of this dismal conversation and hoped for an excuse to go to Dodger and eat actual food. She had the chance as the evening shadows invaded the unlit room. Rune called for the clearing of the meal. She wandered away. As she squared away her saddle and contemplated the food bag, one woman appeared.

"It is nice to get news," April-Sky smiled, looking at Dodger in awe. "I have never been this close to a horse."

"Where did you grow up?" Brandi postponed her snack.

"In Rosedale, Toronto, my parents were dirty rich and ate meat and everything. When I became a vegan, they made fun of me and wouldn't listen. My idiot father got abusive and served meat-only meals to bug me. I met Rune when I was sixteen, moved out and lived with the others. I never saw my family again." She did not seem sad about it.

Evening deepened. Stars populated the sky.

"See the star rising in the east?" April Sky pointed somewhat east of overhead to a brilliant blue star Brandi recognized immediately. "That's Vega." She sounded reverent. "She's our guiding light; her spirit holds our souls and forgives our trespasses on her world. She's the guardian of Gaia. We are her soldiers. Summer is her season."

Brandi thought of Vega as a guiding light, but not as an object of worship. Brent James taught the class in Weyburne about the major stars and constellations and how the Earth orbited the sun and the other basic details of the solar system. He had shown how to navigate and tell time and dates by the stars. After the liberation of Flesherton, he helped Brandi draw sky charts showing the local night sky each month. The institute made these charts standard teaching tools. Soldiers learned how to read the maps. Jeff, Ted and others had copies.

Brandi carried the twelve in her folio. Many nights, she oriented herself on a high hill, planning her direction of travel. She used the position of the stars as a rough clock, although the exact time was no longer a big issue. Only the military found clocks useful to coordinate operations.

The charts kept track of the seasons. The Institute had an official astronomer and calendar watcher who could correct people's errors but kept the old system of dates and the change of leap year. Everyone abandoned the useless concept of daylight saving time. People got up with the birds and went to sleep with the sun. April Sky talked about the healing power of Gaia and her mystical goddess, Vega.

"We find the star important as well." Brandi extracted the midsummer sky chart from her folio. We use it for navigating.

"That is science; science is bad." The woman repeated a catechism. "You insult Vega by using her for mundane things. You can't claim Vega by putting her on paper!"

She said this so forcefully Brandi became apprehensive. Irish Lake came to mind once again. Her host looked skyward and uttered strange words, asking Vega's forgiveness for the traveller's sin.

"I had better get back." She turned, dismissing her relationship with the visitor. "Vega will be at fullness soon and shine her light upon the water. I must be ready at the circle." Brandi followed her down the dark trail. They parted ways at the woodshed, where Brandi would sleep.

Chanting rose from the garden where log benches encircled a large multicoloured granite rock. A hand-ground, black granite stone sat on top, with its hollowed-out surface filled with still, clear water. The seats curved around the north side of the mirror bowl. The star's pulsing light, at the zenith, would reflect from the water's glassy surface at the climax of the ritual. Darkness covered all except for the pale light of the waxing moon sinking below the trees to the west. Bright stars carpeted the sky.

With the chanting in the background, Brandi sat on the doorstep of the shed. Dodger stood contentedly and would soon lie down. She marvelled at the brilliant night sky, feeling restored by the calm evening air. Bats flitted overhead, making no dent at all in the large population of night insects. Brandi casually munched on dried pork. The treat-filled the hole left in her stomach. As she ate, Brandi pondered this fresh evidence of the need for human spiritual fulfilment. It was not clear how this fit into the daily struggle for existence. She found the question interesting.

Brandi did not see the pair of eyes staring around the corner, their disgust and anger lost in the dark shadows. Once again, she was about to experience the dangerous end of the spiritual stick. The sudden stopping of the chanting brought Brandi back from her reverie. She rubbed Dodger's ear as she passed, heading towards the corner of the shed towards the garden. A loud voice brought her up short.

"She's a meat-eating heretic!" Ruen spoke loudly.

"Shhh," a female said. "She will hear you." The voices became subdued. Brandi crept closer to the circle.

"...was eating meat." Echo spoke. "I just saw it."

"She has put Vega onto paper," April sky's voice rose. "They have desecrated the guiding light. She has a gun and murders animals and put steel shoes on her enslaved horse."

"Kill her," the quiet words cut right into Brandi's gut. She fought back nausea. "Let her die by her own rules." Rune's voice commanded. The murmur of agreement pushed Brandi physically backwards. "We'll do it at first morning light, while she sleeps. She won't suffer as her victims did. The horse will run free and enjoy the rest of his life."

Rune sounded generous and caring. Brandi could not help but marvel at the stupidity of condemning Dodger to a short life, alone and abandoned. She crept silently back to the shelter; her eyes tearing in fear and sadness. Desperation gripped her. It would be too dangerous to attempt the overgrown trail in the dark. Dodger could not safely get through the tangle of bush.

The slight movement of a watcher just at the tree line decided. She would need the light to help her and would have to force her way through. She got her gear together, ready to run.

Although she was fit, trained to fight, and much stronger than these people, she could only handle a couple before they overwhelmed her.

It was a fitful night. Brandi tried to appear to be sleeping but kept the door open and sat with her back to the wall, watching. Rest could come later, hopefully after putting a long-distance between her and this danger. She watched through the opening as Vega slid silently behind the trees, signalling the morning stirring of the birds and the start of a new day.

Dodger snorted and struggled to his feet, disturbed by approaching strangers. In the dark recess of the shack, Brandi prepared. Breathing slowly, she fought to stay calm. The sound of someone doing a poor job of sneaking towards her resting place raised a thin smile. The rustling sounds stopped as if they were waiting. Two figures stopped near the horse in the growing dawn light. Brandi came out of the shed cautiously, making sure that no one was to either side. Her backpack and folio bag both hung from her shoulders, so her hands were free. She could easily shed these two encumbrances if it came to a fight. Brandi held her rifle ready with the safety off.

"Move away from the horse," Brandi commanded as she glared at the woman closest to Dodger. "You... saddle the horse." The skinny woman tried to obey but needed help from the other to lift the saddle onto Dodger. They pulled the strap as tightly as they could and cinched it up. "Now back off." The pair obeyed. Brandi hoped the saddle would survive a getaway.

A shadow moved on her right. Rune rushed at her, his arm raised and a knife ready for a chop thrust. Brandi fired a bullet into the ground at the man's feet. He skidded to a stop, dropping the knife in surprise. The bolt snicked another round into the chamber. Luckily, the bullet had not hit a rock and injured Rune. Brandi had no desire to hurt anyone.

"Over with the others," Brandi barked the command, taking control. She moved to Dodger's flank and checked the girth strap. It would be sufficient for a short gallop. The others must be nearby. They would soon recover from their surprise.

Brandi had Dodger at a canter before her right foot found the stirrup. The pair slid by the last of the shocked women. A light nudge from her boot heels and Dodger sped up the weed-choked laneway, deftly avoiding the standing burdock and ubiquitous bindweed. It was a getaway worthy of an old western movie, but Brandi did not think of heroics. The Vegans chased her, grabbing rocks and sticks as they ran, but Dodger and Brandi disappeared as the path curved through the trees, pursued by shouted curses, threats and the sound of rocks hitting leaves. Brandi concentrated on avoiding any disaster with the trees.

Damn it! I had to waste a bullet and didn't even save the casing, she thought, but let out a whoop of victory as they left the tangled laneway, bursting onto the wider roadway.

A few hundred meters down the main road, she stopped to reset the girth; the nearness of her death hit her. She clung to Dodger's mane until her trembling stopped. Brandi hoped this narrow escape from death would be their last.

"You're the best, Dodger." Brandi hugged the big horse and swung back into the saddle, focusing on a safe, warm bed at the James' and a hug from bubbly little Stephanie who called her "aunty".

***

"I didn't leave a thank you note this time." Brandi laughed. "Unlike the Irish Lake congregation, the Vegans are capable of murder."

Her story captivated Jeff and Ted, who had waited in Flesherton for orders after the negotiations. The news of the truce cheered Brandi.

"The Vegans are under the jurisdiction of the new Saugeen Authority." It relieved Jeff that he did not have to take charge personally. He felt he could not deal fairly with people who tried to kill his sister. "They don't seem to have any morals." He frowned at Brandi.

"Oh, they have morals within their own beliefs." Brandi had puzzled over this on the ride home. "They're so caught up in their certainty they believe heretics should die. It is like the crowd at Irish Lake, except these folks will do it. Those others thought their god should do it."

"Make sure you tell the Saugeen people these folks are frail and underfed. They won't eat meat, but they could get some grain and flax oil to them. Without help, they won't survive."

"How can you care about people who tried to kill you?" Ted exclaimed.

"It's my job," Brandi smiled at Ted.

"I don't like your wandering about alone," Jeff frowned.

"I have to ride alone to contact people. It's a good thing when I find groups like this, although I would be happier if they weren't ready to kill me." She chuckled. "We must care for isolated and strange communities. If we oppose the PLM, we need to help and understand, not isolate and repress. I'm sorry, I'm lecturing you."

"You're right, Little Sister. I once told Dad you are way too deep for me." Jeff laughed. "It's your job, as you say. Listening to you helps us believe in our job."

"A couple more things." Brandi remained serious.

She recounted the rumour of slavery near Hanover and wrote the rough location. Then she described the burnt-out farm and razed village.

"Saugeen territory requires help." Brandi smiled. "Many times I wished you two heroes rode with me."

Brandi left to spend a happy day at the James' house. Another harvest would start soon. Brian Young greeted her with smiles and the news that his father would visit soon. Little Steph eagerly showed Brandi her drawings and writing. Steph's journal looked suspiciously like Brandi's.

"You are someone's heroine," Samantha James smiled.

Brandi reached Kimberly the next morning. Warren summed it all up.

"Those folks care about the world ecosystem, but have forgotten that humans are part of it. Nature is a great loop, and we all must balance on the path making allowance for all species, including ours. Nature does not value one species above another. We are what we are. If humans are indeed thinking and wise, we represent a new experiment in the flow of life. We are the first species entrusted with determining its future."

Chapter Seven

It was one of my most wonderful experiences. Barry and Brian Young, reunited, seemed to affirm what we were doing. I,m learning a lot about work from watching Barry, and his attention to detail encourages me to be more careful. He reminds me of Jim Handley. The railway work is a nice rest from the fighting.
From a letter to Brandi Shadly from her brother Jeff.
- The Brandi Shadly Archives

The grand project began with little notice. Jeff Shadly waited in a cool September rain, looking east. Several armed men stood with him. They had camped overnight to the north of Proton station, up the old rail line, and expected the engineering gang from Dundalk to arrive. Jeff did not like the misty conditions with visibility only a few hundred meters. Fog would obscure a large, hostile force. His backup snipers hid much closer than he would have liked. The last time they would bear arms this far south. The two-kilometre disarmament zone would take effect at noon, with the old Proton station at the centre point.

The workgroup appeared through the rain, plodding towards Huron with no armed guard. He recognized Barry Young. Jeff and Ted had recruited Barry as a spy and brought his son, Brian, to safety before the fighting last fall. One other man looked familiar; the rest were strangers. Ted and Jeff reminded each other they did not know Barry. Shadly remembered the other man; the coward who ran away from the fighting almost a year ago. Two surveyors and labourers accompanied Barry and the coward.

"We surveyed this far last fall," Barry Young spoke to Jeff. "Workers from Dundalk are preparing the roadbed. We will move ties and rails up from Weyburne this week; then they'll begin laying track north of the town and repairing a bridge. They'll make it here before we finish surveying the rest of the line."

"That sounds good, Bob." Jeff looked back down the line.

"Barry," Young said. "My name is Barry."

"Oh, I'm sorry," Shadly smiled; pleased with his little ruse to make Mike think they were strangers

"We set up camp three kilometres towards Flesherton. Do you want to go there first or work your way up?"

"Might as well get started here," one surveyor said. "We won't have to walk it twice. Where the hell did we leave our mark last year?" The men located a chiselled cross on the old station footing, and so the work began.

"I sure miss the GPS," the one complained, "and laser transit."

The men's ability offset the primitive equipment. They could have laid track on the existing bed with little surveying, but Barry Young demanded meticulous detail.

"The old C.P.R. surveys have disappeared. In the future, when we're long dead, someone will have the information needed to make repairs."

Jeff escorted Barry and Mike northward. Barry took his time, carefully looking over the right of way, noting where more fill would be required, and where to clear trees and debris. Every time he found a problem, he left a small orange flag impaled into the gravel with a handwritten number on it. These markings coincided with numbered notes in his book. The surveyors would mark these numbers on their map. Every culvert and bridge received careful examination.

Clearing trees would occupy the winter but gravel and culvert cleaning and repairs had to wait until the frost came out of the ground. Barry knew the few weeks of work this fall would save months of stopping and starting when track work began.

The lunch tent stood at an old railway junction. Another rundown roadbed arced away to the west.

"This is Saugeen Junction on my map." Jeff consulted a frayed sheet. "It heads off towards Priceville and Durham."

"When we return from Owen Sound," Barry gazed down the older trail, "we'll explore this. It might be a way to go west."

Mike treated the whole thing as a Sunday outing, but an armed force for lunch shocked him. Jeff found a few minutes alone with Barry Young.

"How's Brian?" Barry asked. "When can I see him?" The pair walked away, pretending to look up the branch line.

"He's in Flesherton," Jeff smiled. "You can see him tonight. We'll billet you in town. We couldn't risk you sleeping there."

"Yeah, Mike's a danger, and he'll have to be in my billet." Barry had not had the chance to warn Jeff earlier. "He's the political spy. The snake has watched me since Orangeville. He's sleeping with Angel's wife."

"If that's true, he's stupid." Jeff thought of Stevie Hunter. "He'll be dead if Angel finds out. Angel enjoys killing."

Jeff used a simple plan to separate Mike and Barry. One of the female soldiers flirted with the PLM hack, allowing Barry the chance to slip away. Brett James opened his door when Jeff knocked. Before he could even say hello, Brian shot past into his father's eager arms. The Huron men waited until the hugs, smiles, and tears subsided. They moved inside, out of sight of prying eyes. Barry could not stay long but would headquarter in Flesherton for a few days and visit each evening.

Jeff had to make amends with the unfortunate female who feigned interest in Mike.

"You owe me big time, Shadly!" the woman constantly reminded her commander. "This guy's a creep."

Months later, Jeff explained, and she forgave him. In payment, she asked to work with a man she liked. Jeff and Jani would attend her wedding.

Barry told Mike it would be useless to get too far ahead of the surveyors, and the engineer kept a slower pace. He wanted to stay near Flesherton for an extra day. Brian had turned into a man, and Barry wanted to enjoy his little boy before it happened.

Jeff arranged for Barry to linger in Flesherton on the return trip from Owen Sound. Jim Handley waited for the engineer to discuss building the stations at each major stop. It took three days of discussion, measuring and designing before Barry Young headed south. Technical details bored Mike, and the woman distracted him. Barry and Brian took a quiet walk in the countryside. They discussed the boy's future. Jeff had suggested that Brian train with a locomotive crew for the upper end of the run. Barry thought it was a great idea.

"Take care," Jeff shook Barry's hand as they parted company at Proton. "It's good to see this progress."

They stood beside a railway car resting a few feet from the end of the track. A pile of new ties that lay crossways on the rails served as a temporary bumper. A substantial pile of un-laid rails sat to one side of the track. The train comprised two flat cars with a small diesel locomotive.

"Take care, Jeff. Hug the boy for me." Mike had hurried off to claim a spot in the warmth of the locomotive. "It will thrill Jennifer to get Brian's note and artwork. We missed all that." His voice trailed off, and he gazed to the north. Young waved at the train driver and deftly climbed onto the flatcar with the workers. The raw October air promised snow. Jeff could feel the east wind on his exposed ears. With two short blasts on the air-horn, the train eased away, and would reach Weyburne before Jeff reached Flesherton.

"Hey Jeff," Jim Handley stood beside the right of way. "Will there be a barrier with the station?"

"There's no barrier in the agreement. Can we set up a few big rocks to roll onto the track to block it? There's going to be a siding on our side so engines can switch ends. Set the rocks between the station and the first switch point."

"I'll put a crib on each side to hold large boulders. One person with a bar could roll them onto the track."

"When will you get going on the buildings?" The men walked along the line towards town.

"I've contracted with the Costello family to bring timber and cut boards from the saw mill at the Beaver. They take a load home for themselves for every ten loads they bring up. We have to feed them as well." Jim laughed. "That's the Flesherton contribution." The pair reached the site of the Flesherton station west of town. A pile of lumber sat beside the old foundations with Costello's heavy wagon leaving towards town.

"I haven't seen Jani or the kids for over two months." Jeff looked sad. "We'll be up for the opening of your station."

"You missed the harvest party, and we missed you." Jim ran a hand along one of the unfinished timbers, cured wood with few blemishes. Jim had seen pictures of old beautiful railway stations built in an earlier time for the former Grand Trunk Railroad and longed to replicate them. A rotunda with a peaked roof was an intriguing challenge.

"Sarah, Kim, and Donnie are coming up here to stay with me. I'll be doing all the stations. Our stay at Longview is over." Jim had mixed feelings about leaving his trusted friends. He would miss them, but wanted this exciting opportunity.

"I understand, Jim. We'll miss you and will need another family to fill the gap". Jeff had often seen Jim caress the lumber and knew Jim would have a fulfilling winter erecting his design on the old concrete foundations. Jeff retrieved his horse and would be in Kimberly for dinner with Brandi and be home in the morning.

Chapter Eight

Sometimes I go about in pity for myself, and all the while, a great wind is bearing me across the sky. - Ojibwe Saying
From: The Journals of Brandi Shadly; (Volume 5 "Life's Lessons" page 1.)

Brandi and Dodger emerged from the morning mist above the remains of Wiarton and followed the old highway north. The sun soon took the late May chill from their bodies and their spirits brightened in a welcome relief from the dismal experience they endured during three days in the village. Like most places in the ninth spring since the collapse, Wiarton appeared to be someone who had lost a lot of weight, with oversized clothing drooping over a shrunken body. The town once housed many times the current population. The remaining folks rattled about within the oversized place. Everyone had been hospitable, considering this time of late spring shortages, and they gave Brandi fresh fish and wizened potatoes for her journey.

Exploring Karen's old residence burdened her heart. Karen asked her to find the place. It carried wonderful memories, especially of the beginning of her love for Chester. Brandi found the building gutted in what had once been a fine part of town. She drew the razed building with the faces of Karen and Chester dominating the sky beyond.

Brandi usually left Kimberly after the spring planting, but Karen had shooed her away early. A cool spring delayed the fieldwork. Karen insisted they had enough labour at Kimberly and could spare Brandi. The

7

7
656

Institute and Huron Council saw her trip up the Bruce Peninsula as a
priority. They had little regular contact north of Wiarton and hoped Brandi
could fill the gap.

She turned along the shore of Colpoy's Bay, through the small fishing
hamlet with the inlet's name, and then north through land much poorer
than the counties to the south. Limestone bedrock, to Brandi's experienced
eye, had little overburden with thin and worked out soil. Scrubby growth,
older than the economic crisis, covered many fields.

Agriculture had always been tough here. The cool spring weather
magnified the effects of poor soil. Lying between the icy waters of
Georgian Bay and Lake Huron, the peninsula had a delayed spring. This
year, this season had not started at all, and natural vegetation barely
sprouted, and made the cool spring in Beaver Valley seem balmy. The
sparseness of the population upset Brandi, although the land was not as
empty as the ravaged stretch she had seen along the Saugeen. It did not
appear fighting and murder had influenced things here, but the
hopelessness of trying to survive in such unforgiving conditions.

The residents seemed surly. Brandi did not take the rebuffs personally,
but found it discouraging no one offered much hospitality. She passed on a
bit of news, and thoughtful gazes had followed as Brandi moved on from
each encounter. She had left a germ of hope in many people.

After a long ride in a chilly wind, Brandi turned onto a side road leading
to the bay. She let Dodger set the pace along the frost-heaved pavement of
tar and stone and finally turned into the woods at a small creek to make
camp. Weary from the day's hard ride, Brandi slipped to the ground,
relieving Dodger of his burden.

She filled her pail from the little creek, judging the water drinkable.
Over the past few years, streams became cleaner and safer. Dodger
contentedly lapped from the bucket.

It was late in the day. A small hamlet sat down the hill at the water's
edge, but Brandi did not want to arrive at mealtime. After breakfast would
be the best time to arrive unannounced. Brandi stashed her saddle nearby
and set about the business of a fire. Expert fingers sparked flint on steel,
and soon she coaxed flames from her handheld tinder. The fire leapt to
life, and she placed it gently into the little rockery, with bits of kindling
and then larger pieces confirming a warm supper and hot tea. Her small
steel skillet balanced on two rocks with sizzling fat surrounding a

delightful piece of fish and cut-up potato. Brandi poured a cup of water and drew a large mouthful. She leaned back, savouring the peace of yet another camp. T

Despite loneliness, Brandi embraced this life of absorbing nature and meeting isolated pockets of humanity.

If only I could share it with others. Brandi let her mind drift. *Perhaps Karen, like we did travelling the valley and would be wonderful with Jeff.*

There had been nothing in her life to prepare her for the isolation and longing of the road. She closed her eyes, conceiving her next drawing. All was peaceful and perfect.

"Snort... " The sound roused Brandi.

"Crack... " The shadowy recess of the bush spoke. Brandi watched a dark form cautiously emerge from the trees. *A bear, perhaps two hundred kilos.* Brandi had no way to judge. It seemed huge. The bear sniffed the wind, its tapered nose lingering on the smell of cooking food. It snorted again, glanced at the fidgeting horse and moved steadily towards the nearly cooked meal. The huge beast headed directly at her with only a few metres and the steaming pan between them. Panic froze her to the ground. Suddenly, Dodger spooked and reared up, loudly neighing, lashing out at the intruder. The bear stopped, growled ferociously and turned, raising its massive body on its hind legs. Once again, Dodger lashed out, but losing its footing on wet rocks, slipped, falling heavily on its left flank. There was a loud crack as Dodger's left foreleg snapped.

The sound yanked Brandi to reality. The bear paused, confused. She rolled over to her saddle and found the rifle. She continued to roll onto her back, working the bolt to bring a bullet into the chamber, giving thanks to Jeff's thoughtful advice of always keeping it ready. The bear turned, presenting its full chest to her, not over five meters away. Wisps of smoke from the cook fire rose between them. The rifle barked loudly. Brandi could see the spurt of hair and blood from the animal's upper body. It seemed to stand in surprise, poised in uncertainty, eyes wide and mouth in a snarl. The bear collapsed, face forward, its chest covering the log Brandi had planned to use for her seat.

She stared blankly, unable to move. Blood oozed from beneath the carcass and over the log. The animal made no more sound. Brandi waited.

Another crack came from the woods opposite the path of the bear. In shock, Brandi turned towards the sound. Her hand worked the rifle bolt, placing a new cartridge into the chamber, and waited for the creature approaching through the trees. It sounded smaller, cautious. She pointed her rifle at the spot. Brandi's finger twitched on the trigger, her breathing rapid and painful. An upright form emerged from the trees.

"Don't shoot, for God's sake!" a middle-aged, native man stepped into view. His long, greying, black hair flowed over the collar of a rough, red-checked bush shirt tucked into baggy brown trousers. Once he understood the scene by the fire, he looked relieved.

"I heard your shot and thought one of my friends was here." He calmly walked towards the girl. "Are you okay?" He knelt and smiled.

"I am not hurt," Brandi said, and then tears filled her eyes. She sobbed loudly. Her pent-up emotions flowed freely. The native turned from the sobbing girl and quietly approached the bear that sprawled over the small log, eyes open, not glaring or hateful, but perhaps pleading. The man gently nudged the carcass with the toe of his black and red rain-boot, his rifle ready, making sure. Once convinced, he knelt and gently placed his hand on its head between the ears, feeling the ebbing warmth of life. The native's eyes closed, his body still. Through teary eyes, Brandi could see his lips moving, but if he made any sound, she could not hear it. Her visitor seemed to pray.

A painful, squealing cry from Dodger roused them both. The great animal lay on his side, three legs kicking and the fourth at a horrible angle. His eyes peered at them. He, too, appeared to be pleading.

"We must shoot him." The native said simply and quietly, pain on his face. "I'll do it for you." The man rose and began to un-shoulder his rifle.

"No!" Brandi staggered to her feet, her voice forceful, unhurt in body, but with a battered soul. "It's my job. I love him too much."

She approached her old friend and knelt, kissing him on the forehead. Dodger squealed once more in pain, his pleading eyes following her. The bolt on her rifle snicked. She placed the muzzle near his right temple. Brandi's finger trembled. Forever, she would remember every detail of this horrible act. The sound of the bolt placing the cartridge, the strange warmth of the stock touching her cheek, the firm push of the weapon against her shoulder, the feel of the trigger on her finger, and the shock of the recoil. It was done.

For the rest of her life, Brandi would hear the echoing sound of the discharge as it ran away, fading into the trees, carrying her grief and the honour of Dodger's love. Brandi stood motionless, tears streaming down her face. Her heart broke.

She knows George MacDonald looked at the staggered girl, and his heart embraced Brandi. *She understands.*

He went to her and gently laid his hand on her shoulder. They said nothing for a long time. Her feelings needed to find their balance.

"I'm George MacDonald," he finally stood back. "I live down there in our little community."

"I'm Brandi Shadly," she sobbed, choking back tears, "thank you."

"We can't waste these animals." George wondered how she would react. "I must get help to harvest them. Will you be okay for a few minutes?"

She nodded, not comprehending. George reached down and took her skillet from the dying fire. "Dinner's ready," placing the pan into her trembling hand. This simple action defined the new reality. Even in tragedy, people had learned, life demanded.

George disappeared into the bush. Brandi clung to the panhandle for a long time. It was hot, but not enough to burn. She ignored the discomfort. It was a pale echo of her deep, internal pain. Gradually, she calmed. Taking a fork from her saddlebag, Brandi ate the tasteless fare. It had been too long since her noon meal. She placed more wood on the fire, and after dripping the grease back into its pouch, she inverted the pan and let the flames cleanse it. A few weeks before the solstice, the evening light would last for hours. The aroma of rose hip tea wafted from an old tin can, steaming over the renewed flames. Occasionally, she glanced from the bear to the horse and back again. Their lifeless bodies were her only company. The bear seemed not as large or fierce as her first impression.

Brandi contemplated a second mug of tea when the native returned, accompanied by several other men and a woman. Another man led two packhorses down from the roadway. They all looked tired, but strong and purposeful. The men dressed similarly to George. The woman wore a white loose blouse and brown work pants, threadbare with worn knees and small tears.

"This is Brandi," George introduced the others whose names Brandi would relearn later. "She shot the makwa. She had to put her friend to death as well." He indicated Dodger.

Murmurs rose from the newcomers. Brandi could not tell if they were in sympathy, respect, sadness or anger. The answers to these questions would come over time, but for an instant, Brandi became a child and felt she had done some great wrong. A hand touched her cheek.

"It's hard, my little one," the native woman spoke gently and kindly. "Even when you have to do something, sometimes those things are too hard." Brandi looked up.

Kindness and lines of middle age filled the woman's face. Her dark eyes held sadness. Brandi knew loss and pain had visited even here in the remoteness of this place.

"I am Ermine," the woman reminded her. "Do you want to stay or come with me to the village?"

The progress of the work startled Brandi. Two men laboured over each carcass, and they had them half skinned. Their knives, sharp and true, flashed in the evening light, separating skin from flesh. Brandi had seen nothing as disgusting or fascinating.

"What are they doing?" she turned to her new friend.

"They'll take the skin and the heads," Ermine replied, "and then gut them and cut the meat into manageable chunks. The hides will come back, and George will tan them using the brains and oak-water." Brandi felt a deep sadness, but the work intrigued her. She helped slaughter farm animals, but had never seen this process.

George came to the women. "This is a boon to us Brandi," he squatted beside the girl. "This meat will feed us for many weeks, and we are hungry, like your makwa. Spring is a lean time of the year for all life. The bear had hunger, or it would not have risked attacking you. Horse and bear would not be our first choice, but the mamakajiwin, the spirit, has offered it to us. For this, we must be thankful. Go with Ermine and rest. We'll bring your gear. I'll finish the bear hide in your honour. The offal will feed other creatures. We must keep the circle true."

His bloodstained hand brushed Brandi's shoulder. George returned to his work. Ermine took Brandi's hand and lifted her to standing. The white girl seemed to tower over the native. With her rifle and folio on her shoulder, Brandi followed through the trees to a collection of deteriorating houses arranged in two neat rows along a dusty street. A large inlet of dark water lay beyond the village. Her first impression discouraged her, but glad to be away from the butchering. Children's laughter raised her spirits as youngsters played in the evening shadows.

***

Brandi roused from a fitful sleep full of disquiet. One dream lingered. A monster resembling Stevie Hunter's killer, Roger Smith chased her. The half-human beast cornered her. Brandi struggled to insert a cartridge into her rifle but could not get it right. She tried repeatedly as the beast approached, her panic growing at each failed attempt. She woke, startled, sweating and trembling after the nightmare ordeal. The morning light and raucous disputes of birds brought her fully awake. At first, the unfamiliar surroundings puzzled her. Then she remembered the genuine horror and sadness of the previous evening. She sat up with a start.

Outside the small dwelling where Ermine had bedded the girl down, Brandi found her saddle and other gear neatly piled on a small bench. A bucket of water sat ready. She splashed the cool liquid over her face, wetting her shirt and soaking the suspenders of her hemp-cloth pants. An outhouse stood amongst the buildings, and Brandi made a necessary, if not disgusting, visit. She vowed to teach about composting human waste.

Munching on a piece of dried pork and pinching mouldy spots from some half-stale bread, she headed off to explore the small hamlet. Eventually, her path took her down near the water, where a small wharf with several boats rocked gently in the morning swells. Near the dock, she saw George labouring over the bear hide.

"You were praying over the bear last night," Brandi spoke to George, and she stared, transfixed, as his hands worked a slimy substance into the hide. "I've seen nothing like it. I shot a deer, but that was just butchering." Brandi sounded matter of fact.

"It's never just butchering, Brandi. We must respect all living things, especially when we kill them. We must celebrate their life and honour their sacrifice for our benefit. I did not just pray for the bear's soul but honoured the life and purpose of the makwa, the bear."

George looked at the girl and paused the steady scraping of his tanning tool. "Always respect life, my dear, and always in the killing."

He resumed the work and his hands moved in a steady rhythm with the bare metal tool flashing in the early sun.

"We are part of a pond in the stream. We share the water coming in, the food from its bounty, and then our bodies and everything we do, good and bad, become part of the outflow into someone else's pond."

George sounded like Warren Dunne. How had he put it? *We are part of a closed-loop with nature. We can't escape our place.*

"What do you know about our people?" George rested his tired hands.

"Chester Amik told me a lot about his growing up over in Saugeen Nation and other things, and I have a friend living at Chippewa Hill." Brandi peered closer, trying to understand how George worked the hide.

"He's a good man." George wiped his blade on his pant leg. "We would share powwow together. He married that white teacher."

"They aren't exactly married, but they might as well be." Brandi smiled, again aware of the smallness of her world. "Karen Lefevre is her name."

"She has the name of a Métis, but I remember she dances like a city gal." They both laughed, George picturing a circle dance and Brandi a vision of Karen on the Heathcote dance floor. "What else do you know?"

"I read a bit about the clans and the various tribes. Chester lent me a lot of books by W. P. Kinsella." Brandi was proud of her efforts in all of this.

"That crazy guy," George exclaimed, but then winked at the girl and laughed, the lines of his face curling and playing as he smiled. He paused for a long moment. "He wasn't of the people but wrote good stuff." His eyes looked sad. "Those times he wrote about were horrible, worse than today. We're poorer in stuff, and the white man's money no longer comes, but we have a purpose now," he paused again and looked away as if suddenly saddened, "at least those of us who ain't dead."

He turned back to his work. Brandi sat and stared, taking in the man and watching his face. George's concentration deepened his age lines, and he looked sad. The girl suspected his story would mirror the personal tragedy and loss almost all the others in her life had suffered. She created another sketch in her mind, George labouring over the hide. She would transfer it to paper in some future lonely encampment along the trail.

"People remember the old times," George returned to the theme, "some long for the way it was way back. Others hold old grievances." He rubbed his sweaty brow with the back of his animal-stained hand.

"It's true for all of us, all of our people." Brandi felt this conversation was significant.

"Yes," replied George, "but I think times have changed; we all got to move on. Your horse's hide is in the water soaking." George drank from an old Mason jar. "That'll take the hair off. We'll tan it to leather. I'll make you moccasins using the leather for the soles."

Ill still be travelling with Dodger; Brandi felt a small redemption in her broken heart. *He will always be my companion.*

"There are things we need to remember," George had thought about this often. "We ain't going back to the old ways, the recent ones or the long-ago ones. It's good to remember and preserve, though, like language. We need to remember. Words can give us understanding and wisdom, but there isn't any right way of talking. I love my language, but some words are too damned long." He chuckled. "I guess in those days they weren't in a hurry, and big words passed the time. People in a hurry use small words. Maybe in the future, we'll learn to use big words again."

"Karen and I talked about language, but this is new." George had stirred Brandi's interest. "I hope I can learn some Ojibwe."

She leaned forward, grasping the bear hide as George's flashing knife scoured the edges.

"Did you know Indian is a white man's word? We weren't Indians before your ancestors showed up." He did not pause in his work. "Even Ojibwe and Chippewa are not right, made up. Europeans couldn't pronounce our name." Brandi thought of Corrine at Chippewa Hill and wondered. Her friend had mentioned none of this.

"After a while, we all gave up fighting it, I guess." It seemed George had read Brandi's mind. "One name we have for ourselves is Anishinaabeg." George looked at the white girl squatting beside the hide. She seemed to be eager and wanting to help. He wondered if her eagerness applied to all things. His mind passed over his ideas and thoughts from the past few years. His stare made Brandi uneasy. He seemed to consider something important; she waited until George finally spoke. "Our name for us, it means the good people, or the people made from nothing, like the story of Adam in the Jewish book."

"I don't know the bible stories very well." Brandi had never been a churchgoer.

"Damn it, you whites made us all learn religion, and most of you never did." George's face had an expression combining humour and sadness. "We need a word to include us all, you and your people and me and mine, into one. We all must work together. There are too few of us left. Have you ever torn up an old shirt to make rags?"

"Lots of times," Brandi thought it a strange question.

"Ever notice it's harder to tear across the seam where we overlap the cloth and stitch it together?" Brandi nodded. "We have to stitch our two peoples together and get that strength." George's eyes penetrated.

"It will not be easy." Brandi wiped the sweat from her brow with the back of her hand and squinted at George through the bright sunshine. "I've met racists. Outside our territory the bigotry is worse than in Huron."

Brandi decided to raise the issue with the Huron Council. She felt a growing fear. Racism, bigotry, and infighting presented the biggest internal threats. The good folks had to win this one.

"We got the same problem." George's knife worked the last of the hide. "I had to speak to a few big talkers last night." His knife flashed in the sun. "You don't need to worry." He glanced at her as he worked, noticing her discomfort. He could not know her mind had flashed back to the narrow escape with the Vega worshipers, and she now had no horse.

"These are good people. We've suffered. Some are bitter with centuries of resentment to overcome."

Why am I saying all this to this slip of a girl? The fleshing tool paused in mid-stroke, suspended by his thoughts. *There's something about her, something...*

George Macdonald could not reduce his feelings into concrete terms. Once again, the tool flashed in the sun, his question not interrupting the sure strokes playing out across the bear hide. The conversation ended.

The day ended with about thirty adults from the community gathered around a fire. A similar number of youngsters frolicked in and out of the fire's circle of light. Most of the children had been born after the collapse. It encouraged Brandi. Embers blazed high until the night swallowed them. Brandi listened as stories, reminiscences and jokes circled the fire pit, ebbing and flowing as each person felt the need to speak. Many asked the girl to tell her stories.

Brandi talked about the threats from the south and the struggles and successes of her people. Everyone nodded whenever she referred to struggle and hard work, but silence dominated after every reference to tragedy. All paid close attention, welcoming a stranger with fresh stories. Batteries had long depleted, and they did not have the propaganda radio of the PLM. There was an exchange in Ojibwe between two of the men in the circle. George interjected, and the men switched to English.

"Harold and I were fishing out in the bay." The man looked at his friend and then concentrated on the details. "We caught a lot and were happy. A black thundercloud came quick, towering over the trees, there above the town." He indicated a direction, but Brandi was unfamiliar with the layout. Darkness obscured everything beyond the firelight. "We heard the thunder but got careless." An outburst of Ojibwe interrupted the man. Ermine leaned over to Brandi.

"They were greedy, two short of the biggest catch of all, and wanted to brag about getting the most."

"Okay, okay," protests and laughter circled the fire. The man continued, glaring at his accusers. "We were stupid. The wind came up, blowing offshore, so we tried to row down the bay, heading towards one of the rocky beaches. The lightning was fierce, scary." More people interrupted, but this time, they sounded sympathetic.

"We got lucky," the man named Harold took up the account. "The damned waves shot us right up onto the beach over there." Once again, he indicated a spot hidden in the darkness. "Damn, I hope we never lose that boat. She survived okay, and we got to row home."

"I'm glad he did," one woman laughed. "He makes a good bed warmer in winter."

Laughter ended the story but stimulated a few more self-deprecating accounts. One man told of the hunting prowess of another. It had led to the shooting of a large buck deer in a January storm several years before. There had been a desperate lack of food, and the man had saved the community.

Many questions followed her account of Chippewa Hill. Many asked about a missing family member. Brandi could give no news. If anyone still resented the white girl, they gave no sign of it.

"I know an ermine is an animal," Brandi turned to her new friend, "but what animal is it?"

"It's a good-looking weasel," George laughed before Ermine's reply. "Don't let her kindness fool you. We don't let her near the chickens."

Everyone laughed, and some native words flowed, eliciting more laughter. Brandi soon learned that the zingosag were weasels.

"I am the hunter of small game," Ermine smiled at Brandi. "I get rabbits and partridge better than these big game hunters chasing after whitetails."

She nodded towards George and tried to look scornful, but her smile stymied her efforts. "They want to sit next to you because you're now a bigger hunter than they are."

The murmurs from several of the men sounded more like agreement, while others studiously added more wood to the fire. Their silence seemed to reflect embarrassment at not having been better providers. Brandi noted the subtle by-play, cementing it in her memory for a future drawing. She fought back her sadness, reliving the loss of Dodger.

"I'm summer brown now," Ermine broke the silence, holding a lock of her long, dark hair in front of her face, "but when I reach the winter of my life, I'll truly be Ermine." She suddenly saddened. Her voice trailed off, and Ermine stared over the fire into the darkness. The light from the flames sparkled from moistened eyes.

"Her mother," George leaned over and put his mouth close to Brandi's ear, "had beautiful, long, silver hair like an ermine. She died only last winter. Ermine carries her mother's name."

Brandi reached out and covered Ermine's hand with her own. Everyone shared the woman's grief. Silence settled until the crack of exploding spruce pitch and showers of embers reignited the conversation.

The next morning, Brandi rose with the birds. In the growing light of a warm June day, she put on paper the image of Ermine, gazing over the fire with its light shining on her face, her proud eyes glistening and sad.

***

They welcomed Brandi into the life of the village. Ermine understood the girl's grief and found work for Brandi, helping Ermine in her tasks. George had joked when he said that Ermine could not look after the chickens. In fact, the ducks and geese and the chickens were her direct responsibility, as well as pigs. Each family had a few chickens of their own, but the central farm operation provided the bulk of livestock protein. The pigs looked scrawny with pig-food in short supply.

"We don't have enough fencing to let them dig in the weed fields, and we divide the slops between them and the birds," Ermine responded to Brandi's question. "The children gather green fodder for all the animals. We are not sure it's worth the work."

"I once saw some folks growing pumpkins to feed pigs," Brandi recalled the Brysons. "There's still time this year if you have seed. They eat the vines and the pumpkins."

"There's seed, but we thought of them as human food. I'll get the patch going this afternoon."

"Maybe you need more residents to help with the work." Brandi knew the positive effect refugees had on Huron.

"There's a barrier." Ermine stood, stretching from her garden work. "A strong minority only wants Ojibwe residents. Some of us oppose exclusion, but we argue. We can't risk dividing ourselves."

"What about summer workers from down below?" Brandi wasn't sure if it would be possible, but if the community wanted, she would try to arrange it. She thought Corrine might come to visit and change opinions.

"I'll bring it up." Ermine put a hand on Brandi's shoulder. "Your spectacular arrival changed some minds. One of your biggest fans was a staunch purist before. When George described what happened up there, the guy started crying. He had a sister who disappeared in the bush a few years ago. He never saw her again, and he believes you are her spirit. Anyway, he refers to you as nimise; it means sister."

Brandi did not know which of the native men she meant. It made her feel better and yet sad. Her resolve to help became deeper. "I never had a sister," Ermine smiled, "you are my, nimise." Brandi thought of Corrine.

Near the end of the first week of her stay, early in the morning, Ermine took her down to the dock. George and another man were preparing a small aluminum craft, an outboard motorboat lacking a motor. The men placed two sets of hand-carved oars into the slips.

"We thought you might like to go fishing." George smiled, handing a life preserver to Brandi. "The water is cold, and you never know."

Brandi shuddered, remembering the account of the swamped fishing boat. The trio climbed into the little craft, and the two men pulled on the oars, heading to the middle of the bay. Brandi sat in the rear seat, her arm resting on the transom, enjoying the sunshine. They stopped above an underwater reef and dropped four troll-lines with gang-lures behind the boat, two trailing behind each stern corner and the others out wide lashed to the forward seat.

"We depend on fish for food." George checked the last of the lashings. "Everyone gets a turn. It's a pleasant change from the heavy work. Fish have been more reliable than hunting. There are more since the rich folks stopped catching them. Last year, we caught and dried enough for winter. The lake is cleaner than before."

George scooped up a handful of water and drank it. He rowed leisurely from the hindmost position while Brandi tended the lines. The morning passed slowly, broken by landing fish and resetting lines.

"Look at those cottages along the shore," George pointed to a line of buildings on a line separating the water from dark green vegetation on the slope below cliffs that appeared about to pounce on the small buildings.

"Visitors were the economic lifeblood of the area. The whole of the peninsula depended on tourism and retirees. Even our community had a campground. These people disappeared." He did not sound sad. "Most owners never returned after the crash. All the businesses depended on summer traffic or government cheques. When both dried up, the businesses had no hope. I think you saw the same down south." Brandi nodded and pulled another pickerel into the boat.

"We are living by squatter's right. The few white folks at the fire last night are some of the original owners." George smiled and looked concerned, as if he was looking for approval.

"We came over from the main community. It could not support everyone. There's a lot of salvage here and hard work. Water is a gigantic task; we carry it up from the lake." The men exchanged jobs. George relaxed beside the fishing lines.

"Aren't there any hand pumps?" Brandi had seen places converted from electric pumps to salvaged hand pumps. Longview still kept its solar electrical supply. Kimberly and the area had the hydroelectric station. Most other places used hand pumps.

"There are electric pumps around and even some photovoltaic panels and windmills, but we can't get them to work. No one knows anything about electricity. Our one attempt nearly burnt down a cottage."

"A guy at Chippewa Hill knows. I can't remember his name. He's Iroquois."

"I'd ride down there myself in a minute. I'm so damned tired of carrying water." George casually leaned over the edge of the boat and scooped a floating bottle from the water, the rusted cap barely water tight. George stowed it with the fish. It would be of use.

They fished until hunger sent them to shore with a decent catch, two dozen pickerels and a whitefish. Brandi had not had such a pleasant fishing experience since her stay with Corrine. It might become boring as an everyday chore, but gave a chance to relax and reflect.

Spending the morning with George was an enjoyable interlude. Almost immediately upon landing, George called a group together and nominated one of the young men to ride down to Chippewa Hill to entice the Iroquois technician to come north to help. Brandi penned a brief note to Corrine, filling her mandate of connecting people and finding mentors.

"Come and see this," George hailed Brandi as she hurried past his house a few mornings later, intent on learning how to smoke fish. Anyone else interrupting her might have irritated, but she thought every conversation with George valuable. "I have this book of paintings." George held a well-thumbed coffee-table art book.

Brandi sat on the polished red and black granite top step of a once fancy cottage. The stairs had kept their lustre as the building deteriorated. The book contained paintings by Allen Sapp. As she turned each page, Brandi became more and more entranced. George patiently sat as she leafed slowly through the book. She paused at a painting of a team of horses pulling a sleigh. She thought of Jeff and the stone boat.

"This is wonderful, George. I want to do what he did, record reality and the everyday things of life and the grand."

"He was a Cree from out west," George smiled, knowing these images would affect Brandi. He had seen her drawing of Ermine. "Nimise, everyone is calling you nimise now. I will not let you take this book. I have no family album, and this connects me to the past. Will you show your work to me sometime?"

That evening, before the gathering at the fire, Brandi showed George her journal and the images of this trip. He saw power and honesty, and a story unfolding even without reading her notes. One image seemed out of place, a young child, screaming with a look of horror, Brandi's self-portrait from the massacre at Paradise.

MacDonald looked at Brandi. The grief and horror of having to shoot the makwa and her horse had not been the only, or perhaps the worst, ordeal this young girl had endured. She looked so young, so frail, yet she had eyes that seemed to gaze from eternity. Perhaps the spirit had sent the makwa to sacrifice itself to bring this girl to their aid. Perhaps the protection of the makwa manifested mysteriously. Perhaps the makwa brought Brandi to fulfill George's quest. He smiled and felt content.

"Who is George?" Brandi asked Ermine as they did the day's chores. "He's deep, with widespread knowledge and interest."

"George is a chief." Ermine pondered what being a chief meant. "Not in the old movie way, but one man whose advice and wisdom we consider. We discuss everything, but George's words hold weight. He's hopeful we'll survive. He told me he would not force people into doing what he thought was the right thing. We have to do it from understanding, or it won't be permanent. It's the old way."

"They elected George chief some years before the crash. Hotheads took over the council and forced him out. They claimed he was too white." She stooped to retrieve an egg laid near the gatepost. "He didn't fight them, but began discussions about the future and teach about our language and history. When the crash came, and the government money stopped, he opposed the ones who wanted to get violent. We pacifists moved here." Her deep sigh reflected a longing for an easier life.

"George spends a lot of time trying to heal the wounds with the rest of the band. Most of the hotheads went south to fight; those who remain are stubborn. George says time will heal and we will work together someday. So far, those over there are surviving like us."

"I don't think those guys who went to fight are coming back." Brandi had not told the entire story about Chippewa Hill. "When the Iroquois arrives, he can tell you the story. He endured a racist massacre down there and thinks only he and a boy from Chippewa Hill survived."

"Maybe this Iroquois can convince some of them then. We should work together. Perhaps we need to change, too." Ermine headed briskly towards the chicken coop.

***

"Ermine tells me you are leaving." George MacDonald had sought Brandi. They were walking towards the workshop turned barn. Brandi had been in Hope Bay for over three weeks.

"I must, George. It's my calling and my duty to go to Tobermory on this trip and assess the peninsula. Now, I'm on foot. I have to get going. It will take a lot longer." Brandi did not seem upset by the prospect. She accepted it as a fact.

"What's best and worst about travelling?" George led on to the barn.

"They're the same thing," Brandi focused on George, "the quiet and awesome natural world full of non-human sights and sounds and the loneliness of it all. People I meet are interesting; some aren't the nicest."

"I hope we are interesting." George watched from the corner of his eye.

"You all are wonderful," Brandi exclaimed with sincere enthusiasm. "I've learned so much. George, you are my friend. I hope we're friends."

"Yes, my nimise. You're my friend." Brandi smiled in quiet pleasure.

"Your horse was your friend."

"Dodger was my friend and companion. He saved my life once. I loved him." Brandi no longer choked up when thinking of Dodger, but her heart ached for him.

They reached the makeshift farm building, with its fading painted steel reflecting the bright sunshine. George walked around the corner to the paddock. Several horses stood quietly in the morning sun, nibbling on hay.

"That one is yours," George was matter-of-fact as he nodded towards a medium-sized skewbald filly. He whistled softly, and the horses looked towards the humans. Another low whistle brought the filly trotting to the maple rail fence. He rubbed her on the neck, and she drew to him, resting her head against his cheek.

"A few days ago, everyone decided you needed a new horse. We agreed this girl would be the best for you. She's my pet, my gift. I would trust her to no one but you. She needs love, too."

Brandi stood speechless. She had always felt the Institute had given Dodger to her in payment for her contributions. These people owed her nothing. She owed them everything. Her head and heart overflowed. Her emotions became a bubbling stew of humility, honour, doubt, and longing.

"How can I accept this honour, this gift? I owe so much to everyone and especially to you, George." Tears flowed.

"You have already begun paying for it, just by your visiting and your stories." He touched her shoulder. "They have encouraged everyone and lightened our lives. I know you will give us more. Just for us to know about Chippewa Hill and Corrine and the others is a good thing." He paused for some time, as was his habit when about to say something he considered important.

"I am puzzled by the makwa letting you kill him." George did not sound angry or scolding but questioning. "Do you know what the bear clan is?"

Brandi had to say no. "It's the warriors and guardians. We are safe because of them. They give us security, and they learn about medicines and which herbs in the forest will help us. They teach us. The makwa spirit is strong and generous. I think he sacrificed himself to bring you here. From the day you were born, you would meet your makwa, and he to meet you. His death was necessary." Again George stopped. "I cannot give you a clan or a name." He finally spoke. "I cannot ask the people for it. Not yet anyway, and the spirit has not given me a name for you. If you had a clan, it should be fish, giingoo; you are a teacher and scholar, but there is a bear in you too. I watched you shoot your friend. It was almost the hardest thing you could ever do. You summoned the courage to help him, your friend, with the genuine spirit of the makwa. You received it then."

Brandi had never seen George choke up, and she thought he might cry, but his emotion was not sadness.

"I believe you are of many callings. One of them is to be a bear, but you will never have to defend yourself or others physically again. You will protect on a level high above the bravery of the warrior, high above the physical. You will protect our hopes and dreams and longings, ours and yours and your people, everywhere. Pain and sorrow will visit you, and they will be our pain and sorrow. Laughter, hope, and love are what you will hold. You will honour the sacrifice of the makwa as you live your life. You are nimise and my makwa." George had been thinking about this for many days. He now felt content.

"This horse is a gift to one we have embraced as our own, not a payment or a debt owed back. Our payment is in knowing we travel with you." He looked away, back to the horse, patiently waiting at the fence. "She will need new shoes by fall." He now sounded workmanlike. "Put an extra blanket under Dodger's saddle. It's too big."

"I'll have it changed at Kimberly." Brandi reached out to rub the filly's neck. As if understanding, the horse nuzzled the girl. "We have very good smiths and tack makers there. I'll leave tomorrow."

She had the same feelings as each time she left Longview or Kimberly. George's speech and the gift overwhelmed her. George and Brandi remained in the warming morning sunshine. Flies flitted about, pursued by dragonflies. Bees searched the trefoil and clover that flourished outside the paddock. The mist of the morning rose. The humans stood silently, immersed in the living loop of the world.

**

A great gathering of the community filled the clearing on the edge of the town. Every resident had come, seated in a vast semi-circle. Some sat cross-legged, some had old kitchen chairs, and others rested in folding camp chairs, all intent on the circle of people sitting at the focal point of the arc. There had been great competition to be included in the smaller group, but the honour fell to those who had first come to Brandi's aid. George sat at the head of the circle of six people, a smudging bowl in his right hand and a feather gripped in his left. Gentle movements of the feather wafted the fragrant wisps of smoke out to the circle. There was no stirring of the heavy morning air. The aromatic offering filled everyone's nostrils. All were deep in their thoughts. Silence held all until George finally looked up from the fuming bowl.

"What is your wisdom for us?" George MacDonald looked directly at Brandi, sitting to his right. "You have travelled lonely paths, have faced grave danger and risen to the task. You have aimed true and shot the mighty makwa. That was a day of sadness, sacrifice and sharing."

George paused, remembering the emotion of that day. The feather in his left hand commanded silence from the gathering. After a long wait, he continued. "You have embraced us, whom you did not know, and opened your heart to us as we have to you. You have listened as the elders spoke. My little one, you have wisdom growing. We will wait for it to be revealed."

The man gravely passed the feather to his left. Ermine took it in her left hand, and the words flowed from her heart and to the next and the next, on until Brandi, at last, received the right to speak. The girl drew out a multicoloured kerchief, extracted a pinch of tobacco and sprinkled it into George's fuming bowl. An extra little puff of aromatic smoke rose towards the sky. Memories brought Corrine to join the circle.

"I have no wisdom. My journey has just begun. I am too young." Brandi felt honoured George had even asked. "My wisdom is your wisdom, and I will repeat it to all. If I grow to add to it, I will always refer to this time, and Hope Bay as the place where my ignorance faded and my learning grew. My ignorance exceeds my wisdom, as it must always. I owe you all a great debt. No thank-you I give can repay you." The sound of satisfaction came from the other listeners. Brandi passed the feather to George.

"There are no debts between friends." George looked squarely into Brandi's eyes, but his message was for all. "Only open arms and warm hearts. Our daughter, our sister, our friend, you will go on your journey now. Carry us with you, be our eyes and our ears and our voice. Carry the spirit of the makwa. Come back to us often and share your tales, as we will always share our hospitality with you. Let it be so in all of your travels and all of your days."

The circle was complete.

George stood, signalling an end to the ceremony. He turned and embraced Brandi, followed by the hugs of the others. Brandi's tears were genuine and joyous, manifesting a deep feeling of belonging. It felt to her she had been transported back through many generations and given a sacred task. Her duty was to honour all those who were and who would be. She had entered the flow of life and honour bound to keep its course true and safe.

Brandi walked to her new horse and stroked her neck, placing her forehead against the filly's cheek.

"Have you picked a name yet?" Ermine approached to stand at Brandi's right elbow.

"It's the first day of summer today," Brandi turned to Ermine. "What's the word for summer?"

"Niibin," the woman looked at Brandi.

"That is her name." Brandi turned again to the horse and hugged its neck. "My sweet Niibin."

Ermine hugged Brandi one last time. The girl put her left foot in the stirrup and swung deftly onto her new companion.

"Farewell, Ermine," she leaned down to touch her friend's shoulder.

"Farewell, Nimise Makwa." George's voice joined Ermine's.

Straightening, she gazed over to the rest of the group, squeezed her heels against the horse's flanks, and smiled. As Niibin stepped slowly towards the old concession road, Brandi waved, and the filly's hooves found the gravel surface. She began learning her new mount. The sound of the horse on the hard ground slowly faded, and the watching community turned in the morning sun to embrace the work of the day.

Chapter Nine

With a shrill blast from its whistle, a small locomotive pulled several flat-cars and a passenger coach along the track beside the almost completed Flesherton station. As the combination squealed to a stop, Barry Young strode along the planking of the newly completed platform.

"Your stuff is on the second car," Barry called over his shoulder as he hurried towards the passenger coach.

"Thanks." Jim Handley climbed aboard the flatcar to examine a pile of finished hardwood, native cherry and oak provided in some mysterious way by a friend of Barry's who worked for the railway in Hamilton.

The Flesherton station was his first major effort, and Jim wanted it perfect, finished in cherry and oak as his special gift to his friends.

Barry reached the leading steps of the coach in time to have a young girl jump into his arms. He hugged Melissa and then his wife as Jennifer descended in a slightly more dignified manner.

"Brian isn't here. It would have been too dangerous. I'll take you into town in the wagon. He'll be there."

It was the middle of June. Bad weather and lack of material had delayed work on the rail line. Eventually, the PLM authorities in the south had found more rails and ties.

The steel-mill in Hamilton could soon roll one-hundred pound rails. Scrap steel was the main feedstock. Barry Young and Rob Bossley were skeptical that the new rails would be of high quality. Aside from his work trying to design and build cheap and efficient steam locomotives, Rob wanted to ensure the track would be safe.

The cool spring delayed the thawing of the ground, and then the rain had slowed the work. Barry calculated it would be September before they reached Owen Sound. Installing the track on the long sloping loop to the harbour would be another slow process.

"Hello, Jake," Barry greeted the engineer. Their relationship had become even stronger when Young had the man's family moved to Orangeville. The PLM did not trust anyone, and splitting train crews ensured they would not become dependent on any single person. "How would you like to have an apprentice between Proton and track's end?"

"Are you planning to retire me?" Jake smiled.

"No, you're essential, but you have accumulated a year's vacation, and we need relief crews." Barry joked. The PLM allowed no vacation, expecting everyone to work hard for the "good of the nation."

"We want a brakeman. Trains need a lot of hitching and unhitching."

"He's young," Barry chuckled. "His name is Brian, and he's a hard worker." He winked. Jake knew who his protégé would be.

"Things are more relaxed now," Jake dismounted and smiled, "since our bird dog has gone, it seems almost safe." He handed Barry a package. "This is your latest reading material." If Jake knew the books had a deeper purpose, he did not let on.

"Yes, it is good that Mike is no longer with us."

Mike disappeared during the winter. The PLM had sent no one to replace him. Rumour said they had reassigned Mike to a project between Hamilton and Niagara. Barry imagined an unmarked grave in Angel territory more likely. Mrs. Angel no longer appeared in Weyburne, and for Barry and Jennifer, her absence explained it all.

Mike's disappearance allowed the Youngs to move to Huron beyond PLM control. It was safe enough to let Brian train. He wanted to work on the railway and engineer was his ultimate dream. He had a long way to go. Working from the ground up fit his father's idea of how someone should develop. At sixteen, Brian would join a track crew.

The Young family would move into a big, brick house Jim Handley had repaired south of the main street.

"This is a nicer station than in Mississauga," Jennifer Young admired the nearly completed building. "Down there, it's shipping containers."

"I've learned a lot from this one," Jim Handley ran his hand along the rounded top edge of a cherry-wood bench in the waiting room. Jim was proud of the work. He had spent many hours sanding and finishing the interior woodwork.

"I'll speak to Amik." it impressed Barry. "We should have a grand opening ceremony."

"I made the mistake of letting Bob Paisley see this," Jim enjoyed giving the tour. "He wants a bigger one in Owen Sound and is arranging for material. It'll be down by the water, and like this one, with its mirror image joined at the rectangles and rotundas at each end. Sometimes he acts like the PLM, but he insists it would give everyone focus and hope."

"I sure hope he isn't a PLM stooge," Young frowned.

"There are sympathizers up here," Jim scowled, "but Bob's not one. He's full of himself but sincere."

"With Mike gone, I need someone to oversee the track gangs. I'm too busy with the engineering. Can you?" Jim Handley impressed Barry.

"I can do a bit. The little stations along the way need my attention. When Paisley gets his material together, I'll need to be in Owen Sound. My family is upset we'll be moving again and far away from Longview."

Jim took over the supervision of construction, and Barry established an engineering office in Flesherton. Day by day, the track drew closer to its destination. September would be the actual target.

Several dozen skilled workers from the PLM territory rode up the line each day to join a larger number of Huron workers. It would have been more efficient to have the workers camped at track's end, but the PLM authorities did not want their people to become too familiar with the enemy. They built a tent-town near Dundalk and subjected the workers to longer days. The truce agreement did not allow PLM security forces to accompany their people. Instead, a rigorous headcount took place each morning and evening. Surly guards, armed to the teeth, watched every arrival and departure. Huron also did a headcount each day at the Proton station. No one wanted deserters to complicate things, or agents to stay inside Huron. They shared no trust, but everyone relished the quiet of the truce.

Chapter Ten

"The spirit has not given George MacDonald a name for me. The last time I saw him, he said he was sad about it, but every time he thought about me, asking for a name, all he saw was a blue sky with a single shining cloud. In his mind, the cloud was strange because it never cast a shadow on the ground, even when it passed overhead. George giving me a name would be an honour."

From a private conversation between Brandi Shadly and Erin Thomas.

George MacDonald laboured in the morning mist of late August, readying the boat for fishing. He ached from the weeks of bringing in winter fodder for the horses and looked forward to a relaxing day on the water. A snicker made him look up towards the houses where the misty morning sunshine silhouetted a medium-sized horse. A rider with a wide-brimmed hat and long, unkempt hair escaping around it sat astride the horse.

"I must be getting old," George said. "I should've heard you coming."

"Hello, George," Brandi slid from Niibin and walked down the slight incline. "I wanted to see if I could sneak up on you. Who's the Indian now?" She wrapped her arms around her friend. Niibin nuzzled MacDonald.

"She remembers me." George smiled contentedly as he stroked the animal's neck.

"We camped up the hill on the other side of the road from where we first met." Brandi left the reins loose so the two old friends could touch.

"I'm so glad you're back safely." George did not look away from the horse, and for a moment Brandi thought he was talking to the animal. "I've missed our chats, nimise."

"I brought a new friend down, Heather, from up near Tobermory. She's a healer. I'm taking her to Owen Sound hospital to teach and learn."

"Is it Heather Norman? I know her."

"That's her. She wanted to come as soon as I mentioned your name."

"I'm her student," George went back to the boat. "I'll chat with her after fishing." George and his companion pushed off onto the misty bay.

"We want to leave tomorrow." Brandi finally tracked George down after he had spent the afternoon with Heather. Even though she was at least ten years younger than Macdonald, Heather mentored him in the healing skills. "I'm sorry, it's only a day. I must get back to help harvest."

George knew the young woman must be homesick. As much as he wanted Brandi near, as much as he wanted to feel her special importance, he had to let her go. She was not a spirit after all, but a person, no matter how important her calling might be.

"How did it go with Niibin? Did you meet anyone as interesting as us?" George chuckled. His simple, sincere perspective endeared him to Brandi.

"I visited many little communities much like this." Brandi sat on the familiar stone steps. "They're all struggling but surviving."

"There are no official communities up there," George observed.

"They're squatting like the rest of us," Brandi smiled. "There are two places up there learning to make bows and arrows. They are getting low on ammo. I left a few rounds of my calibre, and they want more of everything. Perhaps my friend's, the David's, will sail beyond Colpoy's Bay and trade with them. The people there are getting good with the bows and arrows. I want to help spread those skills. I stopped at the place of spinning silver blades.

"You mean the wind turbines?" George laughed. "Don't go Indian on me yet. I have too many questions for you."

"That's how they describe the machines themselves." Brandi was defensive, embarrassed by her language. "The blades aren't turning anymore. They have no spare parts, and there's no grid to energize them. I will try to get someone from the nuclear station to visit."

"You are like the help wanted ads of a newspaper or the How to column." George MacDonald suddenly saw Brandi's role clearly. He wondered how many other Brandies they needed to unite people.

"I met another makwa, George." Brandi said.

"You're still alive. Is the bear?" George laughed loudly.

"I don't shoot everything I see!" Brandi feigned hurt. "It wasn't hungry. We saw it down the trail near the old camping park at Cyprus Lake. It heard us coming and ran into the trees. Those guys have little stealth. We could hear it crashing through the bush for a long time."

"The big kid on the block," George agreed, "timid, but don't care who hears them."

"I'm glad it happened. I shook afterwards, but it helped me heal. The locals up there offered to take me to Manitoulin. Maybe if I had Niibin a few years, I might have left her. The water looked rough, and they had an old sailboat smaller than my friend's boat in Meaford. I want to go to the island someday, but this wasn't the time."

"I love Niibin. She's a wonderful horse, and we'll be great friends. I miss my Dodger." George could see the girl was tearing up and waited, letting her feelings flow. Life sounds filled the air, and a gentle breeze caressed them.

"I have presents," George disappeared into his house. He returned with the bearskin, tanned and rolled up, so the black, shiny coat was out.

"Feel how soft this is." Brandi held the warm bundle to her face. George touched her head and said something in Ojibwe.

"Here's your other present." George offered a small package wrapped in plain white paper and tied with rawhide strands. She opened the gift, revealing two pairs of moccasins made with precise and detailed artistry. One pair was plain, tied by rawhide strings; George had heat-puckered the edges to water-proof them. The second pair was ornate with beading and a star pattern of quill adorning the upper.

"One pair is for everyday and the other for special occasions." George was happy with the results of the past few weeks' labour. "Ermine did the quill while I did the stitching. You left some footprints in the dust, and we used them to size it up." Brandi could not speak.

"The uppers are deer hide, and the soles are from your horse. The stitching might not hold up long, so watch for it. Ermine wants to keep the horsehide. She says she has a plan for it, and you'll see it another time."

Brandi repeatedly turned the items over. She held the soles of the footwear to her face, and her tears baptized them. She hugged George, remaining silent while her tears of sadness and joy dripped from her cheeks, then she slipped on the everyday pair.

"Moccasins let your feet feel the ground, so you always know your place." George smiled.

"Thank you, George. Thank you for being a good friend."

Brandi left with her new treasures, seeking a place to contemplate her feelings. As she sat in a quiet corner of the village, Brandi smoothed out the paper wrap. She drew a portrait of a noble Dodger with the barn at Kimberly in the background.

The following morning, the community gathered once again to bid Nimise farewell. The circle comprised other than the one of a few weeks previously. It included Heather, to George's left. Brandi again sat to his right with Ermine next to her. The girl wore her new beaded moccasins. George noticed her feet and tried not to be proud. Brandi held a large paper sheet rolled into a cylinder in her right hand. He gently moved the feather, wafting the fragrance from his bowl. The smudge streamed away on a vigorous breeze.

The words were less emotional than those of the previous circle. Each speaker made some comment about how things had seemed to improve since Nimise arrived. The talk was of hope.

George expressed to Heather how he looked forward to learning new things when she returned. He left it to Ermine to give thanks and sum up the feelings, jointly holding the feather in her and Brandi's left hands and sharing a smile. She released the feather to the girl's care.

Brandi unrolled the paper and tore a small piece from one corner, placing it into the bowl and causing a slight burst of new smoke. She handed the sheet to George, a detailed drawing of the man labouring over the bear hide as he tanned it. In one corner was her signature brandy glass but now, for the first time, the lower right corner bore the words "Nimise Makwa". All her work would now have this signature.

"You put yourself into this paper, my sister," George now held the feather. "The smoke carries your spirit. It will mingle in the trees and remain with us always." He paused and looked at Brandi. "We call you Nimise Makwa, a name for your friends to use. I wait upon the spirits for your name. Live your calling, but return often."

The circle rose, and the two women bid farewell. They led their horses up the hill, walking together. George and Ermine knew Brandi's heart. She was feeling Dodger carrying her once more. Heather and Brandi finally mounted. Niibin skittered sideways for a few steps, looking back to George and her old home. At last, they turned to the road and the ride south. It would not be a lonely trip for Brandi. Dodger was heading home.

***

Brandi introduced Heather Norman to the doctor and other students at the Owen Sound hospital. It had become the centre of a network of a half dozen teaching and care facilities. Mount Forest represented the most distant, while Meaford remained the most significant centre.

Brandi headed Niibin on the most direct route to Flesherton and Kimberly. Below Owen Sound, she reached the end of the track. The work fascinated her. She had never seen workers laying the railway track and had no experience with railways. Brandi had ridden in the Toronto subway when visiting her cousins. Somehow, it did not seem to count.

Brandi clambered up an embankment above the work. She retrieved her sketch paper and immersed herself in the scene. A shout caught her attention. Her father hurried towards her. Bill swept her up and hugged tightly, smiling. Brandi cried and smiled all at once.

"I am doing my security detail, supposedly guarding these guys. It isn't clear if I am protecting us from them or them from us. These guys from below are mostly nice, and so I am doing more grunt work than guarding." Bill held her at arm's length. "Your mother can't wait to see you. Will you be down for the harvest?" He hugged her once more.

"I was headed there when I saw this work and wanted to watch and sketch. Where's Jeff?"

"He's down at the Proton border crossing. He'll be home for the harvest."

"How's the construction going?" Brandi glanced past her father and noticed workers watching from below. Whispers carried the girl's name.

"Who is she?" asked one man from the PLM gang.

"It's Brandi Shadly. She sketched Mom, Dad and my little sister on the mower once." Brandi recognized the young man from near Chatsworth. Greetings rose from the crowd.

"Do our picture," one man called out.

"Tell us a story," a woman shouted.

Brandi found a spot further down the slope above forty or more men and women sitting in a broad semi-circle on the renovated roadbed. Cementing the scene in her mind for a future drawing, she asked where some people lived and then began telling related stories. The session lasted for over an hour, interrupted with clapping and laughing at the brighter tales and crying at accounts of tragedies. When Brandi had recounted the events with the bear and the death of Dodger, tears flowed. Bill put an arm around his daughter, marvelling at this strong woman.

"What the hell is going on? Get back to work!" Jim Handley stalked up between laid rails and into the midst of the gathering. He glared at Brandi. Jim felt pressure to complete the track before the harvest stole his crew. He would not be late. Brandi flashed Jim a smile. It did not seem to work.

"Oh, oh, back to work." Bill winked at Brandi. "We don't want to keep the railway tycoon waiting." Jim Handley glared at his friend.

"We have to get this done, Bill," Jim pleaded.

Brandi swung onto Niibin and rode towards Flesherton, with the sounds of shouts and hammers striking steel fading behind her. She could not wait to get to the James' house to create the drawing in her mind.

A few weeks later, they had laid the track all the way to dockside in Owen Sound. It turned from a time of satisfaction into the worst security crisis since the truce. Jim Handley would have to wait to celebrate.

Chapter Eleven

"What's this?" The scene down the aisle of the passenger coach stunned the female border guard when she climbed aboard for her daily headcount, expecting a routine return of the PLM workforce to the other side of the border. The normally packed car held only a dozen scared workers. More ominous, she saw a half-dozen armed Huron fighters, a major violation of the truce that forbids armed troops near the border.

"What the hell's going on?"

The commander handed a rifle to the astonished border guard.

"Most of the workers have no ties and want to stay. They completed the line to The Sound, and this would have been their last trip. These have family who would suffer if they didn't return."

The force climbed off the train. The station guard signalled the engine driver, and the train rolled away with a short blast on the air horn, a poet would say reluctantly in an accurate reflection of the engineer's feelings.

"Spread out and cover the approaches. They aren't ready. It would surprise me if they attacked today. They'll wait for orders. No one ever shows any initiative down there. Get someone on the ramps in case we have to roll those rocks down. There'll be more fighters here soon. We sent runners to the barriers."

The guards symbolically lowered the hinged barrier marking the border. A locomotive would easily smash it; however, no engineer would risk hitting the two massive boulders poised to roll onto the right of way at the far end of the platform.

The little force took cover in the bush and waited. Before midnight, a small railway scooter, the only rolling stock Huron possessed, came out of the darkness from Flesherton, the staccato of its gasoline engine shattered the quiet of the night. Barry Young drove. Chester, Jeff and Ted Macedo rode. The commander of the forward party strode onto the tracks to greet the jigger. Light came from a hurricane lantern burning vegetable oil.

"Chester, we're glad to see you. Where's the rest of the force?" The man seemed relieved to yield responsibility for what might be a war, but thought they had little firepower. He acknowledged Jeff and Ted with relief. Both men had reputations from their exploits behind enemy lines.

"If we're lucky, we won't need more," Chester dismounted. "We have most of them assembling on various fronts. Word will get to Saugeen. Mount Forest will be nervous once the news arrives. You armed fighters must withdraw to the one-kilometre line, as the truce says. The PLM will be upset, and we don't want to give them an excuse. The deserters will not go back without a fight. Barry and his family are staying for sure, but the PLM doesn't want war, at least not right now."

The small force retreated. The young commander noticed Jeff and Ted had no weapons. His admiration for the pair grew.

"We'll wait here and man the boulders." Chester set his pack down on the station platform.

"I have to get back to the Saugeen and get ready to blow up some of my best work," Barry smiled. "I hope we don't. That's a nice little bridge." Barry sped off on the jigger.

"We're staying too." The border guards did not hesitate. One went inside to muster some hot drinks. Ted and Jeff walked up the line towards Dundalk where they could see the kilometre marker on the other side. All was quiet, and the group settled down to watch, too nervous to sleep. As the first light crept over the little station, the sound of an approaching train broke the silence. The station crew stood ready at the boulder drops. Chester stood at the demarcation line. The diesel locomotive eased to a stop just nudging the mark. A look of relief came from the engine driver as he realized there were only three familiar, unarmed men. Two quick blasts came from the air horn, and the man clambered down.

"There's a delegation in the coach," Jake smiled. "They're a little upset."

Six or seven men exited the passenger car, but seeing the three Huron representatives, three of the strangers approached. Chester sat at a small table on the platform. The leader of the trio took the empty chair opposite.

"You got some of our people," the man growled, not bothering with a greeting. He kept his hands in his lap. "We want them back." A threatening edge sharpened his words.

"We have a problem," Chester replied in a friendly tone. "It seems they want to stay. Our policy is to let them stay unless they cause trouble."

"You people are too soft. That's why you'll lose." Once again, he sounded threatening.

Chester smiled at the incongruity. This man was a little smaller than the three men from Huron, cleanly shaven, and probably in his mid-twenties. He looked like he should sell tickets at the Dundalk ice rink, not threaten war. The youngster knew little about negotiating. Amik assumed they had not expected this setback.

"Well, I guess that makes us different from you," Chester replied, still trying to be amicable. "We like people. Even you would probably be welcome." Drawing an opponent down to the personal level might achieve one of two things; either having them let their guard down or lose their temper. In either case, Chester would get an advantage.

"Give them back." The man repeated, at a loss how to proceed and irritated by Chester's insult. "What if I have an armed force on this train and just take them?"

Chester raised his arm and brought it down in a swift motion, with the flat of his hand parallel to the ground. Behind him, the station guards yanked on the levers. Two massive boulders rolled onto the tracks, jamming tightly together and forming an impassable barrier. No engine could safely push them aside.

"We just closed the railway." Chester smiled. "I would suggest you not make more threats."

The young man's eyes widened. He tried to form a threatening snarl.

"You just spit on your face despite your nose." The man tried to sound tough. Chester's laughing response to the butchered saying did not improve the man's mood. He waited as the PLM representative struggled to regain his composure. Chester knew he had scared the lad who had orders to keep the rail line open and failed. All the resources the PLM invested in the line were at risk.

"If you have armed men on that train," Chester kept the initiative, "you are violating the terms and tore up the truce. We're not armed and have kept up our part of the bargain. If you have destroyed the agreement, then tell your superiors we will be free to begin military operations today." The man's skin turned white.

"Do nothing. I'll report back." He said. Locally, the PLM was weak.

"Tell your masters," Chester emphasized the man's position as an underling, "the rail line will stay closed until you drop your claim on any refugees. Tell them we will not turn over anyone except criminals."

Chester stood and walked away. There would be no more talk. The man and his companions returned to the rail car. With a short air-horn blast, the little assemblage of rolling stock backed off to the south.

"Damn, you had me looking for a place to take cover." Ted smiled.

"Me too," Shadly added. "Ted, I feel exposed if you aren't in the bush with that scope focused on the bad guys."

"Gentlemen," Chester put a hand on each shoulder as they walked back to join the station staff, "they need this railway much more than we do. They can't get ships through the Detroit River because of pirates and the fighting along the shore, not to mention there's no Coast Guard to install the navigation markers and dredge the sand bars. They want iron ore. The only way it will get there is down this line. They need this, and they need us. War isn't an option for them. They're tied up in the fighting near Windsor and, despite being their allies, are nervous of the military government in Ottawa. No, they don't want a fight here. We're too small to be a threat and are their safest frontier."

"So, where do we go from here?" The art of negotiating, and what his mother would call "the affairs of state" interested Jeff.

"Well," Chester mused, "word of these desertions will have spread. Not even the PLM can keep it a secret. It embarrassed them and might encourage others to flee, so they have a problem. Despite what I told the punk, we don't want war either. Peace is the best thing for us for as long as we can spin it out."

"What are the odds if they attack, anyway?" Ted did not believe that the PLM would not fight.

"The odds are still bad for us, even in their weak condition, but they won't attack for a while. If we can help them solve their problem, we can get back to where we were yesterday morning. Their problem is saving face and looking strong to their population. They don't care about reality as long as they look strong. I have an idea to resolve this. Hopefully, the next time, they will send someone who understands and is ready to deal."

Chester waited in Flesherton, along with a growing force of nervous soldiers. This incident delayed the harvest, but the grain would withstand bad weather. At least, it was not during haying when the timing was more critical. The Huron General Council, all armed, gathered in the town. Helen directed operations.

Jeff camped at the Proton station with unarmed guards; however, in a risky violation of the existing agreement, Ted's snipers waited within firing distance of the station. A stronger fighting force camped at the edge of the legal zone, and Huron mustered fighters all along the frontier.

They developed a plan to attack from Mount Forest towards Weyburne with Matt's force. Tension and worry weighed heavily.

When another train clanked up to the Proton barrier, Jeff sent the little jigger back to fetch Chester. He had waited for four days and thought there would be no progress. Jeff scowled at the sight of Angel dismounting from the passenger coach. There would be no shooting in the short-term. No one had ever seen Angel anywhere near danger.

Chester arrived accompanied by several members of the Council. The entourage hung back with Jeff and the other guards while Chester walked up to the table that straddled the demarcation line and sat down on the Huron side. Angel carried a small bag. Jeff's faith that the man was not suicide bomber material kept him from rushing up to protect his leader. Angel sat and reached to shake Chester's hand.

"Hello, Amik," his tone was affable. "I didn't think I would have the pleasure so soon."

"Hello, Angel." Chester shook the man's hand. The PLM man's tone reassured Amik that Angel did not want a fight.

"It's a meeting I would not expect." Chester's smile hid his dislike for Angel and his blood soaked operation. "We don't have a problem."

Angel reached down and retrieved two crystal wine glasses from his bag, followed by a bottle of red wine. Chester watched Angel extract the cork. The popping sound startled the onlookers. Angel poured the wine without asking and set a glass in front of Chester. Even though he had seen Angel peeling off the seal and uncorking the bottle, he waited. Angel lifted his glass, extending it towards Chester and making the usual salutation.

Chester raised his glass and, reverting to an even more primitive time, poured some of his wine into Angel's glass. The man returned the favour.

"I know my name sounds slightly Italian, but it isn't Borgia. I might have to be careful when I visit Toronto, but there would be no benefit to me doing something foolish. It's nice to share wine with an equal."

They took long sips of some of the best wine Chester had ever tasted. He pondered Angel's intentions. The man struggled to defuse things and massage Chester's ego. The PLM attached more importance to the railway than he thought.

"Yes," Chester replied, "neither of us wants anything foolish to happen."

"Let me get right to the point." Angel looked directly into Chester's eyes. "We want this railway running as soon as possible. Unfortunately, word spread quickly about the desertions. It makes us look bad and might encourage people to jump ship." Chester sipped wine and thought about how Angel's directness reinforced what he believed.

"We don't care about the men; they're worthless. It's the impact of their deserting." Angel sipped.

The man's straightforward honesty reassured Chester and confirmed the PLM would not be an immediate threat. Angel's disregard for people deepened Chester's disgust.

"I can help you out if you agree to a few conditions," Chester sipped.

"That depends," Angel sounded hesitant. "What can you do for us?"

"The harbour needs to be dredged, repaired and a bulk unloader set up. We can say you assigned this crew to help complete the work and run the harbour. We will assign your people to Owen Sound and use them there until we finish construction. Then, they will go to where they can make a life. Spread that story, and your engine crews would confirm it."

"It sounds good. It would be enough." Angel smiled. He saw the simplicity of the plan. "What conditions do you have?" He frowned.

"The biggest one is no restriction on people coming and going on the rail line. Standard border controls are fine, but let us decide whom we let in here. I will always encourage anyone on business to return, but if the occasional person stays, we don't want this kind of crisis to happen again. Remember, we returned your commandos after the fighting."

"That is no problem." Angel agreed quickly, making Chester think he had already conceded before he arrived.

Angel knew he would have no trouble keeping his local people off the train. If people from Toronto used the train to get away, it was not his problem unless his superiors made it his problem. It might benefit him when the time came for him to try for the PLM leader's job; he could stage a spectacular capture of fleeing traitors. In the meantime, he could brag he opened the railway. It all seemed perfect.

"What other conditions?" Angel hoped they were as easy as this.

"We want seventy kilometres' worth of steel rail and ties delivered over the next year and a locomotive, preferably a steam-powered wood burner."

"For the harbour, we need a power shovel with a clam bucket and diesel fuel to run it for unloading the ships." Angel scowled. "This will benefit you too." Chester saw his opponent's discomfort and wanted to soften the blow. "It'll let us ship wood to Toronto and move your iron ore faster, making you look good."

Angel gripped the table as he thought about the request. It was a major condition. Getting the hundred kilometres of track for the Orangeville to Owen Sound job had been a stretch. Now Huron wanted almost the same amount. At the same time, this hick had given him an argument to win agreement in Toronto. It would be hard, but he could accept it. The steam engine might be an issue. He would have to see if the workshop in Hamilton could supply a refurbished machine.

"The shovel is no problem, but what if you use the fuel to fight us?" Angel seemed honestly concerned.

"We fight on foot," Chester replied. "We don't depend on vehicles."

"We can do it. These are small matters for us." Angel gulped down the rest of his wine and poured another glass. Chester refused a refill and nursed his drink.

"We would not expect the first shipments or the engine before next spring." Chester had noted this was not an easy commitment for Angel and did not want to be overly aggressive. Barry Young could not work on the Durham or Southampton lines until the frost was out next year. The harvest would use all the labour for the next month.

"You will get the shovel right away. We have a boatload of iron ore on its way." Angel smiled.

Angel's announcement of the ship caught Chester by surprise.

"I'm not sure we can have the harbour ready."

"It's a shallow draft with only ten thousand tonnes of cargo, ten-year-old iron ore pellets from Duluth." Angel enjoyed his adversary's discomfort. "We'll get the information to Young. You need to put the crew up for the winter. We can only take a few carloads at a time. The whole thing is about a hundred ore cars' worth. It'll supply us all winter."

"It'll be slow work unloading the ship." Chester was glad he would not be shovelling iron ore. "You need to send us labour for each load."

Chester prepared a handwritten paper in duplicate, which both men signed. Another handshake ended the meeting. Angel walked along the planking of the platform, turned, and gave Chester a salute. The train reversed out of the station.

"Good news. We have peace. You can get those boulders back up the ramps. The bad news is, we have to get Owen Sound harbour ready for a ship in two weeks. If we had known, we could have demanded more."

Chester left on the jigger. He had a job to organize and needed Barry and Jim to get started. Jeff assembled the security force to reset the emergency roadblocks, and returned to Flesherton. The station guards settled into the comfortable routine of train watching and gardening.

**

"What a grand event!" Brandi smiled at the enormous crowd surrounding the Flesherton station. She stood with Sarah Handley and Jennifer Young, waiting for the train. The women's husbands chatted with Chester before the official inauguration of railway service in Huron and the grand opening of Jim's jewel, the Flesherton station with the stimulating carpentry challenge of the circular section.

The brisk October air, several weeks after the harvest, did not diminish spirits, and the occasional snowflake caused no concern. A majority of Beaver Valley inhabitants and many from surrounding areas had gathered on the second day of a three-day get-together, a combination inaugural ceremony and the largest harvest party the region had ever held. Scheduling the event for mid-afternoon allowed for recovery from the previous night's revelry. The crowd grew in numbers and enthusiasm. The railway meant a connection to the outside world, even if to a hostile and dangerous one.

"Here she comes!" The cry went up. A locomotive whistled a long, rising note and then rapid, happy blasts, as it eased into the station. The warning bell on the engine clanged continuously. The border guards at Proton had placed a large sign at the front: "Welcome to Huron". In the cab, Jake struggled to avoid an accident. His brakeman kept shouting, "All clear" as onlookers scrambled off the line. The gigantic machine squealed to a stop with a loud hissing of air brakes. Jake breathed again.

Carrying a book for Barry, Jake climbed down from his perch to back-slapping and smiles. He refused the many offers of cider but promised everyone he would return soon. The train made a regular run twice a week, taking the iron ore south and returning empty gondola cars and a passenger coach and express car attached to the rear. In the first week, several PLM officials had travelled on the train, but the coach now normally arrived empty. Occasionally, people travelled looking for trading opportunities.

Chester made a speech outlining the situation with the railway and the truce with the PLM. He hoped they could achieve something permanent without more bloodshed, but warned everyone to remain prepared to fight. Chester introduced Jim and Barry in recognition of their leadership and hard work. Each man tried to deflect the praise to the other and then acknowledge the work and sacrifice of the residents who had helped. Jim called up Jake and his crew. Amidst loud cheers, Jake could only mumble "thank you".

Piano music drifted from inside the station as Joseph of Longview played an old railway song, supported by a dozen other musicians.

Walt found the piano in a church, and he had it manhandled to the station. Joseph spent a couple of hours tuning it, complaining it had suffered terrible neglect. Walt became fed-up with the complaints and played a blues lament on his mouth organ until the Joseph relented.

"I love the blues, Walt." Joseph had frowned. "Please stop wrecking it."

The two mimicked a father and son. Walt replaced the unknown father, who left a hole in Joseph's heart. The teasing carried mutual love.

"Here's another damned book," Jake handed Barry the package from Rob. "It'll take a snowy winter for you to read them all." Jake laughed and winked. He knew the books meant more than simply reading.

"Come and meet the Shadlys," Barry took Jake's elbow and directed him to Sharon and Bill standing beneath the Flesherton sign. He saw Brandi walking down the platform. "Here's Brandi," Young added. "She's the artist-rover of the Shadly family."

Barry appreciated Brandi's care and friendliness towards Brian who, like most people, adored her. Brandi paused and absorbed the scene for a drawing before joining the group.

Young tucked the book into his coat pocket. Rob had not included a red bookmark for an urgent message. Barry had time to party before work.

"It will be like old times," Jake patted Brian on the shoulder and climbed up to his cab. The train rolled away to deliver the empty cars to the docks. On the next run, Brian would ride in the cab and begin his training.

Music flowed from the station. The party spilt along the platform and onto the roadway. They served refreshments in the storage sheds, and several large pigs roasted over fire pits. Smiles shone from every face. Hope raised people's spirits. The winter would be long, but free of invasion fears. Jeff would get to spend a complete season with his family and finally learn to skate well enough to avoid Jani`s teasing. He would help their hockey team, the "Longview Lungers" earn their first win against the "Thornbury Turbines".

The next year would offer both joy and sorrow, especially to the Shadly family.

Chapter Twelve

The train slid into Flesherton station with little fanfare as hissing air brakes brought it to a gentle halt. The railway had been operating for nine months and in this first summer had become routine. Little children still gathered to watch the trains, few adults bothered. In the eleventh summer since the crisis began, building new lives occupied most people.

Several men quickly unloaded boxes, bulging grain bags, and steel bars and rods. Today, a large bale of cotton fibre went to a local textile operation. The weaver mostly used wool and flax, but the railway opened up possibilities with cotton.

A complex trading arrangement sent wood, grain, and cheese for the cotton from the GTA, where bales of fibre came as payment for products sent south into the USA. No one knew how many times the cotton changed hands before reaching Huron. With no currency, each major exchange point had at least one venue to barter goods, although, as in Huron, a personal IOU could carry weight depending on the issuer's reputation. Old Canadian dollars circulated but had no value in Huron.

Few people travelled these days, but a man exited the passenger car. The visitor, middle-aged and solidly built, stood erect, with a greying, well-groomed beard and short-cropped hair. He moved deliberately and precisely, like a soldier.

He slung a heavy duffle bag over his shoulder and headed into the station, admiring the Handley creation with its rectangular freight shed on one end and the impressive circular office and waiting area topped by a steep peaked roof. He entered the spacious waiting room with its high-backed wooden benches running along two walls and down the middle. A Quebec heater sat near the rear wall.

The ticket counter separated the main area from two office desks. The wall behind the counter supported rows of pigeonholes holding envelopes and small packages. A small man, the stationmaster, ticket seller, postmaster and resident gossip, stood behind the smooth wooden structure examining manifests from today's shipments. He spent most of his time tending an attached farm, but always occupied his post at train time.

"Hello there," the small man smiled in the visitor's direction, "can I help you? We don't see many strangers these days."

The visitor noticed the speaker's furtive glance under the counter. It would be where this seemingly harmless person had a weapon, probably a handgun. It did not matter. The stranger meant no harm and would do nothing to raise suspicion.

"I'm from Toronto," the newcomer replied. "I'm looking for old friends. Ever hear of Sharon and Bill Shadly?"

"What you want with them folks?" Eagerness to have news to repeat at tonight's dinner table overcame suspicion.

"I used to know them, a long time ago, back in the old days." He set his burden on the floor and moved his feet apart, at ease. The stationmaster noticed the slight pause and guessed the man hastily made up the last bit.

This stranger seems harmless, and who am I to interfere? The Shadlys can take care of themselves, especially if Jeff is home. This guy somehow reminds me of Jeff.

The man's bag had faded letters, „P. Maki', stencilled down one side.

"The Shadlys live down in the valley, on a farm." He looked at the stranger. "It's a hike. Are you in a hurry?"

"I've been travelling for a day and night," said the man. "I would like to get there before I rest." He slumped onto one of the wooden benches. "It's been a long time."

"I got a team taking some freight part way. You can ride down to Kimberly. Look up the folks in the old ski resort. The Shadly girl works there. She'll get you to Longview."

The man stepped from behind the counter, strode over to the visitor, and stuck out his hand. "I'm George," he continued. The stranger took his hand in a firm grip.

"Thank you, George; I'm Peter."

"How are you doing, Hank?" Warren looked past the driver of the railway freight wagon to the stranger sitting beside him.

"Hi, Warren," the teamster climbed down and secured the team to the hitch-rail. "This is Peter. He came on the train this morning. He's looking for the Shadlys. Can Brandi help him?"

"Nope, she went south, won't be back for weeks."

"Well, I got to return to Flesherton," Hank said. "If you can't ride him on down, he's got to walk."

"I don't mind walking," Peter interjected, dismounting from the wagon and fetching his bag. He surveyed the scene. Large trees in full leaf shaded the grounds and the long lane they had just traversed. Their wagon had stopped at the front steps of a once elegant resort, now with boarded-up windows and peeling paint. A woman repaired a step.

"I'm Peter Maki," he extended his right hand.

"Your name sounds familiar," Warren grasped Peter's hand. "You look familiar, but I'm sure we've never met."

"No, we've never met," Peter agreed.

"When did you last eat?" Warren began the hospitality ritual. Incidents of genuine hunger were now rare, but the courtesy persisted.

"Breakfast yesterday," Peter replied, "and ate bread on the train."

Warren guided him up the stairs away from a scurry of activity as several of the students unloaded the wagon, hustling the contents into wheelbarrows. Warren glanced back. Several of the packages went to his and Jean's cabin. Perhaps the seeds he expected had arrived.

"We can't take you down the valley for at least a week," Warren explained to Peter. "It's only a morning's walk if you are up to it. Stay and eat, sleep here tonight. If you get an early start, you'll be at Longview for lunch. We have some letters you can carry down."

"That would be fine." With a tired sigh, Peter set his bag near the door. He had been tired and hungry many times in the last decade and scared almost as often. In the welcoming confines of the Institute, he felt comfortable and safe.

Warren led Peter into the dining area where food was always available. The school's irregular hours kept Maud or her apprentices constantly in the kitchen. When Warren introduced Jean, she burst into a smile.

"Sharon will be ecstatic." Jean's eyes twinkled.

"What's up?" Warren asked. "Do you know Peter?"

"I never met him," she replied. "This is Sharon's brother. He was overseas when the collapse hit."

"I knew you looked familiar," Warren exclaimed, looking more closely at Peter. "You have Sharon's eyes."

Warren retrieved a bottle of fruit wine and Jean recounted a brief version of their story while Peter told the general details of his life. He would save the darker moments for Sharon.

The next morning, Jean and Warren hitched a small cart to a Canadian workhorse. Peter squeezed onto the seat beside them, and they headed to Longview.

A meeting had begun on the porch of the old farmhouse to discuss increasing lime production to build another stone residential structure to close the west side of the compound past the barn. Longview had developed into a village of about a dozen families. They needed extra suitable housing. Walt Lefevre noticed the approaching horse and cart.

"We have company," Walt exclaimed, "Warren, Jean, and a stranger."

"Don't tell me we have another farmhand arriving," Debbie Hunter watched the wagon's progress. "We don't have room."

"We can use more labour," Sharon stood beside Debbie, anticipating a rare visit from her friends. The cart reached the first of the stone houses.

"Oh, my God," Sharon suddenly exclaimed, "it can't be... it's him!" Bill jumped to his feet.

"Who?" He did not recognize the stranger with the salt and pepper beard.

"It's Peter," Sharon cried as she raced down the steps, laughing and crying all at once. Her shrieks of joy echoed from the walls. "Peter," she cried as the buggy drew near, "Oh Peter, it's you!"

The vehicle came to a dusty, snorting stop. Peter leapt down and embraced Sharon. They stood back from the teary embrace, hands on each other's shoulders, and stared through bleary eyes, then hugged once more.

Walt helped Warren from the high seat. His old friend seemed weaker than his last visit. The commotion drew old and young from all about the compound. In the happy turmoil, the brother and sister had little opportunity to share private moments. Megan Lefevre eased Jean to the ground and followed the crowd into the old house. Megan, now a strong girl of fifteen apprenticed in the kitchen with Debbie. Debbie scrounged a supply of baked treats that Megan placed on the table and distributed brightly decorated clay cups ready for hot tea.

"How did you know to come here?" Sharon gripped Peter's hand.

"A picture tipped me off." Peter took a rolled-up paper from his bag. "See this?" He unrolled the document. "I found this hanging in the Oakville station. This is you and Bill. I would know you anywhere, sis."

Peter held the picture Brandi had done the previous year at the railway inauguration. It depicted the unmistakable Flesherton station with its sign suspended above the platform. Sharon and Bill, along with the engineer and Barry Young, stood beneath the sign. Jim Handley's face peered through a window as a tribute to the station's builder. Brandi had given the drawing to Jake, and he pinned it up in his home station in Oakville.

"This is an impressive picture." Peter went on. "It's almost photographic. I want to meet this Nymeyesi Mickahwah. This drawing is wonderful. I owe him big-time." He put his finger below the signature on the paper. It said Nimise Makwa. Sharon's eyes sparkled, overflowing with happiness. Peter's comment filled her with glee.

"It's a she. You met her years ago." Sharon giggled. "We'll get your pronunciation right, but Nimise Makwa is Brandi. Look," Sharon pointed to a small icon on the other corner of the paper. "See this? It's a brandy glass. She gave this drawing to the engineer in the picture."

"She has talent, Sharon. She could make a career of it." Peter stared.

"Believe me," Bill spoke up, "Brandi has made a career of it as the Huron Territory's chief scribe and documentarian. She travels everywhere, knows everyone and the entire population loves and embraces her. Brandi has sat in every kitchen in this valley and countless other houses and campfires everywhere. We're proud of her and happy she has found her true calling. She's a big part of what has held the territory together, uniting folks who would have never known each other existed. Without mass media, she's the bearer of news. Brandi and the group she and the Institute have developed travel all over. They share knowledge and tell stories about those they meet, but it's Brandi who stirs up excitement in people. Somehow, her spirit and kindness have captured everyone's love." Bill caught his breath, savouring immense pride in his daughter. "I was on a security detail with a railway work crew guarding workers sent up by the crowd down your way."

"It's not my way anymore," Peter forcefully interrupted. "I won't be going back."

"I see," Bill cast an understanding glance towards his brother-in-law. "Anyway, we had to guard them. One day Brandi came by to watch and sketch the work. When the crew saw her sitting on the bank, they stopped and went to her. First, it was only some locals, but then the entire crew downed tools, and soon they sat on the bank asking her questions and demanding a story. She got out a journal and told them of her latest trip up the Bruce, showing her drawings to illustrate. Those tough men and women sat there for over an hour listening and smiling and even crying when Brandi talked about a baby dying at birth, and her having had to shoot her horse. When she finished, they clapped, yelled, and whistled. It was like an old-time rock concert."

"Jim Handley came along, upset the work had stopped. I know he loves Brandi like a sister, but boy did he give her a hard time. Jim felt a lot of pressure to get things done. Brandi gave me a mischievous smile. If you get up to Owen Sound, visit Jim and Sarah, you will see a drawing hanging over their table. Brandi drew a huffing, puffing steam locomotive balanced on one rail with Brandi pulling the other rail out from under it. The front of the machine is Jim's face, snarling right into your eyes with steam coming out of his ears."

"Be sure to look at the signatures," Sharon added. "Along with everything you see in this drawing," she pointed to the paper, "there's a little pigeon beside the brandy glass. Jim calls Brandi his clay pigeon from when we built our first building here. Sarah hung it up. Anytime Jim gives her a hard time, she points to it."

"There are similar pictures spread everywhere." Sharon continued. "Nimise Makwa has spread smiles, news, stories and a sense of togetherness and well-being to us all."

Peter noticed two drawings over the Longview mantle. One was the picture of the naming of Longview, and the other was a double portrait of a man and a woman. Brandi had added the picture of Matt Long and Brenda after Jeff discovered they were both alive.

After Bill's explanation, there was a pause. Peter's heart grew heavy trying to decide when would be the right time to tell of the fate of their family. He had sad news. Sharon decided for him. She, too, had been avoiding the questions on her mind since she first embraced Peter.

"Do you know anything about Mom, Dad, and the others?" Her voice shook, fearing the answer.

"They're all gone, Sharon." Peter cried, and they embraced. Their tears mingled, and they trembled in each other's arms. Everyone but Bill quietly left the room. The others felt their friends' heavy hearts and sought work to distract from their loss. Memories suddenly cast shadows over everyone.

"I only made it to Toronto two years ago," Peter finally continued, recovering some composure. He had lived with his grief for years and felt Sharon's pain. "Mom and Dad died in an epidemic of some sort. I am not sure which one, but there was cholera, typhoid and a flu thing spread fast and killed quickly." Despite himself, Peter stopped to let a sob pass. "I learned that from their old neighbours who somehow survived. Mary disappeared, and no one seems to know what happened to her or the kids." Peter stopped, as if considering what more to say about their brother. Finally, after taking a deep breath, he continued.

"I came across information on Harry. He threw in with one of the dominant groups, the main one originally run by the last provincial government before the People's Liberation Movement took over. They're a mean bunch of bastards with a lot of blood on their hands."

"We know all about them." Bill wanted to give Peter time to recover. "We fought them to a standstill, with the help of the weather."

"When I finally got back from Europe, I re-joined the military in Ottawa, and they sent me to Toronto as a rep to the PLM."

"Harry worked for the PLM secret police. I'm not sure how high up," Peter whispered. "I found a written order to shoot six prisoners over Harry's signature." Sharon gasped. "I'm sure many of those were murders, but I dug into it. They had no due process, only a bureaucratic trial and execution. Other orders named women and children with his signature, so I got out. I've done things I regret over the past few years. I murdered no one or ordered a murder.

"When I asked about Harry, they cold-shouldered me. I got a woman clerk drunk in bed one night. She told me someone denounced Harry, and they executed him. Harry's in a mass grave east of the city."

Sorrow filled the Shadly home for many weeks. Grief clouded Sharon's and Peter's joy at being reunited. Only the constant demands of work gave them relief, but Longview embraced Peter, a strong, healthy and capable worker. There would be no homecoming party until Jeff returned from Owen Sound and Brandi from the south.

***

Brandi sat astride Niibin, high on a bluff overlooking the mouth of a small river flowing into Lake Erie. From this height, the silver-grey water rested still and silent under a low slate-grey sky. Water and sky melded into a shimmering curtain hiding the horizon.

Concrete breakwaters sheltered half a dozen open boats at the river mouth. Several well-maintained and colourful houses sat near the water. Further inland, where the old highway crossed the river, abandoned commercial buildings stood derelict. This place, once prosperous, now crumbled. She and Niibin made their way down the hill past decaying buildings with faded signs, "The Pickerel Inn" and "Beaches B&B". Before the crash, tourists had flocked to the town.

The pair allowed a wagon to pass drawn by a team of Belgians, working to hold back the weight against the slope. The wagon carried bags of grain and a few caged chickens. Sawn lumber extended from the back. Brandi followed the team into a parking lot beside the rusting lift bridge.

To describe the place as a market would have glorified it with only one other horse-drawn wagon. Two people pushed wheelbarrows from the river. A brightly painted plywood handcart with tireless bicycle wheels and twisted spokes stopped beside the wagons. The people watched Brandi approach through the diffuse sunlight.

"Hello, I'm Brandi," she slid from Niibin, "from up north."

"It's dangerous up there," the woman wagon driver said.

"I had to be careful," Brandi agreed. She offered her hand.

"Joan Latchford," the woman smiled, "how far north?" They gasped when Brandi said she had ridden from the Georgian Bay area.

"You must be PLM," one man bristled. "No one else could get through alive."

"I'm sure not PLM," Brandi tried to sound reassuring. "We fought them off a couple of years ago, and now we have a truce. I hate what they stand for, but we can't beat them. We call our place Huron Territory. It runs from Kincardine to Mount Forest and west of Collingwood."

"The radio brags about a railway to Owen Sound. That doesn't fit your story."

"It's true, sort of," Brandi smiled, "but they run it to our border and then we run it to the Sound. We let their train crews come, but no PLM. We trade wood, food and iron ore down for metal, textiles and exotic food."

"A railway sure 'd be great." One man glanced to where a few old rail coaches rusted. "We got the engine but no fuel, and it just goes to Union. They took the rest of the track two years ago."

Brandi would not mention the steel might now be on Huron right of way.

"I think the PLM is weaker down this way. I stayed away from the big towns. Most folks seem peaceful." Brandi tied Niibin to a rusty cable at the edge of the parking lot. "They said things were horrible for a while."

"Yup." Joan wrestled with the grain sacks on her wagon. "At the start, a lot of city folks came out of London and other towns and tried to farm. They pushed the locals aside and killed some. The ones closest to the towns suffered the most."

"We had trouble here in the Port," said the man with the wheelbarrow. "The local folks weren't too bad once we realized togetherness might be best. A town bunch showed up, and we had a big fight." He lifted a tarp to reveal fresh caught pickerel. "There was some bloodshed."

The man did not continue, as if the rest of the story was too hard. Brandi thought he might have killed someone and would rather not implicate himself. She had seen it before.

"Most of the residents took off. Many were outsiders anyway, like me, and they thought the big city might offer them something. That's over ten years ago now. We've heard what happened in Toronto and other big places, so I guess they're all dead."

He sounded sad, but after so much grief and hardship, people had little capacity for sorrow. Brandi wondered if time could heal this darkness. Her family shadows rode with her.

"I saw lots of ruins," Brandi agreed. "Why is so much land empty? Most folks I met wouldn't talk much."

"Probably because they murdered to get their place." Joan evaluated the fish. "These weren't bad folks, but desperate and did desperate things. Once they found out, it took hard work, and they didn't know how to grow anything, many ran back to town."

"I need a couple of boards and a sack of oats." The fisherman glanced at the wagon.

"Yeah, they killed the folks who knew how to grow stuff and then starved. I saw some eating grassroots." The man with the other wagon joined in. He offered potatoes, a weaned kid goat, and some rusty tools.

"Many of them died. We see a steady stream of people coming now, asking if they can join us." He pulled off two sacks of potatoes for one fisherman. "They're suffering, but mostly polite. It spreads out the food, but it will pay off if they will work. There aren't enough farmhands." He placed a sack of fish on the wagon and went to check out the handcart.

"Why did you come here?" Joan asked Brandi as they made their way to the trading cart.

"It's hard to describe." Brandi once again struggled to define her job. "I'm a recorder and storyteller, visiting folks and telling the news. I am also a teacher, spreading ideas and linking folks up with those who can teach skills. The most important part of my job is to help build a basic educational system in Huron. I came down here because we didn't know this area, even though our sources told us the PLM had withdrawn."

"So you are a spy, then?" The woman did not sound upset.

"More an ambassador than a spy. I don't sneak around and hope my honesty gets me the same." The cart full of paper bags containing coffee, sugar, and other things rare or nonexistent in Huron amazed Brandi. A bag of sugar and one of coffee bought two chickens and a half bag of grain.

"We have had little of those." Brandi did not long for the products but only stated a fact.

"What do you have to trade?" The vendor was eager to move more of her goods. Just two customers made a disappointing turnout for the weekend exchange.

"Nothing you would want, I don't think. In most places, I trade work and story-telling and maybe a drawing for food and a bed."

"We can give you work in the garden, and we need repair. What stories and drawings?"

Brandi opened her portfolio to show drawings from the current trip. One image of a Mennonite buggy angled into a road ditch with weeds growing through the wheel spokes and the skeleton of a horse, still hitched to the rotting traces. Questions followed cries of despair and disgust.

"It was northeast of London. It happened a few years ago; I would say. I didn't draw the skeleton of an adult in the ditch beside the rig. Looked like a bullet in the head, murdered by the PLM. They shot many people up our way a few years ago. A Mennonite family told me eight out of ten of their people had died in some places, even though they didn't resist."

"Is that why you carry a gun?"

"This rifle has saved my life more than once. I never let it out of reach."

"Sounds like some stories in that." Joan looked disappointed. "I would like to stay, but these fish need cleaning. Can you come our way and spend a night with us? We're just up the road near Union. Follow this road up the river, and you will come to crossroads with a big house on the left. That's us." Joan headed her team up the road.

"I'm Ellen," the woman with the cart said, "and this black Yankee is Don, and the others are Pete and farmer Larry."

"I have to leave too," Larry shook her hand. "You come see us sometime. We're west of here along the lake. Here are a few potatoes. Your stories are already worth that."

Larry left his load behind, but took the balance of the fish and a few bags from Ellen's cart.

"I can't see how you can make a go of it, with only two customers," Brandi remembered the vigorous markets in Huron.

"Most folks go to St Thomas," Ellen seemed disappointed. "The PLM still runs things up there. Even though they tax the transactions, growers get more. There's a black market. They use old Canadian dollars."

Brandi had hidden Canadian bills from her Mom in her folio... *just in case you have to phone home for a ride.* Sharon had joked.

"They aren't worth much," Chris added. "A hundred will buy you a loaf of bread. The PLM seems to like them. They want them for taxes first, even before food. It's a mystery to us."

Brandi's dollars could only feed her for two days, but might buy her way out of trouble.

"Privateers from Ohio bring the exotic stuff over the lake. We get good value for it and the fish. The pirates take grain and scrap." Ellen closed her cart. She still had most of her wares.

"I grew up near Cleveland." Don flashed Brandi a friendly smile. "Fortunately, I escaped the gang wars and made it over here. Southern goods mostly come from Cuba. It has an occupied zone on the Mississippi, and they trade in the Caribbean. Unfortunately, soft fruits can't survive the long trip. My friends say they might get oranges picked green."

"This trade over the lake was my doing." Don seemed proud of his contribution. "A few years ago, I went back to find my family. No luck there," he paused for an instant, "but I ran into these pirates who had a nice boat and were looking for customers, so we got them to visit here. They're the last link in the trading chain."

"There's always a much larger market when the Yankee traders are in port. We advertise by word of mouth to avoid PLM customs collectors and their bribes," Ellen said. "Come with me." She headed towards a small, colourfully painted cottage. The men pushed their wheelbarrows towards other houses. Behind the women, Don's deep voice improvised to an old tune: "she talked about her troubles; it's a crying sin, rode a painted pony, and tales she could spin...".

A few seagulls wheeled and squawked overhead.

"We ate those birds at the beginning." Ellen watched the birds for a moment. "We would put a few dead fish on top of a net. When these air rats landed, we yanked the net over them. It was efficient. We didn't have any chickens then. The gulls taste okay."

"A rail line running to St Thomas would reduce the local market, but having it would make us a port. I think we would thrive. No chance of the PLM allowing it," was her final say on the matter. Ellen left her cart in a snug shed and gave Niibin a place under the overhanging roof.

***

We remained with Ellen and Don for two days. The ride up from Lake Erie to Guelph was an uneventful but lonely two weeks. Using an old highway map, I avoided all the major towns controlled by the PLM. There were plenty of people willing to betray someone for money or food. Joan, up in Union, told me I had been lucky in stumbling upon their friendly bunch. The majority would have turned me over to the PLM. For the first time, I realized how dangerous it was this far south. Niibin and I hid many times in bush and never rode up to any dwelling. On thinking back, I was foolish, but the trip was the most important one for me personally and eventually ended the loneliness of my life's journey.

From: "Transitions" (The Journals of Brandi Shadly, Vol. 8, p. 71)

Squealing of metal scraping against metal and the roar of a diesel engine reverberated in Brandi's hiding place. She gripped Niibin's reins. Her free hand massaged the horse's nose. Niibin fidgeted at the loud industrial noises. Brandi had not heard these sounds for many years. In the sunshine, perhaps two hundred meters from her hiding spot, a dozen workers laboured over a jumble of wrecked motor vehicles' rusted, burnt-out hulks; many riddled with bullet holes from a major battle years before. Clouds of red and white dust rose from the work site. A crane on crawler treads lifted the derelicts onto a flatbed semi-trailer. Fifty old vehicles littered this spot. Brandi could see more stretching down the old multi-lane road that joined Guelph with the little-used Highway 401. Brandi had seen no travellers.

Brandi had crossed the 401 a little to the west, sneaking over at dawn, having seen convoys of heavy vehicles accompanied by truckloads of heavily armed fighters. Both she and Niibin wished to escape the raucous scene. She wanted to find a secure camp for the night, closer to the town centre, and fretted at the delay but had learned patience on the road.

Long evening shadows crept over the roadway, and the crew climbed onto the precarious, unsecured load and headed towards town, leaving the crane behind. Brandi waited, making sure no guard lingered.

Using the uncertain light of dusk, she walked Niibin across the old highway and past the machine smelling of hot metal and oil. They reached the cover between abandoned factories. Brandi hoped the black window openings only concealed four-footed scavengers. Niibin gingerly picked her way through tangles of weeds and bushes onto the remnants of a paved street leading to the abandoned university.

Brandi needed to find shelter in the quickly fading light. A clear sky promised fair weather, but thought it more important to hide from prying eyes and roving gangs. In the light of a pale quarter moon setting in the west, Brandi found a deserted barn in the school's agricultural complex. Doorways at each end offered two escape routes. Brandi selected a spot where she could see both openings but remain out of sight. They had options if anyone came along, but she saw no signs of recent visitors.

The two friends nestled on a bed of well-composted straw and manure. A cold meal killed Brandi's hunger but did not satisfy. Niibin found old hay to nose in, supplementing her ration of oats, and the greenery she had nibbled as they travelled. Brandi left Niibin saddled and curled up beside the horse, her senses alert to danger. She awoke several times to random sounds. As the brightening sky drew window openings in the walls, she heard a clanking sound. Something metallic and hollow had struck solid wood.

Niibin dozed, unperturbed. Brandi gripped her rifle. The sound did not repeat. She doubted her ears but then heard distinct footsteps quietly crossing the gap in one doorway. A grey human shadow stopped beyond the door, looking into the barn, hesitating, perhaps considering coming inside, then creeping into the building.

Brandi pressed back into the shadows. She found the safety on the rifle and waited. The person drew opposite the hiding place. In the growing light, she saw a young man carrying a bucket. Brandi decided to let him pass, but Niibin snorted. The figure stopped and turned, looking directly at the horse. He could see the white patches of the skewbald.

"No, you don't," cried a boy's voice. He bolted the way he had come.

"Wait!" Brandi called after him.

The lad ran through the doorway, disappearing to the right. Brandi mounted Niibin and started her briskly out the door. The lad fled towards some trees and buildings. Her moccasin-covered heels nudged the horse into a gallop. Despite the poor light and uncertain ground, they closed on the running figure. Brandi sailed past and swung Niibin around, blocking the boy's escape.

"Wait! I just want to talk." Brandi smiled, barely visible in the poor light. The boy retreated, preparing to run again.

"My horse can outrun you anytime." She tried to sound friendly. "I don't want to chase you. I'm a visitor from up north and just want to talk."

He eyed Brandi as a cornered rabbit might react to the jaws of the fox. His bucket had disappeared. He crouched, breathing hard, preparing to fight. Brandi waited, letting him calm down, hoping his rush of adrenalin would burn out. The boy was scrawny and about eighteen years old.

"I'm Brandi," she said at last. "Who are you?"

"Erin," the young man decided he could not escape and perhaps talking would save him. "Erin Thomas." He suddenly sat down, signalling submission. Brandi slid off Niibin and squatted.

"I'm Brandi Shadly, from Huron. I'm on my way home."

"I have nothing to give you." The boy was calm but defiant. "I have nothing worth much and almost no food. Not much to steal." He thought she was a robber, or as desperate as himself.

"I just want information," Brandi smiled. Erin's face relaxed.

"I haven't had many people to talk to," Erin muttered. "I work on my own. It's safer."

"Are you hungry, Erin?" Brandi guessed the boy had been searching for food. "I have a little if you want to come back to the barn." He hesitated.

"I won't hurt you. I promise." Erin seemed to relax. She could see a debate was going on in his mind.

"Look," she said, touching the butt of the rifle hanging on her shoulder, "if I had wanted to steal your stuff, you would already be dead." Erin seemed to accept her logic and stood. "Erin, walk on the other side of my horse. If you want to run for it, then go ahead. I won't chase you."

She could not tell if he believed her. If she lied, it would not matter. She could always run him down.

He looked around furtively. Daylight came upon them.

"Let's get in there. It isn't too safe here." He strode towards the barn. Brandi and Niibin followed.

Brandi offered the ever-present cold-smoked pork and wild rabbit she had shot and roasted the day before. Brandi ate along with him. He did not hide his hunger. He used his fingers, but ate with an elegance hinting at a good upbringing and some manners. Licking his fingers was just a sign of the hungry times. Plates everywhere seldom left a table without a cleaning with tongue or bread. With food in his stomach, he trusted. Profound loneliness made him crave her friendship. Her heart broke at his wrenching story that added to Brandi's collection of many tales of loss.

"My parents taught here at the university, Dad history, Mom ecology. When the collapse hit, we hunkered down with other progressives in a little commune. For a couple of years, it wasn't too bad."

"A gang of thugs adopted us. We did things for them like cook, mend clothes and scavenge. In return, they kept other bad guys away. They were tough, a couple of ex-bikers, one a cop. I am not sure about the rest, a dozen altogether." Erin drank and wandered to a secluded corner to relieve his bladder. Brandi did the same.

"The arrangement worked until about two years ago. This PLM outfit took over the city. They rounded up most people and wiped out our guardians. The PLM fighters were a mean bunch and came storming onto the campus. They grabbed everyone. Mom and Dad hid me. I haven't seen them since. They're dead."

He said this in a matter-of-fact way, with no sign of tears or grief.

"Perhaps they're okay, maybe slaves, but alive." Brandi did not want to raise false hopes.

"It could be anything," Erin said bitterly. "I grieved it all out long ago." Brandi could see his real and raw suffering despite his brave words.

"How old are you, Erin?"

"I was eighteen in July. I've been living on my own since I was sixteen. It has been rough. I've a little garden and some chickens hidden over there in the back. No one comes around much..." His voice trailed off.

"You seem afraid of something."

"Sometimes there are patrols. They never come close, but if they saw us, game over. You don't want to meet the psychotic bastards." His voice had filled with hate.

"I think you're lonely, Erin. Come with me. You would like it back home." Brandi had taken a liking to the boy.

"I just met you, but I think I can trust you." Erin looked intently at Brandi. "I have nothing here but was afraid to move and did not know where to go. We had a cottage by Goderich. I heard it isn't any better."

"You are right about Goderich, although the PLM is losing its grip there. We're only a few days' ride from Mount Forest, in safe territory."

"Could your horse carry two of us?" He looked at Niibin.

"Not even a skinny guy like you." Brandi laughed. "She's a tough gal, but we'll walk."

"I can get a horse. I've never ridden."

"Can you get a saddle? You will need one to keep you from falling off."

After dark, Erin disappeared and before midnight returned with a nice quarter horse, with a saddle, a sack of food and a backpack. Brandi admired the sturdy mare; whoever looked after the animal had cared.

"This horse belongs to the garrison. The wrangler's a friend. I gave him my chickens, and he fixed me up. They think people won't notice her gone for a few days. I've been stealing from them for a year."

"Will he be in trouble? Does he know about me?"

"He'll be okay. They'll think someone stole the horse. Maybe they'll harass their usual targets for a while and check all the barns." Erin opened the bags strapped to the western saddle. "You're safe," he continued. "No one asks questions except for the goons. No one volunteers answers."

"I see you have some books." Brandi read the titles. Everything seemed beyond what she would have thought about reading. One, The History of the Decline and Fall of the Roman Empire, caught her eye.

"The looters took everything else from the university library, but they didn't bother with the books. A few got burnt for heat. Reading has kept me sane. The library has been my hideout. I wish I could bring more."

"We have books." Brandi wanted to be encouraging. "I know you'll like Warren and a few others to talk with on your level."

"Hey, I am not a snob." Erin seemed hurt. "I learned a long time ago, ordinary people have lots to say, and I've been doing a lot of thinking. Mom and Dad taught me to the grad level, but I played street hockey too."

Brandi could see the turmoil on his face as happy and sad memories battled.

"We'd better be out of town by daylight," Erin wanted action.

Brandi gave him a quick riding lesson in the dark and hoped it would keep him on the horse. She set an easy pace and worried about what might happen if they had to dash for safety.

The fire burnt higher than Brandi would have liked. She had learned fire making by trial and error and mastered the smokeless fire, keeping it low, useful and well hidden. She and Erin camped deep in the woods, and the tinder and wood were dry. Still, the wood smoke riding on the wind could give away their position. She stirred the hot coals so the big wild turkey on her black ash spit would brown up nicely. She shot the bird in the afternoon. It would feed them until they reached the Martin farm.

"Turn this slowly every so often. I want it seared before it cooks." Brandi had put the spit onto shorter support pieces. The heat would brown the skin. Later, she would raise it to stew in its juices.

"I wondered why you had two rifles." Erin turned the spit.

"The twenty-two lets me hunt without alerting the whole damned territory." She stuffed the turkey feathers into a bag. The smaller weapon hung in a second scabbard on the left side of Niibin.

"The big rifle is useful, but I used to pass up grouse and rabbits because you need a head shot with the Savage, otherwise, it won't leave enough to eat. A shotgun makes a lot of noise, so I got the little one." She had brought the turkey down with one shot using open sights.

"You're an excellent shot."

"My brother is better, and his friend Ted is a sniper. He could have got the turkey at two hundred meters or maybe a lot more. Jeff used to tease his kids with a story about Ted threading a darning needle by tying the thread to a bullet and shooting it through the eye. The kids believed that one until they were about three." Thinking about Jeff and home brightened her mood after the long and dangerous trip, and she looked forward to the last two weeks of her summer adventure. "If you have to shoot a bear or a deer, the Savage is just right. You need both."

"Have you ever shot one of those? The university crowd believed hunting was a bad thing, but the smell of roasting a turkey has me convinced. At least there is no bear down here."

"I've shot both and could have had a bear today." Erin looked surprised. "You didn't see those two bruins just after we crossed the Grand River. They ran away into a thick bush. I never want to shoot a makwa again."

The hot turkey with Erin's potatoes seasoned with salt, and wild garlic made a filling supper. Sleep came quickly, but Erin's loud talking and fretting woke Brandi several times. It had been the same the previous night. Brandi sat up, watching her friend with his restlessness. The faint light of the setting moon highlighted his struggles. Joseph's mother had escaped from slavery and abuse. Brandi had seen Ellen in this condition and wondered at the horrors behind Erin's cries.

"Well, if it isn't my Brandi and her young man," Aaron Martin descended from his front porch. He had watched them make their way up the long lane with the setting sun obscuring them in shadow. "It has been two years, my friend." Aaron took Niibin's reins as Brandi slipped from the saddle. He stepped back to look at the skewbald mare. "This is new. That big roan was taller." Aaron did not consider horses as pets and only marginally as friends.

"Dodger broke a leg; I had to shoot him. It happened up the Bruce Peninsula." Brandi rubbed Niibin for reassurance. "I loved him a lot, and it hurt. Her name is Niibin. The Ojibwe gave her to me." Even though Aaron did not attach to his animals, he was once a little boy and felt Brandi's grief.

"She's a beauty, pretty as you. Who's this young man?"

"Aaron, this is Erin." Brandi giggled.

"Different spelling... same effect," Aaron smiled.

Erin and Brandi spent an enjoyable few days with the Martin clan. She entertained with more stories while sitting on the porch into the small hours of the morning. Aaron became the patriarch when his father died.

Barry Young building a railway to Durham excited him.

"We might ship to the city. What do they use for payment?" Brandi explained it was a barter system.

Brandi spent many hours in the garden with the younger women and girls weeding and watering. The most amusing part of her stay was observing the frantic efforts of the adults in keeping the young people separated. The first time she had been there, they had chaperoned the young men in her presence. With Erin along, they were busy babysitting all the young people. The young men, including Erin, spent the days cutting firewood in the bush.

They departed on the third morning with Brandi eager for Kimberly and to have Erin settled in. Aaron walked beside as they rode to the gate.

"Those are beautiful moccasins." He touched Brandi's foot; "horsehide on the soles."

"Dodger," Brandi said. Aaron patted her leg.

"Have a safe trip and come back before two years pass this time." Aaron waved as the two young people turned east towards the town.

Chapter Thirteen

The schoolchildren sat cross-legged on the platform of the Flesherton railway station. Although well-behaved, their youthful energy caused occasional giggles. Samantha James faced them, sitting cross-legged and wishing for a chair. In the twelfth year after the collapse, most adults felt the years.

Every week the school went to watch a train arrive. Samantha liked to take the children out for sun and exercise. Walking the few kilometres to the station provided a natural pleasure, especially now to see a steam-powered engine. They practised singing, with several playing guitar, flute or harmonica as they walked. Samantha taught them a song about the river, written by Joseph of Longview. She longed for Joseph to be in her class and envied Harold for having the privilege of teaching the musical genius.

"She's late today," George stood in the shade, looking down at the children.

"It is supposed to pass through today, isn't it?" Samantha wished they had brought lunch.

"Hello, Mrs. James." Brian Young appeared behind George. He waited to join Jake for the run to Owen Sound. Now that they ran steam engines; the work became harder but more fun. Feeding heavy wood into the boiler firebox built his muscles.

"Hello, Brian, I haven't seen your dad lately." Samantha hugged her former foster son.

"He's building the line to Durham. He's away during the week but home on Sunday. When they start work on the Southampton spur, we'll be moving to Owen Sound."

"I don't think Jake's coming today." George stared down the tracks. "I wish we had a phone." He had no quick way of getting information from along the rail line. When only one train ran, there had been no issue. Now, the engine unit working with Barry Young created the possibility of a collision. The PLM had plans to run two trains and install a telephone to coordinate them.

"There's a lot of upset down south. Maybe the trains are affected." George went inside. The children departed. The missing train hinted at the conflict raging to the south.

"Is Barry Young around?" A train arrived unexpectedly three days later. Jake held a package in one hand and his thick railway gloves in the other. The four-wheel steam locomotive hissed and spat.

"He's at Durham," George gasped after rushing from his farm.

"Give him this," Jake thrust the book at George. "It's important. I have to get these cars up to the port and ready when they can move. There's trouble below Orangeville."

"I sure love these steamers you drive now." George was a big kid when it came to trains.

"I like ,em too," Jake smiled. "But they had no choice. There's a big shortage of diesel because of the Quebec thing." George looked puzzled. The PLM radio carried stories of glorious victories in Quebec.

"We'll be down sometime tomorrow." Jake climbed into the cab. With a shrill blast from the steam whistle and a constant ringing of the bell and the big drive wheels spitting sparks, they moved off towards Owen Sound. George put the book into Young's pigeonhole. A red bookmark stuck out from the pages.

"This confirms everything we have been guessing." Chester held the notes from Barry Young, who had steamed to Owen Sound once he deciphered Rob Bossley's message. "The PLM is falling apart. They overreached and are paying."

Chester scanned the Council. The representatives from Mount Forest and Tobermory were on their way.

"For those who don't know," Chester pulled a pile of paper from the centre of the table, "we have messages summarizing PLM problems."

"Who's sending the reports? Can we believe them?" A Councillor from Saugeen demanded, having suffered more than most under PLM control.

"It's safer if we don't know, but they are trustworthy."

"Who's the connection?" The man persisted. With Barry Young in the room, he was the prime candidate. Chester ignored the question.

"Once we defeat the PLM, you'll know. They are heroes taking personal risk, and I don't want to expose them to capture and torture?"

Everyone had relaxed during the truce. Now, a fresh crisis unfolded.

"Getting on with business," Chester glanced around, looking for questions, "I have to tell you, last winter, the PLM contacted me through Angel, asking if we wanted to help in the liberation of Quebec. I politely told them no. Perhaps some in Huron would like to fight Quebec, but I would rather die fighting against the PLM than with them. The way to join with Quebec is negotiate, not fight."

There was a murmur of agreement, although someone muttered they should teach the French a lesson. These comments were all shadows from the past. Chester was glad Roger LaFarge was not present to be insulted.

"Last Christmas, the PLM and the military junta, the self-declared Government of Canada, formalized an alliance. Sharon Shadly's brother, Peter Maki, had been part of the Ottawa team sent to Toronto to do the deal. I think the military is a bunch of crackers. They used their enclave on the east side of the Ottawa at Hull to mount an attack down the river, trying to capture the whole St Lawrence.

"The PLM sent a sizeable force east of Cornwall and over the river. It all sounded good at first, but by April, it had become a horror. The Quebecers didn't want to be liberated, at least not by Ontario. They fought hard with bigger numbers and better morale."

"The PLM is only keeping troops in the field by terrorising them and threatening their loved ones. Their fighters couldn't care less about this war. The Ottawa group miscalculated, thinking they could open up the St. Lawrence and keep their fuel supply coming. They had been paying the Quebec government for the shipments. They ran out of fuel before reaching Montreal, end of story."

"How does that affect us?"

"To begin with, it has disrupted the railway. The PLM population is restless. There's a power struggle within the PLM, blaming the current leader. This last message says to expect a leadership change. The strongest faction thinks they should attack us."

"Is there any word on whether they'll win control?"

"This message was detailed and suggests long-term in-fighting. The current Toronto leader is losing control. The London people run the Hamilton steel mill and control most food production. Eastern Ontario is strong too. The Toronto faction only controls the PLM infrastructure."

"Toronto always ran things using everyone else's money." Bob Paisley raised the old resentments. The group laughed. "So we worry about the London folks." Bob continued. "What's our chance if they win?"

"Not as bad." Chester retrieved another handful of paper from a side table. "Brandi Shadly made a trip through there last summer. She went all the way to Lake Erie." There was a gasp. Many had not heard the story.

"She's one hell of a brave girl." Stan Gregson said.

"If she shot a bear, I guess a few PLM types weren't too big a scare for her." The Wiarton representative raised nervous laughter. Eyes glanced at Brandi's drawings and the Huron charter hanging behind Chester.

"Well, she did it and wrote a detailed account." Chester held up some papers. "Brandi brought back Erin Thomas, who's now at Kimberly. He gave a lot of information on the Guelph area and PLM strength there. You can read this. I think it adds up to most of the people there don't support the PLM but terrorized into submission. Most will quit fighting if given a chance. I say we create a plan for assassination and sabotage if shooting starts. Hopefully, we would start a rebellion inside their borders."

It sounded plausible, and Huron had no options. Even with the stream of refugees, Huron remained weak, and a guerrilla campaign their only hope.

For all of that twelfth summer, the power struggle ebbed and flowed within the PLM. The contest for control played out on a backdrop of mass unrest, shortages and widespread grief and hatred as loved ones died in the hapless Quebec project.

Brandi Shadly rode through the Saugeen watershed, documenting preparations and establishing a horse-based message service. Aaron Martin satisfied her that the Mennonites had a plan in case of attack. Aaron would take his family into hiding in the dense woods to the north.

Barry Young completed his rail line from Saugeen Junction to Durham and eased Brandi's work. The train from Orangeville became intermittent, and for several weeks, it did not run at all. Jake did not bring any books from Rob Bossley. Barry Young despaired of his friend.

A large lake freighter laden with iron ore sat in Owen Sound harbour with its load still on board. The PLM had always provided payment in gold before unloading the ship. No gold delivery had taken place. The ship had nowhere else to take its cargo and remained tied to the wharf. The crew enjoyed the hospitality of Huron, living onshore because the captain could not risk running diesel generators. He would only power up for an hour a day to run the bilge pumps. They waited, hopeful of payment and watching the occasional trainload diminish the dockside piles.

The subtle indicators of trouble suddenly reversed, and the crisis passed. Without fanfare, the railway returned to schedule. According to Jake, the London faction had taken over the territory from Windsor to the western edge of the old city of Toronto. They controlled the railway and the steel mill in Hamilton and intended to continue industrialization.

Jake handed Barry Young a book from Rob, who confirmed the end of the immediate crisis. The PLM territory had fragmented into an uneasy alliance of various factions. The old leadership still controlled Toronto and territory that ran from Lake Ontario north to Sudbury and North Bay. It was not clear if the former leader had survived.

Good agricultural land made the London PLM a separate dictatorship. The east now fell under the military government in Ottawa. The tragic loss of life the opposition forces had suffered was the best news for Huron, making the dictators too weak to have military ambitions. They only fought along the frontier with the USA and considered Huron a friend.

Throughout the thirteenth winter, the London faction evolved. It was not powerful enough to maintain control through terror and had become more benign and democratic. Their ultimate end came with the warm spring weather. Mass demonstrations occurred in front of the leadership's London enclave. After feeble attempts to suppress the mass opposition, the guards sided with the people and ousted the leaders. Rob's messages told of bloody retribution and a "People's Convention" in London.

Angel's control of Dufferin weakened. He had been a firm supporter of the PLM but now depended on another faction for survival. The man had not visited Weyburne for some time, and his guards retreated to the enclave with supply trips to Orangeville.

The Huron Council made plans to liberate Dufferin County.

Chapter Fourteen

"Let me hear no smooth talk / of death from you, Odysseus, light of councils. / Better, I say, to break sod as a farmhand / or some poor countryman, on iron rations, / than lord it over all the exhausted dead (Achilles)."
"My mother loved Greek myths. She quoted this often."- Erin Thomas in a private letter to Brandi Shadly.

I'm still sorry we didn't get to exact the ultimate revenge on Angel and his family. Despite everything that has happened in the years since, my discovering the murdered Quinn family is the one horror that won't go away. Revenge for their murders and for me having to live with the memory would have been sweet.
Matt Long quoted in the diary of Brenda Kovacs-Long

"Those are our people on the platform." Matt Long stood beside Jeff Shadly in the lead gondola car behind the hissing steam engine. Early morning mist, softened the town's silence.

"We overran the town but aren't strong enough to protect it and liberate Orangeville."

"My force will secure Weyburne and go down to Orangeville." Jeff looked back at the one hundred fighters in the open cars of the train. They wore army camouflage fatigues, but officially represented the new Huron Mounted Constabulary, signified by a circular shoulder patch of red linen bearing the lettering, "HMC". Council wanted to claim PLM territory by police, not an occupying army. Jeff had the titles of Chief Constable for Dufferin County and Deputy Chief Constable of Huron.

Brent James became a chief magistrate for the annexed territories. He carried a warrant for the detention and investigation of PLM functionaries, including security forces and the families. Based on Maud Dillingham's accounts, they charged Angel with murder.

"The town's okay. Al Wright's acting leader. He calls himself Lead Citizen. He says we're too small for a Mayor, and there's nothing to chair." It showed a spark of the old Al Wright wit.

"Until you step onto the platform, my group's the government here." The train finally squealed to a stop. Weyburne station had none of the flair of a Jim Handley creation. The unfinished wood had deteriorated.

"It's been ten years since I left here." Jeff glanced around. The station made this part of town unfamiliar. Only the silos from the feed mill suggested the location. The PLM had cut down all the town's trees.

"There aren't many of the old crowd around," Matt sounded sad. "Al is the only one. The rest disappeared. Some ran away; others went off to fight for the PLM. Angel enslaved some or murdered them, like Evy. Al calls the place The Corners."

"Let's get set up," Jeff said. "I don't want to use the old town hall. Angel spread terror from there. Let the locals get accustomed to being safe first." The older men agreed to Jeff's authority. Jeff posted two constables at the station to give legal status to Matt's guards. Jake remained on the platform, waiting for orders.

"I can't believe we survived these thirteen years," Al Wright said. He looked defeated despite being safe.

"It was hard," Jeff said. "Are you okay, Reverend Wright?"

"I'm fine, my boy. I'll live long enough to testify against these murderers." Al's eyes flashed. "I owe Evy."

"We charged Angel with the murder of Evy, her husband, Roger Smith and his son."

"It would be ironic one bastard hung for killing another bastard." Even in the memory of the violent, horrible deaths, Al could not help laughing.

"Angel holed up in the hills," Matt interjected. "If we had been stronger, they would all be dead by now."

Jeff heard Matt's anger. Throughout the past few years, he had been professional. With the impending victory, Matt felt free to hate.

"We'll get them." Jeff trusted his constables. "Let's go look?"

"There's a guard on their barriers but spread thin, with the major force dug in around the Angel compound. We're not sure how many."

"Let's capture some prisoners." Jeff signalled his force to move. "Remember, this bunch is guilty of murder and rape. They know they'll hang and fight to the finish."

***

Jeff's group created some tense moments when it activated a hidden tripwire. With no explosion, they assumed it had signalled a listening post. Jeff left several constables in ambush, and a hostile patrol arrived to check on the signal. Used to false alarms caused by animals, Angel's force was careless, but it did not surrender and only one survived.

Huron attacked the barrier from behind and killed only one defender. Soon after the fighting ended, sniper fire from high on the hillside killed a Huron constable. Two captives ran, using the sniper fire for cover. Jeff's force was not prepared to shoot unarmed men in the back, but Angel's snipers deliberately killed both fugitives, unmistakably in black uniforms. One of the bound prisoners also died before Jeff realized they intended to kill all the prisoners.

Stan Gregson and Brent James interviewed captives in the old pharmacy. Stan, too old to be a constable, had volunteered as an interrogator, hoping he could avenge Stevie Hunter's murder.

Jeff set up a perimeter, with pairs of constables evenly spaced on a half-kilometre radius around town. He feared Angel might decide to attack. Murdering the captives highlighted their cruelty.

Late that night, Jake raised steam and headed to Owen Sound. Bret and Stan had learned the enclave in the hills held several hundred fighters and desperate members of several families. Jeff needed more troops. Roger LaFarge would bring another few hundred fighters from Meaford.

During the four days it took for reinforcements to arrive, Brent and Stan created a list of dozens of people to charge. Some of the prisoners talked, giving a detailed picture of Angel's operation. None of the prisoners could identify the murderers of the Quinn family.

Jeff set about exploring Weyburne with its pitifully small population of less than three hundred. Over eight thousand people had lived there at the onset of the crisis. Fire had destroyed some abandoned houses, and bullets pockmarked several others that Jeff designated crime scenes.

The train returned with two hundred fighters under Helen's command and Ted led a contingent of snipers.

"It's all over for these guys." Jeff stood at a table in the old pharmacy. Helen, Ted, and Matt examined a rough map.

"They've retreated inside the main compound. It's well fortified. Machine-gun posts give overlapping fire. They've something heavier too, three-inch mortars and a fifty calibre mounted on a truck."

"They aren't worth anyone else getting killed." Helen wanted to keep her volunteers safe.

"That's my feeling," Jeff nodded. "We can try to talk them out."

"They have supplies and several hundred defenders. They could hold out for months." Matt wanted a quick solution. He planned to move home to Weyburne with Brenda.

"Let's make them run for it." Helen opened a map of Dufferin.

"Angel's a coward. Where would he and his family go?"

"They will want to get to Simcoe. The railway south is out of PLM control, even if a few sympathizers in Orangeville would help them. The PLM controls the territory to the east." Helen puzzled over the map. "I see three roads. If we funnel them into one, into the open, it might not be too bloody."

"I don't think Angel will leave, but some might try to escape." Brent James suggested. "The prisoners say morale is abysmal and most fighters would defect. One prisoner's a real fanatic. He won't cooperate and wants to escape. We can tell him we intend to kill them all with no mercy, then let him escape so he can tell them the way east is open."

They devised a plan placing Huron forces on three sides of the Angel enclave and set an ambush up to corral the deserters. They would feed the prisoner the plan, minus the trap, convincing him the Huron force was afraid to get between Angel and the PLM.

They brought the unsuspecting prisoner into the room for more questioning. The force commanders remained gathered at their table, planning their moves. The dupe thought his captors were arrogant and so sure he could not escape that they talked openly. They spoke angrily of killing all opponents with no mercy, including the prisoners. Angel would have done that, making it plausible.

They had a problem letting the prisoner escape without suspicion, but used the man's arrogance against him. The captive believed he had outsmarted these hicks. The sudden rearrangement of his accommodations did not arouse suspicion. He saw it as careless stupidity when they locked him in a room at the back of the store, separated from a storeroom by a flimsy, framed wall. They put him to work cleaning the building, letting him scout out the details, and he soon knew the storage space had an unbarred window overlooking an alley. When he stowed his cleaning supplies in that space, he carefully shut the door. After dark, he broke through the flimsy wallboard and was out through the storage room window. The guards checked every two hours, so he would be well into Angel territory before they missed him. Jeff and Matt watched from the backyard of a house as their messenger scuttled to freedom.

Two days later, the first deserters appeared east of the Angel compound. After a week, the exodus ended with gunfire from the estate. Over two hundred Angel fighters, workers, and slaves had become prisoners in Weyburne, securely held in the old high school with Angel's high-risk security forces carefully guarded. Former slaves received extra care. The worst cases went to Markdale, where Stephanie Hunter worked as a doctor.

It required two weeks of siege before the Angel compound surrendered. The burst of a mortar round severely wounded one Huron fighter, but other casualties had only cuts and scrapes. Huron snipers shot several of the Angel defenders operating machine-gun posts.

Angel denied them the chance for revenge. He committed suicide along with a brother and a son. Captives led investigators to murder victims' graves. Amongst the skeletal remains, they found Angel's former wife and her lover, Mike, the railway man. Garrottes encircled the neck bones.

Jeff led a police force to Orangeville, establishing the rule of law for the disorganized residents. Huron administrators would remain until a local government could evolve.

Brent James set up shop in the abandoned Weyburne town hall and developed a triage system. They isolated the worst suspects and formally tried murderers and rapists.

Different justice awaited captives guilty of lesser crimes. Many wanted to head south to find loved ones. Healing circles, similar to the ones used after the liberation of Flesherton, allowed victims to confront the guilty.

Once they satisfied the victims, they released these individuals. If there was any material loss, the culprits had to make amends. Money did not exist, and restitution meant the individual had to work off the debt. Brent James ruled on fair compensation. He did not tolerate abuse or slavery.

Huron's system took over later. For theft, it was a defence to claim a need. In these cases, offenders gave labour as payment. A similar defence in crimes against people causing injury or death was self-defence. If a person injured another, the matter always had to come before a justice who would decide if a trial should take place before three judges.

A jury always observed the trials but only to ensure fairness of, not decide on guilt. Whatever the verdict, this seven-person jury only needed a majority vote for an appeal before three Huron councillors. This system had spread throughout Huron Territory. There had been no murders since the defeat of the Flesherton mob, but crimes of property, drunkenness and family abuse had increased. As the external threat eased, unity weakened, requiring a robust but not a centralized legal system.

By the end of a long, miserable winter, they had tried all the prisoners. Evidence required careful checking as prisoners tried to save themselves by lying about the crimes of others.

The court convicted four PLM fighters of murder. One was the only surviving murderer of the Quinn family. On a bright May morning, out of town, out of sight of the public, they executed the murderers by firing squad. Even if there had been a mood for leniency, they had no prisons. Willard Dick, Matt Long, and Stan Gregson volunteered to be official observers. Volunteers from Helen's force made up the execution squad.

Six captives went to exile in PLM territory. The rest stayed in Huron territory, most in the custody of residents to work off debts. The remaining residents began the daunting task of rebuilding their lives in freedom.

Chapter Fifteen

When we boarded the train in Flesherton, the spring after we defeated Angel and PLM, I was eager to see my old hometown and the Wrights. This excitement soon turned to sadness. I thought I was going home. The house still stood, but my home wasn't there anymore. Our new family home was Longview. Only later, I realized my place was everywhere. I could never go home because I was never away from home, no matter where I was in the territory.
"Days of Recovery" (The Journals of Brandi Shadly, Vol. 9, p 31)

> *Our old home is never there*
> *We can't find it though we try*
> *Only memories bring it back*
> *Shadows linger, ,til we die*

Joseph of Longview: "Travelling Home," Transcribed in "Songbook Three: Shadows in the Valley,"

"We call it The Corners now." All Wright waved his gnarled walking stick at the ghost buildings on Weyburne's main street. Gaping window-spaces stared blankly. Al leaned on his cane and surveyed the group. Warren Dunne and Jean Bennett were perhaps his closest friends from all the hardships. The Shadlys, Bill, Sharon, and that delightful daughter Brandi were dear to him.

He puzzled at the girl, now a mature young woman. Her eyes startled him with their depth, understanding, and curiosity. She seemed different from the others. They focused on the immediate. Brandi raised a question, a possibility of hope. He must speak to her. Perhaps it would ease the burden in his heart.

"Weyburne's no more," Wright spoke with a tinge of sadness. "There has been too much suffering and pain." Al looked at the town hall, and a tear came to his eye. The sunlit facade mocked him. "I couldn't help any of them. I couldn't help Evy."

Tears trickled down Al Wright's cheeks, and he sobbed. Ester Wright put an arm around her husband. Jean and Sharon joined them. Everyone felt his loss and shared his guilt. Despite it all, they had been safe. Evy's sacrifice had been on another level.

"You did all you could, Al." Bill Shadly spoke. "You took enormous risks and saved a lot of lives. Everyone knows. We're grateful. You're a hero."

"Celebrating heroism is for the public, not the hero." Al better controlled his emotions. "I hope we can honour Evy and all who paid the price."

"I'll try to do that, Reverend Wright." Brandi smiled and touched his arm. "I hope you and I can talk." Brandi wanted to discuss the judgmental believers at Irish Lake.

Several individuals wearing red bush hats escorted three bedraggled people. It reminded Bill of the day they had returned with the three Quinn murder suspects. A contingent of Matt Long's constables had captured bandits. The lead constable was Bob, the Newfoundlander ex-partner in the B and B Xpress. It seemed a long time ago.

"We's got this bunch fixing to raid the grain storage north of town." Bob stopped to shake hands. "Where's Jeff?"

"He's in Orangeville," Bill Shadly was happy old friends had survived. "It's a mess down there, and we have to run the place."

"Just like around here." Bob removed his red hat and spat into the dust. "Some people is trying to settle old scores, making up lies. It's damned hard to sort out. They's had too many years where ratting your friends got you ahead."

The contingent moved off towards the town hall. They would release the prisoners to perform restitution after they pled need.

"Matt Long is now in charge," Al continued, "I'm the titular head, but Matt runs the village. Bandits are a problem. I hope that we'll round them up soon and they join the community."

"There're a few drunks. Some people couldn't cope otherwise. There's a lot of pot-growing, but no one cares, except some folks might starve to death, getting high or drunk. Violent drunks are a problem, and Matt is always locking some up."

"Al has tried counselling," Ester added, "but most are beyond help. We sober them up, feed them, and then they find booze and get drunk. There's too much pain, and there are too many cider makers. At least one still operates in the bush. Matt's trying to find it. The alcohol could be useful."

"We sent lots of weapons to the Meaford base. There are still too many guns and ammunition on the loose." Al walked towards the church.

"We hoped you two would have come up to visit last winter," Sharon said, holding Ester's hand as they walked.

"We weren't up to leaving," Al paused. "There isn't much here, but it's familiar and our home. We don't enjoy moving about much. Come, let's celebrate this reunion." He resumed his halting gate.

They had a wonderful dinner. The Longview visitors brought a lamb to roast along with potatoes and mint flavoured apple jelly from the grower in Heathcote. Ester produced jars of pickled beets and carrots, both hoarded over the years. Shelly and her Mom still lived with the Wrights.

Towards the end of the evening, the conversation flagged.

"Reverend Wright," Brandi leaned towards the old pastor. "I have many questions for you about spirituality and religion." The two moved to the half-darkened parlour. Shelly followed in her wheelchair and sat discretely in the shadows.

"Please call me Al," he smiled at Brandi. "I'm only a man, and you are an adult now."

Brandi related the story of Irish Lake, and that the believers' damning of Al had stimulated her questions about belief and religion. Al quietly sat as she detailed her encounter with the dangerous Vega worshipers and their attempt to kill her. Tears came to his eyes as Brandi related her encounter with the bear and Dodger's death and the spiritual relationship between George MacDonald's community and the natural world, and her horror at Paradise with questions about the Mennonites.

"Al," she stumbled on the familiarity, "why were some people strong and found courage, while others either gave up and died or perpetrated the most unspeakable crimes? Many of the strong ones seem to have no spiritual beliefs and not every believer is strong."

"You are asking a question that has defeated brilliant thinkers for millennia. It's hard to sort out." Al smiled at Brandi's sincerity and thoughtfulness.

"You and Mrs. Wright... Ester had the strength and survived and helped many others." She glanced towards Shelly.

"I don't think I was strong." Al fought back his tears. "Our faith helps us, although I have questioned my faith many times. I am full of doubt." He paused and stared up as if apologizing to his God.

"When I was a child," he finally resumed, "I believed deeply, so deeply I feared hell and became pious because of fear. My Sunday school teachers skimmed the gospel good news part and the grace, but they sure got the going to hell stuff across." He chuckled, thinking of old Mrs. Gillespie and her fervent admonitions to "behave or meet the devil."

Al paused for a long time, remembering those events long ago, still full of emotion and power at the end of his life.

"Going to divinity school was a simple decision. My faith ran deep enough to resist the skeptical approach of most of the professors at the college, and I emerged still a believer. Many of my classmates did not. Some quit. Some took up the ministry thinking they were social workers and psychologists. Those parts are important, but I always believed faith gave it meaning."

"What do you believe now?" Brandi felt honoured; the man she respected talked openly and honestly.

"I don't know." Al looked directly into Brandi's eyes. "I know I have a soul, and there's a happier place for my soul once my body is done. My catechism says I must believe in Jesus Christ to enter heaven. I'm not sure my beliefs will make the grade."

Suddenly, all of Al's childhood fears washed over him, and he cried once more. This girl had a way of digging into the hard places.

"People must seek comfort and meaning where they can find it. Faith seems to instil strength and purpose. Most of all, it gives hope. Some have performed incredible good in the name of faith. Others have committed unspeakable horrors in the name of that same faith. Some get sidetracked into rituals like those you spoke of who lived to maintain their building or the Vega worshipers who could justify any crime against heretics."

"Your native friends have a spiritual relationship with nature and their own generations, past and future. Perhaps this is a mystical way of celebrating the importance of those relationships. There are certain parts of their belief system that explain the unexplainable, the random good and bad events as the work of the trickster, like our devil, perhaps a better explanation for the past fourteen years than a loving deity."

Al Wright sat for a long moment, the darkness hiding the emotions playing across his face. He pondered whether he had abandoned his God or vice versa. He finally spoke.

"I thought I had come to Weyburne to finish out my days in peace and honour, with my faith settled. It seemed I would die as a happy man, confident in my belief. The last years have shaken me deeply. I have seen too much cruelty and selfishness. Many times, I've given people words of comfort only to return home crying inside, full of doubt. Could loving omnipotence allow all this horror? Is there a heaven or a hell? I once wisecracked none of the good books: Christian, Islam, Hindu or other sacred writings explained how we got out of hell once we were there. The point being we lived in our hell."

"My telling the Irish Lake folks you said that riled them up," Brandi smiled despite the dark subject.

"You never studied the Bible." Al reached out to lay his hand upon the book lying on the side table. "I have reread the Book of Job many times in the last decade. The Old Testament is mainly allegory and half-remembered tribal history, but the messages can be useful. Job says we will never have more hardship than we can endure. It doesn't seem to me that a loving God would inflict those hardships. Job just makes me question more. Your fundamentalist friends condemning me are understandable. I question the role of religion in our culture. They embraced it without question. I'm not sure a person believes or will find salvation if they ask God questions. I'll soon find out."

He fell silent. Brandi kissed his head as she departed with more questions than answers. Shelly lingered for a moment, contemplating Al. She knew where she had found comfort. Al Wright remained seated, motionless, staring into the shadows.

***

A society grows great when old men plant trees whose shade they know they shall never sit in.
A saying often quoted by Warren Dunne in his old age, - E.T.

"We put fast-growing species in this bottomland." Warren inserted a living aspen twig into the rich muck of the gully bottom. "These are inferior species, but they grow in this wet. It would be a waste to plant maple and beech down here. Besides, maple might die out with the bugs, killing them off."

He stretched, looking towards the old barn on the ridge. His grey hair betrayed his age. The seventy-four years on his body had slowed him. A crew of twenty worked hard and Jean helped Warren. Brandi dug one-meter maples into the drier ground up the slope.

Brandi noted an air of devotion towards Warren as if he were a hero. He was a hero to her. Matt had persuaded Warren to guide locals in tree planting to repair the PLM clear-cutting and to speak at a meeting about the usufruct system and watershed organization.

"This creek is part of the Nottawasaga," Matt planted next to Warren. "The river is under the PLM, but in the long run, the residents will benefit. If we implement the watershed political model, The Corners will be part of that watershed. With the PLM collapsing, it might happen this year."

Matt oversaw some tougher cases of ex-Angel forces working off judgments. He wanted to make sure things went well. The town's population had increased over the past year, with families moving, either to escape Orangeville and its problems or danger from roving gangs. Some of Angel's forces had stayed after fulfilling their repayment obligations.

"The town is about full up now," Matt stuck a shovel into the ground, allowing Jean to insert a cedar seedling. "We only want to use the old houses on the high ground above the creek. We need the stream for water now that the tower is leaking and are building a dam downstream from the railway and hand digging a well above flood level. It can only supply our current population. We don't want to get any bigger. There's a need for more young women."

"That lets me out." Jean laughed, glancing at Brandi.

"Hey, don't look at me! I'm just passing through."

"There's a surplus in Toronto." Matt said. "The campaign in Quebec killed a lot of men."

"You can only farm out a few kilometres." Warren rested. "We need to go back to the old way and have a village every five or ten kilometres apart, as we do in Huron."

"That's our plan." Matt paused for some water. "Before the collapse, they tile-drained many farms. Now the ditches have filled in, and the tile systems are collapsing. Much of the land is only good for trees."

"That's my favourite ground." Warren smiled.

"I have to go to Horning's Mills this afternoon to meet a few folks." Matt said, "They need security, and there's room there for more families."

"Matt, could you arrange a wagon? I would like to visit the Bruce Trail one last time." Warren looked wistful.

"I'll set that up and armed guards too, because of bandits. You can come into the Mills and teach the folks how to improve the water flow with trees. They want to rebuild some of the waterpower sites."

***

"I scattered Susan's ashes from this bridge." Warren drank in the open woods with its carpet of pine needles and dark green under foliage. Sunlight struggled through the canopy of coniferous needles, dappling onto the soft, brown forest floor. He stood on a natural rock bridge over a narrow limestone chasm, all a memorial to his long-dead first wife, Susan.

Warren breathed heavily after the hard climb up from the road.

"It was in the fall, on a beautiful breezy day, so her ashes spread far. I wanted to do it in autumn so she would come alive in the plants the next spring. She loved the fall here."

Warren knelt and gently felt a fern leaf. Dampness from the ground seeped through his pants. He did not notice. His fingers slid up the stalk with a thumb and finger, forming a ring through which the leaves gently passed. He remembered those nights in the hospital, gently drawing Susan's hair through his hand. There were tears in his eyes as he stood to hug Jean. The sensations of her warm body and the gentle stroke of her hand on his neck drew him back to the present and her ongoing love.

Brandi sat on a wet, moss-covered dolomite outcrop. For once, she could not translate the emotional scene into a drawing. Many years later, through the protective distance of memory, she would capture this moment onto paper. Warren's simple words triggered feelings of grief and loss in the shadowy recesses of her memory.

The next day, the three visitors from Longview stood on the railway platform of The Corners hugging Ester and Al Wright.

"Take care," Al hugged Brandi tightly. "Remember, the spiritual is important. It fills a need we all have. Keep seeking the truth."

"You would love George MacDonald." The girl smiled, hugging Al one last time.

They stared into each other's eyes; both knew they would never meet again.

Chapter Sixteen

"It would be of some consolation for the feebleness of ourselves and our works if all things should perish as slowly as they come into being, but as it is; increases are of sluggish growth, but the way to ruin is rapid."
Lucius Annaeus Seneca, Letters to Lucilius, n. 91.
 As quoted by Samantha James in her newsletter, The Flesherton Flyer (Vol. 2 Number 6)

*O*ne way to follow the story of the attempt to restore the Canadian Federation is through the accounts in The Flesherton Flyer. Brandi kept all the issues of The Flyer. First, Samantha James published it and then her daughter Stephanie. They posted the newsletter in public places along the rail line from Orangeville to Owen Sound and sent copies to most of the outlying centres, where similar efforts at news publishing had begun. Samantha James was one of the first to count years using the date of the collapse on that September 25th as zero, anticipating the official adoption of this system by several years. Many residents still use the Christian calendar.
 Erin Thomas in an editor's aside to The Journals of Brandi Shadly

Flesherton March - Year 15 - Flesherton Flyer Vol. 2 No. 6
Readers may have encountered the self-described federalist who arrived in Orangeville by train two weeks ago. He is part of a team from Ottawa recruiting delegates to what they describe as a Canadian Federal Reformation Convention scheduled for Ottawa after spring planting. This

*fellow has been drumming up support up to Owen Sound. There is to be a
public meeting there tonight, sponsored by the General Council, to
entertain the man's proposal. A special train will pass through Flesherton
about two in the afternoon.*

*From a different source, The Flyer has learned that the situation in
Ottawa has not changed. The military government has collapsed. The
junta lost most of its weapons trying to conquer Quebec.*

*To regain legitimacy, the military commanders, in year fourteen,
requested the former elected Prime Minister to assemble an interim
government. They swore in Prime Minister Harridan, the last elected PM.
Harridan asked the last Governor-General; His Excellency, Mr. Donald
Cerise, to resume the post from which the military coup had deposed him.
Mr. Cerise graciously accepted the honour and then proceeded to re-
swear Harridan and his cabinet to their posts. They used the former oath
of office, referring to the King of Canada. As far as we have been able to
find out and based on the accounts of P. Maki, the King and his family
died by murder many years ago.*

*Our opinionated informant, whose name we cannot mention, stated the
government has been issuing decrees but cannot enforce these orders. In
Ottawa, people see this as a sham. The locals joke the only actual parties
in Ottawa are Friday night at 24 Sussex Drive. To counter criticism that
he has no legitimacy, Harridan has called for the convention to re-
institute Parliament and re-establish Canada from sea to sea.*

Please note that The Flyer does not pretend to be unbiased.

We will report on the Owen Sound meeting in the next issue.–SJ

Social note

*Constable Holly Rieu of the H.M.C. and Mr. Jason French have
announced their status as spouses of each other and are thus to be
married, as per Huron custom. They will live on the French farm near
Saugeen Junction. Holly will perform her duties from there. Holly
renounces usufruct claim to her current residence on the 30 Side-road.
The happy couple requests your attendance at a party in the waiting room
of the Saugeen Junction railway station next Saturday from 1 P.M. to
whenever. Bring food and drink. Please try to behave.*

Owen Sound March - Year 15 - Flesherton Flyer Vol. 2 No. 7

*It was a raucous meeting in the Huron council chamber on Wednesday
and well worth the price of admission (free). An overflow crowd*

surrounded the Council building, standing in a snow-flurry and straining to hear. Shouters acted as a human loudspeaker system, doing an adequate job, save for the editorial comment and laughter.

Local freehold farmer Robert Myers put himself forward as the Huron delegate to the Ottawa convention. Mr. Henry Baird, the emissary from Ottawa, welcomed the representative, describing him as "an excellent example of a right-thinking individual." Some in the audience allowed that Mr. Myers had never done much beyond the minimum to help the people of Huron. Most people agreed, if they held a vote, Myers would not be a delegate even without opposition. Mr. Myers made an emotional and somewhat lucid argument for the rights of the individual landowner and the need for a strong federal government to reintroduce the rule of property law. Most of Myer's fellow property owners attended and shouted support at his every word. The man received his loudest applause, and most vociferous boos when he assailed the Huron General Council with the words: "You are nothing but a bunch of communists. We need a strong federal government, not a bunch of anarchists like you."

Opposing speakers felt the project was a waste of time. Surprising support came from a few independent first nation attendees who thought a new Canadian government might reinstate the old treaties and their compensation payments. These individuals did not represent any native community organizations, and Chester Amik expressed considerable scepticism about their understanding of the situation. This reporter overheard Mr. Myers whisper: "Don't think those Indians will get any freebies; they've freeloaded off Canada long enough"'

Chester Amik took a motion to send an official delegate to Ottawa. The motion was soundly defeated, leaving Myers with no mandate. Amik told Mr. Myers he had no authority. If they decided anything in Ottawa, Huron reserved the right to vote on it.

Myers defiantly responded, "You'll just have to come along and do it if Ottawa says so, or else." A general shout from the onlookers said, in cruder terms: "You will have to make us."

Myers and Baird appeared to be in good spirits and defiant the following morning as they boarded the passenger coach, trailing the usual loads of iron ore and firewood. Mr. Myers has graciously agreed to forward dispatches from the convention.

Market update

David Trondheim reports a healthy crop of spring Suffolk lambs. People may order such for delivery in September. Prepayment of two days of labour during spring planting for each animal purchased. Satisfaction guaranteed. Place your order before they are gone. David will begin planting May 10th, weather permitting.

Brampton April, Year 15 - Flesherton Flyer Vol. 2 No. 8

Reports passed on by our delegate from somewhere in the GTA reveal the journey to Ottawa has paused west of Toronto. The radio station in Oakville seems less biased now and is reporting some fighting along the east/west railway corridor north of the city. The PLM is retreating north. Our delegate waits for the line to re-open, as it is the easiest and safest way to get to Ottawa. The radio says the line will operate by the end of the month. The flow of refugees has increased at the twenty-six and Devil's Elbow barriers.

Local events

A tragic fire destroyed the house at the Constantine farm, leaving the family all dead. By the time neighbours saw the flames and arrived, the fire had died down. The cause is uncertain, but the H.M.C. believes it started in the chimney. We advise everyone to check and clean all chimneys and pipe systems. The H.E.I. provides mentoring about wood-fire safety, and about how to build and maintain systems. Please see your local representative. The property on the tenth line will be available for usufruct allotment once the investigation is complete. We know the Constantine family and feel deep sadness.

Ottawa May, Year 15 - Flesherton Flyer Vol. 2 No. 10

Mr. Myers and Mr. Baird arrived in Ottawa in the middle of May. They report they are living at Rideau Hall, along with other delegates. Mr. Myers describes the grounds as a farming operation. All the decorative trees became firewood, and the flower gardens converted to vegetables and the lawns used for animal pasture. The compound was the residence of the Commander-in-chief of the military government. Some rooms have been "tastefully decorated in deep red with enormous beds and mirrored ceilings and walls." These sumptuous accommodations were for the female staff of the operation. Senior military personnel have told Mr. Myers this is proof of how well the junta treated people. More worldly cynics might think it evidence of something else.

Our delegate sleeps, along with twenty other delegates, in one of the unused banquet halls. Myers reports the food to be plentiful and decently prepared. Local farmers and other suppliers are donating copious amounts of food and strong drink to the gathering. Myers says the only thing they seem to want is government favours once they re-established Canada. He tells us, in his last letter; he is developing a list of favourites to whom he owes some gratitude. Bob Myers has never been a politician, explaining his easy sharing of this type of information. We eagerly await his next communication.

Local news

The poor spring weather has permitted limited planting so far. Those fields on sand or gravel and well-drained have allowed seeding in most instances. Many of the marginal operations are not doing as well, although horse work instead of heavy tractors has allowed working the much wetter ground. Farm operations "chisel tilling" instead of using the mouldboard plough have fared much better. Two weeks remain in the prime planting time before the mid-June deadline. Everyone is hopeful of finishing the work. HEI classes will resume a week after planting but will break for haying as usual.

Ottawa July, Year 15 - Flesherton Flyer Vol. 2 No. 13

Our latest missive from Robert Myers tells of slow progress in Ottawa. Near the end of June, three separate delegates appeared from Quebec. At first, the support from the French-speaking regions for restoring a federal government encouraged everyone. When they realized they were rivals from different locations, the excitement turned to disappointment. The Quebec government did not send a delegate., and the language barrier magnified the problem, as there was no simultaneous translation of proceedings. The three could not speak English effectively, and none of the other delegates could speak French. A bi-lingual army officer translated. The officer lacked education, and he struggled with many words and seemed to have his own opinion. Mr. Myers could not say if the translations were accurate and unbiased.

These delegates only had interested in the federal government making payments to their particular region of Quebec. The counter-argument, there was no money to distribute and they would have to wait infuriated the trio. They fought amongst themselves more than with the other delegates. It came to a head, one night, with the murder by stabbing of one of the three. The next day, one of the two remaining Quebecers fled, claiming he would be next. The third man remained. Everyone regards him with suspicion, believing he is the murderer.

This communication mentions warm summer weather has encouraged much social interaction with trips to isolated cottages in the Gatineau and excellent parties on the grounds of the Prime Minister's residence. Prime Minister Harridan has a large entourage of helpers and supporters. There are always many young women to facilitate these events. We are glad that our delegate is finding some pleasure along with the obvious hard work. This communication told of the outbreak of a fever disease in the southern part of the old capital along the canal and Rideau River. Stephanie Hunter in Markdale believes the symptoms detailed in Myers's letter show malaria. Several dozen people have died because of this outbreak. We wish Rob Myers safety.

Mail Service

From our detailed communications with Bob Myers, it should be obvious that there is some mail service. No post office exists, but for several years, the train crews have been willing to carry letters and small packages. With the freeing of the complete system from the Quebec border to Windsor, this is now quite effective. As has been true in Huron for many years, most station agents will accept these packages and give them to the train crew, usually the engineer or brakeman. As our readers are no doubt aware, our Flesherton station has facilities for storing and holding letters and packages. It might be a good idea, from time to time, for everyone to check with the local station agent to see if some surprise is waiting. Ben the Postie from Heathcote and his family, will contract to do this for barter. There are other such services available. The agents and the engineers expect a small payment from the sender with extra if you want your message to change hands on its way. The amount and type of compensation depend on each agent or crew, but a small parcel of dry grain, flour, or jug of hand-pressed cooking oil is usually sufficient. People tell us they always appreciate a jug of hard cider.

Ottawa August, Year 15 - Flesherton Flyer Vol. 2 No. 16

Several delegations struggled into Ottawa at the end of July. The first was a single man from Newfoundland. He bribed his way through the territories south of the Quebec/New Brunswick border, eventually making his way via the former states of Maine and New York and crossing the St.

Lawrence River upstream from Cornwall. It cost him a good amount in bribes and some labour to earn his passage and to keep his horse. This bedraggled chap said Newfoundland was only interested if it meant some support from the rest of Canada. This fellow is unique. He seems to be the only delegate sent and mandated by an authority in control of the territory he represents. He intends to stick around right to the end of the conference, confident he will take good news home. Stories from this man confirmed the observations Peter Maki has already shared with us about the desperate situation in Newfoundland. (See the Flyer Vol. 1 No. 1) The Newfoundlander highlighted the absence of anyone purporting to represent Prince Edward Island, Nova Scotia or the part of New Brunswick not joined to Quebec. He claimed this area was under the influence of powers representing the former northeastern USA.

Late arrivals from northern Ontario and the prairies were the last representatives to attend. Mr. Myers reports they had an arduous journey. Those who came from Alberta and the prairies rode horses to Winnipeg. The railway runs intermittent trains between Winnipeg and Sudbury. The train ride was relatively comfortable, with accommodations in a freight car and recruiting people along the tracks. Many towns from Thunder Bay to Sudbury joined the group. They travelled from Sudbury to Ottawa by horse-drawn wagons along old Highway 17. It was unfortunate that the rail line between the northern town and Toronto was unavailable. The PLM controls the territory and does not allow safe passage.

There is some discussion between Huron and the new southern government of a joint effort to eliminate the PLM. Chester Amik has passed on the mood of the General Council. They believe we should defend ourselves but let the PLM destroy itself. You have all met some of the recent refugees from the east.

Security scare and changes

Readers may have heard about the sabotage at the Thornbury micro-hydro site. An agent of the PLM, posing as a refugee, entered Huron Territory via the twenty-six barrier. At his first opportunity, he damaged the generators and circuits at the Thornbury dam. The attack has set back flour and machined parts production. It will take time to repair. The culprit awaits trial in the Owen Sound jail. In response, a security force pushed east beyond the barrier and entered Collingwood proper. The PLM has declared the town an open city. Our representatives have agreed. We have pulled back to the barrier, and the PLM has withdrawn to Weybridge, Elmvale and south to Angus. Huron now supports refugee camps east of the barrier between the escarpment and the lake. Only the neediest of persons come into Huron, and this will last into the near future with intensified patrols along the escarpment.

Ottawa September, Year 15 - Flesherton Flyer Vol. 2 No. 15

Bob Myers reports little progress through to the second week of September. The meetings have bogged down into bickering about regional rights and benefits. The only agreement was the promise to give northern Ontario the status of a province. Some delegates from the north and west did not want Sudbury or North Bay considered northern, but in the end, the boundary became the southern extent of the French River watershed. Bob has boasted he sold the Huron concept of watersheds to the rest of the delegates and indeed the watershed organization has been the one aspect of Huron innovation Mr. Myers has embraced. We think he enjoys being able to say "no".

Western representatives have been lobbying hard to raise an eastern army to help defeat the substantial Chinese forces occupying the oil and gas-producing areas. Bob explains it seems like a winnable project. The Alberta delegation brought an individual of Chinese origin who claimed to be a deserter from their army. This man stated the Chinese military has few supplies and morale is bad. He claims the force comprises conscripted peasants with poorly trained officers. The best Chinese forces go to Australia, Siberia and Viet Nam, and suppress the rebellion in North West China and Tibet. Because of the retreat of the mountain glaciers, the summer flow of the Yangtze and Yellow river has decreased to the point of crisis. From his testimony, the invading army has split off into roving battalions all down the North American west coast who are foraging to stay alive.

In Alberta, roving militias from former USA territory complicates the situation. Much of the original population of Alberta went south to survive over a decade ago. Prime Minister Harridan and the remnants of the Canadian Armed forces support a fight, but most of the delegates decided there are not enough people in the east to mount a credible army. They have pointed out; we struggle get rid of criminal groupings like the PLM. Myers quotes one delegate as saying: "If we end up fighting the Chinese army, it will be after we have grown enough troops. Give us twenty years." The Chinese deserter's words worked against the cause. Everyone decided the Chinese would soon collapse and withdraw without a fight.

Harvest News

Despite the poor spring, it appears there will be a bumper crop of flax, barley and oats harvested under these wonderful, sunny September skies. The council fears this might have the effect of restricting trade due to lower local demand; however, many operations tell The Flyer they are planning to hold back extra breeding stock, especially sheep and goats for the winter. There is already more interest expressed from the south in trading for grain and flax products. Specialty steel from Hamilton and some exotic luxury foods from the tropics are on offer. Our local weavers are hoping for extra cotton, which is especially useful in the manufacturing of undergarments. We all need them, especially women. – S.J.

Flesherton October, Year 15 - Flesherton Flyer Vol. 2 No. 22

Mr. Robert Myers has arrived home. In his opinion, the effort to re-establish Canada has failed. He graciously agreed to an overnight stay in our home for an interview with this reporter. We repeat a brief excerpt from this conversation, expanding our coverage of the convention. Those interested can read the complete interview in the waiting room of the Flesherton railway station. It is too long to repeat fully here. You will also find several Nimise Makwa drawings to illustrate some of the information from Ottawa. Some of you will find her renditions somewhat irreverent as she reflects the skeptical views of this writer. To paint the scene, Bob Myers sat in our parlour surrounded by several visitors including Brandi Shadly, Karen Lefevre and my daughter Steph.

Me: *"Bob, you left with such hope. What happened?"*

Bob: *"In the end, there were no resources. Every delegation didn't want to commit to paying taxes but was only interested in benefit. I admit we were the same. We all wanted some benefit, and we never found it."*

Me: *"What do you think were the original intentions of Harridan and the military?"*

Bob: *"The military was desperate after losing in Quebec. They called Harridan back to fix what they broke in the first place and maybe try to avoid future repercussions. Harridan just wants to be Prime Minister and have all the trappings of power. I think he's an incompetent jackass."*

Me: *"What happened at the end?"*

Bob: *"Delegates drifted away. Some had a long way to go before the winter. Others just gave up. The folks who supplied us with food and drink decided we would not be successful and cut us off. That's when I left. It would be no fun starving in Ottawa."*

Me: *"What are you going to do now?"*

Bob: *"WE freehold landowners must defend our rights and legal ownership of our property."*

Me: *"Don't you remember the stories from Brandi about the massacres of individual land rights people along the Saugeen? Huron is not like those murderers, of course."*

Bob: *"They were stupid and fought individually. We must stick together."*

Me: *"Would you expect Huron, with its benign policies, to attack you? Would you attack us?"*

Bob: *"If they ever did, we would be ready and fight."*

Bob did not answer my last question.

Other news -The End of an Age

Many of you saw a blazing streak in the sky a week ago Tuesday. There was considerable speculation it was a meteor or some missile a crazy government somewhere had fired off. Many blamed the Chinese as the only country powerful enough to use missiles. Warren Dunne supplied this explanation:

"We saw the re-entry and burning up of the old International Space Station. I had watched it regularly every few weeks at sunset or sunrise. A few months ago, I noticed it flashed brighter and then dimmer as it reflected the sun. It looked like a blinking light, and I guessed it tumbled out of control. I knew the end was near for the whole thing. From the way it travelled, I would say bits of it must have hit the earth's surface in Northern Quebec and maybe drifted into the Labrador Sea. It was quite a show. I could see my shadow for almost a minute. I hope they got the crew off after the economy collapsed. They would have been long dead before the re-entry. It's the end of the space age."

Chapter Seventeen

Brandi despondently stared out the open door of the little cabin. This wooden-clad structure, now worse for wear, had at one time been chic tourist accommodation. Snow piled in huge drifts, with more falling, streaming sideways on a northwesterly gale. Winter had trapped her just below the upper tip of the Bruce Peninsula.

She had taken a risk of making this late fall trip, but several newly trained medics from Tobermory required help to get home. Brandi and Niibin escorted their wagon but now paid the price for this adventure. Visiting Ermine, George and other friends at Hope Bay had delayed her into the winter weather, preventing her return.

"You're lucky it didn't catch you on the trail." Brandi's host shut the door against the fierce wind.

"I need to adjust my attitude, Lisa." Brandi slumped onto a chrome kitchen chair. "I always make the most of the things and have the chance to draw snow scenes." She laughed with improving humour.

"You'll get to split and pile wood too," Lisa poured hot tea. "We only had half the pile cut and stacked. The rest is under the snow. It'll get too wet lying loose. We need to split and stack, but not until this blows over."

The door burst open. A few women and a couple of men ranging in age from early twenties to late middle age hurried inside wearing an assortment of raw and tanned fur garments intermixed with old bush coats, ear-flapped hats and mittens. They shook snow onto the rude carpet at the door and shed winter coats in the woodstove's warmth.

"We heard Nimise Makwa was here," one woman began. "We thought we might get some stories." The speaker spread out the makings of sourdough along with a jug of maple syrup on the kitchen counter. Eggs appeared along with strips of meat.

One man laughed. "Biscuits and egg delight ought to pay for a few wonderful tales."

The woman deftly mixed dough, and soon small round pastries were cooking in an open pan. Wonderful smells filled the cabin. Brandi translated the scene into a drawing, and the visitors later became the subjects of individual portraits. One man was native, a Cree who had somehow ended up south of Lake Huron. He opened a package wrapped in soft fox skin and revealed a small dream-catcher. Pliable twigs formed a tear-shaped oval with crisscross webbing done in delicate strips of deer hide. Grouse feathers adorned the outer edge, highlighted by blue plumage at the apex, and soon hung in the window on a rawhide thong.

"Your stories will always find remembrance in this, Nimise." The Cree sat on the wood box near the window and looked expectantly at Brandi.

She began by telling the origins of her nickname, of the honour, the obligation of bearing the spirit of a much-loved Ojibwe sister. Her story of the encounter with the bear and the addition of the makwa name brought tears to all eyes. She told how this became her spiritual obligation, and she felt the responsibility to teach, listen and keep safe everyone she encountered.

"Is Nimise Makwa your official Indian name?" One of the white women asked. Brandi snuck a peek at the Cree. He did not seem to take offence.

"It's a casual name my friends at Hope Bay used. George MacDonald would be the one to give me an Ojibwe name. He says the Spirit has not told him. I have to wait." Her disappointment poked through.

"Ojibwe could never make up their minds." The Cree laughed.

Brandi decided George MacDonald would like this man. She would steer him to Hope Bay.

This first afternoon became another and another, as Brandi's stories seemed to have no end. Many visitors recounted their adventures, and Brandi's folio bulged. Her journal fattened with the richness of the tales. The group of listeners varied according to work demands; always there was food and laughter. Many nights they gathered under stars that snapped out of the cold, black sky as Brandi told her tales. A blazing fire always warmed the listeners.

Many of Brandi's drawings found their way to the homes of her audience. Over the winter, during breaks in the weather, she visited several other hamlets, travelling by snowshoe, guided through the hampering drifts by the locals. The resilience of the people and the decline of old technology impressed Brandi. The people here lived simple lives and thrived, healthy and happy. Isolation and hard work were central to these communities. Brandi learned how to snare rabbits and other game animals, make sourdough and find food hidden in the drifts.

"We don't have a lot of complicated decisions to make in a day," Lisa said. "We work to eat and be warm and have fun, but seeing the same old faces is boring."

Brandi understood loneliness. She realized her role as a storyteller and communicator of news filled a hunger here beyond the reach of the radio transmitter in Oakville. In this remote land, she also found another student to become a recorder and storyteller. She arranged for this young girl to travel down to Kimberly in the summer to hone her drawing and writing skills. The girl had been making drawings on scraps of paper and strips of peeled birch bark using homemade charcoal sticks.

Skating on frozen ponds was popular, but the most widespread pastime, winter or summer, was lacrosse using homemade sticks and a rawhide ball. The sticks were just one product of a small family producer of snowshoes, skis, poles and dip-nets for the smelt harvest in the spring. This food source was important even in southern waters. Many species had recovered after years of industrial exploitation and habitat destruction. Smelt, whitefish and pickerel were becoming familiar staples for local diets and a trade item in many small markets. Persistent declines in the lake level had introduced some worry, and it appeared invasive species might destroy the natural abundance of these inland seas.

"I know it has been horrible," Jason the stick-maker said to Brandi one day while she helped in the workshop, "but this decline in the human population has helped the animals."

"Is it there are fewer of us hunting?" Brandi had conversations with Warren Dunne about the issue; this subject felt familiar and important.

"That's part of it," Jason worked as he talked, curving the wooden hoop of a snowshoe. Sweat formed on his brow, and his dark brown beard soon became soaked. The craftsman was a philosopher. "I notice the bush is in better shape and the water is cleaner than before. I think we humans had more impact by destroying habitat than the actual hunting and fishing had on reducing numbers. Both were huge, though. Every time I hear a grouse drumming now, I think he is thanking us for dying off."

The laughter was genuine, but both understood the irony in the statement and the grief it implied. "Our relying more on game animals up here now goes against what I just said." Jason extracted a wooden stave from a tub of hot water and bent it around pegs set into a plank. "Our population has stabilized, and there's a balance. About as many die as are born. There are a few stillbirths." The young man's eyes were sad. He and his wife had lost a little one two years before and a two-year-old from pneumonia.

Brandi's drawing of this scene captured the sadness, and yet she had his face portray wisdom and peace. She left this image with the family. Years later, she saw it in their home, framed by a curved piece of red oak beneath which hung a thin slab of clear maple-wood. The words Nimise Makwa straddled an image of a bear, burnt into the maple.

"There's another problem." He finished bending the supple wooden strip back on itself and hammered a peg into the board, fixing the piece to cool and set. "We don't have enough new boys and girls for marriage. There's a risk we'll get inbred. You can't stop natural desires."

"Do you want me to send up a few wagon loads of girls?" Brandi laughed to ease the man's embarrassment. He searched for the strength to say what was on his mind. Talking about sex with a young woman was difficult.

"No, girls going south could get pregnant." He briefly silenced Brandi.

"You can send some down for training," she laughed, to overcome her embarrassment. "They could return educated, and pregnant."

"Is there room here for new settlers?" She thought of a more practical solution. "We could send refugees to add some diversity."

Brandi headed south in early April as soon as the drifts had melted. She escorted a trainee heading for the Meaford medical school, a young woman. The artistic girl would follow later with her mother. Homesick from a winter away, Brandi hurried. After another delightful rest at Hope Bay, the second week of May found her introducing the recruit to Doc Adams at the hospital in Meaford.

"I have a message for you," Adams retrieved a letter from his office. "This arrived yesterday." Brandi recognized Karen's precise handwriting and eagerly devoured the note. Her face darkened and her eyes glistened.

"I have to go right away." Brandi hurried out the door.

Chapter Eighteen

The trees still grow
Though we are worn and weary
The trees still grow
Though we are spent and gone
The trees still grow
Reaching ever skyward
The trees still grow
Carrying...
Our loving hearts along.

Joseph of Longview: "The Trees Still Grow," ("Songbook Three: Shadows in the Valley,")

"Megan Lefevre, bless her scientific mind, once said we grow faster than trees. Yes, we age quicker, but trees slowly carry us along, tying generations together. I wrote The Trees Still Grow. when I was only ten years old. My piano playing was good, by then, and I wrote lots of tunes and words. Warren, along with Walt and Willard, took me on a walk down the lane after supper during one of your visits to Longview. Warren explained about the trees he and Willard had planted. They were nicely growing five years later. I have dug out the words and finished it. Please accept this and my love."

Excerpt from a letter sent by Joseph of Longview to Jean Bennett–the HEI archives

The sun blazed high in the sky as Brandi turned Niibin into the driveway leading to the Institute. Budding leaves from the river-willows and maples lining the roadway lessened the solar heat. She let Niibin walk slowly. Halfway up the drive, she slipped off and walked along beside her skewbald friend, holding the reins loosely, stretching her legs from the stiffness of the four-hour ride over the hump from Meaford. The loose, uneven gravel crunched beneath them, with the stones tickling the moccasin covered soles of Brandi's feet. Niibin snorted and tossed her head, recognizing home, nuzzling Brandi's neck as if to say thank-you. Brandi had pushed her friend on the trip from Meaford, and now the little horse deserved rest. A familiar figure rose on the front porch of the main building. Karen scurried down the broad steps.

"Oh my sweet Brandi," Karen exclaimed. "You have come just in time." The women hugged. Brandi kissed her mentor on the cheek, squeezing her tightly, smiling and speechless. The women had forged the bond between them long ago. Brandi felt a sisterly love as they held each other.

"How is he?" Brandi finally asked.

"He's weak and fading fast." Sorrow filled Karen's face. "Winter hit him badly. I think it'll be today."

"I must see him," Brandi's voice choked. Her heart filled.

Karen led Brandi towards one of the outer cabins. Most residents shared the main buildings, but some of the older staff lived in separate single-storey stone buildings. Brandi tied her horse to a water tap and made sure the Herbert Bucket was full of water. The girl paused and stared at the bucket, remembering Warren had named these buckets.

So many wonderful memories,

She slipped the blanket and stirrup girth off Niibin along with the side pouches containing her precious journals, letting her horse rest in the dappling sunshine. The two women mounted the cabin porch and knocked lightly. Jean Bennett gave Brandi a long, loving hug.

"Come with me," Jean whispered, "he has asked for you. Fresh spring air flowed gently through open curtains into the gloomy interior. In the shadows, Brandi made out the bed.

"Warren," she said gently. Warren stirred and turned towards her voice.

"Hello, my sweet Brandi," Warren's voice was quiet and barely audible. The young woman bent near and smiled.

"Hello, Warren," her voice steadier than she had imagined it could be, "I had to come."

"You have made a dying man happy, my dear. I never had a granddaughter, but in my heart, you are mine." Brandi sobbed; her eyes teared. For the first time in a long, long time, she thought of her grandparents.

"Warren, I have loved you as if you were my grandfather." She paused and found it hard to speak. "I don't want to say goodbye."

"It has been a grand time we have all had my dear," Warren eased his head up a bit, "and even though it has been so hard, so very hard, all of us together have made it the best of times." His head rested back on the pillow and his eyes closed for a minute. In the silence, Brandi could hear a robin warbling outside the window. Warren beckoned her closer.

"Give my love to everyone, my dear. I wish I could have seen Sharon and Bill one last time." He paused again. "Remember the loop, my dear. We are part of it, even when we are gone. Keep the loop safe." He paused for a long time. "Please ask Jean and Karen to help me outside. I want to rest under the big maple."

The women summoned a man from the garden, and the four carried Warren in his bed outside and placed him in the shade under the leafing silver maple. The lightness of the burden amazed Brandi. Her friend had faded.

Warren stared up into the lightly greening branches as if evaluating the tree. His hand, somewhat distorted by arthritis, reached out, and he touched the flaking bark. The familiar roughness raised a smile, and Warren remembered back in Toronto touching many maples.

So long ago, he thought, *so long ago.*

Jean brought out a stool and sat beside Warren's bed. Karen and Brandi gently kissed Warren's cheek and silently withdrew up to the main building to comfort each other. Jean held Warren's hand. Her heart filled with sorrow knowing that her mentor, her friend, and her love was passing away. She smiled into the face she loved and, leaning down, kissed his warm lips. Warren stirred and smiled.

"WD, I don't want to lose you." Jean's voice was soft.

"Sweet Jean," Warren's voice was clear but weak, "You will always have me, have the memories we built together. Please hold them all for me." He paused, breathing quietly. "Your love sustained me through all of this hardship. More than that, you restored my empty heart those many years ago. You let me love Susan, the memory of Susan, and I still cannot fathom your generosity to allow that to me. She filled my heart. I thought nothing else could get inside, but when we met, it was as if my heart doubled in size and you filled it with your warmth and love."

Warren lay silent for a long time, his breathing shallow but easy. Then he opened his clear eyes once more and looked into Jean's glistening ones.

"She has always been in my heart, but I am looking at the woman I love, my... Sweet... Jean."

His eyes closed, and he gave a slight sigh. Jean felt his hand go limp and weigh heavily in her own. High in the tree, a light breeze stirred the branches. The leaves danced. Sunlight and shadow played over Warren's peaceful face. Jean held his hand and wept.

Chapter Nineteen

You were someone I always loved. I was the same as all the other little boys, first loving you as a sister, loving you as a friend, lusting after you as a woman, and then finding that loving friend once more as life led me down another path. There was never a time I was happier than those few minutes we walked up the Longview lane from the swimming hole that day so long ago. You, Megan and especially Kim made me feel safe and wanted. Whenever I play the song, it is that day and you I remember. I wrote this with you in mind as you travel far from us. Happiness...
From: Joseph of Longview, letter to Brandi Shadly. The Brandi Shadly archives.

*Footprints in the dust
Old carpets on the floor
Open arms of trust
No lock upon the door.*
Joseph of Longview: "Longing for Longview," ("Songbook Three: Shadows in the Valley,")

*Other than Brandi, no one else in Huron Territory is as revered and only known by their single, given name more than Joseph of Longview. His piano playing, composing and songwriting are legendary. - **E.T.***

Brandi Shadly stood in a cool morning drizzle. Niibin's reins passed loosely through her right hand. Her left arm wrapped around Megan

Lefevre's waist. The young girl sobbed as the two looked down at Warren Dunne's resting place. Handpicked wildflowers covered the fresh, red clay. Someone had placed a white Christian cross at the head. About a meter beyond was a freshly planted silver-maple sapling, Jean Bennett's work, her offering of love.

"I know it hurts." Brandi drew Megan tighter to her hip. "When they murdered Debbie's husband, Stevie, I felt the same way. It destroyed my world."

"He taught me so much." Megan sobbed, wiping her tears from her cheeks. "He was so gentle and encouraging and loving. He had so much more to tell me."

Brandi looked down at the girl. Her own heart grieved. She shared Megan's feeling of loss.

"I have discovered there is always so much more we would have wanted to say." Brandi thought of her friend Al Wright, who now rested beneath the yard of his old church.

"We can still talk to him in our heart and remember. We must always remember. If we do, Warren still lives. He will live until the last of us are gone. Actual death only comes when those who remember are all gone."

The young women stood silently. If Megan had looked up, she would have seen Brandi's tears. Brandi released the girl and nuzzled Niibin, making little clucking sounds at her horse. "I must go now. Work with Jean and Karen and don't be afraid to cry. Warren would want you to keep going in the direction he showed you. It will be the greatest parting gift you can give him." She hugged Megan one last time and swung deftly onto the horse. "I love you, Megan, and will be back in a few weeks." She and Niibin moved off towards Longview.

Brandi needed Longview. She needed the arms of her parents and the companionship of all those she loved. Her Dad and Mom and the others had all been to Kimberly for the funeral. They departed two days ago. Even in their grief, the spring work had called.

Niibin made steady progress down the old road. They stripped away all the asphalt and carted it down to Thornbury to extract the bitumen. The surface was firm, the compacted underlay of fine material from the paving process. Niibin found the footing easy compared to most of the trails she and Brandi had travelled. Brandi sat silently in the saddle, rocking slightly at Niibin's smooth gait. As they moved along, she noted the fresh green grass glistening in the light spring rain. She remembered the first time she had seen these roadsides, with her shadow seeming to chase her as she sat on top of the wagon towed by the old school bus. Today, the shadows filled her heart. Darkness rode with her in the misty gloom of the valley.

Al Wright had died during the winter. Ester described the cold, sunny day, with a bright blue sky and large snowflakes drifting down, seemingly from nowhere. She said Al slipped away, watching these gentle visitors and quietly singing an old hymn about going home. She felt angels had come for their faithful servant.

Brandi's relationship with Al had not been as close as with Warren, but she had loved both men. Her numbering of those who were ageing deepened her melancholy mood. Willard was now in his sixties, and Ellen had failed. Kathy had remarked once; she did not know how the frail woman had lived so long.

Corrine came to mind. Sadly, Brandi felt she would be the next to go. Her smoking had finally caught up and confined her to bed. Stan had sent a message for Brandi to come soon. She did not know if she could say goodbye once again.

Warren's passing became a way-marker for her and the community's progress. Brandi knew it signalled the beginning of a change in leadership, involving her generation in running the affairs of the territory. Part of her heaviness came in realizing her parents were ageing, now in their fifties, and she, Jeff, Don, Stephanie and the rest were moving to the forefront. Kathie Nelson had handed over all travelling duties to others and only worked in the clinic at Longview.

Brandi did not see herself as a leader even though most people throughout the territory would gladly listen to the young woman's advice. Council members sought her out repeatedly, and she had often made presentations to the General Council. She spoke for ordinary folks' everyday issues. The Council itself had aged. A young woman from Hanover represented fresh blood.

Stephanie Hunter led doctors along the railway from Chatsworth to The Corners. She was an adept surgeon and had worked as far south as Orangeville. Some people called her "the railway doctor".

Jeff, now the Chief Constable of the Huron Mounted Constabulary probably had caught up to Brandi in the distance covered on horseback.

She thought of Jeff as she turned into the Longview lane. The sunburst out and lifted her spirits.

Niibin came to a stop at Brandi's gentle check. The girl sat astride the horse just short of the archway constructed a dozen years before. Contemplating the structure and the weathered signboard, she tried to recall her mixture of sadness and joy the day they raised it over the Longview lane. She slipped from the saddle and led Niibin to the right-hand post. Brandi rested her palm against the wood, remembering Warren's hand had touched the same spot the day they dedicated it. She looked down the lane where the gentle lines of trees, Warren's trees, ran along the lane. They had grown since those days and now cast a shadow across the roadway. Brandi walked on, leading Niibin and listening to the rustle of the almost opened leaves in the light morning breeze. The shadows of the trees alternated with bright sunlight as she walked towards the compound.

Past the gap between that first stone building and the newer structure on the other side of the road, Brandi entered the large courtyard. The old house still stood to the right and the barn off to the left. Now another building of multicoloured bricks closed most of the far side of the yard toward the hill. Longview constructed the building with salvaged brick from abandoned houses, cemented together by mortar manufactured by the charcoal and limekiln by the river. This multi-family dwelling allowed the residents to abandon the old bus and mobile homes. The Thornbury foundry furnace had claimed them as feedstock.

The new buildings looked solid and permanent. Time took its toll on the house and the barn, although bitumen recovered from the roads now protected the wood. Brandi remembered the bare, weathered wood from last year's harvest. The odour of petroleum assaulted her nostrils.

She led Niibin to the barn. The little horse would get a vacation for a few weeks and some excellent care from one of the Smithsons. All of those youngsters had taken to horses, and Don and Muffin mentored them as farriers and trainers. JJ had joined the HMC, following his hero Jeff, and served double duty as a farrier and constable in Heathcote. Brandi placed her gear inside the tack room beneath her loft and gave Niibin a long rub down and brushing. The little horse relished a feed of oats as her mistress restored her coat.

Everyone laboured in the fields to the west of the lane, planting flax. They had perfected a technique of inter-planting with either soy beans or other legumes. Longview had earned a reputation for high-quality flax fibre and oil, making it their main trading crop. On a half-hectare in sight of the house through the gate, poppies had sprouted. The harvest of latex would be the feedstock for the hospital laboratory in Meaford.

She would go into the house soon and visit with whoever worked in the kitchen. The size of the community required several people every day in the kitchen gardens and preparing the meals. Longview kept the community lunch and dinner, but each family took breakfast at home.

As she stepped from the barn, whirring sounds reached her ears, coming from the granary, a recent construct behind the barn and up the western slope. This new building had a large winnowing and thrashing floor protected by a gently sloping roof extending from the building housing the grain bins. Brandi found a lone figure sitting in the shade of the thrashing floor, feeding grain through a strange wooden contraption.

"Hello, Joseph," Brandi smiled as Joseph looked up, startled. The sound had masked her approach. "Is this your new piano?"

Joseph flashed a big smile framed by his black, sweat-shined face. He looked healthy. The light singlet that he wore revealed muscular arms and strong shoulders. Only when he stood could she see the limitations of his legs. He reached her with more agility than she would have believed and hugged her tightly.

"I am so sorry about Warren." Joseph hugged her again. "I loved him too." The two stood silently for a moment, soothing their emotions. They did not speak of Warren again until the years had healed their loss.

"I've seen nothing like this contraption." Brandi examined grooved wooden slats fixed to a leather belt powered by a treadle.

"It's a seed cleaner," Joseph sat at the operating position. "Willard and I designed it from an old timer's story. It slopes down, and oval wheels make the slats shake? I feed the thrashed oats or barley seed in here and run the belt. The heavier grain flies off into the clean bin, and the lighter chaff and little seeds like clover or mustard ride in the grooves and then fall underneath." To emphasize his point, he scooped a hand full of gleanings from beneath the machine. Amongst the bits of chaff, hulls and straw bits, Brandi could see little round black seeds and others she did not recognize. "This saves a lot of weed pulling and we get cleaner crops."

Joseph worked the pedal as he poured a bucket of grain into the device. Clouds of dust rose as a steady stream of grain seeds flew into the bin. His legs easily handled the work.

"This strengthens my legs. I'll never ice skate well," Joseph sighed, "but I walk better. I can't do fieldwork, so cleaning makes me useful."

Brandi left him labouring away and headed for the house. She paused at the old tap. It had a sign saying not to drink the water. The pumps stopped working two years before when the power inverters failed. Wash water came from a large pond in a swale up the slope. The house water was potable, drawn by a hand pump into a cistern and from there piped into each of the dwellings. The salvaged piping would last for many years.

With electricity gone, food preservation became an issue. An icehouse stood behind the old kitchen, beside the woodshed. Every winter, Longview harvested ice from the ponds and the river and entombed it in sawdust and straw. The blocks of ice surrounded a meat locker, cooling smoked meat, vegetables and butter.

The tap and the Herbert bucket reminded Brandi of a conversation with Warren down by the river as they repaired the flood-damaged turbine.

"We can never defeat the second law," Warren had grumbled as he examined the turbine. "We use energy to build stuff and have to keep fixing it. Once we can't fix it, we lose all the original energy. Eventually, everything stops working, even us."

Brandi climbed the old steps.

"Hi, Mom," Sharon was on kitchen duty. Having Brandi home would be an excellent cure for her grief. They hugged, and their tears mingled, mourning Warren and the long-lost family. Jani came from the icehouse, carrying the makings for lunch. More hugs and tears followed. Jani was older than Brandi, but the two behaved like sisters. Jani's belly revealed the baby inside her. This baby would be her fourth, although they had all shared the grief when the third little one died within a day of birth.

"You sure look pregnant. You have a habit." Brandi teased.

"Someone has to make the grandchildren." Jani patted Brandi's work-hardened stomach and then rubbed her bulging belly. "When are you going to find Mr. Right?"

Brandi frowned at the reminder of her loneliness. Coming home always helped. The weeks would hurry by with the fieldwork filling the days, while conversation and sharing of friendship made the evenings golden. Brandi spent many hours in her loft, drawing, writing and thinking.

She produced a series of drawings looking out her window, over the farmyard that had changed into a village square. Little Bill, now a growing twelve-year-old, was her favourite subject and constant companion. His earnest efforts in helping with the work and his teasing love for his aunt formed a deep impression in Brandi's memory. The boy had tried so hard to emulate Brandi and draw, but he just had no feeling for it. His art lay in the harmonica, and the guitar had come naturally to him. Many pleasant evenings passed with the adult conversation going on in the courtyard while the music of Little Bill, Walt, and Joseph drifted from the old house.

The conversation often stopped to listen to the young learner making the occasional misstep, the older man feeling each soulful note from his harmonica and Joseph, the seeming too young genius, talking through his piano. Little Bill would work with Joseph often, helping on the thrashing floor and spending many hours playing music.

Brandi spent a long time on one particular drawing using her largest piece of paper. It depicted, on one-half, Joseph sitting at the seed-gleaner facing away from the centre with Little Bill handing him grain. The other half of the image had Joseph at his piano facing the opposite direction, with Little Bill standing and playing the guitar. At the seed machine, the pair was joyful and smiling. Playing music.,they were serious with deep concentration, but with shining eyes.

Several days before she planned to leave, Brandi and Jani climbed the hill behind Longview. It was a hard climb for the pregnant woman, but they finally reached a small meadow, the occasional home to the goatherd. It was just freshening in lush, late spring growth. In a week, the smaller children would bring the herd up.

"Sometimes, I feel sad." Jani sat beside Brandi. "I wanted so much to go to Weyburne, but I couldn't. I knew nothing was there for me anymore."

"I searched for news of your family," Brandi touched her hand, "but no one knew."

There had been ugly rumours, but no proof, and Brandi would not hurt Jani. From Maud's stories, everyone knew Jani's father and brother had died in the early fighting. No one could say for certain what had become of her mother, but the stories of her living at the Angel estate and the sexual innuendo suggested tragedy. Jeff had searched for news of his wife's mother. There were no clues in the debris of the Angel estate.

"How did you get the strength to come with us?"

"I hated my dad then. He was so stupid and mean." Jani's voice blended with anger and longing, reliving those feelings. "I didn't realize; I loved him too. Mom always took his side." Jani wiped her tears with the sleeve of her shirt. She looked at Brandi.

"We have all lost so much and so many. If it hadn't been for everyone, especially for your mom, I would never have survived. Sometimes at night, I think about them. I feel so lonely when it's quiet, and Jeff's away. Many times I've wished I could be like you, free and roaming around, living a meaningful and interesting life."

"My life is interesting," Brandi agreed, "but it's no less lonely or more meaningful. It's lonelier."

Brandi paused, remembering the nights alone under the stars with only her horse, bringing Dodger to mind. After all these years, she felt sadness.

"I have a job to do. People think I do it well and I have an obligation to you all. When loneliness grips me, I think of you all, often, the friends I have met and the hopeless people I have somehow brightened. Believe me, Jani; many times, I wished I was here and had never left. I always come back when I need your strength. Longview is the one place where I take in strength and never have to give it back."

"Jani, you are the source of so much of my strength and happiness. If I have any sister at all, Jani, it is you. Sacrifice is not a word. Everyone is living with sacrifice. We are forgoing most of our desires for the needs of many. Our reward is our physical survival. We are the generation suffering the most. We still carry the shadow of the past when the individual seemed more important."

"We suffered a loss, but there is hope. You are the mother to most of Longview now. I see you happy with the little ones, and they adore you. Those teenagers, especially the girls, respect you, and you are teaching them so much. Mom, Tina, Kathy and the rest are turning over the mothering to you, my sweet Sister. I know Mom loves you as if you are her daughter. Look at your children." Brandi paused and looked directly into Jani's wide-open eyes. "They're happy and content, never having suffered our loss. Sure, they will hunger for excitement, socializing and breaks from boredom and the work. We must provide fun and receive it too. They'll never understand the places in our hearts where shadows of our lost life make us grieve. If fortune smiles on them, they will never lose their family and never have to flee a great danger as we did."

Jani sobbed, and Brandi gripped her hand.

"I have travelled throughout Huron, up the Bruce and beyond. It's the same everywhere. There's no happiness over the hill greater than the joy to be found here. That's why I returned here now. I lost my wonderful friend when Warren died. I needed to come to you all, to be held, soothed, and let my grief find its way out. Being with you, the kids and the rest of my family gives me hope and seeing Debbie reminded me of the bravery required in facing loss. Even though my heart broke when Stevie died, how much more did Debbie endure? Seeing her finding new happiness reassures me I will too."

Once again, Brandi paused, her mind slipping back to her lost extended family, and warm memories replaced grief, but there was the longing.

"Longview brings Warren back. There's much of his handiwork here. The healing began when Niibin and I trotted up the lane, recuperating in the presence of those trees Warren planted so long ago. The sound of the wind through the branches whispered his voice, and the songs of all of our ancestors forever living, telling us all is well. We just have to keep listening, Jani. We have to keep listening."

Brandi's voice trailed off as she gazed across the valley at limestone cliffs, gleaming grey-white in the afternoon sun. She remembered how she had felt the valley wall confining her the first year at Longview. Suddenly, she felt humble, remembering Warren had told her the rock was hundreds of millions of years old. She caught her breath and trembled. For the first time, maybe, she understood. Brandi stood, took Jani by the hands and pulled her up, giving her a long embrace.

"My sweet sister," she choked, "thanks for listening and being here. Wherever I go, I'll always remember this day. One day I'll write it down, so you will know the comfort your peace and this place gave to me just this instant. I don't understand it yet. It's the greatest gift I've ever received. Thank you, Jani Coswell Shadly."

The two clambered down the hill to the growing complex of buildings that made Longview. Laughingly, Jani related the latest exploits of her youngest son Liam, playing his games and teasing; even at three years old, wanting to feed the chickens and "be big". Brandi had had no children "yet" as she told Sharon and Bill, but it amazed her how this new generation kept the old desire of children to grow up too soon.

> *The trees are growing*
> *Climbing in the sun*
> *With our spirits soaring*
> *And the work undone*
> **- Joseph of Longview**

Chapter Twenty

Don't sit under the apple tree
With anyone else but me
- From an old song.

Brandi dismounted at the Institute stable in Kimberly. Niibin had been reluctant to leave Longview, having befriended the great Percherons and the lively Canadian horses. Now, she seemed eager to renew her acquaintances in the upper valley. Two quarter-horses, part of the original Costello endowment, trotted to the paddock fence snorting greetings. Niibin was soon in the pasture, nibbling grass and playing horse games.

Brandi found Jean standing at Warren's grave, hands on her hips.

"It is peaceful here," Jean turned to Brandi. "I come here when I cry. He comforts me."

Brandi stared down at the plot. The picked flowers were now shrivelled and frayed. Bird poop adorned the cross. Jeans' maple sapling had leafed.

"Warren would love the bird droppings," Jean smiled. "Once, we were in the seed gardens in Weyburne, and a bird pooped on his head. It disgusted me. He laughed and said the loop had closed." Jean had a catch in her throat.

"He told me not to make a monument of his grave, just to remember him and honour him by living. I'm going to plant trees in his honour. For the rest of my life, in my spare time, I'll plant trees. He loved Tamarack. He said it reminded him of people. No matter how ugly we might look in hard times, we would at our end show golden glory. I'll plant Tamarack."

Jean rummaged in her apron pocket and extracted an old photograph, Warren's picture, of Susan on the rock bridge.

"Warren asked me to keep it safe, remembering him and as thanks for love large enough to include Susan. Warren was the last person alive to know her. She finally died with him. I feel as if I knew her too, just by loving the man she loved." Jean paused, searching for the right words. "Please promise, when I am gone, you will burn this picture in a beautiful place in the memory of the three of us. No one else will remember."

Brandi hugged Jean, accepting a duty to honour those who went before.

It became a stay at home summer for Nimise Makwa. The hard winter and the grief of Warren's passing had temporarily taken away her desire to travel. The young girl from the northern peninsula arrived, and Brandi took the eager, homesick girl into her care. To replace the almost exhausted paper supply, her first lessons were in papermaking. Salvaged paper sources had depleted. Flax became the dominant material for paper.

Brandi took her charge to Longview to retrieve gleanings of shorter flax fibre left after the scutching. Kathy Nelson focused on the girl's weakened and unhealthy appearance and soon had her on a proper diet of flax products and goat's milk. The doctor told Brandi in no uncertain terms the girl was not to have too much of the junky starch-heavy diet of the Institute and to make sure she had good nourishing food. Brandi promised Kathy not to tell Maud Dillingham her cooking was inadequate. After the laughter, Kathy lightened her language, admitting, after Longview, the HEI served the best food in the valley.

Towards the end of July, Brandi noticed the girl spent more time in Erin Thomas' seminars concerning human history and its ecological consequences. Brandi approved that approach. Artists and recorders needed to think beyond their experiences and have perspective.

Nimise had spent many hours listening and discussing with Erin. She liked him from the moment she first talked with him. Their time together on the trail had bonded them. The five years since increased her respect for his ability and understanding.

Erin simply loved Brandi. The six years' difference in their ages kept him from expressing his feelings, but his heart longed for the woman.

"Erin, do you think what happened to our world was like the collapse of the Roman Empire?" Brandi plucked one of the riper apples from a tree. On this warm sunny afternoon in late August, the fruit had ripened. The pair had climbed the eastern slope above Kimberly, to one orchard. The air lay heavy with summer haze and no breeze. Bees ranged all about, tasting sweet oozing from fallen apples and gleaning nectar from the asters and goldenrod. Brandi had made the excuse of checking the crop. In reality, whenever she felt her wanderlust stirring, she had to get out of the village and commune with nature. The two had been talking, and Erin naturally followed. Brandi being home had made his longings more urgent. He resolved to tell her before winter.

"I think all overly complicated structures must collapse." He remembered a lecture his dad used to deliver to first-year students. "No two are alike. The common connection is they become too complex and unsustainable. The exact cause varies, from a natural disaster, loss of resources or the eroding of the unity of the population. All of them probably apply. It happened to our industrial economy."

Erin picked an apple, and they shared the sweet fruit. Brandi looked into Erin's eyes; strange feelings gripped her. She touched his hand.

"Erin," she said. His name mingled with the sounds of the bees. In the moment's silence, high up the slope, a bird called out.

"I love you." Erin's words were barely audible, with no idea where he found the strength. Her touch drove fear from his heart. He dared not breathe.

Without a word, Brandi wrapped her arms around the young man. They embraced, tenderly at first and then more fervently. Their lips found the others'. Brandi's tears of happiness washed both their cheeks.

"Erin, I had not thought my feelings for you were this kind of love, but it's true. I've loved you ever since that first ride together. I love you."

They found the ground beneath the fruiting apple tree, their bodies pressing close as they dissolved into each other, absorbed in fervent loving, kissing, sighing and giggling at missteps as they explored the unfamiliar. Surrounded by nature, as if part of the ongoing process of life, they consummated their love.

They remained there, embracing happiness too long denied until the waning sunshine raised cooling breezes and sent them home. When they walked into the dining hall, Karen smiled. Even though their hands were only slightly touching, she knew. Karen thought of herself and Chester.

"Congratulations," Karen said. Brandi and Erin blushed and smiled. From that day on, every one of Brandi's drawings had the Nimise Makwa signature under a small apple tree. The branches of the tree spelt out "ET" in subtle letters. Her long loneliness had ended.

Flesherton September, Year 16 - Flesherton Flyer Vol. 3 No. 19

Good News!!! Nimise Makwa is married!!!

Brandi Shadly and Erin Thomas have announced their status as a couple married under Huron custom. The pair will continue to live and mentor at the Huron Ecology Institute, Kimberly campus, with Nimise still travelling extensively. Longview will host a celebration in the couple's honour at this year's harvest party and invite everyone. Please bring food, drink and your accommodations. Those of us who love Nimise are unspeakably happy. Come, party, and stay for a delightful visit!

Side note by Samantha James

All the single young women in the region will be happier now the young men who had secretly loved Nimise are available. Good luck girls!

Related news

The death of Warren Dunne has highlighted the passing of time. Erin Thomas has assumed the title of "Mentor of Historical Ecology" at the Institute. He will interview as many of the founders of Huron as he can find under the title, "The Voices of the Founders". He will travel in the territory and receiving visitors in Kimberly. I encourage anyone with a story to tell to visit or invite Erin to their home.

Chapter Twenty-One

The watershed is the fundamental expression of the interconnection of ecosystems on the ground. Human organization, including our political units, should base themselves on the watershed. The Great Lakes basin is the main watershed that includes us all.
Warren Dunne, in a letter to Chester Amik, H.E.I. archives

The little steamer slipped its lines and eased backwards out of Port Elgin harbour. She wore a dowdy dress with plenty of rust and peeling paint, but had an air of dignity. A good-sized crowd lined the wharf, shouting farewells to the throng at the ship's rails. A short blast of the steam whistle echoed around the harbour as the vessel turned towards the open lake.

Brandi stood beside Chester, watching the shoreline recede. The deck vibrated as the shaft, slightly out of balance, turned the propeller. It felt strange not to have Niibin beneath her, but this was a special trip. The railway from Owen Sound had brought them to Port Elgin. This steamer from the Michigan shore carried them to Port Huron to a convention. Brandi longed for Erin's embrace, but this gathering was important.

Representatives from the independent jurisdictions of the Great Lakes would attend. Michigan local governments proposed an overall organization responsible for the Great Lakes. They met in Port Huron because it was central and more secure than the remnants of the larger cities. Every jurisdiction sent security forces. Jeff commanded a contingent of the Huron Mounted Constabulary. The luggage and kit were impressive, with tents, portable kitchen and food supplies.

"Our aim is simple," Chester spoke to a circle of people sitting on the stern deck. "We want an organization to protect the water and administer security in the Great Lakes Basin. We don't want a central government dictating from above but to keep the organization as weak as possible while still capable."

Everyone remembered the fiasco of the Ottawa convention. All opposed to creating a new federal government rejected restoring the old one.

The steamer was an old coast guard boat retrofitted with a pair of compound steam engines burning wood or coal. The bulky wood limited the range of the little ship. It took on fuel at every stop. She followed the shore, keeping the speed below fifteen kilometres per hour to conserve fuel.

Re-named the SS Lake Huron, her captain relished telling the story of salvaging the boat from its retirement as a floating restaurant. The steamer had travelled to Manitoulin Island and down along the Bruce Peninsula before reaching Port Elgin. They retrieved delegates from Kincardine and Goderich before heading directly to Port Huron. Other representatives from southern Ontario would travel to Sarnia by train.

No navigation lights guided them, so the little ship waited near the river inlet until morning, with just a small turning of the propellers to push against an easterly wind and the subtle current. The captain watched his barometer falling and hoped they would be in the river before a storm. The ship slipped downstream once the dawn made the banks visible and turned, in light rain, up a smaller river into the heart of Port Huron.

They saw a dismal scene, with little visible activity on a derelict and decaying shoreline. A small abandoned building, with a fading and peeling blue and white facade, all the windows gone, stood along the riverbank. The weathered sign hanging askew above a gaping doorway read Black River Bistro. The odd tree branch bobbed amongst the raindrops on the muddy water, and a pungent odour rose from invisible raw sewage.

"I'll see if I can teach anyone about humanure," Brandi spoke to Chester as she watched people gathering along the riverbank.

"It smells like they need to." Chester focused on the crowd.

Green gardens appeared on both sides of the little river. SS Lake Huron eased into a concrete wall, rubbing gently against logs hung as bumpers.

The crew flung ropes over the side and secured the vessel to two handy trees. A throaty blast from the steam whistle announced their arrival to the crowd gathered in the drizzle. The Ontario contingent descended the gangway onto the concrete pier and Brandi concluded a boat was not routine. The crowd parted for the official host. A round of handshakes followed amidst the offloading of supplies.

Jeff's force set up the field kitchen. The hosts housed everyone in an old college dormitory with cooking tents on the lawn. Jeff provisioned for a two-week meeting, but his experience had taught him to prepare for more. He set out to locate extra supplies. Brandi accompanied her brother into unfamiliar territory. Owen Sound was the largest town she knew. For all of its decaying appearance, Port Huron was impressively urban.

Following a street parallel to the river, past burnt-out buildings, pockmarked by bullets; they came to a park and an intersection. A fading sign said "Glenwood and Poplar".

Jeff stood in the middle of the intersection and looked all around. He amazed Brandi by describing the scene of a major battle. He pointed to a large multi-storied apartment complex with most of the facade showing gaping wounds from heavy weapons. The remnants of dug-in positions spread throughout the parks. Houses and other buildings showed signs of suffering from gunshots, probably from people in the apartment building. Some had burnt to the ground. Jeff estimated the fighting had occurred at least a decade before, with no burnt smell from the wood.

When Brandi asked, the locals referred to it as "The Battle of Black River", a confrontation between the remnants of a Michigan National Guard unit and a local private militia. The Guard unit had prevailed. The militia had heavy weapons, but the Guards had more and better training. This fighting at the apartment complex was the militia's last stand. Time had not healed all the hatred; however, most supported the government that resulted from the Guard's victory.

A farming operation flourished amongst the remnants of the battle. While Jeff sought the farmers, Brandi turned away from the river. The roadways kept their asphalt surface. The pavement showed signs of both powered vehicles and animals. She found several shops open, a bakery, a butcher shop and a general store. A small building with a large roll-door and boarded up spaces where large plate-glass windows had once fit intrigued Brandi. A sign tailored from fragments cut from other mismatched signs read, "Dentist–Denturist". An old yellow sign with the word, "Muffler" peeked out from beneath. A small hand-painted board read, "Prepaid only–Port Script or goods for barter. No greenbacks accepted. Check our competitive rates."

An arrow pointed to the entrance. Brandi pushed through into an anteroom with a faint odour of motor oil and alcohol and a few old chairs along the walls. LED Christmas bulbs cast a dim light. No one was in sight, but the doorbell reverberated through the interior.

"I'll be right out," a disembodied, strangely accented male voice echoed through the gloom. "Take a seat."

Brandi sat in a comfortable padded chair opposite a large piece of plywood that filled a window opening and listed services and rates.

Cleaning–1 chicken; 1 bushel of vegetables; 10 PN; or 1 day's work
Extraction–as above
Cavity filling–2 chickens; 2 bushels of vegetables; 20 PN; or 2 day's work

The girl suspected most patients chose extraction. The notice detailed several more procedures, including the fitting of hand-carved teeth. Beneath the rates, smaller scrip informed the visitor, "Talk is cheap, and we provide plenty of it." Brandi smiled and settled in to wait.

It is strange, she thought, *a person could seem appealing through something like a sign.*

An older black man appeared from the interior. Judging his age was impossible, he appeared younger than what Warren and Al had been, but older than Brandi's father was. Brandi had no reference to judge his age.

I don't know many black people; she thought. Then a revelation shook her. Joseph's family and many friends were black, and Don was at Port Stanley. She had not thought about their colour.

More to consider. Brandi would discuss it with Joseph.

The dentist moved slowly, yet with an air of vitality. A white smock covered most of his body with the front neatly buttoned except for one missing fastener, with an old-fashioned ballpoint pen, backed by pieces of paper, protruding from the breast pocket. He sat on a padded bench opposite Brandi.

"My, you are a cute, young thing." His eyes twinkled and did not hint at danger. Brandi had been the target of many flirting comments and sexual advances, including an attempted rape in Centreville. The man did not seem dangerous. Still, the Savage hung from her shoulder.

"You remind me of my uncle, Peter." Brandi smiled. "You have a strange accent."

"I am a peach tree in an apple orchard." The man laughed at his joke. "They transplanted me here from The Beautiful State of Georgia thirty years ago." He said it with a hint of sarcasm and longing. "I never learned to sound like a Yankee." He smiled once more, studying the girl and wondering at her slightly unfamiliar accent. "The girls loved it when I was younger, but a lot of folks can't understand me. That's probably safer for me." He laughed loudly. "But your voice is unique, too. Are you from Sarnia? Canadians have a distinct sound."

"Not Sarnia but up north," Brandi liked this man, "here for the meeting."

"Ah yes, it's the get together going to solve all of our problems." This time, he sounded sarcastic. "Oh, I'm rude," he stood and extended his right hand. "I am William Hammond Bond, the third, DDS, Ph.D." Still smiling, he gripped her hand. "Call me Hambone like everyone else. I'm a not too bad dentist, bean weeder and chicken plucker."

"I'm Brandi Shadly, traveller, drawer, writer, listener, teacher and general drifter. Oh, and I can pluck a chicken with the best, especially if it means I get to eat."

"I take it you didn't come in here for dental work?" Hambone took a step towards the interior doorway. "Why don't you come and I'll show you around. No charge for the talk." He pointed to the sign and disappeared through the doorway. Brandi entered the repair bay of the muffler shop. The place was clean but kept the odour of motor oil. A single string of white LED Christmas lights ran along the back wall, providing enough light to see. A reclining dentist's chair sat towards the back. It had a large lamp reflector fixed to an adjoining stand. Clean linen lay on shelves. Wheeled carts held dental tools.

"This's my clinic," Hambone turned with a sweeping gesture. "I salvaged everything from the medical building a few blocks over."

"Why didn't you just work from there instead of this old car shop?" Brandi asked.

"Two things," he casually spun the chair as he spoke. "Those modern high-rise buildings aren't workable, needing elevators and sophisticated electrical, plumbing and such. The ground floor is best for everything and maybe two or three floors above for living. It's all walk up now. There's a good air compressor here, and we have adapted the drills and other things to run on air."

As if to make his point, he grabbed one of his power tools and made it spin with a loud whirring and the hiss of air from a drive unit beneath the chair.

"The corporation running this muffler shop had a green thing going before the crash and installed a living roof, rainwater collection, and photovoltaic panels, along with a solar space heating system. It isn't luxurious but a lot easier than some setups. I share electricity with three other operations. Some call us the four horsemen of the reconstruction."

Brandi understood the reference and the joke. Since she had become interested in the role of spirituality, she had read many books, including the Christian Bible. Although she had not found this research much help, it taught the codes spoken by believers.

"We don't believe there is any reconstruction." Brandi examined some of the special tools on the trays. "Most think we must build something new, something more permanent than what fell apart."

"Of course, there won't be any return to the old way." Hambone felt comfortable with the idea. "Those who hope so live in the shadows. They'll eventually come around. People who wanted the old life committed suicide. Anyone thinking of returning to normal is nuts. When they finally realize it's over, they'll step into the light."

"It's hard to give up hope," Brandi leaned on one bench. "We've lost so much. I'm lucky I have my family. My grandparents, cousins, uncles and aunts disappeared; just Uncle Peter came back."

"I lost my whole family," Hambone said quietly, but even in this light, Brandi could see his sadness. "They had gone to visit back in Georgia that September. All hell broke loose, especially in Atlanta, where they were. No one could get out past violent mobs, punks, gang-bangers, and even the cops. I had stayed in Ann Arbor for the start of school. When they didn't come home, I rushed south. I couldn't get past Ohio. There was no safe way. I never saw my wife and children again. I still hope for a miracle."

"You said, Ph.D.," Brandi wanted to change the subject. She had been at this point in a conversation many times. Pursuing the details became too painful, making it better to focus on something else. "You're a professor?"

"The University of Michigan School Of Dentistry, a young hotshot with a knack for teaching and ran their charity clinic. They recruited me because I had set up free clinics back home. They gave me a Ph.D. in sociology after I convinced them I knew something about helping folks."

"How did you end up in a muffler shop in Port Huron?" Brandi laughed. The situation seemed bizarre.

"I became paralysed with grief." He sat on a stool near Brandi. "Hell, it paralysed the whole damned university. It took a few weeks to get folks moving. The majority ran once pay stopped and food disappeared. Most of us who stayed moved into student dorms. Before long, we were getting guns and fighting off looters. Once the mindless looting stopped, after taking all the useless computers and things, they ignored us. No one thought books were worth stealing." He caught his breath.

"Soon, we became raiders looking for food and recruited a few tough guys. As long as we fed them and turned a blind eye, they behaved and gave us some thug firepower." He did not seem enthusiastic about this development. "We survived the first year and built gardens and a little farm. Some agricultural folks from the state university fled to Ann Arbor and joined us when Lansing went up in flames."

Brandi did not know the local geography.

"So how did I get here?" Hambone rubbed his chin and scowled. "Academics being academics and Ann Arbor being Ann Arbor, a fight developed over how to run things. Ideologies caused big fights between feminists, Marxists, free-enterprisers and some who wanted to invoke brotherly love with guns."

"In the second winter, the hatreds became entrenched. I considered myself part of a practical option, but some could not cooperate. In the spring, three rival farming groups exchanged shots claiming the good ground." Ham scowled and paused for a few moments. Brandi dug out dried beef and offered some. Ham took it with thanks.

"I'll fix you a little snack later," He mumbled as he ate. "A few of us decided it would not end well, so we gathered up, stole supplies, and headed out. We came this way to avoid the danger in Detroit. Fortunately, we chose the right militia group to join and that guard detachment finally wiped out a dangerous gang. The Guard unit wasn't progressive, but the gang had murdered the commander's family, and he wanted revenge. The battle weakened them, so the rest of us took control.

"The guy running the General Store came from Ann Arbor. He was an electronics professor and is Mr. Fix-It for the power equipment. He has a salvage and repair operation in the back with a hand full of trained techies."

"The folks in Ann Arbor finally came to a peaceful arrangement. They have a fortified zone there now and make it their mission to save the library and the knowledge. It's like a medieval monastery on a grander scale. I returned a couple of years later to get information. It's a town of thousands, an army, and fields and farms surrounding it. There are rumours you have a similar setup in London, Ontario. I hope it's true."

Brandi puzzled over the effort to keep the accumulated knowledge of the past. It was part of the Huron Ecology Institute's purpose. Native elders performed the same function for their older wisdom.

"Come out back and see my farm." Hambone held the door in an old gesture of politeness.

***

"I must admit I didn't give this meeting a hope in hell of doing anything." Hambone smiled at Chester and Brandi. The little group sat beneath the canopy of the Huron eating pavilion, enjoying a tasty stew with freshly baked Spelt bread and raw goat's milk. Jeff spooned steaming portions from a large pot. The commander could not escape kitchen duties.

Two weeks of hard work produced an agreement. Hambone and Brandi had become good friends. Their friendship helped fill the hole left by Warren's passing, and it pleased her that Chester had met "Ham".

"Well, we haven't re-created the Roman Empire," Chester took some bread, "but we have taken a big step to secure ourselves and the lakes."

"I'm done with empires," Ham glanced around the table. "I hope we keep the centre weak."

"This agreement doesn't establish a central government," A woman from the former state of Wisconsin smiled at the big black man. "We've created rules and an organization to protect the water and maintain security along the watershed boundary."

"They accepted the idea of organizing based on watersheds." Chester looked off into the distance, contemplating the enormity of the concept. It would be Warren Dunne's greatest legacy.

"The territory boundary is the Great Lakes Watershed. Establishing the exact line is hard. We decided the edges should be a grey zone shared with adjoining watersheds. Some boundaries are safe, but the Niagara frontier and south shore of Lake Ontario are unfriendly. There's a huge refugee problem southwest of Chicago. In Ohio, an undemocratic group controls the river watershed boundary, but it wants to trade more than fight. They're the top end of a series of semi-warlords from Lake Erie to the Louisiana Cuban territory."

"The refugees make a big problem and an opportunity. We need population, but the refugees are diseased, and some violent. We must move slowly."

The diminutive woman from Wisconsin pushed her greying bangs and moved beside the dentist, reminding Brandi of Jean and Warren.

"It sure would be nice to have friendly neighbours," Ham contemplated the woman and thought of his missing family.

"We have to deal with hostile frontiers from Quebec to Buffalo and be prepared for an attack from the southwest. Behind those refugees, there's drought and famine." Chester continued. "We have committed to sending supplies, but we will only send troops if it threatens the lakes."

"I don't think it will get too serious," the woman from the west replied. Once these desperate people know we would give them refugee status, they come around quickly. We have seen brutal fighting."

Jeff recalled the bloodshed of his experience at the twenty-six barrier.

"A few Mexicans survived the drought and made it here. Millions fled north to die of starvation as Texas dried up." The group fell silent, imagining the hellish south-west.

Chester broke the silence. "Hostile forces have made the Mississippi and Missouri rivers a boundary. Freight flows for a fee, but it might take generations to unify the drainage basin."

"I hear we call ourselves The Federation of the Great Lakes," Ham had tired of bad news.

"The name came easy." Chester relaxed. "Once we decided there would be no formal federal government, just a coordinating council, everyone said yes. The council will meet here yearly, with a coordinator who can call emergency meetings."

"Will you bring the ratified treaty back here?" Ham asked the woman from Minnesota.

"For sure," her gaze lingered on the big friendly dentist, "I'll insist."

"I finished my work and leave tomorrow." Brandi missed Erin.

"I have a present for my friend, Hambone." Brandi unrolled a large drawing. Ham's portrait on one side and a detailed sketch of his clinic opposite sandwiched a cartoon of a pig's head, smiling with a full mouth of human teeth, wearing a scarf decorated with a maple leaf. Brandi wrote beneath, under an apple tree, "Thanks for the free talk. - Nimise Makwa".

Chapter Twenty-Two

I stood on the Canadian shore watching Ham row his little boat back across the river. It was a misty day, and he quickly vanished into the haze towards the far shore. The sun would burn the river fog away, but we had no time to wait. I headed up the embankment with Ron, my reporter friend, to a railway passenger coach tail-ending a freight train of a dozen carloads of scrap from the old oil refinery and a boxcar of trade goods from Michigan. A baggage Express car separated the coach from the other cars. As the steam whistle blew an urgent double blast, we climbed aboard and found seats. The decrepit ruins of Sarnia's industrial glory slid past.

From: "The circle grows larger." (The Journals of Brandi Shadly, Vol. 11, p 76)

Brandi rode the railway from Sarnia to Hamilton with a radio reporter from Oakville. He could not send live reports and wanted to broadcast news of the meeting.

"I have not seen one of these before." The young train conductor stared intently at Brandi's railway pass. The small bright yellow card read, "Unlimited Travel–Anytime–Any train" and on the back, "Please show Brandi Shadly (Nimise Makwa) all courtesy and help." over Chester Amik's signature and that of the head of the Ontario Railway Company, Robert Bossley. No other such pass existed. It impressed Ron, who had paid a good amount of railway script for his passage.

The railroad had instituted scrip paid for with barter or labour promises at all local stations. Passengers bartered with the train crew at flag stops. The baggage car stored goods traded for passage according to the script value of goods and labour, with one script unit being equivalent to one hundred kilometres of travel but with a minimum fare of ten kilometres. Script and barter rail travel represented a drain on a person's surplus.

"Until now, I've only used it in Huron." Brandi hoped the young man would not think the card a fake.

"It's an honour to have you on my train." He handed the little document back to Brandi. "I have a notice telling about you. If you had boarded without the card and convinced me who you were, I would have given you passage."

"How would I do that without photo I.D.?" Brandi laughed.

"What's a photo I.D.?" the young man responded.

"Times have changed." She mused aloud. "You are too young. You must have been a little kid when the crisis started, but the world I lived in until I was thirteen used photographic identification for dozens of things. This card would have had my picture on it."

"We still have photography," Ron sat opposite Brandi, and the coachman leaned on the seat-back, eager to listen in. "Some photographers are good, but they make their materials, and it isn't too portable. I've seen cards with pictures. The PLM used them. Everyone over twelve years old had one. We called them a Show Me."

"I've always lived down this way." The railway man eased into the seat beside Ron. "We had a travel-pass with no picture. The only photographer I know lives in London."

"A guy photographed the Federation convention." Brandi secured her pass in a leather wallet. "His work impressed me. He liked my drawing, and we discussed papermaking."

"That guy was great," Ron added. "I saw some of his portraits." He looked at Brandi.

"What's it about you that has everyone so excited? After I met you, I started asking around. Everyone from up north… it's as if they worship you. They called you Nimise Makwa or just Nimise, except your brother, who calls you his kid sister. He's proud of you. I can tell."

"I'm just a girl travelling around sharing stories and ideas with people." Brandi paused, realizing that she was no longer a girl but a woman. "I like people; most of them seem to like me. When I visit, I share the work and tell stories, pass on information and ideas about how to do things, listen to their stories and make drawings. People have little outside contact in many places, so they welcome a visiting storyteller."

"What's this Nimise Makwa name?" The radio reporter sensed a story to use on air.

"It's Ojibwe and means Sister Bear. It's a casual name. I don't have an official native name. My mentor, George MacDonald, is waiting on his spirits and the people for my name."

The scenery rolled by as they puffed across flat farmland and through long stretches of summer green forests. Brandi told of the day she met the makwa and how she received her name. The story enthralled the pair. Other passengers migrated to nearby seats. No one wanted to leave. When one couple got off at some remote stop, they handed Brandi a note with their names and location, inviting her to visit. She promised to do her best.

Hours passed on the slow train, and before they reached London, the sun threatened the western horizon. The trainman disappeared briefly, returning from the baggage car with a hot meat-pie and hard cider. Other listener produced refreshments as Brandi related tale after captivating tale. The railwayman did not leave the train in London when his replacement appeared but remained on the train, refusing to miss any of the stories. Other passengers reluctantly left, but fresh faces replenished the audience. It went well into the night until Brandi finally succumbed to fatigue and nodded off in mid-sentence, the sound of the train clicking along the tracks drawing her into a deep slumber.

Ron could not sleep. He took out paper and excitedly made copious notes of her stories, forming a plan in his creative mind. Brandi had opened her folio and used the illustrations to enhance her talk. Ron looked at the images one more time. He stared at the sleeping woman and understood why her friends had held her in such esteem. Besides these other things, she was beautiful.

"I hope we meet again." Brandi hugged Ron. "It was exciting being at the birth of the Federation."

"It sure was," Ron agreed, "but you made the ride back even better." Brandi blushed at the praise. She reached into her folio and pulled out a small drawing. She had awoken early with the first rays of the morning sun. Ron and the trainman slept opposite her, their heads resting against each other, with Ron's notes slipping to the floor. She sketched the scene, adding the face of another early riser peeking around a seat with her eyes peering out of the paper.

"This is for you, Ron." She handed him the drawing. "I always enjoy telling stories. You were a great audience."

The realism and honesty of the drawing overwhelmed Ron.

"Who's the man under the apple tree?" Ron had come across one of Brandi's drawings of Erin, stripped to the waist and plucking fruit from the branches. Brandi always teased him he had picked her like an apple.

"That's my husband." Her warm smile always accompanied thoughts of her love. Ron appeared crestfallen, and Brandi chuckled despite her desire not to be cruel. Many young men fancied her. She only loved Erin.

"Don't worry," she said. "There will be a wonderful love in your life, too. Be patient." She hugged him once more. "We'll meet again, Ron."

The man smiled, thanking her repeatedly as he dismounted.

Brandi and Ron had parted at Milton, another town looking like a small boy in a man's clothes. Uninhabited ruins surrounded a small living core. Ron took a local coach to Oakville. Brandi's train turned south to Hamilton, delivering its load of scrap to the steel mill. The trainman had left in Kitchener to ride a westbound home.

***

I had never paid much attention to the radio broadcasts. Although receivers were widespread and Longview had one, we mostly listened to the newscasts and the occasional advertised discussions and debates. The radio played much music as filler, but with electricity scarce, most people in Huron did not bother listening. The exception was a live music jam session Joseph liked. I remember spending evenings listening with Joseph in the parlour of the old farmhouse of Longview. Many times, he would go to the piano and play along with the music coming from the radio. I enjoyed his playing more.

From: "Conversations with Brandi Shadly," in the "Voices of the Founders," series by Erin Thomas

One highlight of my life was travelling to Oakville to perform on the radio. Brandi arranged my debut with her friend Ron. After the first live broadcast, people and musicians started arriving at the studio wanting to listen or play. It lasted about two weeks, with sessions every day. In the end, I got lonesome for Longview and reluctantly came home. That led to my annual Christmas broadcasts and the Flesherton summer music jamboree. These are the highlights of my year. I have made many wonderful friends through my music.

From: "Conversations with Joseph of Longview," in the "Memories of the Second Generation," by Erin Thomas

"Is this you he's talking about?" Rob Bossley, looking greyer and wrinkled from age and the stress of running the railway, sat behind his large work-cluttered desk. Brandi sat opposite in a comfortable stuffed chair. They listened to a small radio receiver sitting on one of the oak shelves lining the walls of the large office.

This is the second instalment of The Tales of Nimise Makwa. The response to our first show last week has encouraged us, and we promise more. If we are lucky, we may get Nimise herself to come and chat.

Ron had wasted no time in developing this project, and it had only been about three weeks since he and his hero had parted in Milton.

"He sent me a message last week asking for my permission. I told him to go ahead, but if he lied or made me look stupid, I would shoot the pencil out of his hand." Brandi chuckled.

Rob examined the girl's face, looking for a clue to seriousness. Her rifle was never far from her, although she did not carry it in town. According to the radio drama, she was capable of such a shot.

The broadcast continued with this second instalment entitled "Escape from Weyburne". Brandi was pleased. Ron had not only captured the serious aspects of the story but also included her humour and irony.

We must caution our listeners. Future episodes will have some laughs but also heart-wrenching sadness and grief. Ron was into the closing remarks. We will look at the recent dark days of conflict from the opposite side from where most of us experienced them. These stories will be each week, and with luck, will never end. Good day to you all, this is Ron Prendergast speaking.

"I liked it," Rob smiled. "Of course, I've heard you spin your tales directly. He sounded like he quoted you."

"He has a great memory," Brandi admitted. "I guess he'll be asking me to be on the radio sometime, but I will have a price." There was a gleam in her eye. "We have a young musician at Longview who is wonderful and only seventeen years old. Ron will have to give him some performance time, too. You should hear Joseph on piano, fiddle and guitar." She paused for a moment, looking at Bossley. "Why don't you come up for the Longview harvest party this year? Barry Young and his family will be there. Jennifer told me you were a talented musician. Joseph would love playing with you."

Rob rubbed his chin. He had been contemplating turning over the railway's day-to-day operations to someone else. One woman was ready. Even though she had briefly been his lover, it did not affect his judgment. She was a strong, smart mechanical engineer.

"When do I come?" Rob suddenly stood and peered out the window towards the smoke and glow of the ironworks. He regretted not having any family. Perhaps retiring to Huron would help. His engineering work would still be possible from there.

"The last week of September, plan to stay for two weeks. We finish the harvest by the end of the month, but we always hold the party after the twenty-fifth."

"Please take this book to Barry Young. Tell him the library is empty. He'll understand."

It puzzled Brandi. She had not heard of Rob's role as a spy. Brandi hugged Rob. She had lingered for three weeks visiting the affable fellow and touring the wonders of his industrial establishment. Although understanding steel, iron and all the pollution kept the trains running, it saddened her. Brandi drew dark images of this place.

Her train passed the Erindale yards and reminded her of Kathy Nelson's escape. In Orangeville, she claimed a place in the steam-engine cab with Brian Young and Jake.

"Heard your stories on the radio." Jake sounded shy. "It was good." He pushed the throttle forward, and the engine snorted as the mighty drive-wheels spun and the enormous mass moved. Brandi made self-deprecating noises, but spreading her efforts wider pleased her. Years later, Brandi discovered the resulting impact of the myth of Nimise Makwa and the reverence for Brandi Shadly.

Radio coverage led to a growing interest in the Huron Ecology Institute and a flow of attendees from the south. The visit of the archivist from the university enclave in London encouraged Karen and Erin. It thrust the HEI to the forefront of efforts to preserve useful knowledge and spread learning throughout the new federation. The Institute soon had to budget for railway script to cover frequent travels. An unexpected effect of this more direct contact with the western regions to the south was mounting pressure to complete the railway from Port Elgin to Goderich, joining the existing line to London. This new infrastructure would soon prove worthwhile in dealing with the dangerous uranium fuel from the nuclear generating site.

Chapter Twenty-Three

It was a hectic winter at Kimberly. Extra students arrived soon after the harvest party. Several new mentors arrived on the campus. Before the new year turned, we had established classes in cooperage, passive solar devices such as food dehydrators, more blacksmith and forging instructing and electronic salvage. The metalworking moved to the Thornbury foundry, requiring my presence to teach the teachers. Not every mentor was good at working with students, and some had to learn how to teach and encourage slower students. One of my important duties was to teach several of the instructors how to read and write. Spring planting seemed like a reprieve, and when the offer came for me to accompany Chester, Jeff, and an engineering crew on a diplomatic train trip to northern Ontario, I leapt at the chance. Karen and Erin had headed off to London at the invitation of the library crowd there, so everyone seemed to get a reward. Samantha James took charge and ran a writing workshop that summer. I almost wished I had stayed to learn from her, but then, I would have missed several wonderful experiences.

From: "Conversations with Brandi Shadly," in the "Voices of the Founders," series by Erin Thomas

Windblown rivulets rippled over the deep purple darkness of the river. Late afternoon sunlight glinted from the changing surface, creating patches of dancing diamonds. Unhurried currents carried odd bits of flotsam along to the west. Dragonflies flitted about the stream edge, searching out unsuspecting victims. The insects' gossamer wings glowed against the deepness of the water. The murmur of deer and horse flies competed with the cries of sandpipers and the faint rustling of the aspen leaves along the high bank.

Brandi reclined in the warm, August sunshine, protected from the light northerly gusts. It had been oppressively hot for several weeks, but overnight an intense, stormy cold front swept through the region, chilling bodies adapted to the heat. The heavy rains removed the sweet smell of wood smoke. It had been their constant companion for the entire trip, even as far as the Moose River. Forest fires seemed to burn everywhere and had delayed their plans more than once.

This languid stream was the Spanish River, still tamed by concrete dams. Nearby, two bridges crossed over, one carrying an old roadway, and slightly further away, another supported the rail line. A steam locomotive, fussing and hissing, sat at the far end of the second bridge. Brandi could see Barry Young and his engineering crew evaluating the structure, repeating a common event on the trip.

Chester Amik's purpose had been to meet leaders. Young's mission was to evaluate the rail lines for safety and decide on essential maintenance. None of the territory north of Muskoka was officially in the Great Lakes Federation, but contact had been positive. They intended the railway work as a show of good faith and the benefits of joining. Barry took his job seriously. Lives were at stake operating a railway. He would do his best to reduce the risks.

"Hello, young lady," the wavering voice rasped slightly, betraying the man's advanced age and startled Brandi. She had not heard him approaching and twisted about to look up. An old man smiled down at her. He carried a birch-wood fishing pole with a string line wrapped around the shaft; the hook safely stuck in the end. A scraggly grey beard covered his face. Long, greasy, grey hair fell from under a dark, floppy, wide-brimmed hat. His crudely repaired brown pants hung down to an undone pair of well-worn leather boots. A threadbare, red-plaid bush shirt hung over his waist, tucked in behind crude suspenders. Brandi had long since learned never to judge by looks, and she thought of George MacDonald.

"Hello." Brandi smiled in return.

"You don't mind if I just go down here and do a bit of fishing?" The stranger asked as he descended towards the water. He seemed quite agile.

"I'm Brandi," she extended her hand. "I wasn't fishing anyway, just watching that lazy pike down there sunning like I am."

"My name's Albert. I've been on this river most of my life and seen a lot of those big, old, lazy Northern, no use trying to catch that one right now, and I want some smaller pickerel or white fish. I can't eat so much lately." Albert sat beside Brandi, fishing forgotten.

"You with that lot over there?" Albert indicated the train. "That thing scared the bejeezus out of me," he chuckled. "We haven't seen a train in a long time, never steam."

"Yes, I'm with them, inspecting the lines to see if they're safe. We're on a diplomatic mission of sorts from the other side of the lake around Owen Sound." Brandi sat up, so their eyes were level.

"Well, that's no matter to me now," Albert spat at a daisy, struggling to grow on the steep embankment. "I don't have long to go."

"Tell me about the river." Brandi did not want to discuss anyone's imminent death.

"I've been here since they used to drive jack-pine down to the mill. Never saw the loggers who drove red and white pine saw logs down here. Before my time, before they tamed the thing with those dams. I used to work on the dams. They still generate electricity at all of them, but parts are getting scarce and no place to get them. Workers live at the sites, and they get to use the power themselves. Funny how it works." He paused as if remembering a time long past. "They had little towns way back when I started; then they tore them down. It's a full circle. Workers are rebuilding them. Good came of this collapse, if you ask me."

Albert fiddled with his fishhook. "You young folks are going to have a nicer place than what we smashed up. Glad it's gone." His voice rose with emotion. "It was a hell of a bad thing; Everyone was out for themselves. Not that it was heaven before, but people were together, and the bad ones stood out. Then it got so you couldn't tell the bad from the other takers. Now you got to be a giver to make it."

Brandi nodded her head. Albert seemed to sum up much of what she believed and reflected a lot of what allowed people to survive.

"Anyway, all the corporations are long gone around here, the mining companies, paper companies and the junk sellers. I hope you folks aren't planning to restart that nonsense." The old man stared intently at Brandi.

His face was a combination of hopefulness and anger. He looked over at the train and said, "Don't do it by accident either."

Brandi reassured Albert that they had no desire to go back to the old way. She outlined the recent history of the southern part of the province and threw in several of her own stories. Taking out paper and pencil, she captured Albert's image. As he described the dams and his hunting and fishing experiences, she drew a background of a large concrete dam with leaping fish and birds and animals. There was much laughter as the two talked. Brandi was thankful the inspection took all afternoon. The call of the steam whistle came too soon.

"Here's something for you," Albert dug into a breast pocket, extracting a crumpled slip of paper inscribed with a short poem. "I know it by heart, and I am glad I found someone to share it. I have more poetry and writing, but no time to get it now."

"I wish I could see it all. I'll be back one day." Brandi stood and shouldered her folio.

"I'll be dead by then," Albert sounded at ease with the thought. "Where can I send you my stuff? I don't have any family left." Sadness drew shadows across his face.

"If the trains are running, send it to Nimise Makwa, Brandi Shadly, at Kimberly Huron Territory. I'll get it. I would like to write to you."

"Just address it to Old Albert at Rooney's Crossing, west of Sudbury. It'll get here if they get the train running." There was a pause. "It's all tied together, you know," Albert's face said. This was important. "The river, forest, fish, then, now, you, me, life, death. It's one big circle."

Brandi hugged the man, ignoring the odour of his unwashed body and clothes. She slipped two pieces of paper into his hand. They were drawings.

"Thank you for the stories." She turned and hurried away.

The whistle blasted a more urgent call. Brandi jogged to the bridge just as the engine crossed over and began the struggle up the grade away from the river. She swung onto the steps of the slowly moving coach and turned to wave at her friend. Albert intently dipped his line into the water. He did not turn to watch them leave.

The little train went west to Sault Ste. Marie. Brandi spent the time drawing Albert fishing beneath the dancing aspen leaves. His form was ephemeral, with the lines of the far shore passing through his body. A big

Northern Pike lay sunning in the water, eyeing the man with a speculative gaze.

Chapter Twenty-Four

Three figures made their way cautiously across the old swing bridge linking the mainland to Manitoulin Island. A guide escorted Brandi and Chester on the long walk from Espanola, now called Espy by the locals. Chester had met with the inhabitants, while Brandi managed several drawings of flamboyant locals and a wedding sketch for a happy couple. They repaid her with a wedding feast of venison, Spanish River pickerel and other delicacies. The celebration seemed long ago as the trio walked through a cold, soaking mist onto the island.

Jeff stayed with Barry Young and rode the train back home. They would be warm and comfortable, probably heading through Orangeville. Brandi shifted the weight of the Savage on her shoulder and hunkered down against the wet. She did not envy Jeff. Searching was her calling. It was not the most uncomfortable she had ever been.

Three days later, they arrived on foot in the small native community of Sheguiandah. To call any community on the island native or non-native no longer seemed to make sense. Most communities of survivors were mixed and integrated to the point of populations not being distinguishable.

Brandi visited with an Ojibwe family named Patterson. One local in Little Current had learned of Brandi's drawing skills and her mission. He told her a young boy, his nephew, had exceptional talent. The girl carried a letter of introduction to the boy's mother. Sitting in the Patterson kitchen, Brandi was not sure.

Mrs. Patterson was a pleasant, earnest woman with an enormous smile and sparkling eyes. Her hands spoke of hard work. Behind her excitement were the typical signs of the fatigue of daily living. She glanced at her brother's letter. Brandi's purpose enthused her.

"Joseph has great talent, but no one here to teach him. He tells marvellous stories and makes good drawings. We chat many times, and he tells me his dreams; he longs to do something great. Joseph wants to be a teacher like you." The woman glanced at the letter once again. "We have heard of you, Nimise Makwa. Our friends from the peninsula have told many tales. It would honour me if you took my Joseph with you."

The young boy sat on the opposite side of the big wooden table. Joseph was small and stretched his arms up to the tabletop. He appeared nervous and hopeful.

"I can carve and play the guitar and paint, and I write stories, and they call me Crow because I am so small I get picked on." The words gushed out in a torrent. Brandi smiled.

Joseph placed a small wooden carving on the table, pushing it towards the strange woman. It was a lifelike and delicate rendering of a beaver, done in cured birch wood and polished to bring out the wood's natural colour.

"This is the last one I have done. I can show you more." Brandi gently lifted the piece and turned it over in her hands. It felt fine and warm.

"I'm travelling with an Amik." Brandi smiled. "He does not look as elegant as this." She gently laid the piece back onto the table and reached down to take out a sheet of paper and a pencil. "Would you like to try my paper?" It was a bit of a test, but Nimise wanted the small boy to feel as if it were only drawing time. "How old are you, Joseph?" The boy put the pencil to paper.

"I was twelve in June." His hands raced. An unpolished but passable portrait of Brandi grew on the paper's surface. The shading was not quite right, but the work impressed. Only a few minutes had passed.

"You are young." Brandi stared at the paper. Her heart ached as she remembered herself at twelve, struggling to draw and make pleasant pictures. "I am not sure you would enjoy being so far away from here. It may be all winter and a year before you get home again. No, I think twelve is too young. Maybe next year." The boy looked devastated.

"You become a man at thirteen these days," Joe's mother said. "If he doesn't go now, he will end up chopping wood and cutting ice like the rest of us. He will work too, but he must tell our story. I bore him to tell our story and to teach. The day he was born, I ate fish. He writes too. Joseph, go get the lady one of your stories."

Joseph disappeared, reappearing with a homemade folio of birch bark and rawhide. He leafed through the contents and proudly handed a single sheet of paper to Brandi. She read the few paragraphs. Tears welled in her eyes as it told, honestly and directly, of a little boy fighting against his small stature to befriend the bigger kids. The last paragraph ended with: "I was too little to keep up, always trailing behind, but I watched the others walking and running, and I learned how to walk and run better."

She quietly handed the story back to Joseph. Brandi had decided.

"We must leave in the morning. It's important to make the crossing before the fall storms."

Joseph's mother hugged Brandi tightly in heartfelt gratitude. Joseph quietly disappeared to pack his most precious possessions.

Three days later, a small steam-powered vessel turned in from the open water to run up Hope Bay to the small settlement Brandi knew so well. They had barely passed the outer cliffs when they met a small sailing vessel tacking up the easterly wind towards the lake. As was the custom, the powered boat heaved to and let the smaller craft come alongside. With no radio communication, it was a courtesy to stop and inquire about needs. Brandi recognized John and Jane David, smiling and as friendly as ever. The pair declined any help, but they spotted Brandi at the rail.

"Come to Meaford at the end of September. There will be a big party at the condo." They both laughed at their oldest joke. "We are finally retiring for good. We're tired and can't compete with these big brutes." Waves and more smiles accompanied their departure. The steamer resumed its course up the bay.

Even though the ship had a shallow draft, it stood off the little village. Brandi was happy seeing this place and its many memories. A handful of small craft headed to the larger boat. One carried George MacDonald.

George struggled up the flimsy gangway, straining under the weight of a bag of dried fish. The ship's crew organized trade goods to lower to the tiny boats. Brandi and George hugged. She always felt healing in George's presence. Suddenly, he stiffened slightly, looking over Brandi's shoulder.

"Do you forgive me yet, George?" Chester's voice came from behind Brandi.

"I was never mad at you, beshwaji," George smiled, but looked as if he had seen a ghost from his past.

"You didn't come to the wedding." Chester's eyes twinkled.

"That's because there never was a wedding. You were too cheap." George chuckled. "Speaking of which, I'm still out two beers and a burger from the last pow wow. I expect you to even up." The men hugged. "It has been too long." They said in unison.

"I never told you I was interested in Karen." George turned to Brandi. "We were all at pow wow together. This Indian sent me for more beer and made his move when I was gone. He and Karen disappeared and left me holding three beers and a thing of fries. You caused my headache, too." He tried to glare at Chester. "It wasn't even my brand."

"You survived." Chester looked serious. "I hear you had it rough." He glanced at Brandi.

"Lots of them are gone," George responded, frowning. "We're okay now though, and the folks at the Cape, too. It's like the old legends coming true. Makes you believe in the trickster for sure." George MacDonald put his hand on Chester's shoulder. "But we are building a new future. Maybe we'll get it right this time."

"I didn't know you had children." George turned to Brandi once again. Joe Patterson pressed hard against her, homesick and shy.

"This is Joe Patterson." Brandi hugged the young boy. "He's coming with me to improve his writing and drawing. Joe will be a giingoo and a makwa. He's from the island." She did not need to explain which island.

George knelt and gazed into the boy's eyes; staring so long, the lad flinched and turned away.

"There is no end to his soul," George glanced up at Brandi. "He will hold the sacred bond even more than you, Nimise Makwa. His children will be the future."

Joe buried his face in Brandi's thigh, not comprehending the prophecy. Brandi's tear splashed onto the boy's dark hair.

"Miigwech" she whispered. "I will take great care of him." A short, urgent blast from the ship's whistle signalled the captain's impatience.

"Come down to see us on this thing." Chester hugged George once again, tapping his foot on the boat's steel deck. "Make it soon. Karen would love to see you."

"Keep some beer in the fridge." George hugged Brandi and knelt to the small boy.

"Listen to Nimise Makwa, but find your separate way. There are many paths to the high ground." His eyes teared, and he hugged the boy tightly.

The little party from Hope Bay descended to the boats as the steam winch raised the anchor. The flags on the mast stood straight out from the east, and the ship's master wanted to make Wiarton before any weather blew in. With another shrill blast, the vessel reversed away and turned tail to run back up the bay.

***

The trains began regular service to the north in the spring following my visit. Before the summer had become full, a large package addressed to Nimise Makwa arrived at Flesherton station. It was full of poems, brief stories and the history of the Spanish River, along with precious keepsakes and photographs. A small envelope contained a brief note. It read: "I have no family left, and you won my heart. I know my memories will be safe and treasured in your keeping. I will soon join the big Pike sunning in the stream. Remember me, as I dream of you in my eternity."

Signed simply, Albert.

In my life, I have had the privileged to meet many wonderful people. It's as if I have many grandfathers.

From: "Conversations with Brandi Shadly," in the "Voices of the Founders," series by Erin Thomas

The year of teaching Joseph Patterson became one of the happiest Brandi experienced. The lad's diminutive frame earned him the name "Joe Too-Little" which became a term of endearment. Joseph bore it as a badge of honour. He was the best student drawer and carver at Kimberly.

One episode made him feel "too little". It was the first time his namesake, Joseph of Longview, visited. Joseph Paterson played the guitar well. When Joseph of Longview finished playing both piano and guitar, the little boy felt insignificant. The young man from Longview hobbled over to Joe and handed him the guitar. Brandi had told him all about Joe Too-Little.

"Please play for me." He listened intently as the young Ojibwe boy tried his best, performing a tune Joseph of Longview had never heard. Joe's mentor retrieved his guitar and played the same tune, note for note, with added emotion. Joseph's strong, black fingers created sounds the Ojibwe boy had never heard before.

"You are an excellent player," the mentor told the young boy. "When Brandi and Erin finish with you, please come to Longview. I'll teach you some tricks, and we'll play together." Joe Too-Little sat in numb silence. It was the beginning of a lifelong friendship.

Joe stayed almost two years at Kimberly, finally spending a summer at Longview, helping in the fields, playing music and learning from Joseph. He made his way home as a tall young man, full of confidence and humility.

Chapter Twenty-Five

Pandora was given a beautiful box that she was ordered not to open. Consumed by a curiosity inflicted upon her by the gods, Pandora lifted the top and all the evil contained inside escaped and spread over the earth. She tried to put the evil back inside, but the whole contents had been loosed upon the earth. Only one saving grace remained inside. After all, evil had been released, only Hope remained.
From: my father's imperfect memory of the Greek myth.–Erin Thomas

While Brandi travelled south, Jeff and Chester went to Port Elgin in answer to an urgent summons.

"I've something to show you." Maurice Pasterczak, the ageing chief nuclear engineer from the inoperative generating station, sat at a long table. Papers scattered along the surface included a world map with hand-drawn arrows and many sets of charts and tables. "I have several things. When I finish, you must come out to the plant to see the rest."

"This data came from our radiation monitoring system. We got anomalous readings for several years, but we did not trust our instruments. We had no chance to re-calibrate for many years. This spring, we decided the readings are qualitatively valid, even if we can't verify the levels." He picked up a few sheets of paper and handed them to Chester. "Don't worry about the actual numbers. These are esoteric nuclear units, but look at the trend; see the monthly spikes? Each sheet covers a year. The past twelve months have the highest readings yet, but years one and four and the other years stayed higher, just no spikes."

"What does it mean?" Chester read the numbers with no understanding.

"Here are daily logs for the three years with spikes. The link is wind direction. These are for one isotope, Caesium 137. The regular spikes all correspond to the westerly or a south-westerly wind. We have," Maurice said quietly, "a power reactor failure somewhere to the south-west. I would guess California. It looks like it happened six years ago and is intermittently putting radiation into the air."

"Are we in danger?" Chester showed anger and fear. He had always hated nukes.

"Not according to our old standards," Maurice smiled in irony. "As an insider, I can tell you the standards were more wishful thinking than science. We believed if it didn't kill you right away, then it was safe. The fact is, no one knew. It's been a grand experiment on the world's species. Except for three disasters, we had no data to convert opinion to real limits."

"The radiation won't kill anyone here. God knows what it's like near the failure, but the Iodine and Xenon data seem to show a major disaster. We can't tell without mass analysis, and the lab was in Toronto. All the scientific support for the nuclear industry disappeared in the crisis."

"What else do you have?" Chester could see many papers on the table.

"We went over our data back to the beginning of the crisis." Maurice picked up three more sheets and handed them to Chester. The sheets had titles: "Plutonium" "Zirconium" and "Strontium." "These summarize sixteen years from year four to now. See the spikes of all three in year fifteen and sixteen? Here are the monthly data readings for those years." He handed two more sheets to his visitors. "There are three spikes in year fifteen with tailing off and one more spike in year sixteen." Again, Chester had to ask for an explanation.

"These are the signatures of a fusion bomb." Maurice mustered all of his engineering profession to keep from sounding hysterical. "Without detailed mass data, we can't say much more. I looked up some stuff in our library. The data suggest a Russian weapon, but I am sure the Chinese ones look the same." He pulled one more sheet from his pile of bad news, pausing as he looked it over, preparing his next words.

"We detected what looks like a lot of carbon isotopes and a mess of other stuff we can't separate. Our opinion is someone used ground burst hydrogen bombs about four or five years ago. Perhaps either their missiles failed, and they exploded on their launchers, or someone used them like land mines. We still detect a fallout tail. There might be more cancer deaths in the Great Lakes."

"That would be horrible." Chester frowned. "All we can do is pump people full of morphine and watch them die."

Unfortunately, Maurice had more news.

"I want you to come out to the plant. We have a radiation hazard of our own." He escorted Jeff and Chester out to a railway handcart. Jeff pumped the vehicle down to the generating station. They donned coveralls, breathing apparatus, and gloves.

"We don't have any radiation emissions, but the containment and storage are ageing." They walked towards a complex of low buildings beside the reactor containment structures. "We have spent fuel in large, engineered canisters. The final bundles extracted from the reactors are in the water, but the pools and canisters are deteriorating. We need to dispose of it safely before we lose electricity to run the equipment."

"How long do we have?" The enormous scale of the plant awed Chester.

"Perhaps we can keep the wind turbines running for ten years." Maurice took them into a building containing large, upright structures. "After a few years in the pools, the fuel is relatively safe, and we move the waste to these canisters, but they're full."

"So we have ten years to find a site, convince the locals to take the stuff and move it. What else do we need?" Chester tried to reduce this horror to a solvable problem.

"We can't make fancy transport containers designed years ago. We must encase small quantities of the stuff in good concrete and find a deep mine to put them in. Then we hope it doesn't leak for centuries. Poisonous residual chemicals might be a bigger threat than radiation."

Maurice made it seem like a casual conversation. He consulted a logbook. "There are about a million kilograms of spent rods and many tonnes of low-grade stuff ranging from work boots to mops. We can put it into barrels and encase them in concrete." He paused and looked at Chester with an even grimmer expression. "The two plants east of Toronto have to get rid of theirs, too." Chester gulped and looked at Jeff with panic and desperation.

"That seems like an impossible amount of concrete. We're only producing a little for building." Jeff knew they could not scale up the small Portland cement operations.

"We designed a packaging facility." Maurice seemed to think they could do it. "We'll lay a spur line to this building. As we empty a canister, we'll bring bundles from the pool. It has all cooled below safety levels. The oldest stuff is in the back and is only dangerous at close range. Our people know what they're doing. Thank God they're still here."

"We had nowhere to go." A woman technician's eyes smiled through the respirator. "Maurice, I have double-checked and so far, no hot spots." She held a radiation detector.

"When can we start?" Maurice asked.

"It can't go that fast." Chester frowned beneath his mask. "We need approval from everyone, even to start, and someone has to agree to take the stuff, or we need a Plan B to deal with it right here. The political and moral questions will take time to resolve."

The General Council summoned Maurice to Owen Sound. Shortly after, he joined a delegation to the Federation of the Great Lakes at Port Huron. Similar problems haunted old American reactors in the lake's watershed. They would bury Michigan radioactivity in local salt formations.

Ontario found a mine with railway access in the Great Lakes watershed. It would not be acceptable to put such dangerous material into someone else's drainage system, even though some wanted to find a place north of the James Bay divide. They could not build a special shaft in an ideal rock formation. This option had died amidst general opposition years before the economic collapse.

A delegation visited Sudbury to investigate old mines. They met with all the local leadership and delegations went down the Vermillion and Spanish rivers to explain the hazards and ask for permission. They overcame initial opposition with promises of food and jobs as well as providing diesel fuel for some land clearing and farm restoration, but they could not guarantee absolute safety. Maurice felt badly. No one had the full knowledge to make an informed decision. Locals would do the work directed by experts from the south.

Water filled all the mines. Fortunately, there were still a few engineering employees of the local mining companies. Their knowledge shortened the process. One mine northwest of Sudbury had a spiral roadway descending into the ground, making it more practical than trying to restore a hoist-way.

The generating stations on the Spanish River could supply electricity. Crews began installing large electric pumps and the mine sprang to life. One of the most impressive parts of the effort was the assembly of a team comprising electrical operators and linemen; mechanics and metalworkers; miners and engineers. A village grew at the mine site. It had taken over a year to repair the electrical lines and make other equipment operational.

"It's as if we're salvaging people." One leader said as he gazed at a large crowd gathered at the ceremony to start the pumps. Two trainloads of spectators came from Sudbury. There would be a gigantic party celebrating local ingenuity and effort. After two decades of despondency and struggle for survival, people felt part of a greater purpose.

No one worried about the risk to future generations. Everyone believed nuclear waste was safer at the bottom of McNeil Mine than on the shores of Lake Huron or Lake Ontario.

A lottery determined who would push the start button. After the speeches, a small dark-haired girl disappeared inside the control shack, and soon water gushed from a fifteen-centimetre pipe. The crowd roared.

The flow entered a sophisticated filtering system. A layer of larger crushed rock sat on top of a layer of virgin glacial gravel underlain with a thick bed of river-washed sand. Downstream, a layer of crushed limestone mixed with charcoal acted as a filter. Maurice hoped this arrangement would keep all pollutants in the mine water from reaching the watershed. The final stage was a large open lagoon, sized to hold at least half of the water in the mine. Engineers calculated they would pump out ten million cubic meters of water if they drained the whole mine. Bulrush plants grew in the lagoon in the hopes they would act as biological filters. Privately, the engineers believed dying bulrushes would mean the wastewater was toxic. They had no other way to test the water.

The pumps had to stop to extend the pipes and to inspect the exposed cavity for safety. Added to this was the unknown constant inflow of water. The mine records showed low seepage. The deeper the pipes went, the less efficient the pumping. It might take a year to drain the mine. Repair crews for the pumps would remain in place until they sealed the mine.

Huron Territory saw a frantic work of another sort. The safest way to move the nuclear material followed the shortest route. Barry Young and

Jim Handley built one of their last railway projects, a line from Owen Sound to Collingwood. The old rail bed ended at Meaford. Beyond that, Jim laid track on the highway right of way.

Maurice Pasterczak developed an expensive, detailed protocol for train movement. Every shipment required three trains. A leading unit, of a few gondola cars of limestone gravel, preceded the actual shipment, and a third followed with a repair crew and steam-powered lifting equipment. Maximum speed would be thirty kilometres an hour, reducing the risk of rupturing containers in a derailment. Gondola cars carried a dozen one-tonne containers, with only one-hundred cars per trip and similar trains ran from east of Toronto. Armed Huron Mounted Constabulary, commanded by Jeff Shadly, guarded the trains, dominating Jeff's life for five years.

At the Bruce nuclear station, the first shipment of high strength Portland cement came at a high cost by boat from a cement kiln in Ohio. Southern Ontario tapped food reserves and shipped steel rail from Hamilton to the uncooperative operators of the cement works.

They added lead from vehicle batteries to the concrete for radiation shielding and steel bars inserted halfway from the core to the exterior of the concrete coffins, conducting heat from nuclear decay away from the centre. Eventually, the mine would flood and dissipate the heat. A clay coating, applied at the storage site, would protect the concrete from acid in the water. One material in abundance in the Sudbury region was blue clay, leftover from the last ice age. Limestone would fill the gaps to help neutralize the water.

The details required Maurice to travel to Sudbury frequently. Drainage of the mine stopped after nine months, cut short by the inability of the pumps to lower the water level beyond a thousand-meter depth, but there were enough dry tunnels to accommodate all the radioactive containers. The first shipment headed north eighteen months after the decision to use the old mine; it signalled the beginning of years of unease for everyone.

***

"The concrete containers should last five centuries." Maurice Pasterczak was slumped in a comfortable railway coach seat opposite Brandi, his tousled grey hair creating the impression of a wild man. Much repaired wire-rimmed glasses perched lightly on his nose "We can't be certain. Such a long time lets us minimize our responsibility." He continued in his philosophical mood. "In five centuries, someone will live with the consequences of our handiwork."

"This nuclear mess has been a costly one to fix." Brandi found the elderly engineer to be a deep thinker. He reminded her of Rob Bossley.

"We had to do it," Maurice exclaimed. "Many generations will live with a threat to the Vermillion and Spanish River watersheds, all because our generation was too selfish to take ownership of the problem. Damn it!" Maurice exploded. "Our stupid, careless enthusiasm allowed the development of the nuclear industry. I've heard people call them the greedy times. Accurate, I think."

"What's the schedule now?" Brandi sketched his animated face, adding his quote about greedy times.

"Normally, we would drop the gondola cars at the mine, hook onto the empty ones and others filled with scrap for Hamilton, starting back right away, but this is our last trip. These containers hold the low-grade residue, boots, gloves and other contaminated stuff. We'll stay here for a few weeks. Once we set them into the mine, the experts, including me," his tone was deprecating, "will oversee sealing the hole. We placed the high-grade stuff so that if there was a massive failure like an earthquake, the material can't come together. I could never make a critical mass, but it could create more heat and maybe make nasty chemicals. We estimate the drifts will collapse onto the material in a few centuries but have no clue as to the exact timing. We are piling the coffins of low-grade stuff on top of each other, making a wall to protect the dangerous ones. Holes will let the water through when we flood the mine. It gets warm naturally in a deep hole like this. We don't want a thermal failure and flooding will remove the heat. We can't seal the hole in case there's a gas build-up. Best to let her breath on her own."

"Why do you men make things feminine?" Brandi asked.

"Mostly, when men are working, there are no women around. We like women, so it fills the gap." Maurice grinned.

"That's not the story I've heard." Brandi chuckled.

"Well, it's my story. I'm sticking to it." Maurice waved at Chester as he entered the car. "This is our last trip." Maurice made room for Chester.

"It's mine for sure," Chester sat. "I'm retiring."

The news startled Brandi. Chester had aged. He had been forty-two at the start of the crisis and the twenty-five years since had aged him.

"Who will take over? Will there be an election?" She finished her portrait of Maurice and started one of Chester. She had in mind a compound image across the page, showing what Chester looked like when she first met him until today and captured his aged look.

"There'll be an election." Chester peeked at Brandi's drawing and frowned. He would have to check a mirror. "I've asked your brother to stand. We need young people and no one is more experienced than Jeff is. The rest of the council is too old. Stan Gregson will step down, too." Chester sub-consciously smoothed his hair.

"Jeff has agreed," he smiled. "We must negotiate with Quebec and the hostiles south of Lake Ontario. He's up to the travel and stress."

The train lurched to a stop well short of their destination. No one paid too much attention. Gunfire suddenly erupted to the front and stirred everyone to action. Chester hurried forward to investigate. Maurice squinted out the window, watching for trouble. Brandi reached under her seat for the Savage. She hoped her brother was safe. Silence fell they heard no more shots. It reassured Brandi that only one gun had fired. After about thirty minutes, Chester returned with a relieved look.

"There was a blockade on the tracks," he sat as the train lurched forward. "One guard fired a warning. When they saw the HMC firepower, the protesters decided the shooting wasn't a good idea. The people working at the mine are concerned they'll be out of work. They had given up farming five years ago. These folks thought we would abandon them. I explained we planned a permanent group to watch the mine. There would be work for everyone, with electricity for as long as we can supply it."

The mention of the generators stirred memories of the Spanish River. Brandi made a new plan. Once they arrived at the mine and she recorded the last deposit, she would search for Old Albert. Chester, Maurice and Jeff would be busy for several weeks, allowing ample time.

Chapter Twenty-Six

My brief, fortunate encounter with Albert on the Spanish River became a nick- point in my life. It drew my attention to the crumbling shadows of the past and increased my understanding of the quiet dignity required to survive. Albert's relationship with the river and the natural world highlighted the importance of our place in nature. When I discovered his sharing and generosity with others who had not earned his gifts, I saw the living example of the attitude we must have to live as a community. Albert seemed to be the embodiment of the ideas Warren Dunne, George MacDonald, and Al Wright espoused. He must have suffered terrible personal loneliness.

From: "Deepening Roots" (The Journals of Brandi Shadly)

Hissing steam and squealing brakes announced a freight train at an unimposing level crossing. The railway station was a weathered wooden bench. A cluster of deteriorated cabins stood some distance away. Brandi swung from the cab and waved thanks to the crew.

"We'll be back in two days," the locomotive belched steam and black smoke, easing off in a shower of sparks with a dozen gondola cars of scrap. It passed out of sight through a rock-cut towards the river.

"There's no Albert around here." The middle-aged man rubbed his unkempt beard and eyed the young woman in the big hat. Gun-toting strangers made him nervous. Brandi was crestfallen. She had imagined Albert to be a well-known local character.

"Remember, Albert, who used to live over there in the woods?" A tall skinny woman spoke from her seat on the porch. "He died this spring. Old enough, he was too."

"I remember now," the man rose and leaned against a post, staring over at the railway tracks. Brandi decided he suffered from senility.

"Did Albert have any friends?" Brandi felt frustrated.

"He was a loner, didn't get close to anyone. He lived over there in the shack in those birch trees."

The woman nodded towards a small grove of trees towards the river. The white trunks contrasted with dark spruce beyond. "No one's been there since they buried him. He was good at fishing. We miss his fish."

Brandi headed toward the trees. She wondered how these lazy people survived. Perhaps the comment about the fish explained it. They mooched off more ambitious and generous friends.

"Be careful around that shack." The woman shouted. "He was weird. He's haunting the place!"

Ignoring the woman's ominous warning, Brandi picked her way through the birch copses growing from decaying, squared off stumps. Someone harvested the parent trees a few decades before. She saw the dark shape of a small cabin made of round logs. At the front was a nicely fitted door flanked by a well-crafted window divided into four small panes of glass. The log shack showed skilled workmanship with close-fitting joinery, and linseed oil-covered all the exposed wood. Compared to the weathered, decaying structures near the road, this was a wonderful cabin. A small pile of weathered wood chips lay on the ground in front of a wooden bench that rested beside the door. Brandi imagined Albert whittling in the morning sunshine.

She lifted the wooden latch-handle. The door swung silently, moving smoothly on hardwood hinges whose hand-carved pegs rode in lubricated sockets. The green canopy above the cabin muted the afternoon sunlight, deepening the interior shadows. Brandi's eyes adjusted. The one-room contained a small wood stove and a table and chair beneath the window. A handmade bed, covered in dishevelled blankets, sat against the far wall. It was where Albert died. A slight musty smell suggested a lack of use. Woodworking tools hung on another wall and fishing equipment lay across the ceiling joists. Hardwood pegs fixed into the clay chinking of the logs supported everything.

There had been no looting or salvaging. It seemed the local superstitions, and perhaps an aversion to work, had protected Albert's possessions. Amongst the fishing -gear Brandi saw the wooden pole Albert had carried years before. She sat on the maple-branch chair, remembering the stories he had told. Brandi made tracings in the light dust on the table.

Brandi spotted papers tucked onto a shelf, her letters thanking Albert for his gifts, promising to take care of them. She had sent a drawing of her and Albert sitting on the riverbank under the aspen. She found no trace of it until she explored his rough bush shirt hanging at the foot of the bed. A pocket held the neatly folded drawing, much worn from frequent handling. Smudge marks appeared to be from raindrops; Brandi realized they were tears. On the back, she found a poem written in ink with a precise hand.

> *I dreamt I had a daughter*
> *Living here with me*
> *Sharing smiles and sorrows*
> *Beneath the talking tree*

Her eyes watered. These few words conveyed such profound loneliness. She carefully folded the paper and placed it in her folio. Amongst the things he sent to her had been several pictures of a young woman with little children. A similar photograph hung above the bed.

Daughter, she stowed the photograph safely away.

Brandi wandered outside and explored the space surrounding the cabin. She found Albert's vegetable garden. It seemed to have been prepared the previous autumn but not planted. Two potato plants dominated a sunny spot. Likely, a few tubers escaped the harvest and had taken advantage of their reprieve from Albert's dinner table. Beyond the garden rested a long mound of recently dug soil with a crude cross at one end. She reached down amongst the weeds and grasped a handful of dirt, letting the cool dampness kiss her fingers and the peace caress her heart. From somewhere, a blue jay called. A chipmunk chattered its annoyance.

Albert told her he loved the river valley, and she now knew why. Thoughts of Warren surfaced. Brandi felt a special timeless unity with the world the two men represented. Even in death, these men taught her. A fish splashed in the river beyond her view. The blue jay called once more. The wind rustled birch leaves. Brandi felt an overwhelming privilege at being allowed to stand in this place. She knelt down and neatly carved a small heart onto the cross. Little feet scuttled in the leaves. A chipmunk stopped a meter away, staring expectantly into her eyes.

"Hello little fellow," the small animal did not flinch at her quiet voice. "What do you want?"

The ground squirrel sat back on its haunches, raising its forepaws. Brandi slowly reached into her pack. The little creature scuttled back a few paces but then resumed its polite pose. She withdrew an apple, cut a slice, and extended her hand. The animal cautiously took the food. Instead of hurrying away, it sat, nibbling the succulent offering. Three more pieces and then the creature took the last and hurried away toward the trees.

Albert had fed these creatures by hand. Now, his animal friends were his constant companions. Reaching into her folio, she removed the photograph and her drawing that held Albert's poem. She read the words once more, committing them to memory. Then she dug into the mound. Brandi laid the two images in the hole and covered them with warm, moist dirt. She sighed. Sunlight and shadows danced over the grave.

Albert, you will never be lonely again.

Her friend would forever rest in his beloved valley. She felt happiness.

***

The dismantling of the mining infrastructure around Sudbury had a great impact on my thinking. Seeing those carloads of scrap metal heading for the Hamilton steelworks reminded me of just how much we depended on the accrued wealth of the past, so much leftover re-melted and put to humbler uses. We all knew we were depleting the store.

From: "Deepening Roots" (The Journals of Brandi Shadly, Vol. 20, p 11)

"What are you drawing now?" Jeff leaned over to look at the paper, attracted because Brandi normally drew horizontal images. She aligned this one vertically.

"I saw this returning from the Spanish." Brandi turned the page, giving Jeff a better view.

"Yeah, we went to see that stack a couple of years ago."

Jeff reached for the paper and showed it to Chester and Maurice. The group had almost reached home. Their train had turned at the Oro junction and headed west towards Owen Sound.

The image showed the tall chimney dominating the skyline west of Sudbury. It had suffered from years of dormancy, and everyone knew it was only a matter of time before it crumbled. The stack was beyond anyone's capability to bring down in a controlled way. Brandi expressed foreboding in gloomy light and shadow. Birch trees framed the distant chimney. The tree limbs grasped at the stack, dragging it to earth. She introduced a subtle imbalance into the scene, creating a feeling of unease, reflecting her feelings about the structure and the shadow it cast over the land.

"Things from the old days are crumbling or being salvaged." Chester's mood reflected the masterful drawing. "What we aren't tearing down is falling on its own."

"We're gradually using up the leftover stuff," Jeff added. "It's harder to keep things going."

"In my racket, we depended on high-tech stuff." Maurice studied Brandi's picture. "Computers and electronics were the heart of our methods. We've kept critical components going for twenty-five years, but we have to say goodbye to more and more of it. You don't know how relieved I am to see the last of the hazardous waste buried somewhere a little safer."

"What are you going to do now?" Brandi had not been part of the discussions about the nuclear site.

"The containment is still radioactive," Maurice replied. "We need knowledgeable people watching it. Most of us plan to farm there and warn people away. It'll be a job for our kids and grandkids too. Our people have expertise in electronics, electricity and other engineering and can do metal and woodworking. We'll mentor younger folks through the Southampton campus of the HEI. These smart kids might use technology better than we did. The whole industrial infrastructure has been non-existent for years." Maurice watched Brandi finish her drawing. Her signature intrigued him. "We had already dismantled most of our ability to make stuff in North America," he went on, "and we can't rebuild any electronics industry."

"The return to horses has simplified technology." Jeff loved talking about his favourite animals. "If we can make hardened steel and iron castings, we should be good."

"At least it's mostly local," Chester added. "Sending steel produced in the bigger mills for local manufacturing would be the best arrangement."

"I am not sure maintaining industrial activity is good." Brandi had been struggling with the issue. "It makes us vulnerable. There's danger in restarting industry with all the pollution and powerful, rich people."

"Warren Dunne and I had many discussions about this." Chester had the nagging feeling Brand was correct. "Warren said this post-industrial phase, as he called it, would be necessary but unsustainable. We seem to run into shortages and insoluble problems with technology more frequently. You hit the bigger issue, though, about rich people. Powerful elites are dangerous. Industrialism strengthened it, but elitism grew from agriculture and private land ownership. Parts of the Federation are downright dictatorial. A few are what I all feudal fiefdoms. It's scary."

"What am I getting myself into?" Jeff smiled. "Maybe I should leave you on the hot seat, Chester."

"Your generation has to take over." Chester said. "You're the best candidate. Just work with others and listen to all ideas before deciding. Then lead by convincing everyone to do the right thing."

"George MacDonald keeps saying we have many paths to the high ground," Brandi packed up. "I think we must keep an open mind but follow the right principles. Warren hoped the watershed organization would prevent harm to others or the ecosystem. That should be the test of everything we do."

"Sometimes we have to shoot," Jeff and Brandi had not argued recently.

"You won't have a simple job deciding when," Brandi frowned, "just keep the trains running for longer."

As if on cue, the coach lurched to a stop at the Thornbury station. Brandi hugged everyone and stepped onto the platform, waving as the train puffed west, taking her brother away to Owen Sound.

It would be a few hours walking to Longview in the August afternoon sunshine. The journey became longer. Everyone knew Nimise, and she had to visit as she walked. A substantial entourage accompanied her beyond Clarksburg before fading away. Joseph's sisters, Hope and Grace, had been heading home, and Brandi was glad of the company. The pair had become beautiful young women. Brandi recalled the destitute little girls who had arrived so many years before and felt the passing of time.

Chapter Twenty-Seven

The harvest party the year Jeff became the leader of the Huron General Council restored me. For the first time in many years, all of my living family was together. My brother Peter, who had paired up with Joseph's mother Ellen, celebrated as if to make up for all of those years of sadness. Jeff, Jani, Brandi and Erin fit together so nicely. My grandchildren filled my heart. Little Bill, who was now a grown man and his little sister, named Maggie because Jani thought Maud too old-fashioned of a name, was a woman who looked so much like her mother. Our youngest grandson, Steven Mathew Jeffery, looked like his grandfather. I would sit looking at him, remembering those student days when Bill and I first met. The family doted on Bill and me to the point of embarrassment. They sat us in comfortable chairs and brought us everything. We couldn't keep up with the youngsters, but we enjoyed a few waltzes and even jived to impress the kids. They were rewarding us for our hard work and loyalty to Longview.
From: "Conversations with Sharon Shadly" in the "Voices of the Founders" series by Erin Thomas

"Remember the first harvest party?" Bill leaned over so Sharon could hear through the din. He squeezed her hand.

"It was as if it had been Warren and Jean's wedding reception." Sharon smiled, her eyes following the quick steps of the dancers. "It seemed to be the end of our Weyburne days and the start to building Huron."

Little Bill dancing cheek to cheek with Grace, Ellen's youngest daughter, and now a woman a few years older than her grandson, caught Sharon's attention. "Look at our grandson," she poked Bill and giggled. "I think little Gracie has him hooked."

"So, conspiring with Ellen worked." Bill was pleased.

Hope and Grace, Joseph's two sisters, were two of most hardworking and loyal members of Longview. Everyone thought they might be the most beautiful young women in the valley. Hope had a string of suitors but liked a young man in Thornbury. Bill would be sad if she left the farm, but he wanted nothing but happiness for her. Ellen and her children had suffered so much. His face clouded as he thought of the racism in pockets throughout the territory and hoped the women would see no more suffering.

"Little Bill is just like you." Sharon laughed. "If I hadn't seduced you, we never would have gotten together. He's shy and trusting. Grace loves him, Bill. They'll be fine."

Bill tried to deny it, but knew it was true. He leaned over and kissed Sharon, holding her until the music stopped. Jani, Erin and Brandi drew up chairs. Little Bill and Grace appeared with drinks, fried chicken, and potato salad. Jeff stood with Chester. Several others grouped around the pair.

"Dad's in the jackpot now." Little Bill looked in his father's direction. "Those vultures are looking for favours." Chester and several of the Councillors had come down to Heathcote specifically for the party. The hangers-on were local growers and others who wanted to curry favour with the new Chairman. They had invited themselves to the party.

Jeff seemed to handle things well. He had spent years working with Chester, starting with the negotiations with Angel and the PLM. Chester coached Jeff and was sure of his choice. As Commander of the Mounted Constabulary, Jeff had gained diplomacy and wisdom.

"When are you going to move to Owen Sound, Mom?" Little Bill knew it was inevitable his mom and dad would leave Longview.

"Not before spring." Jani's face was a mixture of sadness and happiness. "We are moving in with Jim and Sarah for a few months. Kim is moving, so there will be space."

"Do you know why Kim's moving, Brandi?" Sharon snuck a look at the stage where Joseph led the little musical band in a jazzy two-step.

"Sarah said she wanted to study medicine. I guess she's going to Meaford, or to Maxwell to be with Stephanie."

"She's coming to Longview to work with Kathy first. The excuse is, Kathy is getting old and needs to mentor someone to replace her at Longview." Sharon grinned. Everyone but Brandi seemed to be in on a joke. "She and Joseph," Sharon glanced at the stage, "are moving in together."

"That's wonderful!" Brandi said. "How did I miss it?"

"They met again when Joseph went up to Owen Sound to perform. Kim invited him to stay at the Handley's house, and they fell in love. They all used to run around, swimming and playing. The little girl and the little boy grew up but kept that baby love."

The group looked towards the stage. Kim sat below, looking up at her love. Joseph's big smile shone over her. Brandi was certain he played better than ever. All the other musicians smiled as if they knew they were part of something special.

"Joseph came to Walt about a month ago asking for advice. Walt, Willard and Warren substituted for his father, I think. He asked Walt if he thought it was a good idea. The way Walt tells it, he didn't take three seconds to say yes."

"Kim won't be going home after tonight. Jim and Sarah are coming down for the ceremony. Joseph's piano playing church lady made him into a Christian before she died. The congregation will sanctify the marriage. There'll be a party at Longview."

Sharon drew Brandi and Erin close. "We know you did it in the new tradition," she hugged them, "like Jeff and Jani. Bill and I did it, for our parents, in a church with all the trimmings."

The mention of the long-dead parents did not cause any sorrow. Memories were too sweet for sorrow to spoil the mood. The grieving had ended several years after Peter returned.

"Joseph and Kim's experience will be different. There are many people getting religion."

"Yes," Brandi had been paying attention to the growing spiritual movements, "but not all are traditional. There are some similar to those Vegans without the judgement, and some of the native spirit beliefs are spreading, filling a need that physical survival alone cannot. George MacDonald's beliefs started me thinking about it."

"Before Ron Pierce died, he asked that we bless his remains." Bill sat forward as he spoke. "An elder from the church prayed over his grave. I like to think Ron is resting better for it."

Bill had helped Ron, Roger Smith's former employee, survive the demons behind his alcoholism. The last few years of Ron's life had been happy. The man had certainly contributed to Longview.

Jeff escaped his entourage and came to hug his Mother. Maggie and Stevie appeared, and the whole family stood and hugged. Spontaneous applause erupted from the crowd. Everyone recognized the deep significance the Shadly family had for the valley. Joseph slid into a heartfelt rendition of Longing for Longview, singing the words from memory with his voice conveying deep emotion.

It was the last time the Shadly family would all be together and able to hug one another.

The spring after Jeff became head of the General Council seemed to mark a turning in my life. It was the beginning of the passing of many older friends. Since then, it seems there has been more loss and grief than happiness. These deaths are my own shadows that will go with me to eternity. Except for our love, only when I returned to Longview are new babies and the growing youngsters able to give me genuine joy.
From: "Conversations with Brandi Shadly," in the "Voices of the Founders," series by Erin Thomas

"When we try to pick out anything by itself, we find it hitched to everything else in the universe."
John Muir (an old American naturalist of the early industrial era)

The young man delivering food opened the door into Jean Bennett's little cabin, the one she had shared with Warren. He hurried to get help. Brandi was eating breakfast when he found her.

Jean sat in her wooden rocking chair, almost as if she slept. Her hand held a worn brown leather bag. Brandi's dear old friend had gone.

"I don't know what the bag is." The young man was reverent, but lacked Brandi's emotion.

"It's an old seed bag." Brandi gently removed the object from Jean's hand. She turned it over, thoughtfully, knowing it had been Warren's. A brief smile crossing Brandi's face puzzled the young man. Jean's last thoughts had been of Warren. He had died, feeling her loving hand in his; she had gone holding her love close. Brandi reached down, stroked Jean's grey hair, and finally, her tears came.

A few weeks after she lost Jean, a message came to Brandi from Hope Bay. George MacDonald had contracted pneumonia and died during the winter. Her heart broke. Another rock in her life had crumbled. She felt a growing hollow, only filled with Erin's steadfast love.

"I have to go to Hope Bay," Brandi told Erin the day following the news. "I have not seen Ermine in a while, and I cannot lose her without saying goodbye."

Niibin would make one last trip back to her birthplace. Brandi had intended to retire the little horse, but now it could wait. The filly was game as if she knew the trip's purpose. Fortunately, it was a cooler spring, and they had an easy ride. Niibin had not enjoyed sharing the road from Meaford to Owen Sound with a snorting noisy steam train, but otherwise, the pair rode easily.

"Welcome, Nimise." Ermine took the reins as Brandi dismounted. "I've missed you." The two women hugged. Brandi's old friend now truly had ermine hair.

"It has been much too long." Brandi choked.

As she approached the bay along these old familiar roads, her grief had increased. She rubbed Niibin down and, after settling her with feed and hay, asked to see George's grave. Ermine took her down to the lake. George lay under a large cedar tree within the sound of the waves from his much-loved bay, serenaded by birds frequenting the cedar branches.

"He wanted his grave here," Ermine spoke softly. "He talked about you just before he died." Ermine sobbed slightly. "He gave me this. He said this is your name." She handed Brandi a torn piece of meat wrapping paper. Brandi unfolded the paper, feeling its failing crispness.

Butcher's paper. She remembered George's words: *It is never just butchering.*

She read, "When sunlight shines through dancing leaves, do not see the shadows, but see the light. You are, Seeker of Light."

"He loved you as a daughter." Ermine had composed herself. "He remembered the little boy with you on the boat a long time ago. George said you were gathering fuel for a bright beacon for the future."

Brandi sat on a large rock watching the sunlight dance over the mound of rocks marking George's resting place. A red rock full of feldspar flickered and glowed as if his heart still beat. She knew it was an illusion; it seemed real.

"In his last words, he told me the story of when he was young and they sent him into the wilderness to learn." Ermine gazed across the bay. "His father tried to follow the old ways. Near the end of his ordeal, when he was half-crazy with loneliness and hunger, he dreamt he saw the morning star rising above the trees, so bright it cast shadows. Then, George said, a great bear stopped and looked right at him. The makwa beckoned him to follow, but fright paralysed him. It disappeared into the shadows, and the day swallowed the morning star. It filled him with great sadness and haunted him for the rest of his life until he met you." She found a seat near Brandi. "Then George beckoned me near and said: My bear returned and gave his soul to Nimise. She has carried it everywhere, and the light of the morning star has spread further than my most wonderful dreams. I have been content since that day."

"I was speechless. He smiled. George never spoke again but looked content even in his laboured breathing. He died that night."

Ermine's tears returned, and her sobs mingled with those of Nimise Makwa. They remained beside George's grave until sunset and the evening stars appeared in the sky.

Brandi lingered in the community. The nightly socializing at the fire pit invigorated her. The children who had been playing in the shadows when she first visited now sat in the circle with their tales. New young voices and laughter filled the darkness beyond. The circle remained unbroken. Brandi had new stories to tell. When she recounted her meeting with Albert and his passing, all fell silent. A young man approached her.

"The waters of that river mix with our water." He laid his hand on the older woman's shoulder and looked deeply into her eyes. "Nimise, Albert's spirit is here with us. It touches George's spirit, and they live by the water. Hear the sound of the waves." He paused. They heard the soft lapping of water onto the shore.

"The water carries their spirits and reminds us they lived and we are to remember. Their waves change the shore every time they touch it. So are we to change everyone we touch and be changed by everyone who touches us. It is our honour to the dead and those living."

Brandi looked into the young man's eyes and said, "George's spirit has found a new home."

Her quiet words ended the talking. All sat in silence until the untended fire burnt down and no longer cast shadows. Brandi would never sit in that circle again.

"This is for you." Ermine held a large piece of leather containing a detailed image done in quill, coloured and precise. On one side was Brandi's face. The opposite end was a very accurate rendering of Dodger's head and between was a representation of the Hope Bay village as it had been then. "This leather is from Dodger," Ermine said. I have worked it, so it is soft. I have had it hanging in my house for many years. We will not meet again. I want it to go home. Remember me, as I will always remember you." The women hugged. Their tears mingled.

"I love you, Ermine."

"I love you, Nimise Makwa. Carry the light far."

Brandi swung onto Niibin and climbed the hill heading home. She twisted in the saddle looking back until the turn in the overgrown trail hid her friend from view.

Chapter Twenty-Eight

We buried Maud beside Jean and Warren. She and Jean had been close, and it seemed fitting since she had no other relatives. Willard rests in the little Longview cemetery near the entranceway he and Warren built many years before. It was a growing list of losses during the first four years of Jeff's presiding over the territory. Even so, he achieved good things. Jeff helped to solidify the Great Lakes Federation and spent several weeks each summer in Port Huron participating in discussions over the protection of the lake water and security. His contribution to the latter is well known, but for me, his helping to negotiate the treaty with Quebec was the high point. For once, there seemed to be no threat of trouble anywhere in the Federation. The peace, of course, was not to last. Looking back, the birth of Jeff and Jani's granddaughter was the most important event. I still remember Jeff holding her on the Longview porch, just as he had held her father, Little Bill the day he had been born.
From: "Conversations with Brandi Shadly" in the "Voices of the Founders" series by Erin Thomas

"We have to stay focused." Jeff tried to bring the meeting back to the issue at hand. There had been frequent episodes of upheaval throughout Huron and severe fighting in parts of southern-Ontario. With reduced external threats, internal divisions had begun to surface, focused on the conflict between usufruct organization and freeholders who wanted their land to be "worth something".

The freeholders had formed a network throughout Ontario and felt strong and confident and became the biggest challenge Jeff's administration faced. The meeting erupted after learning the local freeholders had stolen the land deeds for the defunct Grey County and claimed ownership of it all, demanding their right to govern.

"The facts are," the Councillor from Owen Sound shouted, "someone broke into the archives and carted off most of the deeds. We must punish this theft and treason." There were murmurs of approval, and although Jeff agreed, he tried to remain objective.

"We need facts first, and then we can enforce the law. I have to remind you; there is no treason law, only arrest provisions to prevent violence."

"There should be a law," several members exclaimed.

"Has the HMC tracked down the deeds?" Jeff turned to J.J. Smithson, acting commander of the Constabulary. They usually did not allow armed police to attend but made an exception for this issue.

"We've traced the culprits to a farm south-west of Chatsworth. A usufruct family they forced out says armed freeholders have gathered there."

"What have you done so far?" Jeff liked J.J. and thought he would become Chief Constable.

"We are waiting for orders. There are several dangerous spots. We have a train coach of constables waiting at Saugeen Junction to either go to Durham or back this way, depending upon where the trouble starts, with a force here in the Sound. The leaders near Chatsworth concern us most."

J.J. handed his reports to the clerk. A murmur came from spectators obscured in the gloom at the back of the auditorium.

"They have committed a serious crime. To deal with them," Jeff glanced at his fellow Councillors, "we need public meetings before we send in the constables?"

"I say we get them now," a member shouted. "These people fought us from the beginning. They want it all for themselves, and they bought a few usufruct holders' support with promises of the deeds to their land. They act like the PLM. I move we order the HMC to arrest them."

"I second the motion." Another was vehement. "They've been harassing my brother down there for years."

"I have a motion and seconded," Jeff followed protocol, "discussion?"

"Here's all the discussion you need!" A shout came from the shadows followed by exploding gunshots. Jeff silently collapsed, and several other councillors fell to the floor, screaming in pain.

JJ had his handgun out and pointed before the volley had ended. He sent four quick, well-aimed bullets towards the attackers. The shooters had not considered the armed constable. Three went down, mortally wounded. A fourth shooter disappeared behind the seats. Forcing himself to keep from rushing to aid Jeff, J.J. cautiously made his way to the back of the room. The three he had shot did not move. He heard a whimper and a chair scraping just off to his right. Peering around the back of a seat, a handgun pointed in his direction. Beyond the gun, J.J. saw Will Sullivan's face, contorted by pain and anger. Blood oozed from the man's left shoulder. Sullivan had remembered his combat training and J.J.s first bullet caught him going to cover. Will's finger tightened on the trigger as the barrel of his handgun rose. J.J.s weapon spoke and Sullivan died.

J.J rushed to help Jeff, too late. Tears filled his eyes as he tried to help others. When consoling Jani and the Shadlys, he pointed out Jeff had not suffered. The bullet had penetrated his heart.

A volley of shots from outside disturbed their work. J.J. recognized the initial shot was from a rifle or shotgun. The responding volley had been from handguns, the standard semi-automatic issued to the Constabulary. In less than a minute, all was quiet. He lost a constable to the initial shot, but his guard had brought down several attackers and pursued more. The freeholders intended the attack to be the opening of an uprising.

There had been much to do after the attack. Jani rushed to the meeting hall, and J.J. stayed to comfort her as he issued a flurry of orders. Fast riders went to Longview and Paisley, the home of the second victim. The wounded went to the Owen Sound hospital, and a train dispatched to Maxwell to fetch Stephanie Hunter.

Ted Macedo in Meaford received orders to call up a security force. Everyone expected the rebels to stage a major attack. J.J established armed positions around Owen Sound and along the railways with local volunteers acting under temporary orders.

A nervous twenty-four hours passed before he deemed it safe to take care of the bodies. Bill Shadly arrived by train from Thornbury. Brandi rode a passing ore train from Flesherton to support Jani and take Jeff's body to Longview for burial.

Brandi hugged Jani as the two watched his beloved Mounted Constabulary place Jeff's coffin onto the train. The men, in full uniform, climbed into the freight car to sit with their friend and ex-commander on his sad ride home. Brandi, Jani, and Bill rode in the same coach Jeff and Brandi had shared from Sudbury five years before.

The women cried for the whole ride. The Longview clan waited with wagons for the final few kilometres. The young were sad and crying. Brandi and Jani struggled to hide their tears, trying to comfort the young ones. Little Bill hugged his mother and held her tight, riding in an open wagon. Walt, frail and shaky, insisted on driving the big Percherons pulling the wagon with the coffin. Bill rode in silence beside his friend.

"He loved Percherons," Walt said as they started. "It's fitting that they take him home."

***

With no embalming, it was important to hold funerals promptly. Many people wanted to say goodbye to Jeff, and the burial waited an extra day. The family said their farewell, then closed the coffin and stored it in the icehouse. On the morning of the funeral, it sat in the parlour of the farmhouse where friends passed to pay their respects; a grieving crowd filled the Longview courtyard on a warm, late-spring day, bright and sunny, mocking the sombre gathering.

"We'll attack south tomorrow," J.J. stood with Walt and several others. "We have them contained but need reinforcements. Ted and Helen have gathered about five hundred volunteers. We'll take the train to Chatsworth and march overland. The HMC is working its way up from Durham, so they can't escape."

"I hope you kill them all," Walt was unforgiving.

"It may come to that," J.J. Smithson fought against the shock of that terrible day. He had not killed another human before, and he was not eager to kill again. "Too many have died already. Jeff's killers are all dead. We have the bodies on ice in Owen Sound and will try to trade them for the surrender of the families."

"You're a hero," A bystander exclaimed. "You should get a medal for shooting that scum."

"I don't feel like a hero," J.J. scowled. "I feel terrible."

A commotion announced the bringing of the coffin from the house, accompanied by the Shadly family. Gracie carried Jeff's grandson. His granddaughter walked beside her mother.

There was no flag of Huron. A beautifully woven linen spread adorned the simple pine box. A thick carpet of Forget-Me-Not blooms Strewn over the top obscured the coffin. Brandi had created a new drawing of Jeff incorporating one she had made years before at the Weyburne Christmas dinner, one of him with one of his favourite Percherons, and the final part showing his swearing-in as Chairman of Huron Territory. The flowers framed the drawing centred on top of the box. Six constables carried Jeff and gently placed him on two wooden trestles at the foot of the stairs.

"Can we please come together?" Joseph's loud, clear voice sounded from the porch. "The Shadlys have asked me to conduct a service. I have religious convictions, but I know many of you do not. Jeff had a simple faith. He believed in the good of people and that honesty would prevail. No one here did not love Jeff, and no one here he did not love. He once told me, he almost did not take the Chairman's job; he just wanted to live at Longview."

Joseph's voice cracked. He paused to compose himself. "Jeff has come home for good, to sleep here amongst us, and we will feel his loving spirit, his fun, his friendship, and his strength as long as we have breath. When you touch a piece of a harness or lift a stone onto a wall or rub down a horse, remember Jeff did those chores countless times."

"If we knew someone would soon be no more, we would remember each trivial detail, each smile, each hug, each word of encouragement and each bit of sound advice. We have lost our friend, our brother, our husband, our father, our son, but we have him with us, always. The grief will pass. It will seem slow and painful. Loving memories of Jeff will mend our broken hearts."

As Joseph spoke, Walt stood at the back of the crowd softly playing Amazing Grace on his harmonica. Even to non-believers, the sweet, mournful notes comforted.

Bill stood to deliver the eulogy. He recounted many of the known facts and achievements of his son's full life and the many victories, dangerous trips he had made and returned from unharmed.

"Many years ago, a Mennonite friend told me that quiet wisdom and worth came from listening to fathers. I never knew what wisdom I should have been telling Jeff. It bothered me for years. However, the year he became Chairman, Jeff took me aside at the celebration and said the greatest thing I had ever given him was to trust him to be a man. It began when we made that first long walk to the Beaver Valley, and it grew over the years, as I had entrusted Jeff with decisions and planning at Longview.

"Life," Bill concluded, "consists of small events that add up to something big. We are proud of our son and will miss him forever."

He went to sit beside Sharon, sharing her tears. Joseph rose and taking his guitar played, singing a sombre rendition of Longing for Longview. He added a new stanza:

> *We send our sons and daughters*
> *We send them out, our best*
> *They toil in sun and shadow*
> *Til they come home to rest*

Six strong constables, four men and two women, raised the coffin to their shoulders. The Shadly family took their place behind the casket. A formation of constables, all of whom served with Jeff from Weyburne to Port Huron to the McNeil mine, formed up two abreast in front. The Longview residents fell in behind the family.

Don Hunter came from the barn, leading a large Percheron stallion and took a position beside the casket. Polished leather harness with sparkling steel hardware contrasted with the magnificent animal's dark coat that glistened and rippled in the morning sun. Jeff had trained the enthusiastic horse to harness. Without warning, the horse moved sideways and put its nose to the casket, nudged it slightly, snickered and snorted, tossing its head. The great Percheron then stood quietly.

Debbie Hunter joined her son. Stephanie was not there but in Owen Sound, fighting to save the life of one of the wounded Councillors.

The procession passed through the opening between the newer stone buildings. At the far end of the lane, a large contingent of security forces swung off the main road. Ted and Helen marched grimly at the head of the troop. They snapped to a stop at the Longview sign, beside the small graveyard, and waited for the funeral procession to arrive. Some of the troop came from Jeff's original training platoon, while others seemed to be barely adults. The old friends had tears streaming down their cheeks. All had rifles slung over their shoulders, and all the rifles pointed at the ground. In the rear, a frail Roger, crippled by arthritis, rode in a supply wagon pulled by two Belgian mares. On Helen's command, everyone doffed caps.

Almost every Longview resident had shovelled dirt to dig the grave. Two whippletrees that Jeff had made stretched across the hole. The bearers gently rested the coffin onto these supports. The troop broke rank and gathered at the graveside, surrounding the residents and family. Little Bill retrieved a sprig of flowers and Brandi's drawing. On command, four of the bearers raised the casket on two stout linen ropes while the remaining two constables removed the supports. Joseph stepped forward, and as the coffin slid from view, passing from the bright afternoon sunshine into the shadow of the grave, he sang O Danny Boy. Tears burst out from every eye.

Suddenly, Sharon leapt towards her son's disappearing coffin.

"NO! NO! NO!" she cried, reaching towards the now vacant space. Bill and Peter rushed to her and could support her as she collapsed into their arms. She lay inert in Bill's grasp. Roger brought his wagon forward, and they took her back to the house.

"Mom seems to sleep now." Brandi had come out of the house to find comfort with friends. Ted joined Brandi, seeking to heal his own broken heart.

"I should have shot Sullivan the day we captured Flesherton," his eyes flashed anger and hate, "when he murdered the guy who had surrendered."

"You couldn't," Brandi wrapped her arm around him. "You aren't like him, a murderer. Jeff would not have wanted you to murder, even now." Ted sobbed on Brandi's shoulder. Her tears burst out in response.

"At least J.J. got them all," Ted finally managed, the revenge no consolation for the heartbreak. "When we trained, it seemed like a game." Ted had composed himself slightly. "That illusion ended the first time we were at the barrier, but we seemed so strong and invincible. Jeff and I shared all those dangerous, exciting adventures. We helped each other through so many horrible memories. I love him, Brandi."

They hugged as chatter from the mourners passed around them, unheard.

***

It was not a long campaign to quell the freehold insurrection. An overwhelming force moved against the grouping of farms in the area between Chatsworth and the Saugeen River. The only shooting took place at the Sullivan property. The family turned down the offer of their son's body for surrender.

"Who murdered my brother?" A man in early middle age charged out of the large brick farmhouse brandishing a rifle at no one in particular.

The HMC contingent encircled the homestead. J.J. Smithson had approached the door to make the offer of the body only to be greeted by an expletive-rich refusal. He had just stepped back to the ranks when Will Sullivan's brother burst from the front door.

"I shot him before he could kill me." J.J. turned to him.

"You murderer," the younger Sullivan raised his rifle. A volley of bullets tore into the man. He jerked lifeless to the ground. Shots erupted from the building.

"Hold your fire!" J.J. shouted. "Children are there. Let's wait them out."

The force settled down for a siege. Two days passed with only an odd shot coming from the house. More troops joined after subduing the other rebellious families.

"I don't want to risk anyone," J.J. was adamant. "They can't have much water or food. I guess there are ten people in there."

On the fifth day of the siege, a dishevelled and somewhat confused young woman appeared at the front door holding a white flag. She stumbled, unsure, but finally reached J.J.'s position.

"Dad wants to send out the women and children," she sobbed. "Will you treat us okay? He wants to know."

"If you haven't killed or hurt people, you have no worries." With a relieved look, she turned and waved toward the house. An older woman and six younger children, all in desperate condition left the house.

"Who's in there?" Many lives were safe, but the holdouts concerned J.J.

"My husband and brother-in-law," Mrs. Sullivan slumped onto a bench. "They won't quit. You'll hang them for murder, anyway."

"They'll have a fair trial first." J.J. spat the words.

"Did you bury my sons? Can I see the graves?" To J.J. it put the whole tragic episode into perspective. This woman had lost her boys and would soon lose her husband to greed. A constable took Mrs. Sullivan to her son's grave in the apple orchard.

A shout came from the front. Smoke poured from several windows, and flames soon followed. Glass shattered from the heat and then two shots inside the inferno. The tragedy had run its course.

They allowed the fire to burn out. After two days, it cooled enough to search the rubble. The intense heat had reduced the interior to a fine ash, and only heat twisted rifle barrels gave a clue to where two men had died.

They sent captives to Owen Sound for interrogation, but most of the guilty had perished.

"I talked to the woman," Chester sat with J.J. and Ted. "She said that the planning had all happened here, and they joined with similar groups throughout Ontario. I don't know if the fight is over." Chester turned to look at the remains of the house. "The fire destroyed all the land deeds they stole. Those papers will never cause trouble again. They have reappointed me Chairman until a new council takes over with a new chairperson. We must destroy all old land deeds to prevent them from being the focus of another insurrection. At least they won't have deeds as a rallying cry. Usufruct will be universal. Before I finish my term, private land ownership will disappear from Huron."

Chester stood and gazed across the open fields.

"It'll be Jeff's last legacy. He gave his life to bring us to this last step. I am proud to have known him."

Several horses by the far wind-row, quietly grazing in the late daylight suddenly neighed, tossed their heads in the evening breeze and looked towards Chester.

***

Sharon startled awake from her traumatic sleep. Bill took her hand.

"Hello, my dear." He could barely suppress his grief.

"Oh my," Sharon sat up quickly. "It must be late. Get the kids up Bill. They'll be late for school." Shock replaced Bill's grief.

"Look around," he whispered, "do you know where you are?"

Sharon gazed about in bewilderment, but gradually recognition came to her face. She looked at Bill and when the sudden inrush of horrible memory struck; she burst into uncontrollable sobbing. Bill hugged her tightly and their sorrow mingled. At least her feelings were in reality. He had feared that she had lost touch with it all.

Bill's initial optimism soon faded. As the days and months passed, Sharon lived more and more in the past. Kathy Nelson thought the shock of Jeff's murder had released developing dementia. In Kathy's assessment, the prognosis was not good.

Over the following five years, into her seventies, Sharon sank away from reality, either living in the past or inhabiting a dream world of the present mixed with confused memories.

Jani returned to Longview shortly after the funeral. With Jeff gone, there was no reason to stay in Owen Sound. She resumed her role as mother and grandmother, taking over the position of a matriarch from Tina and Debbie, as they too weakened and could only offer wisdom. Jani's constant support kept Bill strong enough to ease his wife's final years. Sharon had been in the barn when the news of Jeff's death arrived. For the five years she lived after her son's murder, Sharon would never go to the barn.

"There's evil there," she told everyone who would listen.

"Stay away from the barn!" Sharon constantly admonished the younger children. This had been frightened and confused the little ones who found the barn to be a wonderful place. They collected eggs and fed the kid goats and lambs. Parents had to explain Sharon's behaviour. Some of the little ones did not remember Jeff, so even the explanation puzzled.

Not every day was bad. Sharon spent her better days in the kitchen cooking. Her age restricted her physical contribution.

Bill spent much of his time tending to his suffering wife. Frequently, the younger adults who had assumed operation of the village asked for his advice. The older founders of Longview had evolved into a respected trust of wisdom. Bill, Walt, Peter, Tina, and Debbie found themselves honoured at every gathering and celebration.

Sharon always sat in a place of honour, and sometimes she understood. Most of the founding children had moved away, leaving Jani to represent their generation.

Brandi often visited Longview, filling the role of advisor, supporter and Aunt. Her heart broke watching her mother decline, and she spent many hours roaming Sharon's stormy, shadow world. Brandi discovered, the hard way, she could not let her Mom see her go to the loft in the barn. One time Sharon saw her, and Brandi had spent the night calming Sharon's hysteria.

One evening, Sharon, Bill and Jani sat in the parlour, watching the fire dance in the stove. Joseph and Kim visited. He was playing soft, soothing music on the original piano Chester had given to Sharon.

"I hope Jeff gets home soon to hear this," Sharon glanced at the door. Jani sobbed. Bill reached for her hand.

"I love you, Bookkeeper."

"Yes, I have to get to the bank and do Jim's books." Sharon glanced around quickly. "Where's my briefcase?"

She lived another month before mercy took her to peace. All the family surrounded her when the end came. Sharon breathed her last in the familiar parlour of the old house. Every resident of Longview held a vigil in the courtyard, braving flurries driven on a chill November wind. Bill, Brandi, Peter and Jani had been grieving for many years. Finally, their torment ended and Sharon lay beside Jeff and her stillborn granddaughter.

"I never experienced so much grief," Peter Maki sat with all the family the evening after they buried Sharon. "When I heard about Mom and Dad, it shocked and I grieved, but it seemed easier. Sharon's hard passing gathered all my grief together. She was special and dear to me."

Brandi spent much of the next year and a half scurrying back and forth between Longview and Erin in Kimberly. She watched her father weaken. After Sharon's death, Bill lost interest in things, although he contributed labour as much as a man in his seventies could do. In late spring, a year and a half after Sharon died they found Bill lying lifeless in the laneway.

Brandi helped lower her father's body into the ground beside her mother and Jeff. Her family slept together. One day, she would join them, but she had first to honour the gift her family had given.

Brandi lingered several months at Longview after her father's death. She knew time was short and wanted to visit with old friends who would soon be passing. Brandi spent much time with her uncle, Peter. He had failed, and she suspected he suffered much more than he admitted. Kim Handley had replaced Kathy as the doctor of Longview. She told Brandy that Peter had a painful cancer of some sort. She prepared morphine, ready to ease his last days when he signalled the need.

"The old soldier is tough," she said. "He won't admit he has a hangnail."

The only other who carried the memories of Weyburne was Jani. She endured, and had found a peace Brandi could not fathom. Perhaps her children, and now her granddaughter, all living at Longview, were the source of her happiness. Brandi would talk about it with her one day soon.

With Brandi's nieces and nephew, the Lefevre children and their families, Joseph, Kim and several other refugees, Longview was a stable community of twelve families and ninety people. It was a hard world, confirmed by the graves of babies and toddlers. The younger generation had optimism Brandi's generation had lost. New sorrow forged their strength, and became part of the character of any future population.

Chapter Twenty-Nine

Once the dust had settled from the railway fiasco, I could take a train ride to Collingwood and deliver my painting of the launch of the Zephyr. It is hanging in the lunchroom at the boat works, along with several of my ink drawings. Paul is always a gracious host.
From: "Restoration" (The Journals of Brandi Shadly, Vol. 22, p 21)

Karen and Chester retired, making Erin the head of the HEI. Megan Lefevre assisted him, teaching biology and forestry. It had become customary for the friends to gather at Karen's for frequent socializing. Students considered it a great honour when invited to one of these gatherings. They respected the mentors but considered it the pinnacle of their studies to attend any function with Nimise Makwa. Brandi only criticized technique. With a student's subject and interest, she always encouraged. Brandi conveyed a caring and love that earned her the adulation of all students she mentored.

"My job is to teach you how to make paper, draw and write," she would say to new students. "It is not my role to choose your path. You must find it on your own. Then you will teach me and others."

Brandi had not left the valley for over six years. Her family suffering and grief had immobilized her, but Erin recognized the urge.

"You need to go riding," he said. "You are fifty-five years old and have not been Nimise Makwa for many years. Go, and search for the light."

"You have never ridden around eastern Georgian Bay. Perhaps they need a taste of Nimise, and she needs something new."

Karen's wisdom supported Erin's advice. "You've been riding that gelding quarter-horse Don Hunter brought down. Take him. See if he measures up to Dodger and Niibin."

"He's a beautiful horse." Brandi acknowledged. "Muffin trained Dodger, and she prepared this one for me. Don hinted they wanted to ease my grief. They named this one Shade, Shady Shadly."

She paused for a moment, allowing sad thoughts to pass. Brandi carried the last of the Shadly shadows while Little Bill led the next generations through their new challenges.

"Karen, I have so many adopted brothers and sisters," Brandi finally said, "and Muffin and Don are wonderful. Shade is a gorgeous horse and better tempered than Dodger was. I rode him to Longview and up to see Samantha, Brent and Stephanie James. Shade could take me to Lake Erie."

"Keep that trip until I can come too," Erin was listening. "We haven't had a honeymoon yet."

"I'll do the Bay route," Brandi had decided. "It will only be a few weeks and maybe get me going. I'll ride to the bay and up to The Corners. I haven't been there since we planted trees with Warren."

Warren Dunne had been gone longer than any of them had known him, but living on in wonderful, sweet memories.

Brandi headed out three days later. Shade required no coaxing, eager to be on the move. He tolerated a stop at Longview while Brandi visited with her nephews, nieces and, especially, Jani. They had grown much closer in the past few years. They were all that remained of Weyburne and shared shadows that no one else could understand.

Feelings of anticipation replaced nostalgia, as Brandi turned Shade out Longview lane toward Thornbury. She would follow the old highway east to Collingwood, then the lake road to the beach. Brandi had no plans beyond these. Eventually, she would climb the escarpment and head towards The Corners. Brandi no longer thought of the place as Weyburne.

Collingwood had reverted to a lake port with a boat building industry. The new enterprise ignored the crumbling concrete of the old shipyard and occupied a dry dock with a timber wharf near the town. The railway that Roger had blown up in the fight against the PLM brought in the material.

A wooden sailing skiff, a larger version of the boat the David's had sailed sat on the slips and beside that loomed a larger, steel boat, about two hundred tonnes dead weight. Two propellers protruded from the stern. She appeared to be unbalanced and clumsy.

"They're beauties, eh?" The voice startled Brandi. The older man gave the impression of youthful vigour.

"The steel one looks like it should fall over," Brandi glanced at the construction scene.

"Yup, she's a duck out of the water right now; she'll be a good one once we have her floating." The man extended his hand. "I'm Paul Whiting. This's my boatyard."

"I'm Brandi Shadly," she gripped his hand and felt firm honesty. "I would love to see what you're doing."

"I met you once before," he looked at her carefully. "Many years ago, you visited Rob Bossley at Hamilton. I was one engineer he mentored. We had lunch together. I'll show you around." Brandi remembered the event but could not recall Paul.

"You are Nimise Makwa," Paul grinned. "I loved the radio programmes. Are there more to come?"

"I don't know." Brandi had not seen her friend Ron in some years. "There are more tales to tell; many are sad. Ron might not want to do them, and some I am not sure I can share." Sadness crept onto her face. "The happy ones could be though. Maybe I'll see Ron soon."

Paul led Brandi to the work yard. Both hulls were complete, and workers laboured over the trim work.

"The sailor is going into the water this afternoon if you want to watch. I'll feed you lunch. The steamer will be two weeks yet. Rivet work is slow, and there's a problem with the engine mounts. Hamilton sent us some heavy bolts that weren't heat treated. If the steel is right, we'll do it ourselves; if not, we'll have to wait for new ones. The organization down there is weak, too many incompetent people climbing the ranks."

"Do you own this shipyard?" It was a large operation. Brandi could not see how this fit into the usufruct system.

"Nope, I'm just the General Manager. The railway owns the operation. The local Council gave them this site, and the locals would likely have trouble cancelling the agreement now. I've always worked for the railway, at least since the fighting stopped."

A flash of undefinable emotion passed over his face.

"Here's the heart of her." Paul led Brandi into the large shed beside the shipway. "I helped design this engine based on the principles we used for railway locomotives. It's a double-acting two-cylinder engine with thirty-centimetre pistons. At full steam, the boat will do about twenty kilometres an hour in calm water."

Brandi had no reference for the complicated machine. She only knew railway engines from the outside. "We're dismantling it to reassemble inside the boat once it's in the water. We had her running last week and fixed a few glitches. She's a beauty." Brandi decided "she's a beauty," was Paul's favourite saying.

"We'll burn anthracite in her, although, for local work, wood will do." He pointed to a small pile of black coal sparkling in the sun. "There'll be a gigantic pile of that here soon. They use it in the steelworks, and we'll get a few hundred tonnes for our ships."

Over lunch, Paul explained, to Brandi, they would use the boats for freight and passengers where railways were too expensive to build. The rim of the lakes had many settlements, and not all could have a railway. She mentioned her boat ride from Manitoulin and down the Bruce. Paul had made the trip several times.

"Those older, salvaged boats are getting dodgy. We'll bring that one here to refurbish. We plan to build a fleet of ships just like this if this design proves out."

They ate tasty meat and potatoes with the yard workers in a central dining hall. Paul ran a democratic operation. Everyone called him Paul, accompanied by much teasing about his new girlfriend. He introduced Brandi as Nimise Makwa. Some did not know her name, but several clapped and cried out.

"Draw our picture! Tell a story!"

Brandi remembered the time on the railway embankment with Jim's crew and smiled at one of her fondest memories.

Amid cheers, the little boat slid silently into the water, sending ripples into the harbour; she rode high and proud. "Zephyr", written in beautiful script adorned the bow. Brandi froze the scene in memory. She would do a painting.

"Do you see Rob Bossley?" Paul asked as Brandi swung onto Shade.

"He's retired, tending goats up at the head of the Beaver Valley. He comes down to Kimberly to play music, especially when Joseph is there."

"That's great. Maybe I'll see Rob again. Who's Joseph?"

"Joseph of Longview, he's a musician, the best I think." Brandi always smiled, remembering his beautiful music.

"I've heard of him. A few of our people play, and a couple went up there to study with him. We have a darned talented piano player, and she blames it all on him."

"See you again, Paul." Brandi squeezed her legs. Shade responded, heading into the morning light.

***

I had not looked at the picture of Susan Dunne for several years. It only came to mind again in the turmoil of that sad spring when Dad died. Jean had asked me to take care of it and dispose of it with dignity. It was a happy chance that combined her request with my traveling again.
From: "Conversations with Brandi Shadly," in the "Voices of the Founders," series by Erin Thomas

Shade and I worked our way over to the recreational beach east of Collingwood and spent an enjoyable time watching local children playing in the sand. Many people from as far as Thornbury would come to enjoy the sand. The sad remains of the days when this was a thriving tourist destination still stood behind the beach with walls crumbling in the weather.

I worked my way up the river and then took the Pine River valley to Horning's Mills. It was an amazing scene at the headwaters of the Pine River. They had restored the dam system and installed waterpower turbines for sawing logs, grinding grain and electric power. By the time I arrived, it was summer, and they could only run the turbines for a few hours a day. In August, there might be a few weeks of almost no production with the electrical generators only running in the evening to facilitate teaching. School happened in the later hours after the students' daily work. The only school holidays were at planting and harvest times.

The most delightful surprise was the discovery of "Dunne Days". I helped plant tree seedlings in the upper watershed, reforesting old fields that would be useful water catchers. Every June, after the planting and before haying began, the locals held a festival of tree planting in honour of Warren Dunne. They created a nursery to start conifers and hardwoods

*from seed making stock for planting. The celebration ended with a dance
and banquet. The strawberry crop came earlier each year, and the food
centred on that delight with wild turkey as the main course.*

*Warren had made a lasting impression on his visit to teach tree
nurturing. They had honoured him for almost two decades. I had done a
large drawing of Warren leaning on a shovel with some small seedlings at
his feet and large spruce behind him. This picture hung in the community
centre above a quote from Warren burnt into the wood.*

*"Plant different native species suited to the type of ground. Trees
evolved to live in forests, not alone. Keep the forest safe and sacred. It is
your lifeblood."*

*Each year, the water for the turbines seemed to stretch a little further
despite frequent droughts. Warren had explained how trees would help.*

*I gave art lessons to several people who will continue to record their
stories. I taught papermaking using flax and hemp. One or two of the
younger ones will come to Kimberly in autumn to learn. I found their
positive energy restorative and rode away stronger.*

From: "Restoration" (The Journals of Brandi Shadly, Vol. 22, p 78)

Shade stood quietly in the pleasant stillness of the pine grove, munching
sweet, green hay and secured to the trunk of a tall red-pine. Little breeze
reached this far into the trees. Shade answered the occasional annoying
deer fly with a vigorous swipe of his tail.

Brandi made her way through the grove towards the rock formations.
Working from vague memory, it took an hour to find the spot. Moss
covered dolomite formed a jumble of little cliffs, sinkholes and fissures,
framed by several types of fern. The rock bridge appeared suddenly. It had
been hard to see from above, but she crossed over and turned back to look.
She sat on a familiar large boulder and remembered Warren and Jean
standing on the natural arch. She savoured the memories of her friends.

Finally, she searched out dry cedar sticks, tinder and birch bark. The
highest stone in the bridge had a small natural hollow covered with green
moss and damp leaves. Brandi carefully placed kindling into the
depression, keeping a small amount of the cedar stripping in a loose ball.
She struck her flint with the back of her knife. Soon rivulets of smoke rose
from the tinder. She gently blew into it. Bright flames leapt up, and she set
the burning piece onto the pile. Brandi's shoulder bag yielded the picture

of Susan Dunne, a fading kerchief protecting shards of tobacco and a small envelope containing locks of Jean's and Warren's hair. Her right hand paused over the low flames as her left brought the old photograph to the flame, laying it gently and reverently into the fire. Flakes of tobacco followed sending sparks into the air, drawing Corrine's memory from her heart and finally, the envelope containing the hair clippings. Using a fern leaf, Brandi gently wafted the smoke into the fissure and trees, revealing streamers of sunlight penetrating the canopy.

She stared at the flames and smoke; her left hand gently moving the frond, as memories of all of those she had known flowed out. The sweet tobacco smell brought Corrine. There was no sound in the forest's stillness, and even the fire remained quiet. The light from the dancing flames reflected from the damp, grey, mossy rock and silent trees. Burning this one shadow cast light on more eternal shadows and chased them away.

In her heart, the lives of Jean, Warren and the unknowable Susan fused with the lives of the countless past generations. Their strength supported the present and the future. The flaws and errors of their lives, the shadows, passed away in the flame's light. The good of their living mattered, and as the present rolled into the future, it was the duty of the living to strengthen this foundation.

A new light would have to fall to purge the shadows of Brandi's generation. Brandi now understood what George Macdonald had meant. She needed to find new light and destroy the power of these shadows. She clearly saw her role. Brandi had mentored dozens of people like herself to travel and seek the light, to defend against returning to the past. Nimise Makwa, and her pupils, did not need to invent philosophies, ideas or rules to illuminate the people. They simply needed to reflect the light from the people and the light of all of nature.

Her work of three and a half decades flashed through her mind. Brandi saw its unity; its beauty and its truth. The honour, the duty, the call to do this work filled her with overwhelming humility. There was so much more to do. It required many more seekers of light to tell and re-tell the peoples' stories; warnings against retracing the past's shadowy path.

For the first time since Jeff had died, she felt energized and focused. Her memories flowed until the last flame died away, leaving only a small smudge of grey ash. Brandi carefully laid the fern over the spot and allowed her bittersweet feelings to make their way home.

Faint neighing from Shade brought her back to the present. She made her way up the slippery path towards her friend. Later, she drew this place with Warren and Jean standing on the bridge as they had on her first visit, but their bodies were ethereal with the forest visible through their forms. Susan smiled from the rocky ledge behind them. They were all here, resting together for eternity.

Her new mission filled Brandi with urgency; her time was short. She abandoned the plan to visit The Corners. The pair rode easily across the flat land, traversing the little branch rail line that now ran from Dundalk to Singhampton. She found the remains of the long-abandoned Maxwell barrier. Brandi had not been here since the day they fled Weyburne and re-lived the memories. Her Dad and brother had travelled here, seeking a safe-haven. She remembered the laughter when Jani revealed herself as a stowaway and the fear as they surrendered their weapons.

Some of the old cribbing remained, and pocked by bullet holes. There had been severe fighting here when the PLM attacked, the scene of casualties and sacrifice. On a boulder of fine-grained granite, someone carved a long list of names into the stone and beneath wrote, R.I.P.

So many died, she thought. *We owe so much. Rest in peace, my unknown friends. We will try to be worthy.*

Brandi contemplated the teachings of Warren and George. They indeed occupied the great loop of life that connected everything and had to be honoured. Nothing could escape this natural web, especially humans.

Chapter Thirty

One thing I learned from the ride that summer, I was too old for long-distance jaunts on horses. I returned home stiff and sore, and suffered some laughter from students and friends as I hobbled about for a few days. The Council asked me the next spring to visit other territories to survey support for a more central organization. They suggested I use the railway. I intended to leave in May, but the Council had to re-establish my open railway ticket. No one then running the railway knew me, and I had a letter attached to the yellow pass. It took a month. Things had changed since Rob Bossley was in charge.

From: "Conversations with Brandi Shadly," in the "Voices of the Founders," series by Erin Thomas

"I am glad you made it to Dad's funeral," Brandi sat on the crumbling steps of the Weyburne United Church with Matt and Brenda, enjoying the June sunshine.

"It ended a few sad years," Matt was in his sixties, about ten years older than Brandi was. "We never got up there in happier times except for the harvest party. It's great you are here." Brenda and Matt lived across the street from the church. The few residents of The Corners worked for the railway or in supplying the farms surrounding the village. A medical practitioner ran the drugstore and did dentistry.

Farms closer to the rail line concentrated on producing surpluses to ship to urban areas. As one went further away, working properties resembled Longview's self-sufficiency and producing high-value trade products.

"It seems to be quiet here," Brandi had not seen many people since her arrival the previous afternoon.

"It gets busier on train day," Brenda handed Brandi a cup of excellent, soft cider. "The farmers meet the train. We have one celebration a year at Christmas. People seem to like that and come from everywhere."

"What are you two doing now?"

"We're the constables of this crime-ridden berg," Brenda laughed. "There isn't much to do. We garden and look after our chickens and goats. We've got a couple of shiftless bums and drunks. Reverend Kevin takes care of them. We hang around the station at train time watching for troublemakers from outside. If any crooks arrived, they would take one look and hop back onto the train. We have little to steal."

"We didn't even have trouble in the Freehold Rebellion," Matt went on. "Angel eliminated all the old landowners and left no one to claim freehold. The Corners is in the Nottawasaga watershed, and usufruct has taken hold. We're self-authorized squatters. We planted most of the land in trees. The few good farms are doing great. There will be a charcoal operation once the poplar and aspen reach maturity. We think we can export about a hundred tonnes without exceeding the land's ability to replenish. There won't be any clear-cutting."

"Warren would be happy," Brandi finished her drink just as the church door opened. The hinges squealed in protest.

"Hi, Kevin," Brenda waved as the pastor descended the steps. "Do you remember Brandi Shadly?"

"I remember a young teenager," DeSantos smiled. "Now, I meet a woman. I guess we have all grown old." At fifty-six, Brandi was the youngest person on the steps.

"How's your family?" No one had told Brandi that Kevin lost his family. The flash of grief on the pastor's face said it all. "I'm sorry." She was rarely embarrassed.

"I'm past grieving," Kevin smiled. "Come in and let me tell you about it." Matt and Brenda declined, needing to take care of their urban farm.

"Just come in when you are ready," Brandi was staying in their modest house. "If we're in bed, don't feel we're insulted."

The pair headed across the street petting the goats eating weeds and grass on the thoroughfare.

"I see you've changed the name of the church." Brandi examined a hand-painted sign affixed to the crumbling brickwork. It read, "The Church of Atonement."

"Yes, I returned just before Al Wright died. He bequeathed the place to me. While Ester lived, I followed the United Church liturgy, even though I found it stifling. When she went, I changed the services and the name. There's no more United Church of Canada, not even a Canada." His voice had no hint of sadness.

The two passed through the sanctuary into the back rooms. Kevin had a small apartment with a cookstove in the kitchen. A door led to a bedroom. He made an omelette with homemade chutney and steamed asparagus followed by Asian tea.

"I'll start at the beginning," he refilled the teacups.

"Shortly after you fled, Angel and his buddies became brutal. Al and I tried to keep a low profile and give moral and ethical support to our congregations. Angel wanted more. He rounded up every able-bodied person to fight or work on the estate lands. He had taken over the best land; slaves and his allies farmed it. I was young enough to go to the army. They took my wife and children to work in the fields. I have no way of knowing." Kevin paused. Brandi sat quietly. She knew his heart in this.

"Anyway, I was lucky. I arrived at the front at a lull in the fighting. The PLM was trying to clean up the gangs in Toronto and had no massive opposition. Even the fight with the North York outfit ended before they needed my group. One of the self-entitled commanders thought he was important enough to have a servant-slave. He picked me. They didn't treat me well, but no one shot at me. I carried baggage, polished shoes, that sort of thing. As things quieted down, they tried to align with the military in Ottawa. A rival murdered the guy who owned me and took over his possessions, which included me, his soldiers and my ex-owner's wife; lots of that sort of thing going on. A power struggle followed, and the faction my new owner supported won out. That meant the end of peace too."

They came up with the plan of rebuilding railroads and tried to provide freebies to the population. I guess fear only went so far, and they wanted to get mass support. Their perversion of Christianity disgusted me. The plan put people to work making steel, and they needed raw material. We moved to Orangeville following the railway. It frustrated me not being able to look for my family, but I felt safer than in Toronto."

Brandi helped with the cleanup and dishes, taking the dishpan of water and throwing it into the vegetable garden.

"When they tried to attack Huron," Kevin continued, "Things tensed up. The lights going out ended the entire show. Suddenly, everyone was angry, and rebellion broke out everywhere. They rushed troops to the GTA, but we stayed put in Orangeville and manhandled railway freight. I worked hard as a prisoner for several years. My status seemed to have changed from a slave servant to merely a slave. Fortunately, they needed us healthy so provided enough food. Troops from Huron arrived and set us free. Several years later, I came up here, walked all night. We searched everywhere and asked everyone, but my family had disappeared. Everyone we asked denied knowing anything. I'd like to know the truth."

Brandi was sympathetic. Her uncle had provided the sad news about her family, but many families had no news. The common situation often raised a passing sadness with the ageing survivors of the collapse.

"Why do you call it the Church of Atonement?"

"Once my search gave way to resignation, I became angry. My anger and hatred drew me from what my faith taught me. I even spit on one of Angel's former goons. It was unacceptable." Kevin struggled to express his shame at his weakness of faith.

"I sought a way back to my faith. I needed to forgive those who might have murdered my family." Kevin punched a fist into his opposite hand remembering his anger and frustration. He paused for a second and closed his eyes, seeking forgiveness.

"One day, as I prayed, it came to me; I had to forgive them and help the former fascists accept forgiveness. We all needed to atone for our sins." Kevin made a fresh pot of tea.

"I painted the sign that afternoon. Some already attended services, but I had been snubbing them. I changed and knew I could not help them until I forgave them; until I forgave myself. By the time the sign was dry I had forgiven. I felt free. I changed, and it was noticeable. Soon, we had a prayer group going, and these tough men and women would pray and cry. Many would beg me to forgive them. I already had. I heard many confessions of horrible things. None of them knew about my family. It took constant prayer to survive. After listening to people's stories of loss, I saw things in perspective. They were victims as much as they were villains. I think, in fascism, most people are both."

Kevin smiled as if he had just thought of a new truth. Brandi remembered Will Sullivan and his family. Could she ever forgive them? The enormity of Kevin DeSantos' effort hit her hard, deep into her being. *How can I? Do I need to?* The questions brought great unease.

"The congregation grew, and we have the families of these former oppressors, local girls who became their wives, innocent children and now grandchildren. Most have moved to rural properties, but come in for services. I see those innocent little ones and know I did the right thing, but I cry in fear that a new fascist horror might catch them. I pray about it every day."

The hour had grown late. Brandi wanted to be on the morning train. She hugged Kevin and promised to stop again. He let her out and smiled as she descended the steps. It was a clear night with a full moon high in the sky. When she reached the roadway, Brandi turned to wave and saw the most extraordinary thing. Kevin had disappeared inside, but the words, The Church of Atonement, painted white, glowed in the moonlight, burning from the wall. A new light shone onto her path.

There are many paths to the high ground. Brandi thought. *Kevin DeSantos walks one of them.*

***

The night I talked with Kevin DeSantos I had a dream. The result was my painting of a person, me actually, climbing a steep, shady and rocky path towards the top of a high hill with a brilliant full moon hanging above. I sketched the memory on the three-hour train ride to Oakville and then did the painting the following winter. Some say it is one of my best works. To me, it sums up what George Macdonald first told me. Kevin's story illuminated another of those paths to wisdom and reminded me all paths are hard.

From: "Conversations with Brandi Shadly," in the "Voices of the Founders," series by Erin Thomas

Brandi pushed through the front door to the radio station searching for her friend Ron. The walk from the Oakville railway station was easy, but the weight of her pack told. She intended to be away for two months and packed the minimum, including smaller sheets of paper. The requirements for personal hygiene and food added extra weight.

"Can I help you?" The man behind the desk snarled.

"I'm looking for Ron Prendergast. He's not expecting me."

The man called a young boy who ran off to fetch Ron. Brandi sat on a hard wooden chair, lowering her backpack to the dusty floor. The guard eyed her with suspicious interest. Ron appeared and introduced her to the guard, who had her sign a registry and gave her a dilapidated visitor's tag with a broken spring clip. Brandi stuck the object into her shirt pocket. The guard seemed satisfied. Ron ushered her into a familiar office.

"Things have changed," Brandi observed, "but not an improvement."

"The railway runs things," Ron frowned. "It's corporate."

"The name tag seems silly," Brandi laughed.

"Yes, but they are very serious about it. When you leave, pretend you forgot the tag."

They talked about old times, and Brandi filled him in on all of her grief and sadness. He took some notes of a few of her stories. "I would love to do some more tales of Nimise Makwa," Ron was subdued, "but I couldn't do them as honestly. I have bosses above me now, and they have to approve every programme. Once, I asked about rerunning the recordings of your series. One of them said, 'That woman sounds dangerous.' I asked him what he meant, but he never replied. You are too free and uncontrolled. It scares them. One positive thing," he went on. "They pay us in railway script. It lets me buy everything I need and not have to do much gardening. I've even let my chickens go."

"That makes you vulnerable, less self-sufficient." It shocked Brandi. "Railway script is getting to be a bigger deal up our way too. I have some in case I need it. I've stayed with friends but will need to rent rooms."

"It is useful," Ron rose and put on a light cotton jacket. "They accept script in Ontario, with a reciprocal agreement beyond the Niagara River. You should be okay there."

"I'm planning to go through Ohio and Michigan and head to Manitoulin Island. I don't know anyone until Port Huron so the money will be handy."

"Just hide it from view. Don't let anyone think you have any. You can stay overnight. Diana will be happy to see you." They returned to the front where Brandi signed out. As Ron suggested, she turned as if to leave.

"Where is my tag?" The man rose to his feet, shouting.

"I am sorry, I forgot." Brandi returned the tag. They went out, laughing at such hostile formality, but it nagged at the back of Brandi's mind.

Brandi left Ron's house after breakfast. A short train ride brought her into Hamilton, passing a much larger industrial complex than she remembered. Brandi wandered from the railway station to the gated steel-works but could not enter. Reluctantly, she turned toward the waterfront. The mill spewed evil-smelling smoke, and a multicoloured sheen covered the murky harbour water. She could see the impressive array of towers and chimneys of a new oil refinery at the top of the bay.

Jeff's negotiated peace with Quebec had resulted in a steady flow of crude oil from the east. Someone, somewhere, was shipping oil by sea and from Cornwall by rail. Petroleum products paid for coal from the south. Brandi recoiled at the ugly consequences for Hamilton.

Eager to leave this obnoxious environment, she headed to the small passenger terminal on the channel opposite the massive road bridge over the harbour entrance. The lofty structure was red with rust, supported by crumbling concrete peers. The structure might collapse, but plans were in place to dismantle the thing and recycle the steel.

The railway ran the boat service on Lake Ontario. Brandi's pass withstood scrutiny. She shared the vessel with a few travellers, crates of live animals, bags of grain, cut lumber and steel products. This ship serviced small ports along the lake. The steam-horn blasted three short signals, the lines slipped, and the boat eased away from the wharf. It glided smoothly through the harbour. As it picked up speed, Brandi felt a distinct vibration. The ship was new; the same size as the one Brandi had seen on the slips in Collingwood, but the unbalanced shaft and propeller caused vibration and made for an unpleasant trip. They reached Niagara-on-the-Lake at the mouth of the Niagara River and tied up for the night. The next day, the boat would steam to Rochester, profiting from the more peaceful relationship with the North-Eastern Territory. Brandi slept on the ship's upper deck.

She happily parted ways with the vessel in the early morning, making her way to an inn where a railway dollar purchased an excellent breakfast of bacon, eggs, thick fried bread and maple syrup. The settlement attracted railway managers and had several well-appointed inns.

Two more railway dollars bought a ride up to the falls. The friendly driver enjoyed guiding his freight wagon behind a pair of matched Belgium mares. The sturdy horses easily drew a load of wine-casks.

"Those dollars are handy," He accepted the script as the horses eased along. "Folks would rather have them than barter. People don't trust like before. Everything here is cheap, paid for in the script. The railway subsidizes it all."

"Breakfast seemed a bargain," Brandi had enjoyed the meal and the friendly atmosphere of the dining room.

"It ain't all rosy back there," The man nodded over his shoulder. "Them rooms have permanent residents, young ladies you might say. Oh, I'm sorry," he thought he had spoken out of turn. "Hope I didn't offend you."

"There's a bit of that everywhere," Brandi smiled. "It's fancier and more organized here. There's always trade for sex." It was the man's turn to be uncomfortable. He blushed.

"The PLM encouraged it. There seems to be an imbalance, creating prostitution. Not enough sex to go around." She laughed.

"Well, I got my woman, and that's lots for me." The man became uncomfortable and sorry he had raised the issue.

"Up our way, we just make sure that it hurts no one, especially the women or any kids. Otherwise, it isn't anyone's concern. Most folks have mates, sometimes the same sex. If a mate dies, the others usually remarry quickly, and vice versa. No one can survive just living on their own. Women outnumber men, and it has caused a few problems, a little mate poaching you might say. Under our system, it's hard if a couple splits up. There's no property to divide up. Both usually end up having to take their possessions and leave."

"If they are part of a little community like mine, they may stay living separately as long as they don't fight. Most folks know it would be better to work out problems and don't split. We had one murder-suicide though." The memory saddened her. Jeff had investigated the tragedy out past Priceville.

"A lot more shenanigans happen around here," the driver stopped under a grove of trees to rest the horses. He climbed down with a water bucket and Brandi followed. "This money seems to encourage people to try to get more, anyway they can, like those ladies. There are single men around with money and time on their hands. Opening a tavern and a brothel seems to be a pretty good bet." He patted the horses and went to check the load. "The railway and boats let people travel to where no one knows, lets them do stuff... you know." He winked at Brandi.

From all of her travels and the heartbreak she had seen over the decades, this deterioration in society saddened Brandi. People forgot the suffering and sacrifice. The sex and other issues did not bother her. Losing the trust they had sacrificed to protect concerned her more.

The rest of the ride up the river was pleasant, with her driver explaining the sights and some improvements. They converted parks to farms, and the massive hydroelectric stations produced some power.

Because of electricity, Niagara Falls had reverted to its original industrial status. Manufacturers produced electrical equipment, chemicals, and specialty materials and parts for the Eugenia power station.

The driver knew the town and brought Brandi to a quiet, "reputable" inn. In gratitude for the good company, she offered another dollar. His refusal stunned her.

"I know who you are, Nimise. You sketched on the ride, and the radio said you were travelling here. I feel privileged. Thank you for listening."

***

"Good morning, may I join you?" Brandi looked up from her notebook at a big man, a muscular stranger, under two meters tall. He looked a few years older than Brandi did, and "well used" as Walt would have said.

"Please," Brandi indicated the chair on the opposite side of her little wooden table. "There aren't too many people here this morning."

The inn's dining room was empty.

"I'm Frank Tremain," the man smiled and extended his hand, "from the other side of the river, towards Vermont."

"Brandi Shadly," she noted the firm grip. "I'm from the north of here."

"I haven't seen many women travelling alone," Frank looked over a list of breakfast offerings as the female innkeeper waited.

"A double order of eggs, bacon and toast, please, why are you wandering about?"

"You might say, I'm fact-finding," she smiled. "I'm travelling around meeting people and listening. What are you doing so far from home?"

"I am looking for an opportunity, you might say." Frank chuckled. "It's probably not a surprise to you we've gone about as far as we can on salvage and making do. Our territory includes most of the northeast, beyond Maine down to Boston and then west, up through the Mohawk Valley. We've restored some railways and phone communication, reopened the canal to Lake Erie and now want to increase trade."

Brandi guessed Frank's territory needed resources. They had shown no interest in any relationship when Jeff had been Chairman.

"My government sent me to meet with folks along the lakes to pave the way for formal talks."

Their food arrived. Brandi's modest plate of wheat cakes and maple syrup augmented by a fried chop seemed insufficient compared to Frank's enormous meal. Brandi sipped sweet, spruce tea. Frank drank expensive coffee.

"I think they would be interested in peace and security," Brandi told him between mouthfuls. "My brother tried to negotiate; the Federation couldn't find anyone to talk to."

"We've consolidated in the last five years."

Frank slathered generous amounts of butter onto his toast, with a huge spoonful of chutney on the home-fried potatoes.

"We're like the Great Lakes Federation, many local territories stretching from the northeast to western New York under the umbrella of a central council in Ticonderoga. We usually meet once a year, since it's hard to travel. Local governments are important."

"The coast from Boston south is outside our limits, but we get along with them. Most people had their fight knocked out of them, though we keep a strong central army ready." Frank deliberately portrayed strength. Brandi wondered if he bluffed or "held the cards," as Chester would put it.

"The Federation only cares about who's on our direct border." Brandi was glad she had been present at the founding. "Our only concern is with outer border security and protecting the Great Lakes water. Recently, we had some internal trouble. There's new authority to put down any violent rebellion."

"You Canadians always were kinder and gentler." Frank savoured his meal.

"Not always," Brandi thought of Jeff and the horror after the collapse.

"We have goods to trade." Frank could talk and eat at the same time. "There's a factory making smokeless gunpowder. We produce cartridges for our army. There's a cotton cloth industry over on the coast. Ships deliver raw cotton. Those clothes you are wearing look different."

Brandi wore an open woollen vest with a faded horizontal pattern of green and brown over a tawny linen shirt with heavier pants of woven hemp. Other than wrinkling, she found her uniform for the past two decades satisfactory. Poor quality dyes caused most intentional patterns to fade. People often wore clothes made from undyed material. Brandi's wide-brimmed, straw hat hung on the hook behind her; the work of Megan Lefevre who still made straw hats for gifting.

"This is hemp and linen with the wool top. We grow the fibre ourselves, and weaving and tailor businesses flourish. It's all local, although we get cotton from down the Mississippi."

"You have some steel we could use," Frank pushed his plate away, and the innkeeper quickly appeared with the bills.

"You'll have to deal with the works up in Hamilton," Brandi examined her charge, "I know nothing about it." She reached for railway script.

"I wish I could give it to you for free, Miss Shadly," the woman smiled, "but times are tough, and we don't allow the boozing and easy girls in here. We just get by." Brandi laid her money onto the table. "I hate to ask," the woman continued, "but please sign the menu?"

Brandi smiled at the pleasant woman and signed "Brandi Shadly" at the bottom of the paper. The woman looked at it uncertainly, but then she burst out. "Would you sign your other name? You honour me staying here."

Brandi added "Nimise Makwa" beneath her name with a hastily drawn apple tree. The woman reached for the money.

"Let me pay," Frank stopped the innkeeper's hand. The exchange between the two women amazed Frank Tremain. He produced a small gold wafer.

"I'll be here a few days; you can verify this is real. If it's not possible, I'll have railway script by tonight."

He would accept no protest from Brandi. She was not a suspicious person and confident in her judgement of people. Frank, in her estimation, had no ulterior motives. Their host scurried off with both prizes. Brandi retrieved her hat.

"I have a short meeting this morning with the town council," Frank wore a military-style forage cap. "Could we meet later and tour the sights? I enjoyed our conversation and would like to hear more."

This woman, who attracted admiration from the innkeeper, intrigued Frank. He needed to know the story.

"Of course," Brandi had no fixed plan. "I would like to hear more too. It's my job, you might say."

The mists from the gorge dampened everything, so Brandi headed up the hill towards the derelict casino to a drier place to sketch the panorama.

***

When Brandi and Frank Tremain returned after a day viewing the sights, a crowd waited in front of the inn.

"Are you Nimise Makwa?" A young man in a railway uniform stepped towards her.

"That's me," Brandi agreed lightly, "unless she owes you something." The crowd chuckled and stared.

"I have a letter for you." The young man smiled and handed her the letter in his left hand, extending the right one towards her as if seeking payment. Brandi reached for some script.

"Oh no, I don't want money." The messenger seemed horrified. "Please, can I shake Nimise Makwa's hand?"

His reverence shone through even as he mispronounced the Ojibwe words. Brandi shook his hand and accepted the envelope. It bore a simple address, "To Nimise Makwa, Somewhere South." She trembled, seeing Chester's handwriting, almost sure of the contents.

The address stunned Frank. Brandi was a long way from home, and yet it only took her name, a nickname, to get a letter to her without postage. The railway man wanted no payment other than the honoured handshake.

Brandi tucked the letter into her shirt. The sad news could wait; she had been expecting it. In the meantime, the gossiping innkeeper and the loose lips of the railway employee had been enough to sound the cry throughout the large town; Nimise Makwa was present. Even here, on the fringes of the Federation, an admiring crowd surrounded her.

There were requests for her signature and many questions. Proud parents asked if their talented child could bring their work to her. The people's work impressed Brandi. Sadly, many drawings mimicked Brandi's stories.

The gathering persisted until dark, when the happy hotelier brought a table and chairs with a meal for Brandi and Frank. The sizeable crowd was good for business.

"You all have wonderful talent," Brandi looked at the crowd of budding artists. "Just remember to find and draw your own stories. I'm flattered you are spreading mine, but your personal stories from your hearts will be the important ones long after I'm gone."

This reference to her future death seemed to quiet the crowd. They lingered and listened as she gave the same guidance she shared with any student. A candle arrived at her table. The innkeeper hung a lantern beside the inn door.

Brandi saw a young boy, shyly sitting against the building's stone wall, illuminated by the lamp's circle of light. He looked sad and small. She went and knelt. He clutched a small bundle of paper.

"I'm Brandi," she said. "What's your name?"

"I am Billy." The little boy replied, precisely, in a small voice. Maybe eight years old, he seemed tiny for his age and timid.

"My father's name was Bill," she said tenderly.

"So is mine," said the little boy. He smiled as if he understood the coincidence.

"What are you holding?" Her kindness flowed over him.

"I draw," he said. "Are you Nimise? I want to show Nimise." Uttering the words took all the boy's bravery.

"Show them to me." It was not a command, but a request couched in quiet assurance. "Yes, I am Nimise Makwa."

The images were small, real and honest: pictures of a playful cat; a dog scratching its ear; a tree by the falls, complete with mist rising in the sun, and a self-portrait of the little boy looking up at an enormous horse. The boy's body seemed to be one of the animal's forelegs. His technique was untutored but of high quality for such a young person. Brandi's throat tightened, her breathing laboured. She always felt this way when she came across a true, open heart.

"Are your mother and father here?" Brandi glanced around.

"It's only me," a somewhat threadbare man who might have been twenty-five stepped forward. He had lingered nearby, waiting to pounce to protect his son. Brandi rose and shook his hand.

"Can you bring him to Kimberly for me to mentor? He's too young to travel alone."

"We can't afford it," the man had tears in his eyes. "His mother died two years ago. I can only afford necessities. A train ride is out." He seemed resigned to the cruel reality of his life.

"Come with me," Brandi led them back to the table and had father and son sit with her. She reached into her folio and took out her pen, ink and two pieces of blank paper. The railway employee was still lingering in the excited crowd. She beckoned him to her.

"Do you work at the station?"

"Yes Mam," he said nervously. "I'm an apprentice station agent."

"Good," Brandi replied, "do you know what this is?"

She took out her yellow railway pass. The young man had heard of it but had not expected ever to meet Nimise Makwa. She pointed to the line that said to give her all help and courtesy and to extend that to her friends. He held the papers as if not wanting to release them.

"I'm writing a letter of travel for this man and his son. They will travel to Flesherton station on my warrant. I would appreciate it if you arranged that. It would be good if they find transfers easily."

"There will be tickets at the station." He turned to the young father. "You will only need to ask for Peter." He turned to Brandi once more, returning her documents. "My boss wanted to come and deliver your letter but couldn't. I'm glad I got to meet you. Drawing is not my strength; I write. Maybe I could send you some."

"Please do. I would love to read them." Brandi smiled. "Send it to me at Flesherton Station."

She wrote out a letter of travel, her warrant for the train. Then she inked a brief note to Erin asking him to find accommodation for the two and work for the father. She signed it with love and the picture of the apple tree. She sealed it with wax from the candle and handed it to Billy's father. "Give this to Erin Thomas at Kimberly. He'll take care of you. Leave tomorrow. I won't be home for many weeks, but they'll settle you in."

The young man rose, stunned. "Thank you. How can I repay you?"

"You already have," she looked down at Billy, "you already have."

Frank had lingered by the inn door all evening. He had accidentally stumbled upon someone important but not a political leader. Brandi, Nimise Makwa, seemed much more important. People adored her, and he doubted anyone had left this courtyard less than happy at having been in her presence. The innkeepers admired Brandi. They met her needs here with the crowd without even a request. It intrigued him.

As the crowd dispersed, he watched her stand, gathering her things, reaching into her tunic for the letter that had sparked it all. Frank did not miss the cloud passing across her face as she looked at the envelope. She had become sad as if she knew the envelope must contain bad news. They arranged to meet the next day.

Brandi reached her room by the light of a candle and softly closed the door. She laid the envelope on the little table beside the sputtering light and stared at it, wanting to control the message. Finally, she opened it. The words were few, in Chester's clean, firm hand.

Dearest Brandi,

She is gone. She asked that I tell you she loves you, and her love will wait here for you. I love her so much, and I will miss her. Megan and I held her hands, and she drifted into a peaceful sleep and did not awaken. We love you. Do not hurry back. Karen would have wanted you to finish this important job. Many times in our life, when things got hard, she would tell me there would be time enough for tears in the evening sun. Be well.

Love, Chester

Karen's heart had weakened over the winter, and she had dramatically declined before Brandi left. Even so, the tears flowed, and Brandi revisited the memories. She slept fitfully. In the morning, she realized every memory she had of Karen was a happy one. Karen had put her upon Nimise's path and guided her still.

***

Brandi finished breakfast. Frank sat opposite. Her mood was sad. In contrast to the previous day, patrons filled the dining room.

"Can we have the bill?" Frank finally caught the attention of the innkeeper as she hurried past, her arms full of plates.

"Look around," the woman stopped and laughed. "Your stay is on the house. We'll be busy for a long time feeding and lodging people in the place where Nimise Makwa slept. Our business has never been better."

She hurried off. Brandi noticed a lineup waiting at the door. While the other patrons seemed to concentrate on their food, many snuck furtive glances toward the visitors. Despite herself, Brandi blushed. It was not her, Brandi Shadly, who was the Nimise. Nimise Makwa represented an idea, the spirit, the search for the light of truth. She hoped some here understood. She and Frank made their way to the door, accompanied by murmured greetings.

"I thought we left the era of pop stars," Frank said as they passed through the crowd.

"It isn't me, really," Brandi stopped to look back at the scene, "it's the idea there's something bigger, something to feed the mind and soul, some future. Nimise Makwa seems to have become the symbol of that desire."

"I think you're modest," Frank explored the admiring faces outside the inn. "You, Brandi Shadly, have inspired something deep. I want to hear all the tales of Nimise Makwa before we part."

They walked to the railway station and arranged to cross the river by rail and west along the Erie shore with the odd road connection, all the way to Cleveland. It took the entire morning. For lunch, they found a small outdoor fire pit serving roast pork or beef, their choice, and potato drowned in cheese and the drippings from the sizzling meat. Brandi remembered the attraction Maud's Café had for the struggling people of Centreville. Good food and the good company lifted spirits.

Grieving Karen's death, Brandi hoped to have a rest in the afternoon. Once they were over the river, she doubted she would find any respite. As they arrived at the inn, a woman invited them to a theatrical performance in an amphitheatre, built years before as a tourist attraction. In summer, the stage hosted a small group of actors called, The Thundering Thespians.

The play was about Nimise Makwa and had been running for several weeks. Brandi resisted the effort to seat her in the front row, and the pair eased into the back of the stone semicircle. It reminded her of Chippewa Hill. She had attended many performances of the Truth Talker Players dramatizing the struggles of Huron. The Niagara site had a spectacular ambience. The roar of the falls and the rising mists enhanced the feeling.

They called the play, "Sister Bear", a highly fictionalized account of Brandi's first trip up the Bruce. The scene where she shot the bear portrayed her as a heroic figure stalking the animal to protect Dodger. They left out the part of her shooting her friend. The writer had loosely based the story on the radio scripts Ron had used years before, although Ron had related the true story. Brandi wondered if the truth lacked entertainment value.

Being the subject of the play embarrassed Brandi. Still, she saw it as part of the people's story, even if slightly changed. The performance ended with a solid round of applause. People filled the benches, perhaps in response to the word Nimise was in town.

"I want to introduce someone special here today," the actor portraying Brandi stepped forward. "Today, we are privileged to have Nimise Makwa in the audience. Please honour us with a few words, Brandi?"

All eyes turned, searching for Nimise Makwa. No one could locate her. They were looking for the younger Brandi. The thunderous applause diminished until the mature Brandi stood. She had seldom been the subject of such attention. One actor rushed forward and led her to the stage. For another five minutes, the applause and shouting carried on. Brandi cried in embarrassment. Finally, they allowed her to speak.

"Thank you for your wonderful welcome." More applause broke out. Deep down, this attention pleased Brandi. It also frightened her. "I enjoyed the performance, and the wonderful acting." She swept her hand towards the actors gathered beside her on the stage, giving rise to more clapping. "You made me into a heroine. I must tell you; the events were slightly different. Dodger slipped and broke his leg attempting to defend me. After killing the bear, I had to shoot my best friend, and it hurt horribly. But yes, that day began my real life's growth, and from this event Sister Bear, Nimise Makwa arose."

"I want to share one of the most valuable lessons I received from this. It was in these words from my dear friend and teacher, George MacDonald who you generously depict here." Brandi used her hand to show the actor who had portrayed George. The costume and presentation looked more like a stereotypical Iroquois warrior of times past than a modern Ojibwe leader. She doubted the audience would accept George in a red and black checked bush jacket and dirty hunting cap, as he had first stepped from the trees. Still, it did not matter in the message's context. Brandi generously neglected to mention the issue.

"George responded to my questions about his actions with these words: „It is never just butchering, Brandi. We must always respect all living things, especially when we kill them. We must honour and celebrate their life and their sacrifice for our benefit. I did not just pray for the bear's soul but honoured the life and purpose and sacrifice of the makwa'. "

"Now, every time I eat, every time I draw a breath," Brandi paused for a deep breath, "I give thanks for some sacrifice, somewhere in our natural world allowing me to live. It's the world we are part of and must honour, as George honoured the makwa."

"It blesses me seeing so many of you drawing and writing and listening, spreading your stories and those of others." She cast an inclusive look at the actors. "Knowing our story is the most important thing in building a future. A wonderful woman, my teacher and friend, believed in me many years ago. She taught me how to express my observations and feelings and to capture those of others." Brandi's eyes watered. She paused for a few seconds.

"On my travels, I've seen many broken hearts and tears, but many smiles and hearts filled with joy as well. Here in Niagara, I've met many people wanting to carry on this work, binding us all to a common purpose and caring. I believe in you all. I believe you all travel this hard road but will find some joy and laughter to lighten the way. Those of you putting this on paper, if you are honest, caring for all life, you will be Nimise Makwa, Sister Bear. Thank you for the honour of sharing with you."

The applause overwhelmed and persisted. Brandi lingered several hours. Frank slipped away, leaving her to her admirers.

It was dark when she reached the inn and ate the light meal her host had saved for her, at Frank's request. She fell into bed, exhausted in body and emotionally torn between grief and happiness. It was to be a brief night. They departed early towards the Ohio frontier.

Chapter Thirty-One

The fragmented nature of the transportation system south of Lake Erie made an impression. Frank and I walked over the gorge on The Rainbow Bridge, a strange name since the deteriorated structure did not give a happy appearance. A train from a stop near the huge generating station carried us west. The line continued until we passed through Pennsylvania.

Before we reached the Ohio boundary, the tracks ended, and we rode a horse-drawn coach. Somewhere in Ohio, we once again boarded a train but after only a few hours changed into another one. Family estates carved up the whole territory. These ran south for a long way from the lake. The largest was thousands of square kilometres. This property bordered the old urban area of Cleveland and extended much of the way south to the Ohio River. One of the railway people explained the families barely got along. We changed trains at estate boundaries.

We had not intended to stop short of the old city, but the train pulled up at a small place called Willoughby where uniformed, armed men boarded. They ordered us to go with them.

From: "Journey South" (The Journals of Brandi Shadly, Vol. 23, p 118)

"Where're you from and what's the reason for your trip?" The man stared straight into Brandi's eyes. She found it upsetting. He did not appear to be a rough character and wore a clean uniform with a gold insignia on the shoulders. He spoke quietly.

"I'm from Huron Territory, part of the Great Lakes Federation. I'm on a trip to explore other members of the Federation and hear the local views. Our Council sent me." Brandi shifted on the hard wooden chair, happy to be talking after an hour of worry.

"Who do you talk to?" The man sounded suspicious.

"Everyone and anyone," She fidgeted despite trying to appear relaxed. "I talk with leaders and ordinary people. Anyone I meet."

"Do you have any identification?" The question threw Brandi. She carried nothing resembling identification, but she had a letter of introduction and her railway pass.

"I have papers in my pocket. Can I get them for you?" She had decided not to make any sudden moves. The man wore a large revolver, and a similar man questioned Frank at the other end of the room. Armed men stood around. He nodded. She reached into her shirt. Her interrogator stared at the original yellow card.

"This lets you travel anywhere in Ontario?"

Brandi said yes. He returned the paper. She carefully read nuances in people's actions. She immediately relaxed. Returning the paper subtly suggested things would be okay.

"It must be hard remembering everything you learn." He sounded conversational, but it was a trick question.

"I draw and write notes in my journal. I have an excellent memory." Brandi allowed a little smile.

"It would explain these." Her interrogator lifted her art bag and folio onto the table. It startled Brandi. She had not seen them remove their baggage from the train.

The man leafed through Brandi's sketches. He slowly turned the pages, occasionally smiling. The series read like vacation postcards with images from The Corners to just after they entered Ohio. He stopped at one image, a sketch of the teamster on the Niagara road.

"Who's that?"

Brandi recounted the pleasant ride.

"It's good," as if he knew the driver. He laid the paper down and then suddenly asked, "How good can you shoot?"

"I can shoot a rifle." Her smile faded. "Why do you ask?" He picked up the programme from the play, Sister Bear.

"This play is about a young girl shooting a bear. It's about you, isn't it?" The man smiled at his clever deduction.

"Yes, it is," he impressed Brandi with his ability to piece it together. "How did you know?"

"My mother was Ojibwe. I know what Nimise Makwa means. And don't ask how I ended up here." He placed all of her drawings carefully back into her folio.

"What's your friend up to on this trip?" He glanced towards Frank and his interrogation.

"We met in Niagara. He's from east of Buffalo on a mission to get negotiations going with the Federation." Brandi decided lying would gain nothing. Frank had not asked her to lie. The man nodded.

"That's all for now. Would you like a drink?"

Without waiting, he beckoned the guard. In no time, Brandi was holding a glass of sweet wine, accompanied by a plate of decent cheese and sliced white bread. She was not used to white bread but enjoyed the wine and cheese. Frank's interview ended, and they sat together, waiting some time before their captors strode back into the room, smiling.

"Thank you for your patience." Brandi's interrogator was in charge. "We had to be sure you were not a threat. We've been waiting for you since yesterday. People in Niagara sent a message you had left for points west. We had to make sure you're harmless. We must keep the Colonel safe, despite himself." The man stopped short. He had said too much and to make up for his gaffe turned quickly to Frank. "I'll keep your weapon until you leave."

"I have orders to invite you to the Colonel's house. There's a wedding, and he loves to have guests. You two are exotic enough to interest him. Brandi... Frank, I'm Justin, in charge of the household guard. You'll like the Colonel." He shook their hands.

Brandi and Frank wanted to meet people and saw no reason to turn down the invitation. They realized the invitation came as a command. Their interrogation had lasted well into the night, and they tiredly followed Justin into the darkness.

***

Brandi woke after a long, relaxing sleep. She had never slept in such luxury. The hard ground of the trail had been her most common bed, although Brandi and Erin shared a stuffed mattress in Kimberly. Somewhat disoriented, she looked around the room, recalling the night's events. Justin drove them by gasoline-powered car to a large estate, explaining it had been a country club for the "well-healed". The Colonel had led a successful campaign to seize the local territory and made the place his summer estate. It was a mansion, with a large ballroom adequate for the wedding festivities and many rooms including three dining rooms and kitchens.

The house staff assumed Frank and Brandi were a couple and put them in the same suite, but Frank objected. It puzzled the servants he did not take advantage of the situation. The travellers would discover the many household affairs and dalliances. Frank and Brandi would fend off advances from both men and women.

Brandi found orange juice; fresh fruits and baked confections displayed on a serving cart, and she sipped juice when a doorbell sounded. A female servant entered suggesting a bath and soon had Brandi in a large tub of warm water and fragrant bubbles. She remembered having similar baths as a child. Dressed in a snug bathrobe, she found the woman setting out undergarments and a modest, but to Brandi rather revealing sundress. Her mind raced back, and she remembered wearing a dress to a birthday party in Weyburne before the collapse.

"I'll come to take Madam to lunch in a half-hour. It's easy to get lost in this place." The woman gave Brandi an approving glance. "I'll show you, anytime."

Left alone, she explored her rooms. Brandi had never seen such luxury. Plush carpets covered the floor, and vast windows with sheer curtains overlooked well-kept grounds. Large paintings and mirrors adorned the walls. Jenks leaned towards half-naked girls swimming in fountains. She poked her head out into the circular hallway with three closed doors and a large stairway to her right.

"Did you sleep well?" Frank looked rested.

"Very," Brandi replied, "I've never slept in such a bed."

The travellers ate lunch alone, excellent meat pie, French fries and tomato sauce, supplemented with a garden salad. After lunch, a manservant, resplendent in a stiff black suit with tails and a colourful bow tie, escorted them around the building.

"This is the guest wing." They stood in a large entrance way with stairs sweeping up to their rooms. Large wooden doors faced the staircase, and others led to a dining room, kitchen and grand hall.

"The family apartments are past the ballroom." He indicated two large closed doors. "You will dine with Colonel Jenks tonight. In the meantime, explore the grounds. If you wish to go further, ask for Justin. He will arrange a guide. If you need me, pull on the cord." The man disappeared in a flurry of self-importance.

"He's a character from an old movie." Frank laughed.

The grounds were beautiful, immaculately maintained and boring with lawns clipped short. Gardeners pruned the shrubs into strange figures Brandi did not recognize, but later someone said they were a tribute to the Colonel's dead father who had loved television cartoons.

"I like the wild jumble better," she told Frank. "We have little time to do more than plant perennials at our houses."

"I am a rough rider myself," Frank enjoyed simple living, "but the bed sure was comfy. Let's find Justin and get a tour. I can't believe this luxury exists after the horror our places went through. They looted all the mansions back home in the Berkshires."

Frank and Brandi tracked Justin down at the stables preparing a wedding honour guard mounted on matched black thoroughbreds. Polished chrome and bright-red tack complemented the sleek grooming.

"The Colonel loves the trappings of English royalty. I dispatched coaches to fetch the bride and her family from the railway station. They will arrive in royal style in an open Landau."

"Can we take horses for a tour?"

Justin provided princely quarter horses with a guide, a man in his thirties who Justin called "boy".

The novice rider slowed the more experienced tourists. Brandi gave the poor man a riding lesson as they crossed the grounds. They turned onto the grand, well-maintained front drive. The roadway exited the formidable iron gates of a stone entranceway through a high wall surrounding the estate. They traversed less grand gateways to a hedgerow that hid meaner, tree-filled country. The luxury only existed within the estate.

"This is where I live," the man proudly showed a collection of small, ramshackle houses surrounded by extensive gardens; many had clotheslines full of laundry. Chimneys showed wisps of smoke from cookstoves. Brandi imagined the oppressive conditions inside in the summer heat. The little forest screened this rude hamlet from the estate.

"How big is your family?"

"I have a small family," he said, sounding somewhat sad. "We only got six kids. Those folks over there, Pete and Marge, they got a dozen, and there are more like them. Their kids is all out working, bringing in extra." He sounded envious. "We only got two so far who do anything useful."

"Is it crowded?" Frank remained unimpressed.

"They're a mite tight." The guide seemed reluctant to complain. "We got two bedrooms. The missus and I are in one, five of the young kids in the other. The oldest boy, well he just become a man and gittin interested in girls an' all, so he's sleeping on a bed in the main room."

Brandi examined their guide. He had been born after the collapse. He knew nothing about life before. Every adult in the village was a post-collapse baby with no shadows from the lost industrial world. They knew only the existence of the village and lived new nightmares.

Despite the unkempt look, each house had unique embellishments, with fences, modest flower gardens, flags and carvings on outside walls, set off with garish colours. No matter how poor, people wanted to stand out and be special. A more elaborate structure stood up the hill, as poor looking as the others, but larger with sophisticated decorations.

"Who lives there?"

"That's the Deacon," their guide seemed respectful. "He looks after things."

"What things?" Frank had become interested.

"He leads our services on Sunday and runs the choir I sing in." The guide sounded proud. "That's our meetin' place attached tuh his house."

The small meeting hall joined to the structure made the Deacon's establishment appeared much grander.

"He reads the announcements and new rules. We never want tuh not know the rules." He whispered as if saying so broke a rule. "The Colonel has a git together for us at the start and end of summer, just tuh show he cares about us. We wouldn't want tuh miss them either, and Deacon tells us when they are. An' if we get up tuh fighting or something among us the Deacon sorts it out. He keeps it from having the Colonel tuh rule on it. If anything ever gets tuh the Colonel, we's in big trouble. He takes an extra tax from us tuh pay for the settling. Nope, we make sure the Deacon's in charge.

"The Deacon's a good guy. He grooms horses for the Colonel. I'm hoping one day tuh be a groomer too, but fur now, I know my place. The Deacon should have been the one showing you around, but they needed all the horses groomed for tomorrow. We'll be having a big git together of our own up on the front lawn to celebrate this hitchin'. Maybe the Colonel and the bride and groom will honour us by stoppin' by."

"Have you heard of these people?" Brandi took out her railway pass and the letter for the man to examine.

"I ain't ever heard of none of them," he stared at the paper as if thinking. "Maybe this one is local." He pointed at the words: "Huron Territory."

"Thank-you," Brandi said pocketing the pass, "I hope we run into them."

He seemed happy he had pleased her but had a fleeting look of frustration. Frank and Brandi exchanged glances. Few of these people could read and write. Perhaps the Deacon was the only one.

"Do the kids go to school?"

"The Deacon picks some tuh come up tuh his place for special lessons." He developed a strange look. "The good boys and girls get tuh stay and learn to read and write and stuff. The bad ones get told not tuh come back. Most of these get mad and say the Deacon's a wicked man, but they's the bad ones just causin' trouble."

"You work up at the stables," they rode on through the little village. "How are you paid? What do the others do?"

"Up tuh the big house we get tokens. One coin a day, if we do our work good." His tone hinted there might be days they did not get their pay. He showed her a small aluminum disc with fancy stamped designs. One side bore the words: "Greater Cleveland Regional Transit Authority".

At least, Brandi thought, *they reuse.*

"What can you use the tokens for?" They eased their horses past the village and relief from a horrible stench that drifted from the outdoor toilets. Brandi tried to describe the sewage composting system, but only horrified their guide. He was not open to new ideas. They came to a vast field of cattle, sheep and goats surrounded by a rough wattle fence. Young children patrolled the perimeter, keeping the animals in.

"We get tuh buy salt and tools and other things we can't make or grow. See, we grow lots of stuff." He nodded to the pasture and some plots of grain nearby. "We all own our stuff but share the pasture and hay. I got a cow, a goat and ten chickens. The Colonel only takes what he calls ten percent rent of what we grow. Not sure what percent means. The Deacon can't even explain it, but if we have ten steers, he takes one, same with the vegetables and barley. Seems percent is his fancy way of sayin' ten.

"Do you live here all year round?" Frank dismounted to get a closer look at the rich soil.

"Some do. Some of us go with the Colonel back tuh his winter place up in the hills. It's an even nicer house than this, built on the south side of a big hill, facing the sun. It's better there than in the wind and snow here. I work the coal for him, lookin' after them big drawt horses. Hope he takes my oldest boy this year. He's a big lad now and can push a coal cart. With luck, he could stay down there permanent like and take his self a wife."

They wandered through fields, orchards of apple, cherry and pear with many walnut trees. A water-driven gristmill flanked a large granary. The estate had electricity, but not the indentured labourers.

"We best be gittin' back, I was told tuh git you back before the shadows crossed the road, or else." He appeared to fear the consequences. Frank and Brandi had seen enough and willingly followed.

The servant waited to bathe Brandi and dress her for dinner, and the process produced an extremely elegant woman, a self-conscious stranger who stared back at her from the full-length mirror.

"My goodness, Miss Shadly, you will be more beautiful than the bride." Frank's tone teased, but in his eyes, she was indeed beautiful. He felt ill at ease having never attended a black-tie dinner except for military full-dress get-togethers. The servants dressed them to fit in. The Colonel had given an honour by having them attend the pre-wedding dinner but would not allow country bumpkins at his table.

The visitors sat near the foot of the massive main table that held forty people. Colonel Jenks sat at the head, his wife to his right and the bride's father, General Thoms, and his wife to his left. Jenks had never met the two travellers but made effusive remarks inventing the story they had travelled far to attend the wedding. The betrothed couple sat opposite each other. Jenks imposed a rigid ranking system of relatives and acquaintances marching down the table to the lowly visitors. Justin's presence softened their relegation. He entertained the visitors with informative conversation.

The Commander of the guard wore his full dress uniform of red serge jacket, dark trousers and polished black boots. Gold braid hung from elaborate epaulettes on his tunic. A complicated series of interwoven lines made from golden thread adorned his jacket cuffs with multicoloured ribbons celebrating fictitious battles stitched onto the tunic's left breast. The stiff collar pushed tight against his throat. A silver sabre hung from a golden sash around his waist.

"Justin, you look very, uh, elegant." Brandi giggled.

"Don't make fun of me, Miss Shadly." He tried to look scolding, but the rigid sash of braid kinked upward and bumped his chin forcing a smile. "I feel silly as hell, but the Colonel must have a hero as his guard commander. I think he stole this get up from the English royal family."

At the end of the meal, the men retired to an adjacent room while the ladies congregated in another parlour. Justin and Frank accompanied the Colonel. Frank arranged for a formal delegation to visit and discuss an alliance with Jenks. The Colonel never let socializing impede business. After the wedding, Jenks' sphere of influence would include the interests of General Thoms.

Brandi seldom experienced what she called "girly chit-chat" and found the evening less than fulfilling. She discovered Mrs. Jenks was the daughter of another landowner and had married the Colonel in an arranged union similar to her son's wedding. Her marriage doubled the Colonel's holdings and contributed to building their great wealth. Love did not factor into her union or the pending one.

As if to emphasize the lack of devotion in her marriage, the groom's mother accosted Brandi. Her host had escorted Brandi into a private chamber on the pretence of showing her family portraits and telling the family history. There were interesting memorabilia in the room. The woman made some suggestive comments and invited her guest to visit the private apartments for some nighttime fun. Brandi graciously declined; hoping wedding activity would distract the woman. Brandi decided to not stay longer than necessary. She was not a prude but feared the situation could become dangerous.

***

The wedding was a wonderfully elaborate affair. The ceremony took place in the back garden, surrounded by rose bushes and many other flowers. Someone called "The Bishop" led the formalities. He wore impressively elaborate gowns topped by a high, conical headdress with coloured braid and three bird feathers hanging down behind. His booming command of the audience reminded me of Al Wright.

An orchestra of horns and other instruments played old hymns. Everyone sang tunelessly and tentatively to unfamiliar music and words. Hymnbooks had the word Episcopal on the cover. The formalities seemed to last forever. The bride and groom looked bored, standing beneath an elaborate arbour adorned with roses and daisies.

The wedding party appeared at the worker's celebration, riding in horse-drawn coaches accompanied by the polished and prancing horse guard. Frank and I walked around the mansion to watch. A resounding cheer of adulation rose from the gathered serfs. Under the direction of the Deacon, the crowd offered an enthusiastic and joyful song.

"Subservient peasants," Frank muttered to me in disgust.

A photographer recorded the celebration using a large view camera. He took a picture of Frank and me in front of the guards' horses.

Justin had told the Colonel I was a good drawer. Jenks approached me at the party to ask for a drawing of the event. He drunkenly fondled me and made some lewd suggestions. I laughed him off and promised I would leave a drawing for him, and no, not of me naked. I left him my sketch of the previous night's dinner with the hosts appearing regal. The drawing I made later shows them as dangerous, decadent people. I resolved to remain sober and took a moment with Frank to make sure he did the same.

To say we dashed for it would be an exaggeration. The next day the entire court was hungover and sleeping off the effects of the revelry. Justin escorted us to the station along with our possessions. Our usefulness as a show piece was done. The Colonel gave us both beautiful suede-leather, hunting outfits. I don't believe we were ever in danger, but I was glad to be leaving.

From: "Journey South" (The Journals of Brandi Shadly, Vol. 23, p 156)

During the conversation, I told Colonel Jenks we seldom had weddings in our territory since there was no property to divide or gain. I mentioned, if people had religious faith, they would have an elder or pastor sanctify the marriage, and the closest we came to a formal marriage would be the *joining party, with words spoken by someone of stature in the community telling the couple they were worthy of each other. This "populist nonsense" shocked and upset the Colonel.*

From: "Conversations with Brandi Shadly," in the "Voices of the Founders," series by Erin Thomas

"You won't be in trouble for letting us leave will you?" Brandi wanted to get away quickly, but she would not sleep well if she thought Justin would suffer.

"Don't worry, Miss Shadly." Justin smiled as he shook her hand. "The Colonel thinks your ideas are dangerous and wants you gone. He likes me, and so does the missus. I monitor her for him and report what she's up to, so he depends on me. Not that he cares; he just doesn't want some lover to suddenly become a danger. Neither cares about the marriage. I saw the old boy grab you last night. Of course, I don't tell the Colonel everything about what she's up to." Justin winked at her.

"Nimise," he seemed slightly embarrassed, "Can I keep this, and please sign it?" Justin held out the programme from Sister Bear. Brandi added her name and the apple tree to the cover.

Brandi and Frank boarded the next train for the short ride into the City of Cleveland. Neither of them had a clue where to get off, but when they saw the harbour, they decided it would be the best place. Brandi noticed Frank patting his waist through his new jacket. Justin had returned his handgun. She seldom feared, but this might be the most uncertain she had felt in many years. No one here would have heard of Nimise Makwa.

The harbour had reborn as a working enterprise dominated by warehouses for transferring goods between the railway and the boats. Diminutive lake vessels floated at the pier. The place had a feel of purposefulness. Railroad cars loaded with coal rested on a siding. Powerful men, stripped to their waists and covered in black dust lifted coal bags onto heavy wagons. Mule teams drew these into town or to the pier. The travellers' sojourn in luxury now submitted to the reality of ordinary people.

"We need a safe place to stay," Frank hoped to spot an inn. Nothing seemed to be an obvious public house. "I want to find the leaders. Let's ask over at the docks. That's where the action is."

They walked towards the wharf where masts and bridge works poked above the concrete and approached the warehouses through an unguarded gate. Signs said "The Guild" protected the site. A graphic of a clenched fist emphasized the warning.

No one challenged them as they dodged workers and handcarts hurrying between the boats and the buildings. Brandi took a seat on a rusty steel bollard, too large for the small vessels bumping gently against wooden fenders. One particular boat attracted her as she sat opposite its bridge. Workers lowered cargo to the boat's deck.

An elderly black man paced the bridge deck, directing the work, and two other black men, one middle-aged and the other perhaps in his twenties toiled on the steel deck, accepting bags and boxes. A labourer lost control of a large bale of cotton, dropping the heavy load the few meters onto the boat. The large heavy bundle bounced wildly, knocking the younger deckhand against a bulkhead. He gasped in surprise and pain.

"Are you okay, Donnie?" The old man in charge called down. Brandi's eyes snapped up to look at the speaker. The voice seemed familiar.

"Hey mister," she called out.

"What do you want, lady? I ain't buying even though you look like you don't cost much."

"I'm not selling," Brandi ignored the insult. "Have you ever been to Port Stanley, on the other side?" She tried smiling at the fellow.

"Yeah, I used to live there, in another life. Are you looking for a ride?" He seemed interested in a paying fare.

"Would your name be Don?" She knew. Frank came to her side now, used to Brandi's puzzling behaviour. The black man leaned on the railing, staring as if trying to remember.

"Do I know you?" He removed his sea cap and rubbed his head.

"I drew pictures and rode a painted pony." Don had teased her with his version of the old song.

"What the hell are you doing here?" He grinned, and for an old man moved down the ship's gangway quickly, scaling the ladder to the wharf in an instant.

"Brandi!" He exclaimed. "What are you doing here? What happened to that little girl I knew? I would never have recognized you." His engulfed her in a genuine and warm hug. It had been a long time since Port Stanley on the silly, wonderful trip when she found Erin.

"You look good," she finally gasped. "and happy. You were sad then."

"I don't look good, and you know it. I found my family the year after we met." Don smiled, then a flash of sadness. "My wife passed last year. That's my oldest boy and his son Donnie on the boat. Yes, I am happy."

"Is there anywhere they don't know you?" Frank laughed at Brandi and extended his hand.

"Frank Tremain, I'm from Vermont."

Their problem of where to stay disappeared. Don and the boys took their guests home. They lived in a little community surrounded by a wall of old shipping containers, a substantial village with houses built into the steel boxes. A central square comprised treed areas with park benches and homemade playground equipment, as well as an extensive field. Younger children, none older than twelve entertained them with a lively baseball game. Don explained that at thirteen the young began contributing.

"There's a family in Cleveland that was baseball crazy before the crash. The grandfather started making baseballs and gloves by hand once the commercial stuff became hard to get. Now, the family survives making sports equipment. Baseball and soccer are the two big ones. In the winter we have ice skating and hockey. It makes us civilized and brings people together."

"I got the chance to search out my family when a pirate boat tried to raid Stanley." They were lounging on benches in front of Don's house after supper. "Those guys were tough, but I guess they got soft raiding defenceless places. The captain was, well let's just say we dealt with him. Most folks are practical. When we took over, the crew thought joining us was better than being put ashore. They were lazy and not too bright. Once we had our bearings, they got let go anyway. I became captain since I had been in the Coast Guard and knew how to manoeuvre and navigate. When we sailed back here, the city had calmed down. One gang protected my family, in exchange for work. I inherited the boat in the harbour. She's a plucky little thing as long as I can keep getting diesel for her."

"I keep telling you, Dad; we should fit her with a steam engine. There's lots of coal." Don's son had been dozing beside his father.

"You have newfangled ideas!" Don laughed at the irony. "We should get a whole new boat. Princess is about to wear out." Brandi mentioned the Collingwood shipyard. Buffalo had one, but boats were expensive.

"We're part of a group called the Privateer's Guild," Don explained.

"Grandpa was the guy who got it started." Donnie bragged. "He's the big boss of it."

"There's no boss," Don admonished him but gave him a loving look. "I'm the Chairman. Speaking of new boats, the Guild is ordering a couple for next season. Maybe I'll have a new one before I die."

"The whole damned fleet will sink before you go, Dad. You are a tough nut." Brandi enjoyed the family's good humour and intelligence.

"What happened to Cleveland? Why aren't you all Jenks' serfs?" The Great Lakes basin puzzled Frank.

"The city was a battle zone. The gangbangers went at each other, killing and fighting to the death, until the ammo ran out and they had too few fighters to carry on. They made peace, and a stable government evolved. Those guys were vicious, not stupid."

"When Jenks and others conquered their territories, the city was too violent, so they left it alone. Now, we're too strong. We control from Willoughby, where Jenks picked you up, around the lake into Michigan. We're called Erie Shores. More people like Jenks live south of here. We aligned with a few along the rail line to Cincinnati and the Ohio River to get trade goods like that cotton bale. Even Jenks trades with us."

"You saw his coal on the dock. Our fleet controls the shoreline to Erie, and we are friends with the rest. Jenks has no navy or freighters. It's a lucrative trade for him and the Erie folks take Jenks' coal up to Ontario, but he's getting weaker. You might have noticed they're a little strange. The wedding you attended was a good example. The bride and groom are second cousins. If they keep that up a few more generations, they ought to become dysfunctional enough to fall on their own. If it weren't for a few good guys like that Justin working for them, they would have already collapsed."

The evening light faded but the young ones played until they risked injury from a scuffed and dirty ball lost in the gloom. The two younger men left for home. Don yawned unashamedly. "I have to get to bed." He rose. "We're sailing at first light, heading to Leamington and Kingsville with a stop at Pelee Island. I'll show you where you can bunk down. It isn't as fancy as Jenks'."

"Show me the toilet first," Brandi looked a little agitated. "That rich food plugged me up, but your brown bread is working. I need to go."

"We do the bucket system, over there in the little house. Please use a handful of the leaf mould on top, okay?" He smiled at her predicament.

"I'm here trying to start contact between our North-Eastern Territory and others. Who would I see to set up a meeting?" Frank delayed Don's sleep.

"We have a governing council," Don considered how to handle the request. "I'll let the council know, and probably you could just show up. Winter is better when there's little to do, but maybe April before the ice is out. It's slow then. What do you want to discuss?"

"Trade, mutual peace and security," Frank showed Don his letter that explained the trip.

"Erie Shores is part of the Federation," Don looked at Frank. "You should talk to the people up at Port Huron about security issues."

"We planned to travel there. Does the railway go that way?"

"Tell you what," Don sat down, sleep temporarily forgotten. "I love that lady, Brandi, don't ask me why. Today is only the fourth day I have spent with her. I got a few tons of coal on the Princess and no buyer. Port Huron pays top dollar for coal. I'll run you up, haven't been up the river in a few years. Can you shoot a gun? There are pirates in the Detroit River."

"I have a lot of experience with guns," Frank admitted.

"Good. We'll draw something heavy from the armoury." Don stood. You go to bed. "I'll fill Brandi in on the plan."

***

Don and his family took us from Cleveland up to Port Huron. The trip was a relaxing two days. We slept on the deck and took turns on guard duty. Our first port of call was Pelee Island. We offloaded a barrel of diesel, a bag of coffee beans and a keg of cane sugar for six barrels of wine (which we all had to taste to verify its quality) and provisions for the rest of the trip. Don told me the Pelee community produced the best vegetables and bakery products. The collapse trapped an excellent chef there, and he started a tradition of food growing and preparation now entering its third generation.

The sailing was tricky with the lower lake level exposing more shoals and sandbars. A nice young woman came aboard travelling to Leamington. To pay for her passage, she gave us all haircuts. It is why my hair is shorter, and in my old age, I like it. She was to study medicine and disembarked with that helpful bale of cotton.

We stopped at the entrance to the Detroit River, and three small boats rowed out to us. Each carried a man claiming to be a river pilot. They competed with each insulting the others' abilities and claiming to be the cheapest. Don remembered one from a previous trip. The chap secured his little dinghy to the stern and clambered aboard. He wore rough farmer clothes, but for this duty added a battered sea cap with the fading words, "Great Lakes Lines", stitched into the cloth. Don handed him a pound of coffee and another of sugar. Thanks to our pilot, we never ran aground, although several times, he yanked the wheel hard, and the boat heeled over in its sudden manoeuvre.

We had some excitement at an especially narrow place where an island split the river. A small aluminum boat came off the Ontario shore. Two burly men rowed furiously while another sat in the prow brandishing a weapon. I laughed until I saw the gun and heard the snick of a weapon. Donnie aimed a light machine gun at the approaching vessel. His father was standing on the lower deck, ready with an M-16. Frank had drawn his pistol. I took cover behind the wheelhouse.

The man raised his gun, which turned out to be only a twelve-gauge shotgun, aiming it in our direction. Donnie's father fired a brief burst from his weapon into the water beside the rowboat. The oarsmen dug deep and brought the craft to a sudden stop. The armed man almost fell into the water but showed bravado, demanding we surrender. Donnie shouted they had better get back to shore before he cut their boat in two. The rowers backed away and turned tail with the shouts of the gunman berating the others for being cowards. It gave us a good laugh. Other than passing the ruins of the two great crumbling cities straddling the river, we made our way to Port Huron with no more incidents.

From: "Journey South" (The Journals of Brandi Shadly, Vol. 2. p. 201)

The Princess lay snugly tied to the wooden river pier. Don navigated from memory, put them safely in the Black River, and tied to a newer timber pier that protruded from the foundation of the crumbling concrete wharf. The usual interested crowd gathered, and Don searched for trading customers.

"Frank, the Federation offices are in that big building on the bank." Brandi pointed to the old school. "You might find the coordinator there. It has been quiet since the last attack south of Chicago, and he might be out gardening. I'll meet you for supper. There's someone I must look up."

"You know people here?" Frank smiled." They should call the Federation, Brandi Land."

"He isn't here anymore," she said sadly, "but he left his mark."

Brandi hesitated in front of the Dentistry office. The sign still hung there, although faded. A newer notice advertised the services with Irene Wallace as the practitioner. Lower down, a slightly weathered hand-carved wooden sign read: "Talk is still cheap, even if a voice has gone." Brandi understood. She entered the shop. An old woman rested in a soft chair behind a little table. She alertly looked Brandi over.

"What can we do for you today?" The pleasant woman had a disarming smile.

"I'm Brandi Shadly." She squinted as her eyes adjusted to the light from the still functioning LED Christmas lights. "Are you Irene Wallace?"

"Nope, Irene is the new dentist. I am the receptionist." The woman laughed, and then her face became serious. "Ham was sorry he never got to see you again." The woman stood, and her smile broadened. She had known who Brandi was without asking. "He asked me to tell you if I ever saw you again, he savoured your friendship."

Brandi recognized the woman as the delegate from west of Lake Michigan who flirted with Ham at the founding conference. She returned to become his partner. The only letter Brandi ever received from Ham had been bittersweet. He said he had given up hope for his family, but he had found some new happiness. This woman was his new joy.

The two spent a pleasant afternoon and visited Ham's grave.

"When they bury me here, there will be no one to maintain this. We will fade away together like the evening light, back into the shadows." The woman knelt and pulled a few weeds but left the prolific bindweed covering the spot. "Ham always said bindweed was his favourite because it was damned stubborn like him. He wasn't a farmer and could love things like that."

The SS Lake Huron arrived and tied up behind The Princess. None of the crew was familiar to her, but when she told about the trip years before, the captain said she had ridden with his grandfather.

"We are heading up lake early tomorrow if you want a ride. How can you pay for it?"

"I could draw you a picture."

"I can't eat a drawing," the man was friendly but did not know Brandi. Her fame had not spread to Bay City.

Frank returned just as Don and the captain of the Lake Huron were negotiating a trading arrangement. The boat from Cleveland offering goods from the tropics and coal was attractive. Some goods came through the newly pacified border south of Chicago, but it was expensive to bring them into Lake Huron. This new market made Don happy and would justify getting one of the new steamers. When he discovered Brandi needed passage north, Don added it to his negotiations and secured a passage for both Frank and Brandi to Bay City.

The captain offered to take them to Manitoulin, but it would cost them since it was not his regular run. Justin had not stolen all of Frank's gold, only the standard Jenks' ten percent. Frank used a wafer to book passage to Little Current. The captain could get a load of lumber from the island. The cargo alone would pay for the trip.

"We won't be meeting again, Brandi." Don's face was firm but sad. "I hope you get back to see the kids. I'll always cherish our friendship."

They hugged, and Brandi walked up the gangway onto the SS Lake Huron. She turned and waved. The crew stowed the ramp and slipped the lines. With the standard three short blasts, the ship gently backed away from shore.

Brandi stood on the stern watching, as the Princess seemed to retreat behind them with Don busy on the bridge. The feeling of another loop closing overwhelmed her.

***

I stood on the deck of the SS Lake Huron as we slid along the North Channel approaching the town of Little Current. It was a clear, windy morning, and the big old swing bridge stood silhouetted against the bright sky. It had been many years since I walked across the structure. The wind blew hard from the stern port quarter. We moved a bit crab-like, trying to keep from blowing towards the south shore. With no radio communication, two shrill blasts from the steam horn said we wished to dock. A flag rose on the harbour master's staff permitting us to land. No other vessel was in port, so we had the pick of any spot along the long wharf. The captain angled us nose in towards the timbers, the engines in reverse letting the wind do the work. The bow touched gently, and then the engines picked up speed as the morning breeze gently nudged the stern against the wooden pier. Lines snaked out, and we were secure with engines stopped.

I always loved watching the skill captains used in docking. One had told me, the trickiest was berthing in a strong onshore wind threatening to wreck the boat against the dock. Our captain blew a full long blast on his steam horn; the common signal to a community a trading ship had arrived. Given the tricky manoeuvre he had completed, it could have been boasting."

From: "Journey South" (The Journals of Brandi Shadly, Vol. 23, p 296)

Frank and Brandi stood on the wharf at the bottom of the gangway watching a steady stream of people make their way down the hill from town. Any ship broke the daily work routine, but the SS Lake Huron, a large vessel, attracted extra attention.

"This community sure looks different from the ones we have seen so far," Frank noted the diversity of dress and the mix of native and non-native faces. He had the feeling of being on a far frontier.

"Nimise... Nimise Makwa!" A loud voice shouted from the crowd.

"Oh no, even here," Frank's voice filled with amazement.

Brandi recognized a man who had been a recent student at Kimberly. He learned to read and writing and had taught how to use black-ash to make woven baskets. The crowd pressed in to see the legendary Nimise Makwa. A man in his late thirties stepped into Brandi's view.

"You don't remember me do you, Nimise?" His quiet voice penetrated the murmur of the crowd. Brandi turned and paused; a smile formed on her face, as she absorbed the man's presence, his mature features transformed to those of a small boy many years before.

"Of course I do, Joe Too-Little," Brandi laughed, "my first son. Have you shot your makwa yet?" They hugged tightly. He had grown to six feet of muscle with long, light brown hair framing piercing dark Ojibwe eyes.

"They call me Joe Giingoo now, Nimise. I have drawn many bears but never shot one. Everyone says Nimise Makwa gave me the bear spirit, and I hold it up for all to share. Thank you for remembering, Nimise. Thank you for sharing your spirit."

Joe hugged her once more with tears in his eyes. A long silence followed with both mentor and apprentice savouring this wonderful encounter. The crowd stood silently. They understood this special moment.

"Show them to me," Brandi finally said, peering deep into Joe's eyes. His folio bag hung from his shoulder. Joe had often heard this command from Nimise at Kimberly and took out a bundle of handmade paper. It felt rich and fine to Brandi's experienced touch.

"Who made your paper?" she asked.

"I do it myself, Nimise," the pride in his skill, learned from Brandi herself, radiated from his face, "from flax. I will give you some. You weren't there when I gifted, and I could not share everything in my heart."

By custom, Institute graduates left gifts in token payment to their teachers and mentors. Joe had left Brandi a carving of a bear done in birch wood and polished to a gleaming brightness. She looked at the bear every day in Kimberly and remembered. He seemed to think that precious work fell short.

Brandi leafed slowly through Joe's bundle of drawings and notes, with many scenes of the rugged and embracing island, Mini Manitou, the home of God. Most drawings depicted people doing everyday things. She found many images of a fair-haired woman with babies and then two young children, and portraits of the children themselves, drawn tenderly and with love. It gave Brandi a feeling of oneness to be looking at this beautiful work. A stiff channel breeze whipped the waves high, ruffling her hair. The water made sharp slapping sounds against the piers. The windblown paper struggled against her grasp. New and old friends surrounded her. The world seemed sharp, and real and good.

She came to the last sheet at the bottom of the bundle. The paper was older, much worn and handled, a picture of her and Erin together leading a class at Kimberly, beneath a maple tree. The love between them was unmistakable. Brandi paused, her breathing became faster, and her eyes moistened.

"How did you know?" she looked at Joe through tears.

"We were all in love with you, Nimise. How could we miss your love of Erin? Every artist you ever taught has a similar image. I carry this always. When I feel down, I look at it and know love is strong."

He paused for a moment. Brandi said nothing. The sound of the wind and waves and chatting people surrounded them. Ring-bills and Herring gulls swooped and squawked.

"I want you to meet some of those I love." Joe broke the silence. He turned, beckoning, and two young children about three and five years old, who had been respectfully hanging back, came forward. "These are my little ones. Chester is five, and this is... "Joe paused as if embarrassed, "this is Brandi. She's three." His look of love overpowered. Brandi's eyes filled.

"Thank you, Joe." Her words choked through a tightening throat. They could not convey the honour she felt. Brandi knelt, spreading her arms wide open. The two youngsters overwhelmed her with hugs and kisses. They knew Nimise Makwa from their father's countless stories and pictures. When she looked up, she stared into the brilliant blue eyes of a blond-haired woman.

"Nimise, this is Annie, my wife and my love." Joe hugged her. Brandi's embrace was heartfelt.

"My dear Annie, you have chosen well. You have found your Giingoo, my little makwa. He is worthy of you."

***

We walked out of town to a large log house where Joe and Annie lived with three generations of family. I hugged Joe's mother and blushed at her repeated thanks for Joe's success. I reminded her, Joe's hard work and her mothering were responsible. Smaller log houses stood nearby. Joe laughingly called the extended family "my school of giingoo". He had a learning circle of local people from toddlers to the elderly. I told him it was Longview in the woods. He said that was no accident. Large open fields surrounded the hamlet, offering protection from wildfires and augmented by ponds near the houses.

Frank found a guide and went to talk to other communities. This civilized wilderness intrigued him. He lived in a world of half-decayed, industrial towns. Frank saw being in the wild as a working vacation, and he filled his two weeks on the island gathering insights into another way of thinking. Joe Paterson embarrassed me with his hospitality. We talked and drew together, wrote and shared many stories.

Joseph`s work did not stop at his home. He travelled every spring, as far as Meldrum Bay on the island and over to Birch Island, Whitefish, Espy and along the Spanish River by canoe in the summer. He told me Rooney's Crossing had become a thriving little community cutting wood for the railway. I asked him to look up Albert's grave the next time he visited there.

One of my sweetest memories is of Joe comforting me when I told him Karen had gone. We explored his Kimberly journals and the brief stories, and the notes Karen had given him. There were times we both had tears in our eyes, mostly tears of laughter.

From: "Journey South" (The Journals of Brandi Shadly, Vol. 23, p 326)

The drumming went on all afternoon and had reached a climax. Brandi did not understand the songs. Joe did his best to explain each one. His mother had assumed elder status in the hamlet and led the drumming with deference shown to her on all sides. Dancers from the various families circled the drum. Subtle variations in their performances matched the changes in the songs. A few dancers wore ornamental costumes while most danced in everyday work clothes. Toward the end of the afternoon, the music ceased. The meat had roasted all day, and the people moved to surround the feast. Brandi looked up from sheets of birch bark and paper that lay in her lap. A little girl stood with one hand on Brandi's knee, shifting her weight uneasily.

"You will be a makwa." Brandi smiled and handed the drawings back to the little girl.

"Tan is one of my star pupils," Joe patted the girl on her head as she ran off smiling. She could now brag that both Nimise Makwa and Giingoo liked her work. "Here's some dinner." Joe handed Brandi a carved wooden bowl containing slices of roast meat and a jumble of roasted potatoes and other vegetables. The utensils were metal. He handed her a clay cup filled with sweet cider.

Brandi smiled and then stared at the things in her hands.

"Stainless steel seems to last forever." She held up her fork. "These may be the last remnants to survive the old way."

It's the last resistance to the Second Law; the thought sounded like Warren Dunne's voice. She paused for a few moments pondering these fading artefacts. Little Chester and her namesake sat nearby. She stared at the little ones. Even Joe had been born after the crash. The experiences these people had were new and vigorous. Memories did not cast shadows over their path. Brandi ate with pleasure.

The village gave the celebration in honour of Brandi and Frank. The visitor from the far south sat further along the circle amongst a group of elders and curious young. Brandi respected Frank as they travelled. He listened more than he talked and yet always seemed to have something positive to contribute.

Perhaps, she thought *negative people didn't survive the last forty years.*

As the light faded, musical instruments appeared, including sophisticated wind instruments mixed with the fiddles, guitars and wooden flutes. Joe and another man came and placed chairs in front of their guest.

"Brandi, Jimmy and I want to share some special songs." Joe plucked his strings and tuned each note. "Jimmy has played with Joseph." No one had to differentiate Joe and Joseph. There was only one Joseph of Longview.

They began with an old Joseph favourite, and soon one after another of his songs poured from their guitars and lips. Others gathered and voices blended in familiar songs, interspersed with songs written by a local.

Darkness overtook the place. Young people kept the fire high. The light danced off instruments and faces. All the musicians now gathered, their seamless blending honed while defeating the boredom of long winter nights. Brandi had heard none of Joseph's songs played with wind instruments and even the fiddle players had embellished the fine originals. Joseph would be pleased.

For the last arrangement, as the young slept in parent's arms, and a waning half-moon eased above the horizon, the band slid into a rendition of Longing for Longview. Tears formed in Brandi's eyes as memories of her friends and family accompanied each verse. At the last verse, the music stopped, and the throng sang, unaccompanied.

The gates hang high but open
The lights are always on
Their loving arms embrace you
You are away but never gone.

Brandi dreamed during the night. She was in her old drawing of Longview with the lane that ran to the horizon. She was walking up the lane to the house. Her mother stood with open arms, but the distance grew greater with each step.

***

We were eager to be on our way. It was a good day's journey down to South-Bay Mouth. A steamer was leaving the following day, missing it would mean waiting another few weeks. Joe had something important to share before he would let us leave. He and Annie, with young Chester and little Brandi, took Frank and me to a small grove of cedar trees. Cut logs formed a circle, with a soft carpet of old cedar leaves covering the earth.

Joe took out a bowl and a crow feather. He made a handful of tinder from shredded cedar bark, and soon there was a small stream of smoke. Joe added dead cedar leaves "for our memories"; sweet grass "for today's blessings" and seeds "for our responsibility to tomorrow".

The feather passed amongst the adults. The two little ones remained silent by their mother's knee. Frank's remarks were full of thanks. As the feather came to me, I took out the faded scarf from my shirt. There was such a small bit of tobacco left. I placed a pinch in the bowl and wafted the fragrance into the trees. I described how Corrine's spirit had now visited the places my body had travelled; an invisible bond again tied together past, present and future. I carefully put the remnants of tobacco away. Corrine and I had more places to visit.

From: "Journey South" (The Journals of Brandi Shadly, Vol. 23, p 329)

"This blow is pretty bad." The captain shouted from the wheelhouse as the little vessel bobbed and pitched on the waves. Whitecaps sprayed over the windward deck against the cabin windows.

"I plan to run on down to the east through Fitzwilliam Channel and then turn into the wind to run into The Tub. It'll be rough when I make the turn. I'll warn you to hang on."

Brandi and Frank sat in the small cabin, trying not to bounce against anything hard. The boat appeared to be substantial at the dock, but now was an insignificant chip in the high waves. On this brilliant, cloudless day, the southwest wind churned the water. The captain flashed a reassuring smile, but a frown crossed his face. The violence scared Brandi. She had not planned to die by drowning.

"You have never seen the ocean have you, Brandi?" Frank did not seem too concerned, although inwardly he was questioning the age and seaworthiness of the boat. "It's worse in the Atlantic."

"If we survive this," Brandi half-shouted, "I would love to see the ocean."

"You come and visit me, and I'll give you the tour."

Suddenly, Brandi rushed to a sliding window and stuck her head out, depositing her stomach's contents outside. Fortunately, she had picked the lee side of the boat. Frank lasted longer before he too threw up.

The captain's warning had not prepared them for the manoeuvre of turning into the wind. They pitched precariously and feared she might capsize, but the sailor knew his ship, and the little boat came into the wind unscathed. The struggle up the wind was one hard landing after another as the hull rose onto a crest and then fell into a trough. They could only hang on and take the shocks through their legs. The dramatic motion cured their seasickness. At last, they slid into the lee of some islands and soon found the protection of Tobermory harbour.

"Wonderful ride," the captain smiled. "I usually charge extra for fun. I'll just include it this time. We leave for Wiarton in the morning. It will be smoother along the east shore."

He was as good as his word, and they made Owen Sound by the next nightfall. The railway operated the vessel, and Brandi's pass had been enough for the passage. The captain did not appear to be a loyal employee. He said, since he had been making the run anyway, he would have carried them free. Brandi had to produce her pass to satisfy a scowling railway agent onshore. She eagerly escorted Frank into the town, relating the story of how it had become a commercial harbour once more. They found an establishment that rented rooms, less polished than the one in Niagara but adequate.

Word had spread Brandi was in town. J.J. Smithson appeared as they ate their evening meal. Brandi had always liked J.J. The tragedy of Jeff's death only strengthened her love of the man. He offered to put them up, but they had settled into their rooms. He set off to notify the Chairman that Brandi and Frank would like some time with the Council.

Brandi introduced Frank Tremain to the Council and gave an outline of her trip, promising a written report within the month. It convinced Brandi small-scale, a local organization still proved superior to a strong central authority. Frank planned to return home and advocate the watershed approach in his remnant of the USA.

"I'll stop in Kimberly," Frank handed her a folded sheet of paper. "This letter expresses thanks. I'll be there soon."

Brian James was not the engine driver, so she opted to ride in the passenger coach. A surly railway official oversaw the car. Brandi thought it a waste of labour. She ignored the man and opened Frank's letter.

Brandi, thank you for making my trip wonderful. I know you just let it happen, and would deny you did anything special, but I fulfilled my purposes so much better in your company. I would have only slept at inns, contacting ,important'people, missing much of the actual conditions. Your presence opened doors for me, and I thank you.

From the beginning, in Niagara, I realized you were a special person. The way you embrace people makes them love you. Several times on our trip, I wondered why I cared so much for you and then realized that I was the lucky victim of the same love you have for everyone. The only judgmental words I ever heard from your mouth were based upon facts and not simply because someone was different. All of this has encouraged me.

I want to send some students from our territory to study with you at the Institute. We can use our own Nimise Makwa in the northeast. Your friend Karen was wise in discovering you and unleashing you upon your territory. I know you grieved her death while on our journey. Please accept my love and thoughts for you all.–Frank Tremain

From: The Brandi Shadly Archives.

Chapter Thirty-Two

From the above details, you can see the concentration of industrial power near Lake Ontario has led to social and economic changes. Many of the problems of our society before the crisis are reappearing, including degradation of the environment and the concentration of wealth. There is much waste involved in the industrial enterprise, and the store of scrap and salvage seems to near exhaustion. We need to conserve and reduce our consumption. The way we are spending this historic resource is not sustainable.

I believe the story of Ohio is a caution how badly things can evolve. The cooperative activities found in Cleveland and Port Huron show local efforts for the greater good can thrive in larger populations. This trip strengthened my belief small local structures focused on the watersheds, with the power exercised at the bottom give the most satisfying and stable results.

The central organization of security seems still to be a good idea, considering the potential danger from the Jenks' fiefdom and others. To protect the lakes, I recommend we change the operations in Hamilton. We must avoid too much central power. On an added note to the above, I have a feeling the railway organization is becoming too powerful and self-serving. It is a threat to us all. Using railway script, although making commerce easier, gives the railway managers new power. Thank you for asking me to make this journey. I found it personally fulfilling.

"Report to the Huron General Council by Brandi Shadly, Year 41"– Huron Territory Archives–Owen Sound

When Brandi stepped onto the Flesherton platform, the railway guard followed her. The man stood beside the steps to the passenger coach, watching as she made her way towards the waiting room. Ben the Postie, now Station Master, unloaded express and baggage. One of his younger children stood ready with a handcart.

"Hi Ben," Brandi set her pack and folio beside the platform bench. She smiled at his son, a boy as handsome as Ben had been as the lone-wolf letter carrier riding a bicycle.

"Who's the railway guy?" They watched the surly man climbed onto the train.

"They put what they call a conductor on the passenger coaches; afraid someone will travel for free. They didn't pick the best guys. You can't have a conversation with them."

The steam-whistle sounded twice, the bell clanged, and the train started away, clanking as the hitch knuckles took the strain.

"I noticed the railway is less friendly," Brandi sat on the bench enjoying the warm sun.

"If I had known it would go like this, I would not have wanted this job. There are piles more paperwork, and they hooked up a telegraph system. I'm learning code."

"Would you rather ride your bike?" Brandi teased.

"Hey, that bike got me the nicest gal in the valley, after you of course." He winked and then turned to his son, "Don't you go telling Mom." The boy laughed and wandered off to help load the freight wagon.

"He's a good one, Ben." Brandi looked past Ben's son. "Where's the wagon headed?"

"Down the valley, via the Boyne, and will be in Kimberly by mid-afternoon."

Brandi sat beside the teamster as he sent his team of light horses off towards Flesherton.

"We have to stop at the Bossley place." He flicked the reins, scattering a few deer flies. "We got a crate for the missus."

The wagon made a quick trip up the lane and circled to a stop in front of the kitchen steps of Rob Bossley's little farmhouse. Rob had attracted a woman about Brandi's age to live with him.

"You remember Agnes," Rob smiled and nodded over his shoulder to the woman as he shook Brandi's hand.

"Agnes was your woman last month," the woman laughed. Her name was Jen, and she had lived with Rob for several years. Brandi visited often and liked the woman. She was one of Rob's old lovers. Brandi teased he was a softy and lacked an engineer's tin heart.

"Rob, I want your opinion." Brandi leaned on a wagon wheel as the driver prepared to climb back onto the seat. "What do you think of the way the railway works now?"

"I'm afraid of it." He looked serious. "They're getting too strong and believe that they run the show in Ontario. The territories have let them get out of control."

"Thank you, Rob. That's what I'm thinking." Brandi climbed up onto the seat. "I hope you both come for the harvest party. We miss your fun."

Brandi made a quick mental sketch of the couple standing in their yard. Rob's unkempt beard played freely over his face, and his wife smiled contentedly, or perhaps smirking in resignation with her eccentric lover. Brandi would have to decide which when she committed this to paper. To one side, peeking out from under a mossy apple tree, a derelict tractor sat nose down on flat front tires. Green, peeling trim set off the old farmhouse, its white clapboard deeply weathered. A rivulet of smoke rose from the kitchen chimney. The big, grey, barn cat scrabbled at their feet.

***

Chester and Brandi stood beneath the trees in the late afternoon sun. The little graveyard had grown, but there was only one fresh grave this year with a simple marker made of oak wood and polished with linseed oil.

"Walt carved it." Chester knelt and stared at the inscription burnt into the wood: "Karen Lefevre, wife of Chester Amik." and "Cry no tears in the evening sun," inscribed below the name.

"I cry anyway," Chester did not look up, "but not here."

Brandi knelt and touched his arm. She extracted a delicately handmade spirit catcher from a little package, neatly wrapped in deer hide. Joe's son, Chester had made it. She gently spread out the circle of wood, laced with fine strands of rawhide, coloured quills and with a delicate tail of feathers. Brandi hung it on Karen's marker. A breath of wind lifted it into the air, and the feathers fluttered gently. The wooden ring twisted towards them and then eased back to rest against the oak. Chester smiled. Brandi's tears dripped onto the still fresh dirt. They walked back to the house in silence.

"I first met your father in this room." Chester eased into a handmade rocker of oak and woven black ash. "I think things worked out okay because of it." Chester picked up a book and read. Brandi slipped off leaving her friend to grieve.

Some days later, Erin Thomas and Frank Tremain sat at a table at one end of Karen's old living room, playing chess, sitting in afternoon sunlight filtering through the large window. Brandi sat at a small table near the big front window where Chester sat with his eyes closed. Her report to the Council was complete. She looked towards her husband and Frank. Brandi stretched and rubbed her sore neck. Lately, it had been harder to sit working for extended periods.

"Erin, I'm going to Longview in the morning to help with the harvest. Come down to the party, and we can come home together." She returned to the paper in front of her.

"I am off in the morning as well." Frank glanced up from a game he was losing. Erin was three moves from a mate and Frank could see no way out.

"A stop in Hamilton and I'm going back over the Niagara frontier."

Chester remained unsettled; his grief still played at his heart. He leaned over to read Brandi's conclusions.

"The railway may be more dangerous to our future than the PLM ever was," Chester said. "At least the PLM was incompetent and ready to kill each other. They did stupid things to destroy themselves. These railway people may be smarter."

Brandi used the harvest as an excuse for travelling to Longview, but once again, she needed comfort from her extended family, and she wanted to paint. In her small and stuffy loft, she preferred painting in the summer, removing the window and venting the fumes from her oils. Fumes and dust affected her more than in her younger days.

I always return here when I need restoration. Brandi read her own words, written many years ago on a small sketch she had done of Joseph playing the piano. It sat in his handmade frame on top of the instrument. Joseph smiled at her as his hands ran smoothly over the keys, tenderly evoking sweet notes. Brandi sighed in contentment. At Longview, at home, the mix of sorrow and happiness always made her whole.

It required a wagon to carry her painting on stretched hemp canvas to Kimberly. She seldom did large canvases, but this one was special. She and Erin hitched a ride with Rob Bossley and Jen on their wagon, brightly decorated with red ribbon. Rob claimed he had always wanted to be a gypsy.

She hung the painting beside the fireplace in the great hall of the old ski resort. The image showed Karen and sixteen-year-old Brandi, walking the valley road from Longview to Kimberly, animation and happiness in their faces. Viewers soon discovered one of Brandi's subtleties. *I love you,* written in the dancing blades of grass and wildflowers. Brandi often stared at the painting and felt Karen's love.

Chapter Thirty-Three

Erin and I had been together for twenty-five years and never took time alone. We were nostalgic for the ride we made from Guelph and repeated it. We planned to go away and explore until we felt the need to return home. Riding Shade would be a wonderful pleasure.
From: Summer of Love (The Journals of Brandi Shadly Vol. 25 p 2)

I cannot remember when I fell in love with Brandi. When I first saw her, I was afraid of her; a gun-toting stranger who rode like the wind and seemed so confident. For the previous two years, since my parents had disappeared, I survived by being quick. That morning I was too slow. Maybe, when she didnt shoot me right away I felt for her. By the time we reached Kimberly, I was a smitten young boy. It took years for me to get the courage to tell her. One smile from her erases all the sadness in my life. Her love embraces me. There is nothing else to feel.
From: "My private journal" The Erin Thomas Archives.

"We've never had a vacation," Erin looked up from the row of potatoes he planted.

"I'm in," Brandi exclaimed as she dug another hole for potato seed. "Did you get the brochures?"

"Old joke," she laughed at Erin's puzzled look. He did not remember the incessant travel advertising. Brandi stood and peered around the garden.

"We can get away after planting. There's lots of help this year. The two Bills are hard workers." Brandi kissed Erin.

"The little one's growing and learning fast. Billy's reading and writing are top-notch, and he's interested in everything." Erin taught the boy world history before the collapse. He wanted to give students some background on the creation of Huron Territory.

"He's a long way from ready," Brandi's thoughts wandered far away. "He needs more time, maybe another eight years." She thought back to the summer she received Dodger and her first trip with Karen. "Someone will need to replace me. It might be Billy."

Her face was unreadable. Erin could not tell if she was sad or being practical. She went back to digging. The concentration on her face far exceeded the simple task. Erin smiled. Brandi's mind travelled far away. He could only see the beauty in her face.

Two weeks later, Brandi and Erin rode up old highway ten towards Chatsworth. They had spent a night visiting Stephanie Hunter and her family. Her grandchildren had all run about, helping entertain, as the doctor and her husband reminisced. The travellers only stayed the night, wanting to be alone and explore.

Brandi dismounted to stare at an embankment. The railway ran beside the road here, and she recognized the place where she had told stories to the fettlers and provoked Jim Handley. Brandi recalled her father sitting with her. She sighed. *There are memories everywhere.* Erin saw her look and put his arm around her waist. He knew this woman well.

They avoided the major settlements, heading for the north bank of the Saugeen and visited many little hamlets and villages, but they loved sleeping under the stars. They travelled light with only the essentials including Brandi's sketching paper and a pan and pot. Villages restocked them with food, but they depended as much on taking the game and Brandi's impressive knowledge of the edible forest. Humans had occupied little of the land. Most people lived in small communities, farming the adjacent fields. These little villages were like Longview. Essential skills such as blacksmiths, farrier, harness making and woodworking existed in most places. Some specialized in weaving wool and exotic animal hair from large numbers of llamas and alpacas. Brandi made many drawings of these strange but loveable creatures.

Brandi's name and reputation opened most doors, although they found indifferent or contrary folks who remained distant. Brandi amazed Erin with her friendly, patient and even-handed treatment of everyone. Many who scowled at their arrival smiled and waved as they rode away.

"Things have changed," Brandi sat in front of the hemp-canvas tent, enjoying Erin's delicious chicken stew.

"People focus on the ordinary now. Their lives have become secure and routine. The villages provide a social life and protection from bandits. Initially, with Longview, Warren thought a defendable compound might be a good idea. Perhaps it will prove so." Brandi moved beside Erin.

"The bandit problem seems to start with communities kicking out misfits. These little places don't like rebels." She hugged Erin.

"They're like the academic world Mom and Dad lived in," Erin kissed her lightly. "Village life can be cruel and full of backstabbing and rumours. They can't stand too much difference. We have to work hard to avoid becoming narrow."

The pair cleaned up the leavings from supper. Since the makwa now roamed freely, they secured their food high in a stout tree away from the tent. Erin burnt the pots clean and rinsed them in a little brook. Their campsite occupied the edge of a meadow beside a dense bush. On this warm and dry evening, Erin and Brandi slept beneath a clear sky.

"I wish you didn't sleep with that thing," Erin nodded towards Brandi's ever-present rifle.

"I learned the lesson the hard way," Brandi smiled, remembering Dodger. "I feel vulnerable without it." She placed it on the side away from Erin.

Darkness fell slowly as the pair snuggled. Stars appeared, and the horses made quiet sounds. Erin spotted a dim object moving amongst the stars.

"I used to watch these with Warren," Brandi rose on one elbow, following the fleeting dot of light. "Some artificial satellites will orbit for centuries. People will forget what they are and make myths." The satellite disappeared, and Erin turned his attention to the rest of the brilliant summer sky.

"What's that one?" He pointed to a bright blue-white star in the east.

"That is my old friend and troublemaker, Vega." Brandi chuckled but felt sad. Her attackers suffered an unpleasant fate. Only one survived the winter and staggered to Mount Forest, but she had not lived too long after.

"You know, Erin, I have hope my journals and writing will keep knowledge alive and superstition will not displace reality, but there's a spiritual part of it all I don't understand; it's a deeper level to explore."

"Your makwa your little bears, are already doing a good job I think." Erin kissed her cheek. "You have made an incredible impact. How many people come to Kimberly just to see Nimise Makwa?"

Brandi slept contentedly. Over the years, there had been many nights on the trail when she had longed for someone, and then later for Erin to be beside her. This summer, she had her longings met. It was already the best of times for her. The satellite passed silently among the stars several times, as they slept.

As they travelled, first to Chippewa Hill and then down along the lakeshore, Brandi was living two realities. Only a few of her old friends survived. Stan Gregson, old and feeble, held her hand at Corrine's grave as they reminisced. Most of the familiar faces were of those who had been younger, and she had not known well; however, their memories and deep friendship for Brandi made for slow progress. Many people desired to visit and chat. Nimise would disappoint no one. They left a tide of new people in their wake who considered themselves friends of the travellers.

Love of Nimise Makwa would be deeper. At the amphitheatre in Chippewa Hill, the Truth Talker Players changed their summer performances to concentrate on the voices of Longview in Brandi's honour. Attendance was higher and more attentive than normal.

At the old nuclear site, her friend Maurice had passed away. He developed cancer a few years after the last trip to the McNeil mine and died in some pain despite the availability of morphine. Brandi's woman friend whom she sketched on her first trip south of the Saugeen now led the compound. Many former plant staff had died of some form of cancer. Erin and Brandi stayed one night and then followed the river through Paisley to Hanover.

The horse races were in full swing when they arrived. The Hanover meet had become a monumental event, and people travelled far to attend. Don Hunter and Muffin were there, along with most of their family.

"Who's minding the ranch?" Brandi and Muffin chatted as the younger grandchildren bounced around.

"The damned horses run the show, anyway; they can fend for themselves." Muffin laughed. "Our youngest son Luke and his wife stayed back. They have a late foaling mare and couldn't leave her. Don wanted to come down," she paused, "maybe this is the last time. If it hadn't been for that, we would have stayed home too. Getting to Durham was okay, but it was a devil getting the horses and all the gear on and off the train. It's about too much for this old gal."

They remained in Hanover for the week of celebrations. This time, Brandi did not have to flee a drunken brawl. Alcohol consumption stayed well under control. Most of the crowd were second-generation survivors. This new cohort seemed to have less resentment. The alcohol brought out more fun than anger.

A familiar friend sought Brandi out. She once again found herself challenged to a drawing contest. The first one had created a precedent. An art show and contest were now an important part of the celebrations. This time, Brandi won but only because her opponent's grandchildren constantly interrupted and insisted on being in their Papa's picture. Brandi's winning image depicted her friend sitting at his artboard with the little ones around his feet. The band of fiddles, guitars, drums and a piano on a hay wagon played flat out for the entire hour. They insisted on a picture as payment. Both artists took turns working on the piece. The musicians seemed satisfied.

Brandi presented her artistic friend with a drawing of him dressed as a cowboy holding a pencil in one hand like a six-shooter and a large sheet of paper in the other. The title was "Quick-draw". His grandchildren laughed, but he told Brandi he would cherish this gift forever. It especially pleased Brandi when a man and woman introduced themselves as the pig-tail pulling brother and sister Brandi had drawn in that first contest.

***

Erin and Brandi stood beside their horses, watching Don and Muffin's mob disappear towards the railhead at Durham. The local roads had long since lost their asphalt, and clouds of dust rose from the horses' hooves.

"Where to, my love?" Erin swung onto his mount.

"South," Brandi turned Shade down the crossing road into a new country for her. They rode for the best part of the day, all the way to the hamlet of Clifford and then swung west. A local had told them of a little lake where they could make a comfortable camp. Brandi looked forward to a swim. Bathing had not been possible in Hanover. No one minded body odours, but she knew cleanliness was necessary to stay healthy. The bonus was frolicking in the water with Erin. Bulrush stalks stood guard along the shoreline broken by a small gravel beach.

They camped on the beach near crumbling cottages. A self-perpetuating vegetable garden provided a few greens and attracted rabbits with no fear of humans. Brandi's small-bore rifle ensured rabbit stew was on the menu. They lingered for several days, savouring the rustic luxury.

The need for supplies finally forced them to leave this little paradise. Lakelet Lake supported a good number of residents. There was a large hamlet at the north end, and a farming community sat at the south outlet. The village of Lakelet proved hospitable. A day's splitting firewood and a drawing of the children earned a week's supply of food.

A short ride from Lakelet, the road crossed a newly restored railway roadbed. Workers had cleared the gravel of vegetation and smoothed the surface. Recent crawler tractor tracks led them up the line to surprise them with Barry Young overseeing a group building a timber bridge over a small creek. A farm tractor loader hoisted salvaged power poles into place. Barry had aged but still kept his sharp mind.

"The railway encourages commercial farming and logging," Barry explained while shouting advice to his crew. "They need food and wood in the cities. The old track beds are being restored, but I don't have enough skilled people. We had more when the PLM tried it. They are burning lots of diesel." He helped nudge a support log into place and admonished the two men in charge of the work.

"There aren't a lot of engineers around now." He returned to Erin and Brandi. "They expect me to train them on the job. I've got six pupils here, and there isn't one worth a pinch. They're as lazy as dead grass and about as smart." He nodded towards the two he had just lectured.

"When we old guys die, there'll be big trouble."

Barry decided the workers could finish without him. The horses trailed the trio up the line, manoeuvring around a washout.

"They're sending a dump truck and a loader to haul gravel to fill these bad spots before the track layers arrive." He stared back down the line. "The fettlers are slow and way behind. I wish Jim were here to get them moving. As soon as we get to Wingham, I'm going back home and not leaving. Rob and I will sit and gossip until we're dead and gone."

The trio arrived at an encampment. The clanking and sputtering of the diesel bulldozer came from just out of sight through the trees where the roadbed split into a wye, and the crawler worked up the right-hand branch.

"Eventually, they want to run that branch line up to the lake. My job is to get to Wingham. This little intersection will work like the one at Saugeen Junction so they can turn the trains around." Barry seemed satisfied with the work. "I recruited most of the labour along the way, and some of these people are smart, maybe short on education but quick to learn. I can let them go on their own now. My official students screw things up more than the country folk."

They stayed a day as Barry's guests enjoying the abundant food. He spent a lot of the railways script, a paying customer for local farms.

"Stable communities use barter, gifting, and trust," Barry mused, "but this disrupts everything. I'm not sure the railway's a good thing. When I buy, folks compete for my business. I see the way neighbours look at neighbours, unfriendly. So far," Barry smiled and winked, "I just buy it all. The railway never told me I had to get the best deal. That'll change I'm sure, but I won't be causing any hard feelings."

"It explains all this good food," Brandi munched a tasty biscuit with her breakfast of ham, eggs and fries.

"That and those Mennonite women cooking, they've been with me since Harriston, earning railway script for the homestead."

"I know them," Brandi glanced towards the cook tent where two of Aaron Martin's daughters laboured over tall tables.

The sound of horses rushing up the improved rail bed interrupted breakfast. A contingent of Huron Mounted Constabulary trotted into the camp. Every young constable rode proudly and wore red hats and light-blue linen shirts with shoulder flashes. The matched chestnut geldings looked as proud as the riders did.

"Bandits stole supplies from a survey party," Barry said. "The cops are hunting them down."

The commander did not seem as arrogant as some constables had become.

"We got a couple of them down in Harriston, trying to sell your tools but are now working off their debt with the tracklayers. The rest are hiding out in Greenock Swamp. They should have gone south. Maitland Territory doesn't have a constabulary. We'll get 'em." The contingent hurried off.

Watching the settling dust, Brandi felt a growing unease about the police force. It was no longer Jeff's. It seemed self-serving.

"After our encounter with Barry Young, our discussions for the rest of our journey, centred on the question of what was happening in the territories, and if they were positive changes. Erin and I disagree many times. He was a well-educated, intelligent person when I found him and much better schooled than I will ever be. He says I know more than he does since I studied under a reality much harsher than his master. We have developed disquiet about the territories."
From: Summer of Love (The Journals of Brandi Shadly Vol. 25 p 101)

Dusk softened the land and raised night sounds. This last night of Erin and Brandi's vacation shaped up to be special. The weather turned warm and dry following the storms they experienced while visiting the Mennonites west of Mount Forest. The sky cleared and the light wind promised a beautiful night under the stars. From their vantage on this high hill, Brandi would have been able to see the spot where she had the unfortunate encounter with the Vega worshipers.

They had been on the trail for two months, riding down to Port Stanley, and spent two days in Guelph vainly searching for the barn where they met. Now Kimberly waited a day's ride away.

"Where do you think the region will go?" Erin and Brandi savoured the last glow of a spectacular sunset. From the fiery red horizon, the sky gradually passed through orange and greens into deepening purples.

"Eventually," Brandi sighed contentedly, "I think technology will diminish. The railway will cease to run. It will limit everyone. I believe it will be a good thing."

"Maybe so," Erin snuggled closer to her, "but it will be a long time coming. No one alive today will see it."

"How can you be so sure?" She watched the bright light of Venus in the west. "We don't exist in isolation. Many people want wealth. The PLM might just have been a rehearsal. Outside forces might attack us, or we'll have to fight some other PLM. I have a candidate." Her smile went unseen in the darkness.

"Yeah, I know, the railway barons. You might be right."

"Something Barry said is bothering me, the large urban areas depending on a vast hinterland. I think that's dangerous," Brandi shivered in the warm evening air, "with the cities overpopulated." She could just see Erin in the fading dusk.

"There's still room on the land. We rode many kilometres with no sign of people."

"There's a sustainable limit. The loop can't support too many humans."

"How do we control our population?" Erin recalled what had once seemed to be an academic debate in the Thomas living room in Guelph.

"If we don't, nature will, again. The collapse led to misery and death."

"How did you avoid being pregnant?" Neither had wanted a family.

"Indian magic did it," Brandi smiled, "and their natural medicines. Not that you didn't try." She laughed easily, without embarrassment. "Not that I didn't either."

"I've been thinking about our conversation near Southampton. The remaining shadows are emotional with our sense of loss and grief pulling at us. The children and grandchildren do not have our shadows. As we die off, the shadows diminish. Salvaged material and technology are fading shadows, as is the knowledge of how to use them. Maybe the next generations will make technology sustainable, or it too will disappear. We have claimed and reused most of the salvageable material. Remember, we couldn't find the barn where we met. They had broken even the concrete up to get the steel out. I believe the railway, steel, oil and everything will diminish until they are gone. Barry said the expertise is dying."

"People invented it once before." Erin played the devil's advocate. "The Institute maintains and improves technology."

"Maybe we shouldn't be keeping the knowledge alive."

"We can't decide for others or dictate. Why should it fail?"

"Warren Dunne used to say, and George MacDonald agreed in his non-scientific language, that everything runs down. Warren pointed out that technology evolved in a world of expanding resources. He insisted things had declined for decades before the final collapse, and it will be impossible to repeat because the easy and cheap resources are gone. I never knew Warren or George to be wrong."

"Where does it leave us?" Erin stared at the bright light of Venus as the planet slipped ever closer to the horizon.

"From all my travelling," Brandi looked up to see Vega hanging directly over their heads, "I believe relationships, community and respect for the natural world are the basis for happiness." A long silence followed as if the future was too large to contemplate.

"I can never really be happy," Brandi looked intently toward Erin's loving eyes. "This sadness always tugs at me, these shadows in my heart. Your love has been such a wonderful help and made me always find a happy thought when I became sad. You fill my darkness with light. I love you."

They embraced, their bodies fusing in desire, as strong and warm and thrilling as the first time on the slope of the valley under the apple tree. Later, as Brandi lay in Erin's arms, staring up at the brilliant stars, she knew the love between people was the reason to live. She remembered Joe Too-Little's drawing and the love he had captured. Somehow, the images of George MacDonald and Warren and Old Albert infiltrated her loving feelings. All the hard work, building and planning only supported love. Laying there, feeling Erin's strength and caring, listening through the darkness to the pulse of the world around them, Brandi felt complete and happy. They slept. Venus slipped beneath the horizon. Amongst the silent flashing stars, a silent white dot passed overhead on its endless journey.

***

The snorting of the horses woke Brandi. Years on the trail had given her a keen ear for any subtle disturbance, but the horses were a bit late. From her position beside Erin, beneath the wool cover her barely opened eyes followed a trio of young people, two men and a woman, moving cautiously into the clearing. The intruders ignored the horses and reached the rope that held the food bag high in a tree. One man released the hitch knot and lowered the prize into eager hands. A small gauge single load shotgun dangled carelessly from the other man's hand. Brandi's hand moved beneath the blanket and released the safety on her rifle.

"Are you hungry?" Brandi kept her voice quiet. This was simply the latest of several encounters with hungry desperados; these did not appear to be threatening. The startled intruders turned, and the armed man grasped the shotgun in both hands, thrusting it towards Brandi as if it was a lance instead of a firearm.

"Get up!" The armed man snarled, but the youthfulness of his voice destroyed the effect.

"Are you hungry?" Brandi repeated without moving. Her hand rested beneath the Savage with her finger lightly on the trigger guard. She noted the un-cocked hammer action of the shotgun.

"Yes," the second man said in a softer voice, "we need food."

The woman pulled the cold roasted rabbit out of the sack, bit off a chunk and passed it to her companions.

"It would taste better warmed up with some rosehip tea." Erin stirred sleepily, and half rose beside Brandi. "We have company, dear." Brandi's left hand tapped a caution against Erin's thigh. The shotgun rose. The man's thumb was reaching to cock the hammer. Brandi suddenly sat up, drawing the Savage from its hiding place and levelling the weapon at the armed visitor.

"I think you should put the gun down," she commanded.

The man gently laid the weapon on the ground. The trio raised their arms with the half-eaten rabbit suspended from a trembling hand.

Erin prepared the fire as the visitors sat safely away from the shotgun. Soon, they sipped hot rose-hip tea from Erin and Brandi's tin cups. The rabbit, covered in wild herbs, sizzled aromatically in the pan.

"Where are you from? What's your story?" Erin removed the hot pan, allowing the meat to cool to finger touch. Brandi pinched mould from some dark brown bread.

"We lived south, in Grand country." The young woman spoke between sips, eyeing Erin's pan. "My family has a farm, but I got pregnant, and they threw me out." Defiance tempered the sadness in her voice.

"We got pregnant." One of the young men hugged her.

"You don't look pregnant," Brandi observed. "Where's the baby?" She glanced in the direction the intruders had come.

"It came too soon, dead." The girl sounded matter of fact, but the sadness in her eyes deepened. "I got too hungry, and we were walking and the baby…" she choked back a tear.

"It was in the spring. Dad wanted me to marry some guy and get his land, but I loved Davy."

"When Cats… Catherine got trowed out; I went with her." The boy reached for her hand.

"What about you?" Erin looked at the second man as he served the meat and bread onto elm-bark slabs.

"About the reverse of Cat's story, I'm number three son. My oldest brother already has a wife, and he'll be takin' over the usufruct on our place. The next one is getting together with a neighbour gal, and they'll stay to help. Along with Grandpa, Ma and Pa and the young ones, it's plenty of help, so I'm out. Pa told me to find my place. We met a couple of months back."

"Yeah, we were slaves together. Some farm family took us in, seemed nice but made us prisoners." The girl finished her food and still looked hungry. "That's where we met Gordy. Soon as we could, we ran for it."

"It was my idea," Gordy seemed pleased. "I figured with three of us running they might get confused. Anyway, I had flint and stole a table knife. The bastards worked us hard until almost dark. I set a fire on the last load of hay one evening, just as it was drawing back to the barn. Once the fire got going on the load, with all that confusion, we ran off into the dark, served „em right. I wish it burnt the barn."

"One of them dropped this pop gun when he ran for water, and I grabbed it. Only has one shell, so we bin saving it just in case." Davy looked longingly at the 110 still cradled in Brandi's arm.

"Where's this place?" Brandi considered asking the HMC to intervene.

"Down near Fergus." Brandi knew Huron would not intervene outside of its territory. She would take it to the Council.

"We don't have any supplies." Cat whimpered. "Could you spare some?" She seemed to assume they could leave.

"Well," Erin looked at Brandi, "yes, but you need a long-term plan. You won't live the winter otherwise. You can come with us."

"I have a better plan," Brandi searched for a way to get the trio started on an independent life. "Head over towards Wingham. On foot, it will take a week. When you get to the new railway they are laying, find the boss, Barry Young. I'll write a letter of introduction. Ask him to give you work. Abandoned farms fill the Maitland Valley. Once you're paid, claim usufruct on one. He might keep you on over winter, but at least you can buy chickens, feed and tools."

Everyone was enthusiastic until they saw Erin and Brandi could only give them a little food. The pair planned to be in Flesherton for lunch with Stephanie James and had little.

"We won't even survive to get there," Davy muttered. "We can't hunt. You don't got shells for this shotgun, do you?"

"Nope," Brandi seemed to struggle over a decision. "Can any of you shoot a rifle like this?" She lifted the Savage slightly. Erin stared at her wide-eyed as he realized her intention.

"I did a lot of hunting," Davy exclaimed. "Dad has an old .303. I could hit a deer at a good distance."

"Here's what I'm going to do," Brandi sighed as if some deep emotion gripped her. "I'm going to give you this Savage," she paused, "but I am not sure I can trust you all the way." The trio protested their good faith.

"Anyway, I have about fifty shells for it and so far only one in twenty is misfiring so it ought to be good. You can get deer or even a turkey or rabbit if you shoot straight. We'll ride out, and I'll leave the gun along our trail about a hundred meters out and the ammo bag, a hundred beyond that. I think you are okay and won't use it to hurt folks."

Erin and Brandi cantered away from the ammo bag but slowed to a walk along the overgrown road to Priceville.

"There's a lot more meanness and selfishness about now. It's spreading into Huron." Brandi sounded sad. "When people don't see a common need, they forget how to live together."

Erin broke a long silence.

"You gave up Jeff's gun, the rifle that made Nimise Makwa." Erin struggled to read his lover's mind.

"They needed it," Brandi said, "and I don't anymore. I'll never be riding alone again. Nimise Makwa must join the grandmothers in the lodge. I'll remember Jeff there."

Chapter Thirty-Four

Erin and I rode slowly that last day, making our journey last as long as possible. We chose the valley route, past Rob's place, stopping briefly to tell him about meeting Barry Young. We ended up spending the afternoon with them and finally made it to the Kimberly barn just before dark, having held hands often on the way down the valley. I am sure the horses thought we were crazy. That fall and winter, we always seemed to be together. Our living room became a substitute campsite. We spent the long winter months in front of the woodstove. As usual, many guests came to share this living-room campfire, but our times alone in quiet chat were golden. Our love had grown deeper and stronger, but Nimise Makwa was not to stay in the lodge for long.
From: *The Outer Loop (The Journals of Brandi Shadly Vol. 26 p 1)*

Early the following spring, Brandi found Erin chatting with students and waited until the group departed.

"We're rehearsing for our retirement," Erin joked as he sat in one of the threadbare stuffed chairs.

"I don't plan to retire," Brandi looked serious. Erin smiled. "I'll teach, even if you have to carry me into the room and everyone has to fetch for me. I'll be an easy taskmaster." She smiled, wondering if Colonel Jenks still commanded his servants.

"We grow our pension every year in the garden and barn. It would be a working retirement." Erin felt weary, thinking of the fast-approaching spring planting.

"The Federation is sending a delegation to Quebec City in May. They invited me. I would like to go." Brandi quietly questioned. Erin turned to her with a serious look.

"You are not asking are you, Brandi? You never need to ask. Your work is most important. We agree on that."

"No, I am not asking," She sat beside him and took his hand. "But I'm asking you to sacrifice a few months of our time together. I want to travel on by myself and see the ocean, find Frank Tremain and see his territory. I'm not sure how long it would be."

"You know I worry about your safety every time you go off on your own." Erin squeezed her hand.

"You sound like my mother," She giggled. Time had been generous, leaving happy memories.

"Your Dad once told me your mother worried the day Karen took you away, and she never stopped, but she was so happy for you. I'm happy too."

In Erin's mind, it was all a foregone conclusion. Brandi was her person, and he loved her. They sat quietly for a moment, as always when memories of their parents surfaced.

In the preparations, Brandi surprised Erin by producing a large stash of old Canadian banknotes.

"Mom smuggled these from Weyburne when we fled." She examined the contents. "I never told you, she pretended to be pregnant. It helped us through the barrier. This is the little sister I never had.

"I'll need spending money and a reserve if the railway won't honour my pass. They gave me a hard time last trip." She counted out thousands of dollars. "I'll take a few thousand for Ben to convert to railway script."

The money exchange took three weeks before Ben received the official script. The bureaucrat overseeing the process asked about such a large amount of cash. He dropped the issue when Ben told him it had belonged to a dead person. Superstition held sway.

Steam-powered the train from Huron, but in Oshawa, they transferred to a dedicated passenger train powered by electricity from the Saunders generating station on the St. Lawrence River that also supported an industrial niche at Cornwall.

At a longer stop in Kingston, Brandi befriended the train driver and, in payment for a tour of his workspace, sketched the man standing in front of his electric locomotive. She compared the quiet, cool driver's cabin to the noisy, hot space she often shared with Brian Young on the Huron line.

Cornwall shocked her. The port and industrial town came with negative features. Freighters and barges offloaded their cargo for shipment on the railway. The large ship canal and locks upstream were beyond repair. It was cheaper to transfer cargo to the railway than to restore the old system. It would be a week before a river steamer carried them to Quebec City.

The group took rooms at a local inn, touted as "reputable and first-rate" by railway managers. It revealed itself as a poorly disguised brothel catering to the sizeable crowd of men who passed through the town. The dirty inn compared unfavourably with the roughest camp Brandi had ever endured. The group had to tough it out the first night. Brandi shared a room with another woman and slept on the floor in her bedroll. Her companion used the bed and suffered bug bites. Before breakfast, the entire group fled the premises and went to ferret out better accommodations. They discovered an old college on the river that functioned much like the HEI and rented out clean dormitory rooms.

"We're off the radar," The woman who ran the school gazed over the lunch table. "We have high standards. The railway crowd and sailors don't like us. Quiet people come here."

Does anyone still use radar? Brandi sipped Asian tea to wash down a delightful croissant.

"I saw similar things in Niagara."

"There's an advantage of being a port town. We get tea, coffee and cane sugar, along with the crude oil and industrial stuff. I give oranges as Christmas presents."

Brandi recalled she last ate an orange at Colonel Jenks mansion. Luxury and decadence always lived together. Brandi told her new friend about the H.E.I. and of her mission in life. While the Cornwall school had similar goals, it also featured traditional academic learning. Brandi's travel plans shocked the woman.

"You're very brave or very foolish." Her face clouded, "I would never consider travelling through such a dangerous country."

Brandi's stories of meeting the makwa and other exciting events earned her a new admirer.

"I have heard of you, but I thought Nimise Makwa was a fictional character and much younger." She smiled. "One of our students once performed a play called Girl on the Loose based on transcripts of some radio show. We thought they made them up."

"The original versions were more or less accurate," Brandi laughed. "Later productions strayed a long way from the truth."

"I want to show you something sad," they walked by the river. "That's an island," her friend pointed to a line of green, visible through the river haze. "It's what's left of a native settlement. When the economy crashed, we had a lot of fighting around here. Belligerent angry types from the native side thought they would conquer more land. They attacked the Yankee side and us. They weren't any too nice, and people fought back. Racism grew on both sides. It became a fight to the death. In the end, the whites outgunned and out-manned the natives. They retreated to the island. Canadian and American leaders agreed to blockade them. We, ordinary folks, thought the siege would make them surrender. It soon became apparent, the leaders wanted to starve them to extinction."

"On this side, there was an internal fight, and the blockade weakened. We got some help over there and bring many people to the mainland. The Yankees attacked the island, and they finish the job. Soon we all fought them. They had more guns and fighters. It looked bad until they turned tail. We found out someone attacked them from the south, and they had to defend themselves. None returned."

"Sadly, over half of the native population died along with a good many from the mainland. The community over there's recovering, building boats, fishing and farming. There's still bitterness, but the school has a good relationship with them. They send students and teachers to us, and we return the favour."

Brandi finally understood why the woman had been so interested in her stories of Chippewa Hill, Hope Bay and Joe Too Little. Those suggested a potential future with unity and respect amongst people.

***

As we slipped down the river, the abandoned downtown of the City of Montreal stood up tall, glistening brightly in the early morning sunshine. From the boat's deck, the old office towers looked shiny and new, as if preparing for just another business day. They stood mocking the future with their past glory, and their seemingly enthusiastic welcoming of dawn's light. They abandoned these tall buildings shortly after the collapse. It was impossible to salvage much of them, especially the glass on higher floors. No one had the proper equipment to make the job safe. The scene startled me.

I had observed Toronto's skyline from further away, in shadow, brooding like Old Baldy in its morning shade with none of this beauty. I understood, for the first time, why people took these structures as symbols of the permanency of their world. They had enthusiastically named them "skyscrapers". Al Wright called them, "the spires of the Church of the Almighty Dollar". They reminded me of a picture I once saw of the hand of a drowning man sticking up from the water, grasping for salvation.

Past the first rush of enthusiasm, I became sad at the thought of the misdirected effort. It seemed to me these were the grave markers of the past and represented loss and grief. After our little ship had moved down the river, I became melancholy. My drawing of the skyline reflects my depressed mood.

From: The Outer Loop (The Journals of Brandi Shadly Vol. 26 p 34)

For the first time in her life, Brandi experienced tides. Their boat, a large vessel compared to the smaller craft on the upper lakes, floated against a concrete pier. At the ebb tide, the gangway angled steeply up to the wharf. Climbing to the dock required grasping the rope handrails and careful stepping onto the gangway treads.

Brandi took in the historic city of Quebec, built many centuries before, between the river and the cliffs. Business before the collapse had turned it to tourism and recreation, but in the wake of the battles for control of the French nation, it reverted to the centre of administration and commerce. The fighting destroyed many buildings in the upper town, including the parliament buildings, the grand, railway hotel and other institutional structures. Smaller, serviceable buildings required fewer resources leaving the ruins of the grand edifices as salvage.

The Federation delegates waited on the wharf as several officials emerged from a large building beside the docks. The structure echoed a ship's superstructure. A faded sign hanging above the entrance read Musée Naval de Quebec. It was the administrative headquarters of Lower Quebec, which comprised most of the St. Lawrence Valley and the major tributary streams. Although there were pockets of resistance to central rule, only the deeper hinterland escaped Quebec's dictatorship.

The leader had been a sergeant in the Royal Regiment of the Canadian forces. He ran a more or less benevolent dictatorship. Like Ontario, Quebec had dissolved into factions, and the police forces had sided with the old ruling elite. There were major elements of the Canadian Armed Forces in the province. At first, these tried to remain neutral. When it became clear the elite forces had aligned with organized crime and became a murderous threat to the majority, the head of the military moved his troops against them. The well-armed military gained control after fierce fighting.

The Quebec forces did not join the junta in Ottawa but seized the opportunity for Quebec independence. Soon after, the forces themselves dissolved into factions. Much of the dissent arose from the arrogant, brutal treatment of the troops by the officers. A Colonel decided the Brigadier was incompetent and led a mutiny at the top. Internal fighting lasted for three years. The sergeant now in charge of Quebec was a competent and inspiring leader. He soon controlled most of the forces and territory and opposed the Ottawa-PLM invasion. Battle-hardened experience, along with their control of petroleum, made the outcome inevitable, and they accepted the formidable task of rebuilding Quebec. They had no interest in conquering more territory, rightly assuming the people in Ontario would eventually negotiate. The significant threat from incessant fighting in the USA finally controlled their ambitions.

Brandi watched the introductions on the wharf. Both parties stumbled over the language barrier, with one poor interpreter struggling to keep up. Jeff's delegation, years before, had the benefit of having Roger LaFarge along as a translator. His death left the delegation at the mercy of Quebec's translators. Trickery did not concern the Great Lakes Federation that only wanted to increase trade. Jeff's delegation had dealt with the security issues years before. Re-establishing the railway over the Ottawa River and trading arrangements were mundane topics.

Other than recording that initial meeting and the kickoff banquet, Brandi was free to wander. Her billet in a historic home near the river allowed easy access to the central part of town. It reminded her of Port Huron, a vibrant town, bearing scars of fighting but the people of Old Quebec had done more restoration and recovery.

A pall of sulphurous smoke spread over the lower town. Her explorations along the St. Charles River revealed the coal docks stocked from mines in Nova Scotia. Coal was a cheaper alternative to wood. Smoke from both hung heavy in the air.

When Brandi climbed the hill and found the desolate ruins of the larger buildings, she understood the ferocity of the conflict in these streets. The historic surroundings of the citadel captivated Brandi. She sat high on one rampart in the warm sunshine, gazing beyond the compound to the silver ribbon of the river. Her pencils flew as she reproduced the impressive scene, hoping to make a painting of it once she returned home.

The drawing had captured her attention completely, but a shadow crossed her paper. She looked up, startled and annoyed, to stare into the intense dark eyes of a young man. The intruder had wild, unkempt hair and a full dark beard. Brandi found his nearness unsettling.

"Excuse me!" Brandi used her best scolding tone.

"Oh, 'scusez moi," he retreated from her personal space. "Je suis Alain Robert, tu's Anglais. You are English?"

"I am Brandi Shadly, from Ontario." Brandi knew little French but assumed the man had said his name was Alain Robert. She smiled and held out her hand. Her annoyance disappeared, replaced by an interest in meeting this native Quebecer. Her poor knowledge of French could not match the man's familiarity with English.

"I draw and paint too." He looked down at her nearly completed sketch. "You're very good."

"Thank you," Brandi smiled again. Sincere compliments were always welcome. "I've been drawing all of my life."

"So I have." The young man said proudly. Brandi smiled. He could have been her son.

He opened a large folder and extracted sheets of paper. Brandi leafed through the bunch. She had done this many times with hundreds of artists and had a habit of doing a quick survey and then returning to give a closer look. Perhaps the man had not noticed, even in her first run through she paid close attention. He seemed to interpret her speed as disinterest.

"You don't like?" Alain sounded more defiant than hurt.

"What?" Brandi looked up, startled. She had returned to the first image. "Oh no, I was just glancing at them and now am looking closer. Alain, you draw as I do." Her smile disarmed the artist. Indeed, the images were very similar to the ones that she would have done. His style used a cross-hatching technique as opposed to Brandi's shading. There was a broad range of images from portraits to landscapes. His capturing of detail impressed. Many of the images were of town life and daily routine. Brandi loved them. One portrait of a nice-looking young woman communicated deep love.

"Who's this?" her eyes lingering on the piece.

"It is my wife," he smiled, embarrassed but proud, "très belle, non?" He slipped into French in the eagerness of his emotion.

Brandi dug into her folio and extracted her favourite portrait of Erin, laying it beside Alain's work. Immediately, both artists knew they had found their equal. No more needed saying; these drawings cried: "We know how to draw love."

As Brandi savoured his work, Alain examined the drawings from her folio. At last, almost surreptitiously, he reached into his pouch and took out a plain sheet. His pencil moved quickly, and several times when she looked up to ask him a question he would give instructions in a wonderful mixture of language: "rest là... hold it... un moment... that's good". Unlike Brandi, he seemed to enjoy talking as he worked. After an incredibly short time, he showed her the image, a precise and warm portrait of Brandi done in her style of shading.

"This is incredible, Alain. I would have to practice your technique for hours to even try it." She held the paper smiling and dumbfounded.

"I will display this in my house." He re-examined his work. "Tell me about those little signatures on your drawings."

Brandi explained the small brandy glass, her little joke and told the story of how Nimise Makwa came to be. Alain reminded her of Joe Too Little, and she told his story.

"Mon frère," Alain exclaimed at the end. "Moi et Joe, nous sons frères."

"I would like to draw your family." Brandi needed to have a drawing to remember this happy encounter. "Can I visit one day before I leave?"

"Come now," Alain leapt to his feet. He was full of impulse and energy. "Eat with us. Susanne will love you."

On the walk down the hill, they talked about papermaking and the need to tell stories and of relationships and those things connecting people. It was Brandi's turn to be impressed. An endless stream of people on the street greeted Alain by name, stopping to talk. When he introduced Brandi, they shook her hand vigorously or embraced her tightly.

"C'est Nimise Makwa de la Terre Haute," was the phrase he used repeatedly when he introduced Brandi. "See," he turned to her after one of the many repetitions of the words, "I know some Indians too. You and I are both on paths to the high ground."

A little boy ran down the street to them, calling Alain "Poppa". He took the drawing bag and offered to take Brandi's folio, smiling with pleasure as she handed it to him.

"This is my son," Alain looked proud. "He is the love of our lives." Then he turned sad. "We tried many times to have more. Perhaps, one day we will again. We lost four others before they were born or when very young. It is too painful, especially for Susanne." Brandi remained quiet. Her heart searched out Jani and the pain of her one loss.

"They tell me we used to have the best doctors in Canada." Alain broke the silence. "Now, we hardly have any, and they don't have many supplies. The medical schools are no more. There is only a little apprentice programme."

Brandi described the system in the Federation. She resolved to talk to the delegation. Perhaps offering to train doctors could be useful in bargaining.

They arrived at a small, snug house. This began several enjoyable days. Alain invited her to sleep in their house, and she eagerly accepted. He showed her around the town and many obscure places. Brandi met more people than she would have on her own. The language barrier had made for lonely days.

The Roberts' stove burnt wood because Alain and Susanne thought coal polluted. Someone had told them that coal mining in Nova Scotia was dangerous, killing many miners; neither wanted to support suffering.

"Besides," Alain said with a smile, "we go up the St. Charles in winter to visit Susanne's family and cut our wood for two months. We bring it down by boat in spring after the floods, and then we plant more trees. It's an excellent bit of hard work." He showed her many delightful drawings of those winter escapes.

Aside from the personal benefit and pleasure Brandi enjoyed, she learned one more piece of information useful to negotiations. Alain told her the ruler; the old army sergeant would soon die. They did not have a democratic system and expected a power struggle. Even though the leader had specifically said there would be no family dynasty, he had several sons who seemed to think otherwise. Alain suggested it might be unpleasant for a few months once the old man died.

Susanne and Alain intently listened as Brandi explained Huron and the Federation. They asked many questions about the watershed organization and the usufruct system. Brandi had sowed the seeds of a popular movement, which would become a growing influence in the St. Lawrence Valley. They understood how a system to keep Lake Ontario clean would benefit those who depended on the river.

Chez Robert was a focus for art, music and talk. The night before Brandi's departure, they held a gathering with music, dancing, laughter and food. Many children of various ages scurried through the throng. It reminded Brandi of a Longview harvest party or the fire pit at Hope Bay.

People are people, Brandi savoured the revelry, *we have more to share than we know, and there are so many paths to the high ground.*

***

Alain secured free passage on a coal boat and sketched out my route south through old New Brunswick. The railway bridge at Quebec was still useable, and it was one of several coal ports along the riverbanks. It was a genuinely sad occasion to leave my new friends, but I always looked forward to new experiences and new friends.

We ran down the river on the ebbing tide. The captain explained with the current they just needed enough headway to make steerage and saved fuel. Steam-powered the vessel, similar to many I had travelled on. This one was by far the dirtiest.

The only clean space was the kitchen and dining area. These spaces were immaculate, kept under tight control by a ferocious matriarchal cook. She prepared excellent meals and everyone called her "ma mere". She would roar with laughter every time and smile broadly.

My guide, Alain's friend and fellow artist, the only one of the crew of six who could speak English, explained Chantelle had no children of her own but was one of a family of fourteen siblings. The cook claimed this family on the boat was too small to keep her satisfied. That was the captain's job. They had shared a cabin for over thirty years.

"Night travel was not safe, and we put into two ports on the way down the river, offloading coal and allowing me to meet many people and see uplifting examples of innovation and community. It made for an enjoyable

trip. We lingered a day in Tadoussac, the captain's hometown. We then took a dirty, old coal-scow in tow and rode the rising tide to a place called Trois Pistoles."

From: The Outer Loop (The Journals of Brandi Shadly Vol. 26 p 68)

"Look there, to port!" Jean Desjardins stood with Brandi at the railing of the bridge deck, enjoying the strong river breeze and the cloud-studded blue sky. He was pointing to a little white ripple almost lost in waves. A dark shape rose above the surface, and a jet of spray puffed into the air. A large tail rose and seemed to wave at the sky before gently slipping beneath the surface. The water returned to its wind-whipped regularity, but suddenly a huge shape lifted from the water much closer to the boat. It rolled slightly and fell back with a large splash.

"A humpback," Jean was excited. "They are more here now. Mostly belugas before, the blanc ones, but this dark one's marvellous."

The man's accent made the scene more exotic. Brandi was speechless. She had never seen such a large animal. Seagulls wheeled overhead, screeching along with several exotic species she did not recognize. The birds trailed between the boat and the scow, occasionally diving to scoop up a delicacy stirred up by the ship's screws.

Perhaps, Brandi mused, *that's what attracted the humpbacks.*

"I think the whales are social and like us," Jean had extracted a small wooden board and was sketching with a homemade charcoal pencil. "This one's always here to say 'ello if we are on the tide. Watch for the big notch in its tail. Listen to our engine."

Brandi concentrated. There was a slight regular thumping sound coming from below. She could feel it through the steel deck. It seemed the ship talked.

"I think they know it is us from our particular sound. Hey, look! La!" A massive form had broached high into the air a mere hundred meters from the vessel. It rolled, and the mighty body slapped back onto the water in a shower of spray. The tail showed a large distinct notch. Near it, a much smaller form attempted to mimic the first creature. "Le bébé," Jean grinned, and his hand moved faster over the sketch board. "I guess she's a she. This will become a painting in the winter."

The mighty animals accompanied the boat for hours and seemed to enjoy the company, surfacing and broaching several more times. Only when they turned in towards Trois Pistoles did the whales disappear.

"That was wonderful." Brandi looked back to the river and then turned towards the approaching shore. "I had given up hope I would ever see this. I love it all; the sea, the smells, all of those birds and your whales." She smiled at Jean.

"Ah yes, c'est marvelleux, but it is changing. I hope not to be worse. The water gets higher. When I was little, we lived near the shore. See the falling of the banks." Jean pointed to the water's edge near the wharf. "The sea level has risen, and the tides have ripped into the shore. My hometown, down the river, is mort. My house is gone, in a big winter storm."

As they eased the old scow into one side of the wharf, Brandi noticed a much lower dock made of stone cribbing. Now, at high tide, that dock was underwater with a few small open boats secured to large wooden posts floating over the jetty's surface.

"How fast is it rising?" Brandi asked Jean.

"Peut être, a half-meter since I was a boy, I am forty now. C'est fast." Jean seemed sad and frightened. He was certainly perplexed. "I don't know why it's like this."

Warren Dunne and Brent James had explained climate change. They thought changes could come quickly, especially sea-level rise. Brandi stared into the gathering dusk. The river fused with the sky in a deepening grey haze. Suddenly, the wind chilled her. Brandi shuddered and headed below to join in the evening meal.

Chapter Thirty-Five

I left Jean on the wharf at Rivière du Loop. He gave me a seashell with a picture of the boat he had painted on the smooth inner surface. My offering was a sketch of him standing at the ship's rail, his drawing board in his hand with the notched tail of the whale descending into the water behind his shoulder. I hope I captured his smile in the warm way I felt it.

The train ride from the St. Lawrence to the Bay of Fundy was long and not without incident. Our engine broke down, and we spent half a day in a little, isolated village. The population was mentally slow and sickly. One of the train crew made a deprecating remark about the place. In broken English, he explained to me this was "hillbilly country". These people had lived in isolation for generations, with only the railway as a link to the outside. They became inbred and weak. I resolved to make sure that we had no similar places in Huron. My optimism grew as our journey resumed and with our late night arrival at the border.

The sign proclaimed the place as Deersdale. We went to the station to identify ourselves. It reminded me of my interview with Justin in Ohio, except the atmosphere was more relaxed. Several armed guards patrolled the platform, but they seemed unconcerned.

I dropped Frank Tremain's name to the skeptical border agent, but he simply returned my documents from Huron and commented he had met no one from our territory. Apparently, he didn't consider me a threat. We crossed the Miramichi River, entering North Eastern and Atlantic Republic territory. I was in Tremain country.

The trip down the Bay of Fundy from Saint John was interesting and peaceful. I had many more whale sightings and enjoyed a school of dolphins playing with our little ship. It was the largest vessel I had ever boarded. As we made our way south; however, the water became rougher with a constant rolling swell overlain by growing waves and soon tossed the ship wildly. The travellers sharing the lounge told me it was a small vessel for the ocean.

"Night and my spirits fell together. The ship rolled in a growing sea, and I felt sick. Before midnight, it had become so rough one could grab the stair rails and, as the ship fell, simply hop onto the tenth step up. Unfortunately, my condition kept me from moving around. To prevent being embarrassed, I locked myself in a toilet and threw up many times. Later, someone told me braving the deck and breathing fresh air would have been better. I endured the night in misery while the ship bounced along, well away from the Maine coast. My stomach settled as we ran into Portland harbour in daylight to a town larger and more active than Quebec City with huge ocean-going vessels moored to the outer wharves. We tied up with modest steamers and several large sailing ships. Happily for my stomach, I soon stood on firm ground."

From: The Outer Loop (The Journals of Brandi Shadly Vol. 26 p 90)

"Brandi Shadly!" The loud, familiar voice startled Brandi as she stood on the railway platform, waiting to leave Portland. Frank Tremain beamed as he strode down the platform accompanied by a small entourage. They hugged. Brandi had spent two days exploring Portland. She planned to head west, thinking Frank would be in Ticonderoga, although she had only a sketchy idea of how to get there.

"I hear you booked a ticket to Boston." Frank looked serious. "I'm glad I caught you here. You don't want to go to Boston. They're doing their own thing, and we're barely on speaking terms." He smiled again. "Let's get onto this train and out of here, but not that coach; it goes to Boston. Come up here with me." Frank took Brandi's arm and guided her forward to a coach and an express car hooked behind a few freight cars. "We always run combinations." Frank had noticed her glancing towards the engine. Most folks stay put these days, and little demand for dedicated trains."

They entered what looked like the living room of a house, furnished with elegant drapes on the windows and lounge chairs with low tables. Frank ushered Brandi to a chair, and a young woman came to take her gear.

"Set her up in cabin B, Stella." The woman disappeared towards the front of the car.

"You're now my guest, and I want to treat you as the special person you are. Rail is a comfortable way to travel. I came on business anyway, but I wanted to find you. I'm sorry I didn't greet you at the ship."

"How did you know I was coming?" Brandi wondered if the man might be telepathic. Frank's laugh reminded Brandi of their previous trip.

"I knew just after you crossed the border. We have a functioning telephone system. The agent informed us of a strange old woman who had travelled from Ontario via Quebec and claimed to know me. Once I saw the report, I knew, and no, I don't think you're an old woman." He laughed even louder, infecting Brandi with his humour. "You didn't believe that we met by chance did you?"

"It spooked me," Brandi relaxed in the comfortable chair. The train lurched and moved. She noticed that the large, serious men now sat in cubicles near the rear door of the car.

"These are my bodyguards." He followed her gaze. "There are Colonel Jenks types who would like to run things. We need to be careful."

Brandi recalled Jeff's death. Perhaps the North-East was more practical than Huron. Frank must be more important than the mere envoy she met two years previously.

"Have you had breakfast?" Without waiting for a response, Frank called out, and Stella reappeared. He ordered his favourite breakfast of bacon and eggs with home fries. It satisfied Brandi with some eggs and toast. A large coffee pot appeared along with fine china, not as classy as the Jenks but impressive.

"After breakfast, Stella will take you to your room; you can freshen up and rest. I have to work. As you might guess, I have a few more duties than I had two years ago."

Stella showed Brandi to her quarters. The elegant room had a soft single bed, a comfortable chair and a writing table making it a bedroom study, complete with a railway toilet and shower stall. The stream of warm water surprised Brandi who spent a luxurious twenty minutes in the soothing heat easing the effects of her nauseating night on the ship. She donned her nightshirt, slid into bed and drifted into a healing sleep.

***

Ships that pass in the night, and speak to each other in passing, Only a signal shown, and a distant voice in the darkness; So on the ocean of life, we pass and speak one another, only a look and a voice, then darkness again and a silence.

From: A poem by H.W. Longfellow (American poet of the nineteenth century CE)

Of all acquaintances I met during my travels, Frank Tremain remained an enigma, a man of power and influence who understood the ordinary person. Frank is a democrat and believes everyone's voice counts. My personal experience of the man was of one who listened as much as he talked and judged only after learning all he could. Frank is a combination of Warren Dunne's enquiring mind and Chester's leadership ability. Many times, I have wished to sit and chat with him once more. Our travels together seem to have been all too brief. This last time was little more than those two days on the train. I doubt I will ever see him again.

From: "Conversations with Brandi Shadly," in the "Voices of the Founders,"

"Did you sleep well?" Frank smiled across the lunch table as Brandi sat opposite her friend. "I didn't want to wake you, but three hours is a double sleep cycle. Your day would be upside down if you stayed too long."

"Thank you. I didn't sleep on the boat, and I'm still out of sorts. How far have we come?" Brandi accepted coffee to relieve her dry mouth.

"We are about halfway to the junction near Boston. We'll turn west there and head for Troy. The tracks are rough. The train can only do about thirty."

"It looks faster." Brandi glanced out at the landscape sliding by.

"Thirty miles an hour," Frank laughed. "Metric folk have a unique sense of speed."

"Pound for pound, metric is better." Brandi laughed at Warren Dunne's old joke. Frank joined in.

Lunch was tasty and the food plentiful. Stella, who seemed to be the only person working, served the meals. She then brought out her food and sat beside Frank. The men at the end of the car laughed as they ate.

"I never introduced you earlier," Frank glanced at both women. "This is my daughter, Stella. She's as beautiful as her mother and the best cook I know. She is even better than my wife." He hugged his daughter and smiled. "Stella is my joy, and we travel together a lot. She cooks to make sure there is no tampering."

"You aren't the Colonel, are you?" Brandi teased Frank.

"Me?" Frank pretended shock and hurt. "How could you accuse your old friend?" They laughed, and Frank explained Colonel Jenks to his daughter. "By the way," he turned to Brandi, "Jenks is still in charge, as are the other feudal barons, but they kowtow to Erie Shores, which controls the territory to the Ohio River. The feudal guys can't do business unless Erie Shores lets them. Justin will take control when Jenks dies. He will join the Federation."

A young man came from the front and handed Frank some papers.

"Thank you," Frank glanced at the message.

"Brandi, I have to do some work. Let's get together in about two hours for a snack. Stella, please give Brandi a tour, show her everything."

The quick tour fascinated Brandi. The front part of the first coach contained bedrooms for Frank and Stella, plus Brandi's compartment. A well-equipped kitchen separated the sleeping areas from the main room with another guard cubicle at the front end. The rest of the entourage slept in the next car in bunks along each side. A galley and lounge lay beyond, where uniformed men and women relaxed. Everyone wore a sidearm.

"These cars are armoured," Stella explained. "The glass is bulletproof. We draw the curtains at night. There's no organized danger, but some backwater places are lawless. It's best not to take chances."

"Are these people, police?"

"Nope, these are soldiers. We all are." She sounded proud of her role. "We haven't created a civilian force. We handle the drunks and thieves, but if anything happens, it usually requires firepower. Maybe the police will be enough when things quiet down. There are hostile groups south of us. Every little valley seems to have an army. The lower Hudson is dangerous. They trade with us, but if they caused trouble, we would be ready."

Brandi thought Huron was lucky. There had been little of a need for the military since they defeated the PLM. The next coach held a communications centre, with two-way radios and wireless telegraph. Sounds of transmission filled the air, and one operator was in voice communication with some unknown distant receiver.

"We have broadcast radio in Ontario but little two-way or telegraph wireless, just landlines."

"This is difficult to maintain," Stella read a message over the telegraph operator's shoulder. She seemed to understand the jumble of dots and dashes that confused Brandi. "It's a big help to Dad and the other big shots. I'll let him explain what is going. A lot of these messages have to do with Quebec."

The boxcar behind the engine tender made a rolling stable with six horses and riding gear. "If we ever have to chase someone, we can send out a force quickly. I'm in the mounted unit." Stella was extremely proud of her skill. "Do you ride?" Brandi smiled and said yes.

Brandi helped Stella in the kitchen while telling her stories of Nimise Makwa. They spent another hour in the lounge looking through Brandi's folio and telling Stella of the trip with her father until Frank returned.

"Stella, did you show Brandi the radio room?" Frank sipped coffee. "Sure did, Pops. I mentioned Quebec."

"I went to Portland to see a delegation off to Quebec City." He leaned back into his chair. "This gives us an excellent opportunity to solidify our relationship. With the south hostile, peace in the north would help."

"I explained some issues." Stella seemed tired.

"Why don't you go have a lie-down?" Frank touched his daughter's hand. "Phil can get dinner, and you just come and eat." Stella left.

"She was up all night trying to track you down. We feared you had already left town. Your sleeping in the hay threw us off."

Brandi had not located a room in Portland and finally convinced a teamster to let her bed down in his hayloft. It had not been the best sleep.

"I was already on my way to Portland when word about you caught up to me. I sent out a memo last year saying if anyone claiming to be Brandi Shadly or Nimise Makwa showed up to notify me personally."

"The message I just received said they have arrived in Quebec City. They have a portable wireless unit that reaches our station on Mount Washington. The negotiations in Quebec are slow but progressing."

"I heard there might be trouble when the head guy dies." Brandi thought Frank would be interested.

"I'll pass it on. We want to be friends with the winning side. Hopefully, they won't be a bunch of murderers."

"I think there's a citizen's group that may push for more democracy. I spread our Huron philosophy of watershed and usufruct. They,re interested but not the ones in power."

"You convinced me two years ago. We have been reorganizing along watershed lines whenever we can. Most people like the idea and they especially like the veto for the bottom end. It keeps us swelled heads in Troy in line." Frank laughed and took a bite of jam covered pastry.

"The usufruct thing is slower. We Yankees like our land even though most of us are squatters; people believe they own the land. We call it freehold. Usufruct sounds too foreign. We've been able to make sure there's no real-estate market, and inheritance is more or less along the lines you have up there. I'm not ready to ask them to consider the territory as the landowner. Socialism is a curse word here."

Frank seemed disappointed. Brandi wondered about his background. He had an education but must have been young when the economic crisis hit.

"Erie Shores Territory is doing the same thing with the watershed organization and landholding. They're closer to your ideas than we are."

Frank excused himself. Brandi returned to her room and sat sketching despite the incessant rocking of the railway car. She captured Portland harbour and wanted to make sure she depicted the many sailing ships sharing the wharves with more modern vessels. She created an image of the boxcar with the horses, showing Stella caressing her mount. It would be her present for Stella.

The train stopped before dinner and had not moved for several hours. Frank showed up late, only joining Stella and Brandi after they had finished. He explained they were at the junction where the railway split with one line going into Boston and the other west to the Hudson Valley. The Boston leadership met with Frank.

"I've invited them to visit."

Stella groaned. This would be one of her father's famous parties. Frank surprised Brandi by asking her to be both an honoured guest and the evening's entertainment.

"I want you to tell a story and show your drawings."

Brandi smiled. She would do what she loved.

"This meeting today is a bonus," Frank admitted before the guests arrived. "My trip to Portland just might the time we made peace both with the north and Boston which controls the coast up Long Island Sound to the mouth of the Hudson. We might get the crime bosses running New York City to change their attitudes too."

The guests arrived, resplendent in dress suits and ties. The women wore formal frocks and shoes with well-coiffed hair and makeup, but the North-Easters had not changed from their ordinary daily garb. Brandi felt like a hick once more in her homespun hemp and linen clothes. Her short greying hair was presentable, but not alluring like these visitors.

The soldiers from the guard contingent wore dress uniforms. In the end, it did not matter. Frank Tremain was an accomplished host and made everyone at ease. The Bostonians were not snobbish. Frank lubricated the event with some strong drink. Chatter and laughter grew louder as the evening progressed. Brandi judiciously limited herself to sipping a hard cider, and, when Frank called on her, she had a clear head with her memory intact.

Her stories engrossed the crowd, and a party planned for only a couple of hours stretched into the night. It only ended when Brandi became fatigued and begged off more talking. The woman from the north had enthralled them all. She received invitations to visit new friends. A few of those invited themselves to Huron and Kimberly. The Bostonians stumbled off, a little worse for wear, into the breaking dawn. Brandi felt happy and encouraged.

"Frank," she paused on her way to her bedroom, "that was like Little Current compressed into a few hours."

"I think so." Frank smiled. "I owe you thanks. You sealed the deal."

The gentle rocking of the train, moving west towards the Hudson, eased Brandi into a welcome and satisfying sleep.

***

Here is my shortened version of Frank Tremain's telling of the history of the Northeastern and Atlantic Territories. This was their history and only of use to us in understanding our cousins living beyond the frontier. In the years after the collapse, the USA fragmented into many smaller regions, most racked by violence as competing forces, ranging from military units to organized criminals, fought for control. Every substantial military base became a power centre, with the naval base in Norfolk being the strongest military force in the east. After the overthrow of the government, the command structure splintered. A Norfolk naval commander assumed the presidency. The Commands west of the Appalachians became regional power structures. The Norfolk forces attempted to control the Atlantic coastal plain. Violent fighting in Philadelphia stopped them short of New York City. In Florida, everything south of Daytona was a climate-change wasteland.

Real fighting only lasted for the first two years, as starvation and violence decimated the populations. Resources depleted rapidly. Fuel for the high-tech weapons got short, and mutinies deflected the fighting internally. Frank did not know where all the nuclear weapons ended up; for a time; some commanders had tried to use them as threats to extort submission. None had ever exploded. Frank thinks the warheads have depleted to uselessness.

Many members of the military deserted. Cholera decimated the central region and spread with the refugees. The northeast behaved the same as the rest, with the complication of enormous masses of refugees fleeing the large cities. The tide of conflict and destruction reached north past Albany and along the coastal region but then more rugged and remote areas of Main, Vermont, New Hampshire and western New York avoided the refugee onslaught. There was fighting amongst local populations. Vermont attracted more progressive and cooperative refugees similar to our experience in Huron.

Frank was a trained fighter with the US army mountain division. His force from Fort Drum stabilized and unified the northeast. Most of the division had rushed south to defend West Point Academy and had never returned. Frank's special-troops battalion stayed behind to secure Fort Drum. Frank eventually displaced incompetent commanders and rallied the soldiers. Vermont and upper New York united easily, although all the larger urban centres had to be subdued and cleared of local gangsters and warlords. After a decade of struggle, some of which saw bitter, bloody fighting, but most of which was a patient negotiation, the territory from south of Albany, west to Buffalo and northeast along the Canadian border including all of Main came under one central leadership called North-Eastern Territories. They stopped at the Canadian border, too weak for an invasion with pacifying captured territory an ongoing struggle. As security improved, it became hard to maintain fighting forces. Most people only wanted to work and look after their own families.

About twenty years after the crisis had begun a delegation representing southern New Brunswick arrived at Ticonderoga, requesting a union and surprised the North-Eastern Territories. The northern French-speaking portion of that province had joined with their Quebec cousins. Since these delegates did not ask for anything other than trade and security, it had seemed like a good way to secure part of the northern flank. Prince Edward Island and Nova Scotia joined under the same terms giving the territory access to an alternative source of coal. Collapse had not decimated the populations of these regions as other areas and they contributed skilled and healthy labour. The name became the North-East and Atlantic Territories, and the capital moved to Troy for better transportation and communication. The security threat had diminished, making the more remote location less attractive.

It took a day to complete the train trip from Boston to Troy. Frank, Stella and I talked for hours. I settled into the Tremain house in Troy and had the freedom to wander. The town was busy but safe, and I explored daily. When Frank told me he had to leave for several weeks, I took my departure, heading west to Buffalo. Frank escorted me ten kilometres north to the boat I would ride along the Erie Canal. The tug had collected a large coal barge beside the railway yard.

From: The Outer Loop (The Journals of Brandi Shadly Vol. 26 p 163-166)

Brandi handed Frank a drawing of a tree growing from the crumbling concrete of a collapsed road bridge. The two friends stood beneath a large spreading tree, shaded from the bright morning sun.

"A lot of the old stuff is crumbling," Frank stared at the image. "Brandi, I sometimes think we are doing the wrong thing with all this." Frank turned and waved his hand towards the town. A black steam engine hissed and sighed in front of the railway station. The locks of the canal burbled behind them.

"I think we are trying to salvage the past, and this is not the actual future. Maybe we are a bridge between the two, and this will give way." He waved Brandi's drawing of the crumbling river crossing. Frank leaned on a rusting wrought-iron fence, somehow spared a trip to the steel mill.

"My friend George MacDonald said something similar." Brandi turned to look into her friend's face, contemplating this philosopher soldier. "He said we were now walking through a forest with two edges. We had left where the old world had stopped, and the forest began. One day, our children would walk out the other side into a new world. For us, he said, where we came from determined our way, but as we made our way through the darkness, the old influences would diminish. We would wander in the shadows. Then, as we progressed, the light from the edge of the new beginning would guide our descendants. One day, they will pass from the shadows into the light. He said none of us living would see that new world." She stared at the little patches of sunlight leaking through the leaves, dappling the weedy ground.

"George named me, Seeker of Light."

"They want to leave soon," Frank sounded reluctant to say goodbye. Brandi had indeed become his nimise. It amazed him that a tough, old soldier like himself could feel so deeply at this parting.

Brandi hefted her pack, and they slowly walked toward the waterway. The superstructure of the boat rose above the concrete skirt as the lock filled. When the lifting operation was complete, a man with a wild beard, and wearing a battered sailor's cap, stepped ashore. His boat was a snub-nosed pusher with a huge coal-laden steel scow attached to its bow. Most sailors would call this vessel ugly, but it's clean, freshly painted superstructure shone in the morning sun.

"Brandi, this is George Armstrong." Frank hugged the man. They appeared to be friends. "Army, take care of Nimise. She's valuable cargo."

"Yes, General!" George straightened suddenly and snapped a classic, military salute to Frank, surprising Brandi. The man expressed a mixture of military subservience and deep friendship. This simple act of respect implied something much more profound between these two men. Frank hugged Brandi and then pulled out a little metal object from a pocket.

"This is a brass candle holder I made for you." He handed her the object along with a small candle made of bee's wax. "I thought you could light this once in a while and chase away some shadows." Brandi hugged Frank as she accepted the gift. They hugged once more.

"I don't think we will meet again, Nimise."

"I know," Brandi turned and climbed aboard the boat.

She could not see Frank's tears, and he could not see hers.

Chapter Thirty-Six

I thought about Jane and John David as I travelled the Erie Canal. They had long since joined many others in their final rest. Their retirement plans had been to take their boat down the Erie Canal to the tropics. They would have enjoyed the beauty and community of this place.
From: "Conversations with Brandi Shadly," in the "Voices of the Founders,"

"It's a little village along this canal," Brandi spoke to George as she stowed a hooked pole against the gunwale. They had just cast off from a lock-side mooring after trading coal for grain and a couple of kegs of cider. The testing of the cider had delayed them a few hours. They were leaving a regular little hoedown as the local folks used the boat's arrival as an excuse to get together.

"It's mostly friendly folks along here," George stared at Brandi as she nimbly lifted a hundred-pound sack of grain and dropped it down to crew-member in the hold. "For an old gal, you're sure strong." They were a day out of Waterford, and he enjoyed Brandi's company. "You handle the pike too good to be a lubber."

"Thanks, I think." Brandi tried to glare. "I'm just an old farm girl."

It was a pleasant evening. George set up his customary, comfortable chair on the afterdeck. A pungent mix of local tobaccos smouldered in his hand-carved pipe. Brandi sat on a chair from the mess. It was past high summer, and the shadows lengthened earlier in the evening. The throbbing steam engine could not mask the evening cries of birds.

"What's your story, George?" Brandi gnawed at a juicy apple and moved away from George's drifting smoke. "You saluted, and called Frank, general."

"I got a wife and two kids back in Troy," George drew something obnoxious through the pipe stem and spat downwind over the rail, the spittle making a satisfactory splash in the water. "We've only been together for ten years, but about the General."

He glanced in annoyance at his pipe, as if the device had said something nasty and laid it aside on the hatch.

"Frank and I go back a long way, but my tale starts way back when I was a kid."

Unable to resist, he picked up the pipe and struck a coarse match, drawing flame deep into the bowl.

"I'm from New York City. My mother and I fled about a year after the start of the hungry time. I was small, only three. I barely remember anything... except being hungry. My father's just a blur. Mom told me lots about him, about how kind and smart he was, and how he worked hard for the city. She never said what he did. Later I found a magazine picture of a man in a fireman's uniform which I adopted as a picture of the father I never knew." George paused for a moment. Brandi had many memories of her father. She began drawing rapidly in the waning daylight.

"It got real bad, and I remember being scared. I know now it was shooting, but all I remember is loud scary noises. Mom ran in one day, grabbed me and hurried down the street. She had a little stroller and stuffed me into it. I cried because I was too big for her to treat me like a baby. She just told me to shut up and kept going, fast. We got to the river. A little powerboat waited with a couple of men in it. We jumped in, and they headed up the river. There was a lot of noise and fire behind us, but I felt safe in the boat with Mom. One man smiled at me and gave me a bit of hard, dry bread. Boy, did it ever taste good. I'll always remember that taste."

George reached down and took one apple and bit into it deeply, his pipe forgotten. He glanced at the wheelhouse where the glowing sunset silhouetted his first mate.

"Better find that old bridge to tie up to," George called up. "It should be right here close by."

"I remember little of the trip except the two men seemed to sit close to Mom. I fell asleep, and I woke up in the trees and the green slopes of the Hudson Valley. I'd never seen so many trees. We got as far as Albany in the boat. One man took us to a small house, and we stayed there for some time with lots to eat, and I found a few playmates. Then something happened, and we ran away, north."

George looked pained and hurled the half-eaten apple into the canal. He snapped at the helmsman about the difficulty of a nighttime tie-up, apologized, and then quietly sat while reloading and lighting his pipe.

"Mom and I walked for a long, long time." A perfect smoke ring drifted away to port with George's satisfied gaze watching it dissipate. "Mom hid when anyone came near and always looked back as if someone was after us. I felt hungry again and mad at Mom for it. She would cry, as if the world was ending, then tell me to shush, we would find something better. A few weeks later, after struggling, begging for food and stealing some, we reached the shores of a big lake. We slipped past an old city, Burlington Vermont I know now, to a town on the lake called Colchester; it has a different name now. I have never been back since I met Frank."

A broad smile passed over George's face. Not even his beard could hide it. The memory of meeting Frank had power.

"We stayed there almost ten years. A man made friends with Mom and put us up in an old abandoned house and supplied wood and stuff. He never moved in but visited lots. Mom took in laundry and sure worked hard. I can still see her out in the cold hanging men's long Johns on the line. Her breath used to puff out in gigantic clouds; her cheeks got red." He paused gathering more memories. "She would come inside and run her hands up under my shirt on my back. I would yelp at the cold and struggle. It,s one of my best memories."

George stooped to scratch a match on the sole of his boot. The sudden flare cast his shadow sharply on the white-painted wheelhouse. Yellow flame drew down into the bowl of his pipe, and Brandi could see his eyes glistening in the subdued glow. The match died. George's shadow merged with the darkness.

"I had no schooling then but had playmates. It hurt because some families didn't want their kids playing with me, but they were still good times. I learnt to fish and snare, and we gardened. Then it ended," Brandi heard a little gasp in the dark, "she died."

Another pause as the boat bumped slightly against the concrete pier. A shout from the bridge stirred the deckhand.

They killed her. Men used to come over and give us food and stuff. At least that's what I thought. They were pretty rough. Sometimes Mom was a little beat up. One night one of them was drunk and hit on Mom real bad. She fell down and never got up. The guy who hit her stumbled out, and that was that. I went for help, but no one would come. I was crying a lot.

"Anyway, next day the landlord comes and digs a hole and buries Mom. Just like that. Then he tells me to git. I didn't want to stay there, but he left, and no one came around for a long time, so I just stayed in the house. When the food ran out, I stole. The garden was good, and that lasted until winter. I had to sneak lots from the neighbours and got caught and beat up a few times. I got smart, and no one caught me again." George sounded proud of his abilities.

"I stayed in the house all winter, and then the guy came back, so I ran off. He threw all of our stuff out, but I sneaked around and got what I liked." George dug into a pocket and extracted a little rectangular paper. He then struck a match so Brandi could see the battered and cracked photograph of a smiling, pretty, well-dressed and well-fed young woman.

"That's Mom in New York." He carefully placed the photo back into a protective leather folder.

George suddenly stood and stretched, with a big noisy yawn. The effects of the long day of humping bags of coal and the testing of the cider had taken their toll. He disappeared into the captain's cabin. Brandi curled up under a covering on the deck. The stars shone down, bathing her in soft light. In the morning, they made their way once again, picking up some steel scrap.

"Tell me how you met Frank Tremain," Brandi helped George stow a large, rusty, steel bar.

"They're still finding scrap to trade." George shoved the bar with his foot. Brandi thought he was ignoring the question.

"Frank was the best thing that happened to me since Mom died, don't tell my wife." He chuckled, but the words highlighted Frank Tremain's status. "I lived on my own for two years." George worked a pike-pole pushing the little boat off a concrete wall.

"It was hard, and I was sad. I missed Mom and had never even gotten to say goodbye. Some of my young friends helped a bit. I was the best fisher in the group, and they often had extra to take home for dinner. In the second winter, when I was fourteen years old, things got rough. I was running out of food and having trouble keeping warm. That's why I took the chance I did when the army camped near the lake. They were a mean-looking bunch, and dangerous I thought, but by March I was desperate. I snuck into a cook tent, thinking I was smart and quick, but these fighters were a few notches better than the local folks. It was no problem getting into the tent, but when I turned to leave a big guy was standing right behind, just waiting for me. He hadn't made a sound. I was so surprised I nearly choked. As it was, I must have looked pretty silly. I had a half-eaten turkey leg hangin' from my mouth, and my arms were full of bread and turkey.

"He had seen I was hungry and let me eat before he nabbed me. Even then, he let me recover and finish the leg. Most of them fighters had family or lost family or memories of being a hungry kid, but they was as eager to shoot as smile too. Then, he took me to the guy he called the boss. That was Frank."

George finally could lay the pole down and give Brandi his full attention.

"Watch that first bend up there," George called up to the wheelhouse. "Remember the old truck underwater by the road."

"Someone killed hisself," George remarked nonchalantly to Brandi, "drove his truck into the canal. They fished a skeleton out when they was getting the canal ship shape. My grammar ain't very good." He sat on the hatch cover and retrieved his pipe. "That's part of the story. I got some schooling after." A puff of smoke sped off on the breeze.

"Frank scared the crap out of me. He said I was lucky his man hadn't shot me right then. Then he asked me my story. I told him about what I told you up to now, with a few more tears and some shakin' too. The damnedest thing, Frank looks like he's about to cry too. He lost contact with his family, him being up at Fort Drum and them down south and all. He understood and said I should join up.

When he found out how young I was, he said I could be his batman. One of my friends had some old comics, and one was this Batman guy. I told Frank I didn't have a costume. Anyway, he didn't understand my thinkin' and said not to worry. The army duds weren't the black cape I was expectin'."

"Well, I became Frank's helper, carrying and fetchin' for him, too young to fight, but I trained and marched with them. We did a lot in two years. First, we cleaned out all along the lake, both sides and then on down this way. We fought lots of small battles and cleaned up thugs and gangs and a few self-appointed rulers. We were unifying the whole thing. That was the start of the Northeastern Territory.

"It was dangerous, dirty work. We got halfway across New York State before Frank gave me a rifle and put me on active duty. I was real proud and went off by myself to tell Momma out loud I would be a good soldier."

George paused for a long time, smoked a pipe full of tobacco, and then continued. "About the end of the third summer, we suddenly start marching hell-bent over to the Hudson and on down a bit. We ran into a big force of fighters coming up from the city. It seems they had plans to conquer the farmland to feed them. They weren't nice and wouldn't talk. It was the biggest battle I ever saw and heavy weapons on both sides. Frank was a good leader. They were just rabble. Still, lots of us were hurt or killed before we done them in." George skirmished with his reluctant pipe.

"We got into close fighting, even hand to hand. In one of these dust-ups, one of their guys got a bead on me. I would have been a goner, but Frank was right there and shot the guy. After that, I told him I owed him everything and would stick to him come thick or thin. I became his bodyguard until the fighting stopped. He fixed me up as a deckhand on a boat, and I travelled the canal. ,Bout ten years ago they made me captain. I married this sweet gal. We live just over from Frank and the missus. Here let me show you a picture of my kids."

George went to his cabin and returned with a large piece of paper. Brandi had been expecting a photograph. It surprised her when he showed her a fine hand drawing of him standing beside a pleasant-looking woman and two smiling children. The picture did not match her skill, Andre, or Joe Giingoo; it was as good as many of her students.

"It looks like you have a talented artist in Troy too." Brandi felt the love the image captured.

"Frank drawed it," George stared at the paper. "He didn't tell you he was an artist." George smiled. "He got lots of talent. You're the gal he told me about from that trip. He thought he was good until he met you. Frank says

you put magic onto the paper and cast a spell over folks. He was right."
George sat and relit the pipe.

They dropped the barge with its cargo of Nova Scotia coal at the eastern
end of Lake Oneida. It was a rough crossing of the lake. The boat sailed
easier in the confines of the canal, not open water. At Brewerton, they
retrieved an empty scow and pushed it west to Buffalo. A load of Ohio
coal would travel east on George's return trip. Brandi stepped ashore on
the Erie frontier, still savouring the community along the canal.

"The railway is useful too," George had explained. "But the canal costs
less to run and doesn't need machinery. They're even fixing the draw
paths along parts of it. Maybe one day, my kids will use animals to pull
these barges. I think things are going downhill, back to the old ways."

Brandi shook George's hand. He was too shy for a hug.

"Tell Frank I'll think of him often and you too," she hefted her pack.
"All the best to you, George."

"All the best to you, missy," the man doffed his sea cap.

Brandi turned and headed towards the railway station, intent upon
getting home. It had been a wonderful trip, but she missed Erin and
Kimberly. Behind her, three sharp blasts of a steam whistle carried
George's last farewell.

***

"Move that stuff," the gruff voice commanded. "Someone might trip
over it."

Brandi had set her pack on the floor at the end of a bench in the empty
waiting room of the Niagara railway. This late in the evening, the only
other people in the room were the guard and the ticket agent. The train to
Hamilton would leave an hour after daybreak.

"I'm just getting a ticket and then I'll straighten it up." Brandi used her
friendliest tone.

"I told you not to leave it there."

The man was big, wearing a pistol and the uniform of the railway with a
shoulder patch saying "Police". He seemed determined to exercise his
authority. Brandi picked up her gear and carried it to the ticket counter.

"I think I need to see some identification." The security guard had
followed her. A side door opened behind the counter. A familiar figure
hurried to stand beside the agent.

"I'll take care of this one. Go grab your break, Bill." The newcomer smiled at Brandi. He was Peter who had delivered Chester's letter. "I know this woman," he glared at the security guard. "I'll take over from here." It was clear Peter was in charge. The others scuttled away.

"Hello, Miss Shadly." He allowed the other man to depart and spoke in low tones. "You can't use the pass. You're on a list of undesirables. They'll refuse passage. Do you have cash? I can't get a free ride past them."

"I need to go to the washroom," Brandi winked at Peter. She noticed the other agent lingering by the door. Brandi retreated into the restroom. Behind the locked door, she took her knife and cut the stitching at the top of what appeared to be a decorative patch on her pant leg. Brandi extracted a thousand dollars of railway script. She placed the bulk of the bills into an inner pocket and a sufficient amount for a ticket, into her jacket.

"Can I get a ticket right through to Flesherton?" Brandi placed some bills on the countertop. They were old worn notes but had the proper embossment and signature.

"I'll give you two tickets. Only show the one to Oakville first, but the train won't leave until eight in the morning." He looked worried. "It would be safer if no one knew your final destination. At Oakville, you'll have a brief wait. Try to be inconspicuous. Board the train to Orangeville at the last minute. They usually won't check your ticket until you are almost there." Peter's voice stayed conspiratorial. The rear door was ajar, and the other agent continued to spy.

"What's his problem?" She did not look up.

"Oh, it was a slow day, and he wanted to do the work. He's a trainee and hopes he might get my job one day if he works hard enough. The poor guy hasn't learned, it's who you know that gets you ahead with the railway. I was lucky, but they won't be promoting me." Peter laughed.

"Your writing is good," Brandi pocketed the tickets.

"Thank you, Miss Shadly. Your opinion means a lot to me. I kept all your letters and the one from Billy too. Can I give you a little thing I've written? It's just in the back. One second." He hurried off, returning quickly with sheets of paper filled with neatly written paragraphs.

"Your writing has improved." Brandi shuffled the papers. It was a short story entitled "Living in the Mist–A Boyhood Memory of Niagara."

"You told me to write what I know, and little details sometimes are the most important. The story is about when I was ten. I'm doing more stories for the Mist series."

"You have the storyteller's heart." She leaned slightly forward. "Write everything in your heart. You are telling it to the future." Peter smiled happily.

"I'm going to read this in the corner and rest."

"I'll stay all night, so these guys don't bother you."

Brandi read the story. It was heartfelt and honest. She found a comfortable position on the hard, wooden bench and slept. The room remained silent throughout the night.

"Nimise," the word came gently. "Nimise!" Brandi opened her eyes. Peter's face pressed close to hers. "The train leaves in thirty minutes." He smiled, yawning. "A few people here want to say goodbye."

Brandi sat up with a start. People crowded the waiting room. Most stood, the closest sat on the floor.

"Some of us have been here all night," a seated woman said.

One of Peter's artist friends had come by to chat, but once she realized Nimise Makwa was sleeping in the corner, she ran off to spread the news. The station filled quietly in the late evening. Many had met her on her previous visit. Once more, people pressed close, some presenting drawings for her to see and others wanting to shake her hand. The collection of excellent images cheered Brandi.

"We have a group here we call, The Club". One told her. "Peter started it. Writers and artists get together to criticize each other's stuff. It's a lot of fun."

"Everyone still talks about your last visit," a young man said as he helped Brandi to the waiting train. "Today will become another legend."

Brandi stood on the bottom step to the railway coach and spoke to the throng on the platform.

"Thank you. You have made the end of my journey a joyous occasion."

None caught the double meaning. Her tired body told her the long journeys would no longer be possible.

"The spirit of Nimise Makwa lives in the mist and the sound of thunder. Nimise Makwa is not me. She's in your heart, making you want to share your stories and protect the world you share. It will always live there."

The engine blew two loud blasts, and the train moved gently away. The cheers and farewells faded in the clicking of the wheels and rushing wind.

Chapter Thirty-Seven

Perhaps my sombre mood came from Peter's concern for my safety. Whatever the source, we made our way north from Niagara through a landscape of desolation and decay. I saw the impact of the decimated population from the window of the railway coach. Much of the housing and other buildings along the railway had only their foundations standing as a reminder of the decline; vegetation reclaimed them. I saw deer grazing amongst these ruins, an encouraging sign. They reminded me of pictures of crumbling castles in England.

One annoying new feature was the radio piped into the coach. Radio was widespread with some local transmitters and the railway controlled radio station in Oakville. Niagara had an especially good factory to make simple receivers. On the train, most of the broadcast comprised insipid music and long-winded recitations of the virtues of the railway. Fortunately, the train north did not have a radio installed.

From: "Conversations with Brandi Shadly," in the "Voices of the Founders,"

"Where are you coming from?" The railwayman towered over Brandi on the Orangeville bound coach.

"Niagara," Brandi answered before remembering her ticket was only from Oakville.

"Why didn't you just buy a ticket all the way?" The question did not seem to be friendly conversation.

"Oh," Brandi caught herself, "I wanted to stop in Oakville and see Ron Prendergast at the radio station."

"Wow, you know him?" The man became friendly. The worship of famous people was widespread. "I like the programmes on there. The company," he said company in a reverent tone "has some great shows. I met Mr. Prendergast once." His chest puffed out. The man sat down opposite Brandi, returning her ticket. "I'm the conductor and boss of the train." He seemed proud of his title.

He subjected Brandi to a monotonous stream of self-important meanderings. Brandi heeded Peter's advice and did not reveal her identity. The pompous man seemed not to notice. Luckily, he had waited until almost at Orangeville to check the passenger tickets. After half an hour, she found relief as he left the train. Brandi found the episode enlightening. The blind loyalty of this ambitious conductor represented what Brandi thought were the dangers of the railway organization.

At the railway section boundary in Orangeville station, new people replaced the Oakville crew. The new conductor, a woman named Hope from Huron contrasted with the obnoxious man. Brandi had met Hope at the celebration of Brian Young becoming manager of the Huron division.

"Brandi, it's a job, but not much fun." The woman had quickly taken care of her duties. "They have tight control of everything. We have layers of bosses and tons of paperwork." Hope dug into her uniform jacket pocket and removed a folded wad of paper.

"I have your name on here. I am supposed to report if I have anyone on this list riding my trains." She opened the paper and showed the columns of names. It shocked Brandi to see the name of every Huron councillor and even Rob Bossley. It listed Brandi as both Shadly and Nimise Makwa.

"I won't be making any report about your trip. Mark was careless. He does not know who you are. He got his job because he's the nephew of one mucky-muck down in Hamilton." Brandi had the impression Hope wanted to spit. "I should talk," she chuckled. "Mom knew Jennifer Young and got me the job. I was born in a refugee camp in Orangeville. Jennifer came down to help in the aid effort and recruited Mom to be her helper. They're great friends."

Brandi suddenly realized Hope would have been born after the collapse. Hope had the hardened, competent look of someone brought up to a life of work and responsibility. Her face did not have a deep sadness marking older people. Despite her negative talk about the railway, Hope had an energetic spark and represented the spirit of her name.

"What should we do to improve the railway?"

"New coaches and steam engines would be nice." Hope cautiously said.

"No, as an organization, I won't quote you."

"We should do something about the people at the top." Hope glanced about. They had no listeners. "They're powerful and scare me."

"Why's that?" Brandi wanted arguments she could use.

"They take us down to Hamilton for meetings, call them rewards for good service, but I don't like them. They try to fill us with a bunch of good feelings for the company, but it's just a big party and they always watch us. I think they want to see who they can trust." Hope glanced around nervously at the thought of spies.

"People party, getting drunk and everything. I think it's encouraged because some get loose in their talk. A few who mouthed off about their dislike of the company lost their jobs soon after. One guy who wanted a union disappeared." Hope shuddered.

"We had rats in the camp when I was young. We learned to avoid the PLM spies. I see the same rats hanging about our meetings and parties, pretending to be friends and get us talking. I try to sound like a harmless, company-loving idiot."

Hope represented the strength of a generation soon to be running things. She had given some actual information for Brandi to present to Huron council and perhaps change the railway. Brandi went directly to Owen Sound to the General Council.

Chapter Thirty-Eight

The Council was in session when I arrived at Owen Sound. The Quebec delegate had returned, and the Council was discussing proposed new arrangements with Quebec. My status as Nimise Makwa gained me special permission to speak. Many of the Councillors were people I did not know, adding to my stress. I carried on despite this strange nervousness. My speech lasted over an hour outlining my misgivings about the growing power, and what I saw as the corrupt, self-serving direction of the railway leaders. I included the questionable goings-on in Cornwall and Niagara-On-The-Lake and discussed the control of the radio station and the poor treatment of both travellers and employees. The news they were on the watch list and the railway considered them enemies shocked the Councillors. I saved that bit of information for the finale. It created the desired effect."

From: "Broken Steel, Mended Path–The Railway Incident" (The Journals of Brandi Shadly, Vol. 27, p 1)

"I don't see this as a big problem," said a new councillor from the southern edge of Huron Territory. "It seems to me; the railway has brought nothing but good things to Huron."

Brandi sat beside the Chairman. They had become friends on the trip to Quebec. He whispered. "That's Delbert. He runs a freight outfit in Durham and sells wood and grain to the railway."

"Who else is in their camp?" She looked around the table.

"There's one other guy who services the engine tenders and the water towers. He used to work with Jim Handley and struck out on his own once Jim retired." The Chairman glanced over the Councillors. "I think the only other problem might be the guy from Feversham, mad there's no railway there. He's a contrarian who usually votes against the majority."

"Jim Handley and Barry Young both warned me about the railway becoming too powerful." The woman delegate from Owen Sound had the floor. "They said the new managers did not see the railway as a service to the territories but as their property and an opportunity to get rich."

"What's wrong with that?" Delbert piped up.

"You don't remember the collapse do you?" An older Councillor slowly stood. "You don't remember the whole crisis and all the pain, suffering and death because a lot of rich folks thought they were more important than everyone else. They sucked us all into that thinking and look at what happened. It sounds to me that the railway people are the same. It's my opinion," the Councillor gazed around the table, "we have to nip this in the bud. I want to propose a motion." There was a general stir around the room, and two voices mumbled objection. "I move," the man consulted a paper lying on the table in front of him, "we send delegates to the other territories in southern Ontario to ask them to consider limiting the power of the railway managers." Nods of approval flowed around the table. Several Councillors seconded the motion.

"I guess talking won't hurt," Delbert spoke up, "but they've always given me a fair price and buy everything I offer. I never have trouble with them, and families depend on my business. We shouldn't upset the apple cart. I say no!"

Delbert slumped into his chair and voted "No". They drafted a letter to all territorial councils and the Federation headquarters in Port Huron.

***

"Once again, I find it useful to use extracts from The Flesherton Flyer to tell the story of the struggle with the railway. Brandi acquired pneumonia shortly after Samantha's death, and we spent the winter and the following growing season at Longview. Pneumonia has become a dangerous problem, and the threat to Brandi was great. Her loft was too cold, and we spent the winter in the first stone building Longview had constructed. Space became available with Debbie Hunter's passing from pneumonia.

Brandi could enjoy her family there. It insulated us from the railway confrontation. Brandi only played a part at the beginning and then at the very end of the struggle."

From: A note by Erin Thomas in The Journals of Brandi Shadly

October, Year 41 - Flesherton Flyer Vol. 27 No. 19

It is with great sadness that we announce the passing of our founder, Samantha James. This talented lady died in her seventy-eighth year on September twenty-fifth, forty-five years to the day, after the economic crisis changed the world. She spent her last days comfortably, enjoying the bright, warm September sunshine. For those of you who did not attend the services, Brandi Shadly read the eulogy. Samantha had been Brandi's teacher in Weyburne for two years after the collapse and before they came to Huron. Samantha was a great mentor, mother and friend. She has no known relatives. Our teacher, our love, now rests in peace in our garden beside her husband, my father. The Flesherton harvest party will be in her honour. With sadness: Stephanie James (Editor)

Owen Sound

The Huron General Council will hold a special session after the harvest to discuss the railway. Delegates have returned from visiting several of the territories, and others sent written communication. There are proposals to restructure the railway and regain territorial control.

December, Year 46 - Flesherton Flyer Vol. 27 No. 23
Owen Sound

The past two months have seen heated sessions of the General Council. Most territories are unsure of what to do about the centralized power of the railway. Most feel the benefits of having the transportation system are huge, and we all have a stake in the system. People remind us, repeatedly, we would not have the sugar, fruit and other delicacies available to make the solstice season so special if the railway did not run. Last month, we detailed the list of benefits to having the line and the risks involved in opposing the company. This may be the majority opinion.

Flesherton

The railway posted a new rate schedule at the Flesherton station with ten percent decreases to the rates paid for wood and grain and a surcharge of five percent to cover loading. They also impose the same increased rates for third-party shipments and mail. The C.O.D. freight rates for goods from the south have increased ten percent. Ben has passed on the reason as being increased labour costs. We have heard rumours of a lot of spending on things not related to the operation of the system. We are trying to find concrete evidence of such expenditures. These new rates will be effective on January 1. The company will only accept Railway Script in payment for passage and mail. The railway will install trading warehouses at each station allowing people to convert goods to script and implement a service charge for such transactions.

Flesherton

The Christian community is once again holding its popular Christmas celebration. There will be a week of gatherings, bonfires, skating if the weather cooperates, banquets, culminating in services in the evening of December twenty-fourth and Christmas morning. Those of all faiths and non-believers are invited. They encourage potluck contributions and musical and artistic participation, with thanks. This event is perhaps the local musical highlight of every year. We understand several of the fine artists from Kimberly will participate; however, Nimise Makwa is ill and not be attending this year. We wish Brandi a speedy recovery.

January, Year 46 - Flesherton Flyer Vol. 28 No. 1

Owen Sound

Huron General Council has demanded a meeting with the railway company related to the recent new rate structure. The Territory does not have significant reserves of Railway Script, and thus can no longer afford to transport the Mounted Constabulary and similar official uses. They dispatched a letter over the Chairman's signature this week past, and the Council awaits a reply. They have postponed the debate concerning the status of the railway pending the hoped-for meeting.

Flesherton

Organizers have recovered various items of apparel and miscellaneous belongings after this year's Christmas celebrations. Ben has these items on display at the station. Speaking of lost things, the Charles family would like their oldest son, and the young woman who enticed John to move in with her at the Tuesday dance to contact the family. The Charles'would like to arrange for the proper nuptials, as they are firm adherents to the

Christian faith. Rumour has it, they should look out the fourth line for the happy couple.

February, Year 46 - Flesherton Flyer Vol. 28 No. 3
Owen Sound

The railway management has refused to meet with any territorial governments. A letter to that effect arrived from Hamilton at the end of January. The company confirmed its fee structure and warned of future increases. They suggest local administrations impose a tax on residents to pay for any increased costs. The railway has offered to lend some immediate operating Script at a rate of five percent per annum. Council will meet on February 24th to consider the situation.

Flesherton

The Charles family announced the engagement between Master John Charles 16, eldest son of Mr. and Mrs. Jack Charles, and Miss Beth Grogan 24, the teacher at the Saugeen Junction day school and proprietor of Junction Farm. Miss Grogan is originally from Kincardine and has no family locally. The Charles plan the wedding for the Flesherton Christian Assembly in early June before haying and will hold a get together in the couple's honour February 14th at the Assembly Hall upstairs from the textile works. The family stresses, they will not allow under any circumstances, alcoholic beverages at the celebration.

March, Year 46 - Flesherton Flyer Vol. 28 No. 5
Owen Sound

Huron Territorial Council unanimously recommends no one sell goods to or ship via the railway. The discussion revealed the new freight rates and reduced prices have eliminated any profitability for the wood harvesters and farm surpluses. They request no one place new orders for goods delivered by rail. The Council has issued a further statement acknowledging the hardship this will place on the textile shops, foundries and other operations requiring material from the south. Work is already underway to arrange shipments of essential commodities during the summer navigation season on boats sailing directly from the Erie Shores Territory and the western lakes. On a temporary emergency basis, units of the Huron Mounted Constabulary will stand at major centres from Dundalk in the east through to Mount Forest and Tiverton.

Council has sent a letter to the railway company demanding copies of any Deeds of Right they might have for all property the railway is occupying in Huron. The Chairman has issued a personal appeal for no hostility towards our brothers and sisters who work for the railway. He notes the dispute is with the management and not the employees.

Saugeen Junction

The severe snowstorm last week has blocked the rail line along the open stretch next to the Cuddle's farm just south of the junction. This blockage may remain in effect for some time as the railway had earlier announced reduced wages for local labourers who would normally work hard to clear the snow. No one is shovelling snow at present. An iron-ore train waits up in Owen Sound, and no can say when it might be moving. A work train from Oakville has headed north, but a large drift south of The Corners is blocking the line.

May, Year 46 - Flesherton Flyer Vol. 28 No. 11
Flesherton

The railway no longer allows us to post this news bulletin at the railway station. They have deemed us "incompatible with the interests of the railway". Activity at the station has declined considerably. We will post at the crossroads and in the usual places in the smaller towns. You will see new notice boards complete with cedar-shingled roofs appearing along the more travelled paths. These, donated by the H.E.I. Jim Handley carpentry-mentoring programme will hold our postings, and other community and personal communications.

Owen Sound

With planting in full swing, the Council has scheduled a meeting at the end of the month. The Chairman informs us most territories serviced by the railway in southern Ontario are complying with the initiative not to do business with the company. Further, the demands from the territories have moved beyond simply redoing the rates and charges. There is now a joint effort to design a restructured railway under direct territorial control.

Longview

Our sister publication, The Thornbury Stream, reports Nimise Makwa is making good progress in her bout with pneumonia. Brandi could help clean seed for the planting. We wish her a full recovery.

June, Year 46 - Flesherton Flyer Vol. 28 No. 13
Owen Sound

In response to the erroneous reports on the railway radio station, the Huron General Council has issued a statement denying there is any intention to expropriate the railway or to evict landholders enjoying the occupation of land under usufruct. Landholders are still subject to the original rules of usufruct and as changed after the tragic freehold revolt.

The Council declares, with the other territorial governments, they never ceded the railway to the present group of managers. All rights of way, rails and rolling stock still belong to the territories that host these assets. Council has sent a joint communication to the railway management and registered it with the Federation. This document states, the managers and all other employees of the railroad are employees of the territories and subject to these governments. The territories have summoned the directors to a meeting in Guelph after the fall harvest.

Flesherton

The Charles/Grogan wedding went off without a hitch. The bride shone radiantly in a flowered cotton dress especially hand-stitched for the occasion by Dot Shepitka. Beth wore a pair of doeskin moccasins, made by a student at Kimberly. She carried a bouquet of assorted wildflowers, and similar flora adorned the band of her wide-brimmed straw hat. The groom wore a new pair of double-weave, hemp bib-overalls, dyed blue, and over a crisp white linen shirt closed at the neck by a red bow tie. Sheila Charles, the groom's youngest sister, was the flower girl. Erin Thomas, who mentored Beth Grogan at Kimberly, stood up for the bride. It was nice to see Brandi Shadly in attendance and looking well.

The couple will reside on the fourth line where they farm and host the Saugeen Day School. As is our custom, the bride will not be taking the groom's name. Yours truly accidentally caught the bouquet. Boys, you will find me in attendance at all local social functions assessing my prospects. I prefer men over thirty years of age.–Stephanie James

October, Year 47 - Flesherton Flyer Vol. 28 No. 21

Oakville

There is widespread unhappiness in the industrial centres of Hamilton and Oakville. Shortages of food, especially grains have developed, aggravated by dwindling supplies of firewood. The radio station in Oakville has been issuing a stream of denunciations of the territorial boycott. It is becoming clear, if the dispute lingers into winter, there will be widespread hardship. There is a tone of desperation in statements from the railway management. Adjacent territories such as The North-East and Atlantic and Erie Shores territories have supported our action and are not shipping to the western end of Lake Ontario. This support has caused a lack of coal for the steel mills and the railway.

Owen Sound

Huron General Council announced in September; they will open facilities to stockpile excess grain and other agricultural products. This year's surplus will provide over a year of reserves of all staple grain. A subcommittee is investigating using this accidental bounty as the basis for a one-season reserve against future crop failures. We may need to ship food south to prevent a humanitarian catastrophe.

Guelph

Delegates from all the territories are on their way to this town to attend the meeting with the railway management. All the representatives have been travelling by horse and not using the railway. Brandi Shadly is still too weak for such a journey, but Erin Thomas has accompanied our delegates.

Thornbury

Our sister publication, The Thornbury Stream reports the Longview harvest party this year was hotter than normal. The venerable old hall in Heathcote caught fire, near the end of the evening, and burnt to the ground. No one was injured, but Joseph strained his back helping several men save his favourite piano. The musician has been the butt of much teasing, suggesting his legs are now strong enough to fork manure. Jani Shadly-Coswell, the business manager of Longview, has announced a building bee in the spring to replace the old structure. Jani confided to me; she cried while watching the old place go up, taking many memories.

October, Year 47 - Flesherton Flyer Vol. 28 No. 22
Guelph

There is mixed news regarding the attempt to have the railway management listen to reason. The company did not send an official delegation, but only one man purported to be an observer. Learning that he was trying to make a list of the attending territorial representatives, they threw the man out of the meeting hall. A band of local youth chased the interloper to the Guelph station, where he escaped on a Hamilton bound train; however, he lost all of his possessions. Included in the spoils was the man's lunch. Guelph locals have dubbed the incident, "The Pork Sandwich Rebellion".

The delegates drafted an ultimatum demanding that the railway managers allow overseers to assume operation of all the railroad enterprises. Each territorial government must ratify this document. Huron will meet in November to consider the approval of this plan.

Meaford

For the first time since the freehold rebellion, the Security Force requires citizens to prepare for their stint of service. Ted Macedo, head of training and operations, is preparing for winter training. Locals are fulfilling their security-service obligations by repairing the facility.

Owen Sound

J.J. Smithson, Chief Constable (acting) has assembled several dozen officers at the Owen Sound barracks. J.J. has stated they will perform routine security related to the meeting of the General Council.

Flesherton

Ben, the Station Master, has announced the railway management has directed him to hold a pre-Christmas children's party at the station to show the company's care and concern for its customers. He will hold the party on the first Saturday in December.

December, Year 47 - Flesherton Flyer Vol. 28 No. 24

Oakville

Food and fuel rationing now exists within the railway trading-zone, including the larger centres from Cornwall to Sarnia. Railway radio reports large demonstrations have been frequent occurrences in these larger centres. The broadcasts blame these incidents on criminals and agents of the outlying territories.

Meaford

In a brief statement, Ted Macedo has told us the training of the first contingent of field leaders is progressing well. In a related story, the Huron General Council will issue a statement in January concerning future efforts related to the railway. The Chairman has sent a personal message wishing everyone a wonderful Solstice celebration.

Flesherton

I please us to announce Brandi Shadly will attend this year's Solstice festivities in the village. She will oversee the art and craft workshops at the James' house. Yours truly will attend there as well and hope the artistic young man who won top honours at the Priceville harvest festival will attend. To avoid some of last year's excesses, we will not serve alcoholic beverages to anyone under the age of eighteen. Despite the fortunate outcome for the Charles family last year, Mrs. Charles has expressed the desire to avoid the possible exploitation of the young and its resulting family upset.

The railway children's party was a complete failure, but Ben will once again play Santa Claus. He will be resident in the church hall every afternoon during the week and preside over the after service festivities Christmas Eve. Several of Ben's grandchildren will act as elves.

January, Year 47 - Flesherton Flyer Vol. 29 No. 1 (Special Edition) Owen Sound

After midnight on January 1, the Chairman of the Huron General Council issued the following statement:

"At six in the morning of December thirty-first, forces of the Huron Territory occupied all railway facilities in Owen Sound, Thornbury and Southampton. They sent trains carrying elements of the Huron Mounted Constabulary and the Huron Emergency Security Force south to Orangeville and to Kincardine and east of Thornbury, securing Railway facilities within Huron Territory with no violence. The forces detained several railway employees at various locations pending their transfer south to the industrial centres. Similar operations took place in the Thames Territory and the Nottawasaga and Bay Territory, the Grand River Coalition and the North Erie Federation. Current information suggests all operations have been successful although there were some casualties in the Grand River jurisdiction. I would like to thank J.J. Smithson and Ted Macedo for their excellent work in organizing and coordinating this effort. Both men have praised the professionalism and dedication of their forces and pleased with the high quality of the men and women under their commands. They will hold a meeting of the Council today, with more announcements forthcoming."

January, Year 47 - Flesherton Flyer Vol. 29 No. 2 (Special Edition) Owen Sound

All the railway system north and west of the Niagara, Hamilton, and Cornwall corridor has been isolated from the influence of the central railway management. Despite recent heavy snows, traffic has been possible using the Durham, Mount Forest, Guelph route to the south. Drifts temporarily blocked the line between Orangeville and Owen Sound, but heroic efforts by residents cleared the drifts. There has been no sign of any counteraction by the railway. In a joint statement, the coalition of territories has announced negotiations with railway management via telegraph messages. Guelph remains the location of the ad hoc administration set up by the coalition.

Orangeville

The troop of H.M.C. in Orangeville, led by J.J. Smithson, surprised a large contingent of railway security forces gathered in the town and detained several hundred without a struggle. It appears the railway was preparing to use this force to secure the line to Owen Sound. We have created a security post south of Orangeville. All is quiet as of this writing.

March, Year 47 - Flesherton Flyer Vol. 29 No. 5
Guelph

As previous editions have shown, little has happened through the winter. The ad hoc group has tried, unsuccessfully, to reach an amicable arrangement with the railway Board of Control. The company rebuffed an offer to ship much-needed supplies of food and firewood. Those tuning into the Oakville railway radio station will have heard references to hunger and sickness amongst the population. It appears the railway is holding the residents as hostages to maintain power.

Owen Sound

The Council issued a call for volunteers to join the security forces for duty until the start of spring planting. The turnout has been high. Ted Macedo has set up a refresher course for most of the experienced members. So far, there has been no announcement regarding the duties of these new troops. Something may happen soon to resolve the current impasse. All other territories are duplicating Huron's efforts, and there has been some action at the Federation level. The onset of spring-like weather has added urgency.

Orangeville

A long train of freight cars carrying grain and flour has been sitting in this town for a week. Recently, a second train arrived with gondola cars of firewood and several freight cars with cooking oil from the Chatham mill. It appears there is hope the railway company will agree to some action to relieve the suffering of its citizens.

March, Year 47 - Flesherton Flyer Vol. 29 No. 6 (Special Edition)
Guelph

On March fifteenth, the ad hoc committee in Guelph issued the following statement:

"This morning we informed the Board of Control of the railway company we are removing them as the operators of the railway and all subsidiary entities including the steel mill, oil refinery and the radio network. As of this time, forces of the territorial coalition have been advancing along the railway corridors and other land routes towards Lake Ontario and the main industrial centres. There has been little opposition so far.

"To support the coalition, the Federation of the Great Lakes has announced that elements of the army of the North-East and Atlantic Territory south of Lake Ontario have crossed the Niagara River and have secured the river frontier from Fort Erie to the town of Niagara. These forces are advancing down the river intending to seize the port of Niagara-On-The-Lake. Other contingents from this territory have advanced north from Fort Drum to support a local uprising in the town of Cornwall. We have no reports of fighting in these areas. Naval forces from the Erie Shores have blockaded the coal port near Welland to apprehend any fugitives. We expect a further statement when more information is available."

Flesherton

Telegraph activity has been brisk. Ben at the Flesherton station has agreed to pass on any relevant information. Coordinating train traffic has become a serious matter, and Ben has been living in the Flesherton station to monitor the telegraph and operate the signals. One train a day has travelled each way since the advance south began. There has been no shooting in the Orangeville area.

April, Year 47 - Flesherton Flyer Vol. 29 No. 7
Flesherton

Since the call-up has affected almost every family, it will be no surprise to hear two trainloads of volunteers passed through this town on their way south. The good news, they were unarmed and are simply to support the distribution of food northwest of Toronto. Stephanie Hunter led a medical team to Oakville and sends word the situation is serious, but we have avoided a medical disaster. This reporter wishes her namesake all the best. Kim Handley has arrived in Flesherton to provide medical services in the areas understaffed by the departure of the Hunter team.

April, Year 47 - Flesherton Flyer Vol. 29 No. 8
Hamilton

A representative for the territorial coalition has announced all railway facilities are now in the hands of territorial forces. Some casualties, including deaths, occurred in the last struggle at the company headquarters. The violence resulted from a misunderstanding of the timing of the surrender of the building. All fatalities were with the railway forces although several others were badly hurt.

Guelph

The coalition has announced all is quiet throughout the Great Lakes basin. Relief supplies have moved forward to the major centres and are being distributed free to needy residents. Long lines exist, but there has been a respectful calm. Transportation away from the railway is limited. We appeal for seed for both vegetable and field crops for the critical local planting season.

Saugeen Junction

Beth Grogan has given birth to beautiful twin boys. Kim Handley attended and says mother and babies are doing well. The young father returned home from duty in the south. Beth thanks her mother-in-law Mrs. Charles for her support at the birth.

May, Year 47 - Flesherton Flyer Vol. 29 No. 10
Owen Sound

Most of the Huron Territory forces have returned home. Many volunteers remain in the south helping the locals with spring planting and organizing food distribution. Council has announced another shipment of food will be required, but this will be commercially. Planting is in full swing. Council has appealed to all citizens to help neighbours who may be short of labour due to absent family members.

Guelph

A new organization called the Coalition of Southern Ontario now exists and based in this town. The working group has one representative from each founding territory. This organization will oversee all mutual concerns of the various local territories and administer the railway and other industrial enterprises. We will constrain it from major decision-making unless ratified by local territorial governments. All resources and infrastructure, such as the railway lines and industrial works are the property of the territory in which they are located. Each territory may operate these assets as they deem fit; however, the Coalition will work to maintain mutually beneficial operations such as manufacturing rolling stock, steel track and locomotives.

Niagara

In a remarkable live broadcast, Oakville Free Radio has reported on the departure of the forces from the Northeast and Atlantic Territory. Our readers may have heard the live interview with Frank Tremain, leader of that territory. Mr. Tremain had assumed personal command of his forces on the Niagara frontier, and many have credited his experienced leadership for the nonviolent operation.

One statement he made is of local significance. When asked what kind of payment his territory would expect for their tremendous effort on our behalf, Mr. Tremain said:

"You owe us nothing. We know if we have a similar need, you will support us. Our territory and I personally, owe a great deal to your Nimise Makwa. This campaign is a small repayment. She has opened my eyes to the possibility of a bright future beyond these problems from the past. Her vision is not one of paradise where hope is realized but of a world where there is hope in sacrifice and hard work. Brandi knows we will pass from these shadows into a better future. In her spirit, we wish a growing and peaceful relationship with all of you who have a stake in that struggle."

Chapter Thirty-Nine

"If I had known Frank was at Niagara, I would have gone south with the forces. I had recovered completely and would have been up for a train ride. A few months later, Stella surprised me when she arrived in Kimberly. She acted as a special ambassador, visiting all the territories in the Great Lakes Federation to negotiate observer status for the North-East and Atlantic Territory at the Federation. The south shore drainage basin of Lake Ontario was firmly part of their territory, but they wanted to coordinate with the efforts to protect the lakes. There was no question we would welcome them."

"The North-East and Atlantic gained a vote in all matters concerning Lake Ontario. Since the lake is downstream from most of the drainage system, they effectively have a vote in all Federation matters. This was a template for later arrangements with Quebec. Stella spent a wonderful two weeks with us but finally left to complete her journey before the questionable autumn weather. She left a wind chime, made by Frank, with the chimes of wrought bronze in the shape of bears in various poses. The sound is like laughter. It hangs on our porch beside the front steps."

From: "Conversations with Brandi Shadly," in the "Voices of the Founders,"

A polished, black steam-locomotive sighed and hissed at one end of the Flesherton station. A long line of passenger coaches stretched back through the station. This train from Owen Sound carried the Huron General Council along with the family of Brian Young, head of the Huron

Railway Commission. Joseph of Longview led a small musical ensemble seated on the platform beneath the weather overhang. The train notice board said; "Train No. 1" and beneath were the words: "Barry, Rob and Jim, coming home."

Brian Young led a large group down the wooden decking of the platform. The band played a tune called "Tracks Through My Heart" that Joseph had composed for Barry Young's funeral. Brian stopped to listen and reached out to take the hands of his mother and sister. The three thanked the players and joined the crowd just past the musicians.

Jim Handley stood, surrounded by Ben the Station Master, Erin Thomas and Brandi Shadly with a fourth man holding a wooden mallet and a shining chisel. Rob Bossley, old and frail, sat in a comfortable chair with Jim's hand resting on his shoulder. The new arrivals stopped beside Jim, in front of three tall objects concealed beneath colourful tarpaulins.

"Welcome to you all," Erin Thomas stepped forward as master of ceremonies. "You all know why we are here. Rob, you are in for a surprise, a pleasant surprise I hope." Rob stirred in his chair and gazed around as the crowd laughed and smiled in his direction.

"Three people are most responsible for the existence of this station and the railway it serves. One person here today hammered spikes into this very platform." Jim Handley smiled at the spontaneous applause. "Another man here designed the locomotive sitting beside us. Rob, you were a driving force behind a lot of this."

Erin touched the man's frail shoulder, and Rob gripped Erin's hand tightly. He stared down the platform towards the living engine, feeling pride in his handiwork.

"Sadly, one of those who played a key role is now gone." Erin turned to Jennifer Young and her children. It had been over a year since Barry died and the grief remained strong. A tear formed in her eye. Brian hugged her tightly. Sensing their grief, Erin moved on.

"Part of the Huron Ecology Institute mandate is to record the history of Huron. As a Mentor of Historical Ecology, it is my job to honour that mandate. When Stephan came to me with the proposal for these sculptures, I agreed immediately. I want to introduce Stephan Reinhart, the man responsible for these creations." Stephan stepped forward and waved his mallet to the applauding crowd. "Stephan is self-taught, but he spent a season with Joseph Patterson at Little Current honing his skill."

"I know everyone wants to get to the food and music, so we'll get on with the formalities." Erin turned to Jennifer Young. "Please remove the shroud from the central figure."

Jennifer gingerly pulled on the corner of the covering. The cloth slid clear, dropping to the platform, revealing a life-size statue of her late husband. They made it of cedar, stained to a light tan and polished, so it gleamed. Barry smiled. His left hand grasped a mechanical slide rule while a pencil rested in his right. His foot was forward creating the impression of a man in a hurry.

"I gave Barry centre stage because he was the driving force behind most of the early work even while enslaved by the PLM." Erin looked once again at Jennifer and then to Brian and Melissa. "The Young family took many risks to help defeat the dictators. They sent coded messages to us, so we knew everything the PLM was doing. If any single thing contributed to our victory it was, perhaps, the risks this family took. Thank you, Jennifer, Brian and Melissa." The crowd burst into applause. Many had never heard about the Young's efforts.

"I now want to ask Kim Handley to come and remove the left-hand shroud." Erin stepped back, smiling. Joseph's left hand played some walking music on the piano as his wife stepped forward. The crowd giggled. Joseph winked in response to Kim's feigned glare. The fiddle players scratched out some notes sounding like a sigh.

"Dad, we have always been so proud of you," Kim grasped the cloth and yanked hard. It flew off and draped over one of her shoulders. Her father's form seemed to leap out, carved in the same wood and finished as Barry. His representation gazed towards Barry Young's statue as if discussing some detail. His hand held a large framing hammer, with his baseball cap on his head. Jim Handley stepped forward.

"You all honour me," he smiled lovingly at his family. "It was wonderful to be part of this massive undertaking. Barry inspired me as a partner, boss and friend." Jim fell silent, contemplating the forms under the overhang. He reached out and touched Barry's wooden shoulder as if asking a question. He stepped back to join his family.

"Rob," Erin turned to the seated man. "We all know the significant contribution you made in expediting the railway and restoring steam-locomotives to everyday use. People may not know, you also risked your life to send intelligence information through Barry. Every time we see a locomotive, it reminds us of you. Will you please unveil the statue Stephan carved of you?"

Erin handed Rob the end of a hemp cord fastened to the covering. The man stared at it for a moment and then gave the twine a gentle tug. Erin discreetly added an extra effort, and the cloth fluttered to the platform.

Rob sat silently as the crowd cheered. In the following quiet, he gazed at his representation. He saw a young, vigorous Rob Bossley, clear-eyed and grasping engineering drawings. Rob's eyes watered as he remembered events, people, and places he had not thought about for a long time.

The three figures looked down the tracks towards the beginning of the line, looking towards the past. Rob pondered and turned his head to look the other way, over his shoulder up the line. Those nearby instinctively turned to follow his gaze. They saw nothing. Rob could see the tracks curving gently around a bend and out of sight. He struggled to imagine the future hidden there. Rob beckoned Brandi. She bent, her ear close to his lips.

"Turn them to look the other way. Have us looking to the future." His voice was barely audible. "I don't think this railway goes where our children must go."

Brandi looked at the carvings, and then, with a smile, looked back to Rob and nodded. She understood.

"Can we hear some music?" Rob spoke to Erin. His voice hardly raised above a whisper. His love of music surpassed his love of engineering. Joseph played gently on the piano, singing an old folk-tune telling the story of when there was no railway in the land. Rob smiled.

Brandi stood beside her friends, watching Billy from Niagara quietly sketching the scene. Several months later, a large oil painting appeared in the station waiting room depicting this day. Billy had captured the instant when Rob had looked over his shoulder at the railway disappearing into the distance. Rob Bossley's expression portrayed a deep yearning and revealed his searching thoughts on his special day.

Beneath the painting, Brandi hung a commemorative plaque. Burnt into the polished wood were the words,

I don't think this railway goes where our children must go.—Rob Bossley, Musician.

Chapter Forty

I thought my travelling career had ended. The bout with pneumonia left me weaker, and I did not feel up to riding. We converted Shade to a harness horse, and I took to travelling in a horse-drawn buggy.

I made a yearly pilgrimage to Southampton to visit Corrine and Stan's graves and hear The Truth Talker Players. Once I saw Billy's painting hanging in the Flesherton station, I knew Nimise Makwa had found a light and could rest. He had progressed beyond my shadow-hampered way of seeing.

Nimise Makwa had one last important job to do, but I would not find out until over five years had passed from the dedication ceremony at the railway station. That task became the hardest I ever had to perform.

From: "Conversations with Brandi Shadly," in the "Voices of the Founders," series

"It was as if a large black bird had flown over the world, covering us all in its cold, terrifying shadow."

From: The Desperate Time, (The Journals of Brandi Shadly Vol. 35 p 1)

"Planting should be underway now." Little Bill stood on the porch and scowled. Snow swirled about the Longview courtyard, piling in drifts among the stone buildings.

"In sixty years, I've never seen snow like this in May." Brandi shivered beside her nephew. He was forty-four years old and had grown children of his own. Brandi remembered the day Jeff held his tiny body, minutes old, on this same porch. Little Bill stood taller than his aunt, strong and fit, his face obscured by a greying, bushy beard. "We had a few cold, wet springs and even some late snow but nothing like this. It's as if it were March." She brushed some snow from the porch railing, feeling the bite of cold.

"This is bad." Bill scowled, and they retreated inside.

Snow lay piled in the yard for a week. Then a promise of spring came as cold driving rain. The drifts melted but left the fields waterlogged. The wet continued well past the June planting deadline. As if a tease of nature, warmth returned with brilliant red skies at dawn and dusk. Everyone rushed to plant the vegetable gardens and attempted to plant grain for animal feed. The early hay crop had already failed, but if they had two weeks of nice weather, hay remained uncut. A great frost and more snow visited in July and devastated the vegetables and grain.

"These colourful sunsets have been happening since Christmas." Even deep in the valley, Erin and Brandi could see the redness of the August sunset. "I think they are linked to the bad weather. Whatever is making the sky red is blocking the sunlight. On clear days, the sky has a silvery haze."

"Erin, it's a disaster. There are no crops in the whole Great Lakes basin." Brandi felt the threat hanging over them all. "I wish Mom and Dad were here. It's like the first fall in Weyburne after the collapse. They had to save everyone. That first winter was hard and sad, but we survived. We need that kind of effort, or many people will die." Brandi shuddered at the frightful vision.

"I've read," Erin hugged Brandi, trying to reassure while sharing her fear, "something like this happened long ago after volcanic eruptions on the other side of the world."

"What do we do right here, right now?" Brandi surveyed the desolate ground where a thriving garden should have been. "We need to get people together, or we won't make it." A flash of Sharon Shadly appeared in her daughter. "We need to take inventory and see if we have enough food then plan on how to deal with shortages. We have to involve others."

Erin could see the old Brandi, the one who ran him to a standstill in Guelph, the Brandi he first loved. The situation was not good but not hopeless for Erin and Brandi. The Institute had enough food for the humans to survive until next year's harvest. In the past volcanic disaster, conditions had improved over several years after one starvation-filled year. The animals were a problem. They had harvested little hay and no grain. Stores of animal feed were dangerously inadequate, and some livestock would not survive.

"We need to plan a cull, eating and sharing what we can." Brandi sounded matter-of-fact, but her heart broke. Snow swirled about the windows even though it was not yet September. Her list of animals to slaughter included several of their horses. The logic of this cruel time meant an older gelding like Shade must be on the list. They had to save the younger breeding stock. One unpredictable event destroyed years of careful management and growing confidence.

"One advantage," Erin grasped a slightly positive thought, "is with the cold we can preserve more meat instead of having to eat it."

"People need to gather," Brandi remembered horrors from Weyburne. Those who went it alone had died.

Every Council created plans similar to the HEI. Many people independently arrived at the same conclusions. The Huron General Council implemented the forcible removal of people to safer places. In the end, the Mounted Constabulary used judgment and simply recorded the people who refused to move. Some lived in remote places impossible to reach, causing more tragedy.

The industrial centres near Lake Ontario benefited from the livestock cull. There were too many animals for local consumption, and the surplus went out by rail. It would not be enough to prevent starvation in these larger places. In November, the rail lines closed. There were no surpluses to share, and armed guards oversaw breeding stock and seed-grain stores. In desperation, some guards ate the seeds and animals they were to protect.

***

Shadows at night are never seen
Shadows at night are just a dream
Shadows of night fly away
In the dawning
Of a bright new day
Joseph of Longview: "Cold Shadows"
Songbook 12 No. 6

"... and the sun rose upon the land. The light rent the shadow into two portions and shone upon our eyes. Our arms lift in thankful joy. Our voices rise to the heavens. God's great wheel still turns above. Salvation warms our world once more."

From: A prayer of thanksgiving said by the congregation of the Heathcote Community Church.

Winter became a relentless horror. Snowdrift piled upon snowdrift. The usual January thaw never appeared. The heavy snows prevented people from travelling and thus stopped wandering thieves and looters. People remained where they were, enduring their brand of misery. Those who strayed too far from shelter paid with their lives as the icy gales showed no mercy.

By March, almost everyone was hungry and weak. Retrieving firewood and dealing with waste buckets became onerous chores. At Kimberly, half of the population of the Institute had crowded into Brandi and Erin's house while the rest remained huddled in the old lodge. These groups had strong mutual support. Cooperation was essential as supplies dwindled and the suffering increased. Even amongst these dear friends, stress strained the strong bonds of caring. In the darkest hours, minor celebrations and entertainment helped. Years later, when retelling the stories, many would recall these good times and not the bad. Brandi drew bright images mixed with the dark. Hope sputtered but did not extinguish.

Spring arrived in late March, bursting out in sunny warmth as if the world were trying to make up for the misery visited on its human passengers. Not even flooding dampened the survivor's thankful relief. Hunting parties and scavenging sorties went out, and the bare ground encouraged. Sadly, Brandi's horrible memories of the first winter in Weyburne became a new reality.

"Where are they going?" Billy and Brandi stood beside the crumbling concrete bridge over the Beaver River. A troop of mounted constabulary accompanied a large wagon drawn by a pair of emaciated draught horses. The group moved slowly, tired and weak. Riders and beasts had survived the wretched winter and forced themselves to duty. The horses looked longingly at small green shoots struggling up in the roadway. The force often stopped to let the horses forage, allowing the constables to fill their hunger with rough bread slathered in animal fat.

"There have been many tragedies," Brandi gazed sadly at the young artist. "They're going to retrieve survivors of a family who refused to come down to the valley. They were good people. I taught them all." She stared into the clear rushing water as if trying to cleanse her mind. "Billy," she finally said, "we need to ride out and visit people."

Brandi sighed and suddenly felt tired. She had not planned ever again to ride the trails and make rough, but despondent people needed her, everywhere, and there had been suicides. They hungered for caring and hope. She turned to the warming, morning sun.

Where were you when we needed you? Her thoughts were bitter. *Did we humans need this hard lesson in humility?*

Nimise Makwa turned to Billy. Her job compelled her to protect and to bring hope and help. "It'll be hard." She had to reach up to touch the shoulder of the boy who had grown a man's body. "Listen, as much as talk. We'll hear many sad and horrible tales and have to contribute to each place. No one has anything much to share this spring. One more thing," she paused trying not to sound self-important. "It may disappoint some it isn't Nimise Makwa at their door. You need to build your relationships."

Billy nodded. He and Brandi had many discussions about the spirit of Nimise Makwa. Billy knew his journey would take paths his mentor never knew, but she had given him the feeling of her feet upon her pathways. He often wondered how she had done it. There had been no one to teach her the way. Once, he asked her about it, and she had merely said, remembering Karen and Megan:

"There's always someone along the way to teach us and bring us toward the light. They tell us at the time what we need to know."

They waited two weeks before riding out, allowing the horses to regain strength. They departed on a misty morning; a fitting beginning to what they both feared would be unpleasant journeys. Bill headed down the valley towards Longview. Brandi had already had a reassuring visit with her family. She set her path up the high hill and eventually to the Bruce. She was not sure she could get past Hope Bay, fearful of what she might find there. Her new headstrong mount demanded much from her ageing body. Billy disappeared into the mist, and then, with great effort, Brandi slung her leg over the saddle. Erin stretched up to meet her kiss and the horse and rider headed up the cloud-shrouded hill.

***

I had not seen the land so empty and yet so full of sorrow. My route avoided the rail lines and the main wagon roads. These had relief trains and convoys to help people. My task was to find the little backwaters and isolated hamlets where desperate people huddled. Many times, I wanted to quit this dark journey and flee home to Erin's love. I had thought I had seen all the sorrow and tragedy that life could offer. I was wrong. The dark shadows of the forest surrounded me, and I became doubtful an end existed. Then, as George MacDonald promised, the forest darkness gave way to the light. It would not heal the thousands of sorrows, but restored hope in my heart.

From: The Desperate Time, (The Journals of Brandi Shadly Vol. 35 p 103)

"Mommy, I found these!" The little girl burst into the kitchen, smiles and pride shining from a gaunt face. She wore a ragged linen dress, her legs covered by stained and torn pants. Old but wonderfully stitched moccasins protected her feet. She held a little bag, bulging with hidden contents.

Eleanor, sitting opposite Brandi at the bare wooden kitchen table, smiled weakly and reached out from under her blanket to touch her daughter. The mother was in her late twenties but looked older, aged by hunger, desperation and grief. Her face was as sallow as the little girl's but lacked the hopeful smile. In comparison, even in her weakened state, Brandi looked robust and well fed. The bag revealed a collection of green leaves, young spring shoots, wild plant bulbs and dried high-bush cranberries. It was all edible. The little girl knew her woodlands.

The room was comfortable, adorned with woodwork, shelving, and some handmade artwork all relatively new, full of love and caring. It reflected people who had been happy and comfortable. The table and chairs were homemade but skillfully crafted and sized with linseed oil. A little bouquet of trilliums and a couple of early dandelions sat in a clay jar with a circular, crochet doily protecting the wood beneath. This room reflected love and care. The soft surroundings highlighted the hopeless desperation of the mother.

A decently sized cook stove sat near one wall radiating warmth as a cast-iron kettle steamed away ready to make more tea. The woman had already consumed one cup of spruce infusion, but needed more, shivering beneath her blanket. A second cup sat on the table waiting for the little girl's lips. A cast-iron pot simmered beside the steaming kettle. It boiled whole barley into gruel to fill desperate stomachs. Brandi had added a few plant roots and salt to make it more palatable. She would add the treasures the little girl had gathered. Brandi needed to get food into these empty stomachs without causing illness. She planned to turn the leftovers into soup, adding chicken fat from her saddlebag. Hunger gnawed at her. This was Brandi's third stop. The first two places had suffered severely, but this house was the first where she had encountered genuine desperation.

Her daughter brightened the mother's mood and gave her some energy.

"What's your name?" Brandi smiled at the little girl who was eagerly sipping her warm drink.

"Aspen," she smiled at Brandi with youthful eagerness, "my Daddy likes trees."

"Where is daddy?" Brandi was almost afraid to ask. Eleanor made a sound as if to answer, but the eager girl rushed ahead.

"He has gone to get help." She smiled proudly. "He is so big and strong." There was a slight gasp from the mother. Eleanor's sunken eyes reflected hopeless grief and desperation.

"Ben left to find food in February." A tear ran down the woman's cheek. "There was a break in the weather, and we were desperate."

It seemed Eleanor apologized as if Ben's decision had been her fault, as if hers and Aspen's desperation had been a crime.

"I haven't seen him since." More tears fell. She attempted to cover her sorrow by lifting the cup to her lips.

"How old are you, Aspen?" Brandi smiled hoping to divert thoughts back to the present.

"Seven," she smiled again and then for the first time seemed sad, "and I have a little brother, but he is sleeping under the flower garden."

"He was stillborn," Eleanor sobbed. Brandi rose and went to the stove as if the reluctant barley required vigorous stirring. Her tears threatened to season the contents.

She spent three days with the pair. They had no proper food in the house, and it would take decent care before they could be on their own, but the mother did not want to leave. She held a spark of hope and her love remained strong. "I can't leave. What if Ben returns? I can't leave the house unguarded."

"Can Ben read?" Brandi had to convince Eleanor.

"Yes." Her tone told Brandi she wanted to go but felt guilty.

"I'll leave him a note so he can find you. No one will touch your place." They would have to leave before the day grew too old.

"Please take care," Eleanor smiled up at Brandi as she sat high in her saddle.

"I will, Eleanor. You and Aspen get strong. Go down to Kimberly, even for a little while. We have room."

"Ben and I have been working hard on that place. I can't abandon it. He'll be back."

Eleanor sounded hopeful. Brandi left the pair with people only somewhat better off than Eleanor and Aspen, but they had kind hearts and knew the family. Brandi waved as the horse moved off carrying her heavy heart, sure the husband and father had died.

By the end of her journey of sadness, Brandi saw a picture of awful dislocation. Whole families had perished, but most of the dead were men. Fathers, husbands, brothers and sons tried to do the manly thing and made desperate, fatal attempts to find help.

The land now had many single mothers and fatherless families. It would cause hardship for years and create unplanned social adjustments. Not all of these changes were pleasant. While the territory would not condone polygamy, it soon lost much of its social stigma. Formerly stable relationships ended as men cast their eyes over newly available, needy women. The legacy of the wretched year would persist for decades.

The Ojibwe village at Hope Bay survived in much better shape. Their ability to fish and philosophy of careful provision against such disasters brought them through. They gifted fish to more needy towns and began a normal season of planting.

No one recognized Nimise Makwa at first. Curious but somewhat suspicious residents of all ages surrounded her. Her horse, a noble-looking Arabian stallion attracted more attention. A middle-aged man came from one house and looked at the woman on the horse. He then strode through the crowd, with the people making way in respect.

"Welcome, Nimise. The spirit of the makwa returns in our time of need." Brandi slid down and hugged the younger man. He was George MacDonald's protégé and had given Brandi good advice so many years before.

"This is Nimise Makwa." The man shouted. His voice echoed from the buildings. "We now know light lies ahead, and this darkness is lifting from the land."

The warm welcome lifted Brandi's spirits healing the constant suffering and grief that had torn her heart along the road. The story of Eleanor and Aspen had repeated in various ways in place after place. So many died or had their spirits crushed. She had restored something akin to hope in most people while reducing her soul to despair. In Hope Bay, she would recharge and heal. Once again, the feldspar heart of George MacDonald's grave would signal the light always shone.

The village had transformed into a mixture of races. The Ojibwe people were the majority but included many Caucasians, blacks and Asians.

One Chinese man interested in Brandi. He alone had survived from a band of Chinese army deserters who had fled Alberta. They had suffered murderous racist attacks along the way until this man, lonely, starving and desperate, reached Manitoulin as the only survivor from his squad. He wanted to get south in the mistaken impression he could arrange passage home.

When he reached Hope Bay, he found a more welcoming community and remained there. His Ojibwe wife bore several children. Now, in his old age, he doted on grandchildren. One of these grandkids, a boy of about fifteen, was a worker in leather and quill. He could already fashion fine garments and footwear, not simply moccasins but boots with hard leather soles and heels as well, all finely decorated with quill work, coloured thread and designs burnt into the leather. A series of drawings done on softened deer hide in quill, depicting village life and the people was his pride and joy. His grandmother, the woman who had married this Chinese traveller, was Ermine's daughter. She passed on his great-grandmother's skill. The boy's vision, as it seemed for every seeker that Brandi had found, had burst out spontaneously. The boy had a following of children who wanted to learn and emulate. Pride filled the old man's face whenever this special boy came into his presence.

"I know your real name," the boy said to Brandi "You are Seeker of Light. Grandma told me about you."

"You are a seeker too," Nimise Makwa smiled. "You are bound to it. Your work tells me." The young man smiled. A tear formed in his eye. It was almost too much that Nimise Makwa, Seeker of Light, approved of his efforts. He dug deep into a pocket and extracted a smooth red stone. It was ice-polished feldspar. He held it out to Brandi.

"This is for you, Nimise. I didn't understand until now why it has been so important to me. Now I know. It is part of his heart. I found it by his grave."

They hugged as she took the treasure. He did not need to explain whose grave it was. Meeting yet another who would carry on her work filled Nimise Makwa's heart. His wonderful spirit lightened and encouraged Brandi on her journey home.

Chapter Forty-One

I awoke one day
In simpler times
The clang and clash long gone
My thoughts were of food
And fire and love
My heart was full of song.
From: A poem by Old Albert adapted to music by Joseph

For years after that horrible season, the whole of the Great Lakes
Federation struggled through a slow, painful recovery. Myths surrounded
the event, along with a growing desire to blame the supernatural. Some of
my Ojibwe friends blamed the "trickster". Others blamed their god or our
sins for bringing just punishment upon us. The more scientific suggested a
volcano exploded somewhere. In the end, it did not matter, although the
event formed the basis for some schisms and hard feelings affecting our
unity. The concrete result is a system of food storage and preparation
against a disaster. Once again, people are pointing to the warmer, drier
summers as a threat. The brilliant sunsets fade.

I spent another season travelling, mostly along part of the Saugeen River
some distance from the railway. It was a more encouraging time. By the
end of the second summer, I was exhausted and unable to carry on. Billy
has been hard at it, and I am encouraged. His drawings are beautiful and
full of insight. I plan to go through all of my journals and drawings, and
with Erin's help try to make some sense of this grand tale. We have
handed over the Institute to Megan Lefevre. I am now at Longview,

watching the harvesters at work, enjoying Joseph's music and celebrating Jani's seventieth birthday. I will remain until after the harvest party and then retire to Kimberly with my love and my memories.

From: The Time Has Come, (The Journals of Brandi Shadly Vol. 38 p 1)

"It seems when I travel now, I'm visiting graves." Brandi looked sad, and Jani shifted to take her hand. The two women sat on the old porch at Longview. The late August afternoon lingered. Most of the residents laboured in the sheds preparing equipment for the harvest. It promised to be the best harvest ever, perhaps a record, since the horrible summer five years before. Gentle music came through the doorway. Brandi closed her eyes and tried to remember how many times she had sat on this porch listening to Joseph play and compose. It soothed, and for an instant, she drifted into dreams.

Grandchildren frolicked in the courtyard, some skipped and sang silly songs. The children's cheerful voices and laughter rang off the barn, echoing back to the house.

Beans for the garden
Beans for the stew
Beans for the honey bee
And beans for you
1...2....3...I...am...OUT!

"We have so many family and friends who have passed on." Jani's tears clouded her vision. They sat silently for many minutes. Kim came out of the house and sat near her older friends. These two had always been her heroes and adopted aunts. Brandi remembered the first time she had seen Kim, babysitting the little girl while her parents were in a meeting in the Shadly living room in Weyburne. She had resented relegation to the upstairs, watching "some little brat" instead of being with the adults doing important stuff. Kim, not knowing where the nickname came from, had enjoyed the attention when, later at Longview, Brandi had often lovingly called her "brat". To Kim, it had been another word for love.

"We are the last of the Weyburne shadows." Jani choked out the words. "We have left a legacy. I hope our grandchildren build a better world."

"Do you remember how exciting it was though, in those first few years we were here?" Kim looked up from her perch on the top step. "So much was going on, so much new and we learned and built and tried new things. It's almost boring now." She smiled as one of her granddaughters ran over with a wildflower. "Now, it's mostly fixing, making do and building new. We haven't salvaged a building since Willard died."

The women glanced down the lane towards the high gate and the little cemetery that held so many memories. There was a section they called "Weyburne" where everyone from the old hometown lay and where, eventually, Brandi and Jani would sleep beside their family. One section held the remains of many who had arrived later, Ellen, the Smithson's, Kathy and Harold, now all gone.

There was another part, much too large, that held small graves representing those lost at birth or very young and too innocent to have deserved such a fate, testifying to the hard life now embracing the world.

Look to the big house
Look to the gate
Jump right in and
Don't be late.
1...2... 3... all... IN!

"After the last five years, I think boring is good." Jani shifted her weight, easing a cramp in her thigh.

"Do you remember Weyburne much, Jani?" Brandi now remembered The Corners when she thought about the place at all.

"I have dreams," Jani looked sad. "I dream of Mom and Dad sometimes, and Maud. It has never gone away." Brandi nodded. Jani carried pain Brandi could not share.

"I can't remember much," Kim spoke up. "I remember the night we ran away and coming here. Then all I remember is here. It seemed like a grand adventure. I'm glad we came."

"Yes Kim, my sweet brat." Brandi smiled. "You represent the new, the beginning of the new at least. I envy you but I would not trade my life, even with all that sadness, for any other. I have been privileged."

"I would change the tragedy," Jani looked at the children playing in the dusty square.

There's my granny
There's my aunts
Got Mr. Smithers
In their pants.

1...2...3...run OUT

"I see Megan still visits," Brandi laughed. "That damned snake just won't die."

Have a bath once a week
Jump into the freezy creek
Wash your nose and wash your toes
Splash around and out you goes
1...2...3...run OUT

Kim's granddaughter and Little Bill's oldest grandson called and waved as they ran past the women on the porch.

"Stay away from the cow!" Kim's voice trailed after the two children, as they disappeared into the barn.

***

Aspen, birch and pine
Blazing October
Colours this heart of mine
Setting feet restless
Upon memory's road
Visiting places that
Be no more
But living wild
Within this memory

From: A poem by Old Albert, (The Journals of Brandi Shadly Vol. 30 p 234)

Brandi sat in the warm morning sunshine, resting in the small meadow above the Longview compound. She would be sixty-eight years old this October. Her summer of rest had ended with the harvest, and Brandi would soon return to Kimberly. She could see the movements of people below through the brilliant reds and yellows of the autumn dressed trees.

Brandi felt weary from both the climb up the hill and the years and all the trails she had travelled. Her tired body soaked in the warmth of the September sun. The cold would soon descend upon the valley, but this warm day restored and raised lingering memories of summer.

Lingering memories still haunt us, Brandi thought, closing her eyes and seeing many images pass before her, dwelling upon a scene at a Thanksgiving table so many decades before.

Her thoughts were sad and full of longing. It had been a hard life, but good in its way. She had many accolades heaped upon her and much love. She was Nimise Makwa, everyone's sister, protector, teacher; open arms welcomed her into all houses in this territory and through much of the Federation. She once again gazed down the slope towards Longview. Taking her quill pen, dipping it into a little red, fired-clay bottle of black ink, she opened her notebook. Her hand traced those ever so familiar movements.

The shadows are softer now, not drawn as sharply as they once were. The end of shadows is near. There are few of us left from the old days. We are the ones who carry the dark shadow of the before time, the time of strange dreams, misplaced desires and past horrors now given way to new struggles. So few of us shadow bearers walk the valleys, trails, and roads now, and even Longview has only Jani left. The rest are gone or are, happily, too young to suffer from the memories, so few remain to remember those now dead and many lying in unknown places, but remember too. The memories will keep us from slipping and falling back. Brandi paused. Tears traced down her cheeks, following the little wrinkles in her skin, dripping onto the paper.

My journals are a remaining shadow, the memory written down. I have longed for them to be a light on the past and a warning not to travel that path again. I long for them to be a guide to tomorrow, so others will record the journey of the future and find the forest's edge. I have many sisters and brothers with paper and pen, charcoal and paint. They walk my trails and find their own. There are many paths to the truth. My life has been to shine light onto those paths. The history will spread throughout the land, and the people's stories continue. Listen... Listen!

Once again, Brandi paused, remembering George MacDonald. The little stream beside her, reborn from an early fall rain, babbled down the rill. A blue jay flew somewhere behind her, complaining through the trees at her presence. Down puffs from milkweed floated over the clearing on a gentle morning breeze, dancing in the sunlight, flirting with the frost browned golden-rod, their fleeting shadows scurrying over the yellowing grass.

With her clear eyes gazing over the valley, she remembered sitting in this very spot with Jani many years before. She saw the cliff, timeless, dominating and sleeping in its morning shadows. The birds, the plants, the wind, the cliff were doing what they had done and would do forever.

Suddenly, a feeling of humility and understanding flowed through the years and touched her once more. She thought of Jani, now mothering all of Longview, sitting on the porch doting over three generations, passing on wisdom and strength. She thought of Warren, her family, George MacDonald and many others. New tears formed tears of happiness.

Brandi once again travelled her roads. She could remember each one in almost complete detail. They passed before her, page after page of memory, friends, family, dangers and joys. Her mind drew these adventures vividly, each one a loop, beginning and ending in the valley, and all forming a blooming flower made from ribbons of time.

Somehow, the morning had passed, and the cliff face glowed in the brilliant sunshine. Brandi opened her knapsack and retrieved the faded scarf and the three drawings she had always carried: a family portrait of her father, mother and Jeff; the sketch of her and Karen on the valley road and her screaming self-portrait from Paradise. From her pocket came the small shining feldspar pebble from George MacDonald's grave and a shard of Dodger's leather, clipped from the quill image Ermine had given her. Tinder smoked, then blown into a small flame and set into a hollow on a boulder of granite, much older than the limestone cliffs. Carefully, she placed dry twigs onto the pile and waited until it made smouldering embers and then took bits torn from the corners of the drawings and dropped them onto the red coals accompanied by Dodger's leather. As their smoke rose, Brandi opened the scarf, took the last of Corrine's tobacco and sprinkled it onto the embers. The smoke grew sweet and pungent, wafting to her face and then across the meadow, joining the dancing seed tufts. Brandi stared at the dying embers, and as the last of the smoke rose, she set the red stone into the centre. Sunlight glinted from the smooth surface, glowing crimson amidst the blackened ashes. She picked up her pen and wrote one last line: *The end of shadows nears; the sun will light this place forever.*

***

*Perhaps the best tribute to Nimise Makwa can be found in a painting by Joe Too Little Patterson. Joe sketched the scene on the Little Current dock depicting the day Brandi, and Frank Tremain arrived. He captured her looking at his drawings with his children gathered at her feet. He reproduced that drawing in oils. This painting hangs in the community meeting-place at Little Current. Joe made one addition when he painted the scene. Over Brandi's right shoulder, standing a little down the wharf is another Brandi... the young woman who first met Joe and brought him to Kimberly. Her eyes gaze out from the surface of the painting over the older Brandi's shoulder and into our eyes. She is challenging us. I cried the first time I saw this painting. Joe, I thank you for this. - **E.T.***

I have assembled this account from all of your journals, letters and other's stories. It is your legacy, my sweet love. Our journey was wonderful, and your love made me whole. It will always be with me, and I pray that our love and your story will inspire others to continue along the path. There are many ways to the high ground. Your journey was one of the best. I miss you and will always love you.

From: The handwritten forward to, "The Journals of Brandi Shadly." Compiled by Erin Thomas in tribute to the memory of Brandi Shadly and completed shortly before his death. (The HEI library copy Kimberly Campus)

Added by Megan Lefevre, Director (retired) of the Huron Ecology Institute

The End

From **The Seventh Path**, the follow on story set a century after **The End of Shadows.**

Prologue
Giving of Her Name

Amidst the drumming and singing, the sound of the stringed gitter danced over the throng, and soon the words of the old song wrapped about the people. *Longing for Longview*, passed down through the generations, the song held only mystical meaning now, with many phrases in old Glish puzzling to the listeners.

Joseph of Longview was simply another of those ancient wise ones. Longview, the home of Nimise Makwa, lost in the mists of time, became a fable, a myth although many knew that the community still thrived in the land of Amik, the river Beaver and the valley of fruit and shadows.

The gathered people were a blending of many races, with some individuals showing the characteristics of several at once: black, white, Asian and the natives of Turtle Island; others seemed to be the unaltered echoes of centuries old differences. No family grouping possessed only one set of racial features.

A woman elder, adorned in a colourful costume of pounded deer hide, dyed quill and feathers, rose amid the throng and lifted high a blazing torch of woven cattail, saturated with spruce pitch.

"Nimise Makwa; you are the ancestor of many names."

The woman's voice, old and wise, strong and sure, rose above the quieting din of the throng, as she slowly made her way to the front. Mother's voice was the voice of the people; they prepared to listen.

The crowd, the entire community called Patterson, sat cross-legged in a semi-circle, mimicking the crescent moon.

The focus of the gathering was a pile of wood and sweet grasses. The tightly knit mound resembled the lodge of the beaver, but with a conical chimney dominating the top of the curve.

Mother's torch dipped, touching the base of the pile. Small flames appeared amongst the sticks and wormed their way into the centre, following a path of pitch-laden tinder, gradually embracing and igniting more of the fuel. Sweet scents of burning grass and herbs wandered over the gathering.

Drumming arose once more, earnest, urgent and heartfelt. Several gitters added lamenting flat notes to the sounds, as if calling to the dead.

The flames climbed higher through the inside of the pile. Sparks struggled into the night and died in the blackness. Silent eyes followed the embers. The glow strengthened, lighting the pile, as if some interior sun spirit struggled for release.

Flames inside reached the top and the base of the round crown, a hollowed out dry cedar trunk filled with pitch and tinder. Fire burst into a torch of white-hot flame reaching to the stars. Embers shot high, rising forever, refusing to yield to the dark, finally drifting down upon the watchers, silent, orange fireflies descending. The circle glowed as if the sun rested above.

The crowd gasped.

Drums picked up an urgent, fast, wild beat of celebration, and the gitters joined with rapid, uplifting chords. Chanting drummers called forth hope and promise.

The old woman turned to face the throng; her white robes glowed. Quill adornments sparkled in the blazing light. Her eyes glistened. A necklace of polished bear's teeth rose upon her breast. She spoke.

"I give you the words of our grandmother, Annie Patterson, when she and Joe Giingoo were told Nimise Makwa had joined the spirits."

Seeker of light
Sister of the bear
Go into the night
We remember your words
Of love and understanding
Embracing all that is living
That lets life be
Spread your light, and we know
Your spirit, your memory is
The end of shadows

"Nimise Makwa, I name you now and forever, Seeker of Light."

Continued…

www.ingramcontent.com/pod-product-compliance
Lightning Source LLC
Chambersburg PA
CBHW061059210726
48294CB00001B/210